The Color of Redemption

By

Lynn Cornell

The Color of Redemption

By

Lynn Cornell

Dove
Publishers

Dove Christian Publishers
P.O. Box 611
Bladensburg, MD 20710-0611
www.dovechristianpublishers.com

ISBN: 978-09975898-1-8

Purinted in the United States of America

The Color of Redemption is a work of fiction. Names,
characters, places and incidents are the products of the author's
imagination or are used fictitiously. Any resemblance to
actual events, locales, or persons, living or dead, is entirely
coincidental.

Book design by Raenita Wiggins

Dedication

I'd like to dedicate my first novel to my wife, Beverly. For years, you had urged me to write when I didn't know that I was a writer. But you kept after me to learn the literary craft and signed me up for my first writer's conference. It was then I realized I could be a writer. *The Color of Redemption* is the fruit of your wisdom. I thank God for your love and companionship.

P.S. I'll see you on the dock.

Chapter One

June 1960

An eerie foreboding had jolted me from my sleep this morning, vexing my spirit—the kind of vexing that made me want to cower under my covers and stay in bed. But, I had to get up. The call of Sunday morning chores wouldn't allow me to nurse my trepidation. Shaking myself, I grabbed my Bible and opened the door to face the day.

A pleasurable sigh escaped my lips as I stepped onto the porch. Like a tapestry stretched across the heavens, a golden-orange sun and puffy white clouds decorated a crystal blue sky, as only God could do. The morning was hot but tempered by a mild cool breeze. Knee-high grass and pink geraniums blanketed the fields in a gentle sway. I loved my farm—God's place of refuge for me. Here my heart is content. Here, I'm safe.

The sight of Maxine interrupted my gaze. I couldn't believe she had the nerve to come out of the house dressed like that. I marched over to our truck where everyone was waiting for me. "Maxine, have you lost your mind? You know that dress is too short and too tight to wear to church—let alone anywhere else. And who gave you that makeup?"

Maxine pressed her lips together. "A friend, Mama."

"You march your behind in that house and change out of

that dress and wipe that mess off your face!"

Maxine narrowed her brows, poked her lips out, and stomped into the house. As if someone had slapped me with a cold rag, reality had struck me with a sobering realization. Maxine was sixteen and budding into a woman—too fast if you ask me. My babies were growing up. Edward, fourteen, primped in the side mirror of the truck, thinking he was God's gift to anything. Timothy, twelve, jostled Ruby. He was immature and at the same time tried to act like a tough black militant. Ruby was ten and milked being the youngest child. I wasn't ready for them to grow up yet.

Gregory paced back and forth. He wore blue jean overalls and a dingy white T-shirt. His hair was matted in tiny naps, as if he'd never seen a comb. He kept darting his eyes at me. "You's makin' me late, Katie, sending that girl back in the house. You know she be slow."

"Stop fussing, Gregory. That girl's dress was too tight—let alone to be wearing to church. You would have gotten there, saw the way she was dressed, and thrown a fit."

"Well, I can'ts be late. I'm a deacon. I'm s'posed to be an example."

Maxine stomped out the house with her lips poked out and her arms folded in protest of the brown flowered print dress she had changed into.

"See, there she is," I said.

"I look like an old grandma in this dress," Maxine said.

Gregory scowled at her. "Watch your tone, Maxine. You is the reason we is late."

I took Gregory's hand. "Calm down. We're not going to be late, and we'll get there with everyone dressed decent and in order." I rose on my toes and kissed Gregory's cheek. Watching his frown turn into a smile made me give him another kiss. "Now, let's go to church, or we will be late. Y'all get in the truck before your daddy has a stroke."

Timothy pushed Ruby and jumped in the back of the truck. Ruby shrugged. "Stop, Timothy, and leave me alone."

Ruby and Edward got into the truck. Maxine followed them and plopped against the back of the cab, pouting. Gregory drove off.

Thank God, town was only five miles away. Gregory parked on the church lawn next to a row of cars. The church was a small white-frame building with four, black-framed windows that never cooled the church and five black-painted wood steps that led up to two black wood doors. The hand-painted sign read *True Rock Missionary Baptist Church*.

Edward, Timothy, and Ruby jumped from the truck and disappeared. Maxine stepped from the back of the truck, primped in the side mirror, and walked toward the church. Henry Lee Scott fixed his gaze on her. He was handsome and well groomed. He'd just turned eighteen and wanted to study for the ministry. His suits were always pressed and cleaned as if specially tailored. He dashed over to Maxine not realizing I was standing behind him.

"Morning, Henry Lee," Maxine flirted.

"Maxine, you sure is a pretty sight. God has smiled on me today."

"Henry Lee Scott, Maxine is too young for courtin'," I said.

Henry jumped. "Yes ma'am, Mrs. Smith."

I turned to tell Gregory whom Maxine was making all the fuss over, but he had dashed off to catch Reverend Sims before he went inside the church. He was flamboyant, wearing a bright green suit. His hair was pressed, and for a reverend, he wore too much gold. But he was a good man. I tried to intercept Gregory from badgering the reverend, but I was too late.

"Pastor, you have the largest church in the county. It's the only buildin' on this side of town that could handle the crowds. We need a rally to stir the people," Gregory said.

The reverend grimaced. "I'm sorry, Brother Smith. I can'ts helps you. You know the people don't want that kind of attention. They don't want no trouble. Things are good for us around here. Why do you want to mess that up?" The shrill of screeching tires sliced through the air. Reverend Sims snapped his head toward the street. "Oh, my sweet Lord."

A red 1960 Plymouth Fury with white stripes on the side and two Confederate flags flapping on the rear tail fins parked in front of the church. The horn blared, and voices jeered. The front of the Fury, sleek like a feline's face, stared at me as if stalking its prey.

Reverend Sims wiped the sweat from his forehead and pressed his lips. Gregory drew his brows in and looked at the reverend with contempt. Shaking his head, he folded his arms and looked toward the car. There was no fear in his eyes. That bothered me.

Four men sat in the car, shouting vile racial slurs. One of the men, wearing a brown fedora, sat in the passenger's seat. There was something different about his demeanor this week. He didn't say a word, but he peered at us with an evil glare. Everyone froze where they stood, eyes glued on the car. It amazed me that this man, just by his mere presence, struck unspeakable terror in our hearts. I looked at Gregory. He nodded, and I nodded back. That's all the assurance I needed at the moment.

The man wearing the fedora locked his eyes on my

husband. He spat a long stream and slapped the car door twice. The engine revved, and the car sped away.

Gregory glared at the reverend. "Pastor," he said, whipping his finger toward the street. "Why are you so 'fraid that you can allow that to happen every week?"

"Let it go, Gregory. They didn't do nothing, unlike the old days."

"Why do you cower before them like that? You always stood up for yourself. Ever since that night they tied a rope around your neck and dragged you from your house ...."

The reverend furrowed his brows. "That's not fair, and you know it."

"You've been 'fraid to speak out against things you knows is wrong."

Reverend Sims looked away. "I'm looking out for my family, the church, and our community." He faced Gregory. "Something you should be doing. I want to be around for my wife, children, and grandchildren."

I wished Gregory feared white people as much as the reverend did. Maybe that would keep him off of the streets of Birmingham protesting. I wished Gregory had the same burning desire to be around for his family as he did for fighting for civil rights. But that wasn't his calling. Stepping between them, I touched Gregory's arm. "It's time for Reverend to preach."

"Thank you, Sister Smith. Maybe you can talk some sense into him because I sure can't." Reverend Sims pulled a handkerchief from his pocket, wiped the back of his neck, and dabbed his forehead. "I'll see y'all inside," he said, walking away, mumbling.

Dreariness draped over the service. From time to time, people, like me, glanced toward the window, wondering if those men had come back. I was glad when Reverend Sims, dressed in a black robe with gold stripes down the middle, leaned against the podium, said, "Don't worry 'bout those men. The Lawd gon take care of us. Go in the joy of the Lawd."

'Thank you, Jesus. Praise the Lord' and 'hallelujahs,' billowed from all over the sanctuary. Relieved to hear those words, I leaped to my feet, but people already crowded the aisle all the way to the door. Folding my arms, I sighed and looked around the sanctuary.

"Hey, Sister Katie," someone yelled.

"Hey, Sister Smith," another woman said.

Church hadn't changed since I could remember. The same light brown paneling covered the walls; the same dark brown light fixtures hung from the plastered ceiling, and people sat on the same scratched-up brown pews. Reverend Sims preached behind the same old wooden podium, and the people — dressed in suits, dresses, and pressed hair — gossiped about nothing.

Gregory pinned the reverend by the podium. They were the same age, forty-five, but had two different perspectives on life. Gregory believed Negroes should stand up to the white man and fight for their rights. The reverend felt Negroes should leave things alone. A lot of people felt as the reverend did. Peering down the aisle, I plowed my way outside, past the hisses and sighs, and stood on the top step, waiting for Gregory.

The reverend came out the back with Gregory hounding him. I walked across the yard and stopped just a few feet from them. Preoccupied with getting his point across, Gregory didn't notice me. I grabbed his arm. "Excuse me, Reverend, you have a good day. We're going home," I said and marched Gregory toward the truck. "Maxine, let's go." Looking around the yard, I yelled, "Eddie, Tim, Ruby, to the truck, now."

The children promptly appeared. Ruby grabbed her father's hand, smiling her "please, Daddy" smile. "Daddy, can we get some ice cream on the way home?"

Gregory gave me his "please, honey" look and scooped Ruby up in his arms. Ruby giggled and hugged her daddy's neck.

"Gregory, I just want to go home."

"Come on, baby, it won't take but a few minutes. It'll be a nice treat for everyone."

I pressed my lips together, but a grin squeezed through.

Gregory laughed. "You can'ts hide that pretty smile. Ice cream it is, everyone."

This didn't feel right. I knew in my gut we should go straight home. It was a short ride through colored-town's row of shabby, rundown framed ranches, old two-story homes, and single mobile trailers. People waved and smiled either from their porches, or as they walked along the dirt road. I waved back. I knew most of the people or was kin to them in some way — first, second, or third cousins.

Gregory drove across the railroad tracks. The landscape instantly changed. Eeriness wrapped around me and pressed hard. This side of town always made me uncomfortable. The streets were paved, the houses neatly painted, and the lawns were well-groomed. Elderly men sat on their porches and scowled. Elderly women stared at us with furrowed brows. Others walked on the sidewalks, ignoring our presence.

"Oh, Henry, you so fine, I's just loves you so," Timothy said.

I glanced back and chuckled.

Maxine hissed a deep sigh. "Ooh, you're so immature, Timothy. I can't stand you."

"Your kids are acting up back there," I said.

Gregory smiled. "What else is new?"

I looked fixedly at Gregory. "You're so preoccupied with protesting and marching you can't see what's going on."

Gregory stared ahead. "Your daughter is in love."

The truck swerved, slamming me against the door. Gregory quickly recovered and grimaced. Ruby giggled, and we both laughed at the shock on his face.

My smile disappeared as we approached the ice cream shack. It was a small square hut with cinder-block walls painted red, white, and blue. It had one walk-up window. A few wood tables and chairs set on the patio. A large Confederate flag draped across the front.

Four men sat at one of the tables, slurping on ice cream cones. I recognized the man wearing the brown fedora, and the red Plymouth Fury parked in front. My stomach sank. He was tall, thin, and wore blue jean overalls with no shirt. I've never seen a grown man's face so smooth and hairless. He drew his brows in and fixed his eyes on Gregory.

Reaching across Ruby, I grabbed Gregory's arm. "We should go home."

But, it was too late. Gregory had already stopped. The men looked at us, still slurping their cones. Their mischievous grins disappeared.

"Hey, ain't that that agitator?" one man shouted.

"What's he doing here?" another one said.

A tall, husky man stood and tossed his ice cream to the ground. He walked toward us, proudly displaying his sculpted physique through a tight-fitting T-shirt. He pointed his finger at Gregory. "What are you doing here, boy?"

Gregory reached for the door handle, but I squeezed his

arm. "Gregory, the children are in the back. Let's go home." I squeezed tighter, praying he wouldn't be stubborn. "Please."

Gregory glanced at the man and looked at me. There was no fear or intimidation in his eyes. That scared me. "We have a right to be here, just as much as them. We have a right to enjoy an ice cream cone with our family. Blount City gots to change it racist ways."

"Please, Gregory. Let's just go home. Please."

Gregory clenched his jaw and stared intensely. It took every ounce of his strength to back down from the men who denied him his rights. Gregory turned to me, teeth clenched. He released the door handle and grabbed the steering wheel. "All right."

Gregory shifted the gear stick and circled onto Route 7. I let his arm go and closed my eyes. It took a moment for my nerves to calm. Glancing back at the children, I gasped. The red Fury bore down on us. I didn't know if Gregory had seen the car, but I was too afraid to ask. Closing my eyes, I prayed he'd go straight home.

The drive to the farm took only a few minutes, but it felt like forever. The Fury's horn blared, taunting us. Maxine closed her eyes and covered her ears. The car rode our tail, at times just inches from the bumper.

Gregory glanced at the side mirror. If he was scared, he didn't show it. He pulled onto the rutted driveway and stopped. The ruts led up a steep hill and disappeared into safety. The red Fury parked in front of the driveway. Thank God, the entrance was cluttered with wild brush, overgrown weeds, and brushwood. I hoped it was enough to camouflage our farm's entrance. I didn't want those men knowing where we lived.

The husky man jumped out of the car and walked toward

the truck.

Timothy jumped to his feet with his fists up. "Come on. Y'all honkies do something."

The husky man pointed at Timothy. "You got a big mouth, boy."

Timothy beckoned with his fist. "Come on, do something."

"Gregory!" I screamed. But, he already jumped out of the truck. I turned around. "Help us, Lord," I kept mumbling.

Gregory glanced up. "Sit down and hush up." Timothy plopped down with his lips poked out. "You got no business with us," Gregory said to the husky man. Timothy leaped to his feet with his fists raised. Maxine yanked on his pants. "Timothy, I said sit down and be quiet."

I glanced at the man wearing the fedora. He had a stare in his eyes that paralyzed me with terror, more than the vile curses and threats they spewed at us. I prayed that Gregory wouldn't say or do anything that would incite them.

He rapped the car door, keeping his eyes locked on Gregory, "Earl Ray, another time."

Earl Ray grinned. "Yeah, nigger, another time." He pointed his finger directly at Gregory and glanced toward Timothy. "You better teach your boy to mind his tongue, or well, you know what'll happen to him." He snickered as he walked toward the car. "You'll come out of your house one morning and find him swinging from a tree."

That wasn't an empty threat. The man wearing the fedora kept Gregory in his sights as the car sped away. Gregory glared at Timothy, got into the truck, and drove up to the farm.

He parked in his usual spot, next to the car. I got out and stretched my arms, relieved to be home, glad to be in the safety of our land. A loud yelp pricked my ears. I winced and whirled around. Gregory had Timothy's head pressed against the truck.

"The next time I tells you to do somethin', you better obey me. Dos you understand me?" Timothy nodded as best he could. "Your foolishness could have gotten us killed. Those men are nobody to play with. They will kill you and string yous up like an animal and thinks nothin' of it. And no one, and I mean no one, will dos anythin' about it."

The red Fury crept over the hill and purred at the end of the drive.

"Gregory!" I shouted.

Pressing Timothy's head, he shouted. "Katie, this boy gots to learn to mind his place."

I pointed my finger. "Look!" The red Fury slowly lurched back and forth, revving its engine in a taunting tease. I wondered what he would do if the car advanced toward us. The engine roared, and the tires peeled dirt. "Oh, dear Lord Jesus, help us!" I screamed.

Chapter Two

The red Plymouth Fury let out a loud roar and plowed over the knee-high grass in a wide circle. Nasty vile slurs flung from the windows with each pass. Earl Ray hung out the side of the car, dangling a noose, hollering, "This is what we is going to do to you, coon."

"Gets in the house, now!" Gregory shouted. The girls bolted toward the house, but Edward and Timothy gawked with their mouths wide open. "Gets in the house, boys, now."

The car fishtailed, making a figure eight. Gregory clenched his fist and looked around the yard. *Don't do it, Gregory. Don't try to fight them. Just let them go.* I tried to will the words out of my mouth but couldn't utter a sound. Thank God, there wasn't a stick lying in sight. Gregory would have tried to drive those men off the land.

Earl Ray tossed the noose, hollered, and slid back into the car. The Fury sped off then screeched to a halt. The tires peeled, a cloud of dust puffed up. The car moved back until it stopped by the noose.

The man with the brown fedora stepped out of the car and pointed his finger. "We warned you 'bout your preachin'. Bad enough, you stirring up the niggers with your freedom crap. But when you step out of your place and preached to good God-fearin' white folks, you've gone too far. You should have kept your preachin' in Niggertown, boy."

The man turned and got back into the car. The Fury sped

away and disappeared over the hill, leaving a cloud of dust looming over the driveway.

Gregory picked up the noose and shook his head. I looked toward the driveway, hoping, this time, those evil men were truly gone. *Oh my God, they know where we live.* Folding my arms over my stomach, I couldn't control the quivering in my belly.

"Y'all come out here," Gregory yelled. The children trickled out and stood on the porch. Gregory held the noose toward Timothy. "This is why you keep your mouth shut around those men. We have enough trouble without them bein' provoked." Gregory threw the rope toward the side of the house and took me in his arms. "It's all right. They's gone."

I squeezed his waist. *I wish I could believe that.*

* * *

I lay as still as I could, hoping for the slightest breeze to brush across my body. Not so much as a breath of air blew. The heat sizzled on my skin, with no relief in sight. The house was quiet, but my thoughts screamed loud and boisterous. Anxiety buffeted my mind.

I snuggled next to Gregory, trying to take my mind off the horrors that had happened earlier. I couldn't sleep. I sat up and swung my legs onto the floor. I couldn't get the image of the man wearing the fedora out of my mind.

Standing, I threw on my dress and stepped into the darken living room. Panic seized me. It was silly to fret this way. I glanced toward the children's bedroom. Snores rattled from inside, assuring me that they were safe—I peeked in anyway.

Swiping the sweat from my forehead, I lifted the latch. *What if the man with the fedora is lurking outside? What if he comes in here for us?* My hand trembled. I pulled the door open, expecting to see tree limbs flailing in the wind, debris hurled by a violent squall, or a raging tempest flinging things about, or worse, the man with the fedora ready to charge in and attack. But, pleasantly surprised and relieved, I stepped outside into a beautiful calm night.

"Ah!" I screamed. Two raccoons scurried off of the porch. "Darn critters. I told Timothy about leaving these tops off of these buckets. Slop is everywhere."

The moon, full and bright, illuminated the countryside with a soft light. Frogs croaked. Insects whined. Owls hooted. I could stay out all night, enjoying the tranquil bliss, but the agitation in my soul kept me in a frenzy. Stepping back inside, I dropped to my knees and buried my head on the couch. I stayed that way for forty, forty-five minutes and stood with no relief. "Lord, what are you trying to tell me?"

I slipped into bed and nestled next to Gregory. He turned, and in his sleep, he held me in his arms. I stayed awake as long as I could. Finally, my eyes sagged as I tried to fight the sleep off. I didn't want the man with the fedora invading my dreams. But, I couldn't hold my eyelids open. As they closed, it felt as if moments had passed.

"Cock-a-doodle-doo" jolted me from my sleep precisely at 4:30 a.m. I tugged the sheet over my shoulders to catch a few more winks. Throwing the sheet aside, I jumped out of bed and slid into a black, flowered print dress and stared into the mirror. Running the brush through my hair a couple of times, I saw no improvement in the image staring back. My eyes are puffed, and my hair frizzled as if I had stuck my fingers in an outlet. Placing the brush on the dresser, I shook my head. "I have too many wrinkles for a woman of thirty-five."

As I walked out of the house and toward the barn, my soul felt as empty as the basket I cradled in my arms. Where were my joy and peace? I wasn't used to feeling this way. Everything felt off-kilter. I wanted to hide somewhere. But this was the place of my refuge. Where would I flee?

I set the basket on the ground and gazed toward the rutted driveway. I'd always felt safe and secure on my land — until those vile men desecrated my sanctuary. They'd stolen my serenity and molested the land, despoiling it of all its tranquility. The image of the man in the brown fedora soiled the landscape.

Leaning against the fence, I closed my eyes. Not knowing how to articulate my prayers, I just quietly groaned. *Lord, I feel like my stomach is being wrenched in knots. Help me understand all of this.* I whispered, "Amen."

Gathering my thoughts, I darted over to the garden; grabbed a few tomatoes, onions, and peppers; placed them in the basket; and made my way to the chicken pen.

"Morning, Ben," I greeted, entering the coop. "You won't get the ax today because you're my friend."

Gathering a dozen eggs, I made my way back toward the house. The place where the grass was matted in a figure eight caught my eye. *They had never come on the land before.* When I opened the door, Gregory startled me. He was slouched in the chair, wearing his usual blue jean overalls, white T-shirt, white socks, and black shoes. He stared in deep thought and hadn't noticed I'd come in. "You scared me, man. I thought you were sleep."

He sat up. "Naw. I thought I'd get up and sit with you for a while." His eyes lingered on me. "You got out of bed early. I don't like it when you get out of bed early."

I snickered, knowing exactly what he meant. "What you staring at?"

"I be starin' at you; that's what," he said. He jumped to his feet and rocked me in his arms. "Don't cheat me out of my lovin', woman."

"You're a mess, a real mess." I giggled, pretending to protest, but I loved every bit of his sporting. "Stop, Gregory. You're not gonna get breakfast if you keep bothering me."

He kissed my forehead and sat in the chair. "I'm gonna get both."

We chatted while I prepared breakfast. I pulled the pan of biscuits from the oven. Gregory liked his food cooked fresh. The smell of fresh-baked bread filled the room and made his nostrils flare. I smoothed butter over the nooks and crannies. His eyes widened. The rice was ready, so I rushed to scramble the eggs, knowing he'd growl with impatience. I set a plate of fried tomatoes on the table. He chewed the crusted treat with delight. I loved it when he was pleased with my cooking.

"I'm drivin' to the city this mornin' to talk to some old friends. Out of the blue, they wrote to me and said they wanted to come to town."

"I hate it when you drive to Birmingham."

"Don't start your fussing." Gregory drifted off for a moment. "After all of these years of tryin' to get them to come, now all of a sudden, they want to have a rally."

"That's good, ain't it?"

"I've been thinkin' 'bout things."

I glanced over my shoulder. "What things?" The question dangled for a moment. Something bothered him. Gregory should have been more excited than this. I glanced over my shoulder again. "What you thinking about?"

Gregory stared at the floor. "I've been thinkin' 'bout quittin' the movement."

Surprised, I stopped stirring the bowl of eggs and whirled around. "Stop playing, Gregory. You know you're not quitting your work."

"I ain't playing, Katie. I've been thinkin' hard 'bout quittin' the movement."

"How long have you been thinking this?"

"For a few days now."

"Those men got you scared?"

Gregory scowled. "No. They got me thinkin' 'bout things, though."

I set the bowl on the counter and studied him. "How can those evil men get you thinking about anything? I wish God would strike them dead."

Gregory frowned and leaned forward.

"They're evil, Gregory."

"That's wrong for you to think that, Katie. Despite what they is, God still love 'em. Jesus loves 'em enough to die for 'em. That's how you gots to see 'em."

"Umm," I grunted. "What else is bothering you?"

He shrugged. "Things."

"What things, Gregory? You're not telling me anything."

"I wonder if God's will is being done in the movement."

"Umm-hmm." I poured the eggs into the skillet, surprised he would even joke about giving up his passion. "I find that hard to believe, Gregory. I really do."

"I jus' feel different. My heart isn't in the movement anymo'."

I finished cooking and joined him. After we had eaten, I made some instant coffee. We both drank ours black. We went outside and sat on the porch.

Gregory sipped from his cup, looking over the land. He caressed my fingers and kissed the back of my hand. "We've had a good life together, Katie. I gots no regrets."

"Lord willing, we'll have many more years together."

"Amen to that," he said. His eyes drifted across the field as somberness draped over his face. "I've put money away for the kid's schoolin'."

"That's nice."

"I want 'dem to have a better life than we have."

Stunned, I turned toward him. "Gregory, we have a good life here on this land. I wouldn't trade this life for nothing else in the world. What's bothering you?"

"Oh, nothin', everythin'." He shrugged. "I jus' want to do God's will, and I don't know if I am, workin' in the movement. I wonder if I've wasted all of these years for nothin'."

"I thought you were doing God's work. You've wholly devoted your life to the movement. You've neglected me, the children, the farm, even your duties at the church. I'm not fussing, but I thought you were doing what God wanted you to do."

"I thought I was, too."

"Then, what's changed?" Gregory just stared at me. "Is it because you haven't gotten the support from the people? I heard Reverend Sims fussing at you for trying to hold a rally at the church. I told you he would never let you have a meeting like that there. He's too scared of those white folks."

"That's part of it."

"Was it those men following us home yesterday? Did they scare you?"

He grimaced. "You know better than that."

"Don't give me that look. Something is bothering you. What is it?"

"I just think the Lord is takin' me in a different direction in life." The expression on my face must have jarred Gregory because he peered directly into my eyes. "The movement ain't doin' this… reachin' people for the Lord. I jus' feel the Lord want to reach people's heart."

I stared at him and looked off toward the hills. "I never liked you working in Birmingham no way. Too many black men are being beaten, tortured, and killed by the police and the Klan."

Gregory looked at me, stunned. "I thought you were okay with me workin' in the movement. Why didn't you say nothin'?"

"You never asked. One day, you just went off to Montgomery, preaching and marching in that bus boycott. You were gone for a whole month. And when you came back home, you only stayed for a week, and then off you went with the car, toting people around Montgomery. I didn't see you again until that boycott was over. Thank the Lord you wrote. I knew you were doing something important. I didn't know what until afterward. Besides, I didn't say I didn't like you working in the movement. I said I don't like you working in Birmingham."

"You never said nothin' to me about workin' in the boycott."

"There was nothing to say. Your mind was made up. All I could do was pray that the Lord protect you and bring you home safe."

"I jus' wish I'd know how you felt."

"Wouldn't have done any good. Once you got a taste of marching in the streets of Montgomery and working with the folks down there, you were fired up. Then you came back here on fire, wanting to march in Birmingham. That's what scared me."

"Negroes are bein' killed everywhere, Katie, not jus' in Birmingham."

I smacked my lips and looked off. "I know that. I don't want you to be one of them, killed by the Klan or the police in 'Bombing-ham'. I just prefer that you stayed here on the farm with me."

Gregory gazed at the land with an empty stare. "The Lord has to change men's hearts. The movement ain't doing that."

"Isn't the movement changing Negroes' lives? I don't know what you mean, Gregory."

"Only after God has changed the heart can you change society. You can't change men's heart with protests and marches. You'll change laws, but not men's heart. They still be hateful. If God change men's heart, that'll solve the race problem, cuz He takes the hate out their hearts and puts His love in place of hate. They's be changed from the inside."

I didn't know what to make of Gregory's outlook. He had been unmovable about his passion for civil rights. "What brought this on? This is not like you."

Gregory glanced at his watch. "Oh, Lord, look at de time," he said, jumping to his feet. "I gotta be in the city at nine, and it be already eight-thirty."

He intended to give me a quick peck, but when our lips touched, our kiss lingered.

I wanted to hold onto Gregory. I didn't want him to leave, now that he had made his decision to leave the movement. I didn't want to risk something happening to him, not when I was this close to having him home to myself. I wanted to tell him how I felt, how troubled my night had been. I was desperate to try anything to keep him here. As he sped away, I only managed to say, "Be careful out there."

I never cared for the struggle the way Gregory did. As a child, I rarely left the Negro side of town. Most of what I needed were there; school, church, and even a small candy store run out of a lady's house. Sometimes, not often, my mother would take me to town with her, but I'd never noticed any prejudices back then. My mother, like all the Negroes, knew her place and never strayed from it. I thought it was natural for society to exist this way.

It wasn't until Gregory had gotten involved in the Birmingham movement that I had come face-to-face with bigotry. Like everyone else, we'd heard stories, had a relative, or known someone who had been beaten, jailed, or even lynched. My own brothers ran into trouble from time to time, but my parents had taught them how to behave—always with their heads down and speaking with a very respectful tone. Gregory never held his head down.

My greatest fear was that one day I'd be sitting on this porch, maybe on a day much like today, enjoying the scenic view, when over the hill it would come, a black and white patrol car, or my sister bringing the dreaded news that Gregory had been murdered.

Chapter Three

A black sedan steered toward the house with a quiet purr. Leaping to my feet, I squeezed the banister with both hands. *Is this the day?* It had only been a couple of hours since Gregory had left, but I couldn't help but wonder: was this the dreaded messenger of death?

How the news could come so fast? *God, please, don't let them tell me that Gregory is dead.* Questions buffeted my mind, forcing me to face a horrible reality. How had he been murdered? Who murdered him? How would I tell the children their father was gone?

Louise smiled and waved her hand as she brought the car to a stop. I lowered my head and blew out a long sigh. *Thank God, this isn't the day.* I threw Louise a quick wave. *Thank God, it's my big sister instead of the police blaring the news of Gregory's demise.*

I worried about Louise's health. She was tall, three hundred pounds, with extra-large breasts. High blood pressure ran on our mother's side of the family. She wasn't taking care of herself, and I feared she'd succumb to a heart attack one day. Louise maneuvered out of the car and stepped on the porch, pausing to catch her breath.

"Whose car is this?"

"It's mine. Curly... bought it for me... for my birthday." Louise pushed out the words between panting.

"Happy birthday, Louise. How does it feel to be forty-five?"

"The same as forty-four." She tossed a big smirk. "Anyway,

I'm only here for a minute. I'm off to see Daddy."

"Ooh, that's a long drive."

"I don't mind. Birmingham is only an hour away." Louise stared at me for a moment. "Anyway, the reason I stopped by...."

"What is it, Louise?"

Her mouth hung open. "I don't know if this means anything, but...."

"Will you just say it? Dag, girl."

"I had a dream last night. It was so real it woke me up in the middle of the night. I couldn't go back to sleep. I saw you and the kids dressed in black. You and the kids had just come from a funeral. You and the kids came to my house and sat in the living room, dressed in black."

I don't know why, but Louise's dream hit me like a ton of bricks. She always told me about some dream of hers, but this one, for some reason, jolted me. It took a moment to respond. Someone was missing from the dream. "It must have been something you ate."

Louise's eyes drooped. "You all right, baby? I didn't mean to upset you."

"I'm fine," I retorted.

"I gotta go. Tell the kids I'll holler at them another time." She made her way to the edge of the porch but turned toward me. "Why don't you come with me? It won't hurt you to get off this land. It'll do you good."

"Girl, I have too much work to do. Besides, I have to cook Gregory's dinner."

"Don't try to hide behind Gregory. You just don't want to go anywhere. There's more to the world than this farm, Katie."

"I'm very content here."

"That's your problem. You're too comfortable living out here, away from everything. All you're doing is hiding from people."

"Bye, Louise. Thank you."

"For what?"

"You're the only one who drives out here to see about me. You've always looked out for me, and you've always let me know that you loved me. I really appreciate it."

"Thank you, Katie. I do love you, and if you got out more, you would see that other people love you, too. I'm going to leave before I start crying." She blew a kiss and got into the car. "By the way, if you had a phone, I wouldn't have to drive all the way out here." Louise sped off, beeping the horn as she passed the porch.

I plopped into the chair, perplexed. *It's just a dream.* But, if it were just a dream, why was my stomach in knots and my heart racing? Looking toward the driveway, where it ducked down to turn onto Route 7, I yearned to see Gregory drive over the hill. I wouldn't rest until I saw his truck. *It was just a dream.*

* * *

A blue truck drove over the hill, bouncing toward the house at a slow speed. I stood to see who was coming. Since Louise had left just a couple of hours ago, she couldn't have come back so soon with bad news. I didn't see a siren on top of the roof — that and the fact it was a truck put me at ease. I was disappointed it wasn't Gregory.

A petite white lady stepped out of the driver's side and brushed her dress. I folded my arms and squinted when Timothy jumped out of the truck with a defiant stare. He opened his mouth to say something, but I held up my hand.

The lady was a little taller than I but much younger — in her mid-twenties, I guessed. Her hair was pinned back in a bun. She moved about, proper and prim. She grimaced as she grabbed Timothy's arm and marched him over to the porch. She wasn't intimidated by his size or his menacing African garb, which he would have to explain to me and his daddy later.

"Hello, Mrs. Smith. I'm Amy Broubaker, Tim's teacher. I know this isn't the usual protocol, and I guess I could have taken him to the principal's office, but I don't want him to get kicked out of summer school. But he won't listen to me, and I'm at my wit's end. He's a good student; he could make straight A's... but… I just don't know what to do with him."

"Ma'am, what has he done?"

She tossed me a look as if to say the list was too long. "Well, he disrupts the class with his constant preaching. He challenges everything. He criticizes everything. He preaches that Negroes are the original man, and all white people are evil devils, and that Negroes shouldn't listen to the white man. Did you know he believes that the white man was created in a test tube and that…?

"The Honorable Elijah Muhammad teaches.…"

"Timothy, hush up," I said, shooting him a look.

Timothy pursed his lips and stared off. Mrs. Broubaker sighed. "I don't have to warn you about that kind of talk. Tim is a smart boy."

"Boy. See, this is what I'm talking about. White people see us as boys and not men."

I shot Timothy another look. "Hush up, Timothy. You're in enough trouble." He quieted down again. "I assure you; Timothy was taught better than that. I'll speak to his daddy as soon as he comes home."

She glanced at Timothy and looked at me. "I just don't know what to do when he gets like this. I would hate for him to be kicked out of school over this. But, if he persists, the principle will expel him. What concerns me the most is… well, I don't know where to begin. I don't know where he gets those views. I have never heard such anti-Christian talk before."

"Timothy was raised in a Christian home. I can assure you of that."

"That kind of talk, overthrowing the white man, killing the white man, the white race is evil isn't safe for him to speak. You know what I mean."

I stole a glance at Timothy and squinted. He maintained his defiance. "I don't know where he gets that stuff from, but his daddy will give him a good talking to. I assure you."

She glanced around the farm. A frown came on her face. I knew what she thought, what everyone thought about the farm. How could we live in such squalor? How could we live in an old and dilapidated shack? How could we stand the unsightly junk sprawled around the yard? How could we bear the stench of slop and animals? But this was my oasis away from the evil world. God had placed me here, and I wouldn't live anywhere else. I loved my house—a shack by most people's standards. But to me, it was my humble palace—a gift from God.

She must have realized she was frowning because she quickly plastered a smile on her face. She locked eyes on my Bible. "You're a Christian?"

"Yes, I love the Lord."

"Wonderful," she said. "I do, too. What church do you attend?"

I thought the question was odd, since there was only one

church Negroes attended. "True Rock Missionary Baptist Church."

"I attend First Baptist in town," she said with a look of hesitancy. "It would be nice if you could come and visit us. It's all so silly — this prejudice against one another." She frowned and let out another sigh. "After summer school ends, I'm leaving Blount City. I'm thinking of heading out west to teach."

"May I ask why?"

"They stick me over here and tell me to teach, but they don't give me the proper facilities or resources to do my job. Don't get me wrong, I love teaching on this side of town, but I hate the politics. Maybe one day they'll integrate the schools like they did in Little Rock. I hate the way things are here. And I hate that Christians can't even fellowship the way God intended." She glanced around the farm again and looked at me. "I don't like it here. In Alabama. In Blount City. I don't like the South. You know how things are here. Both of us are Christians, and I can't even invite you to my church to fellowship. I can't have prayer, Bible study, or communion with you — with any Negro. Whites are not supposed to mix with coloreds. I'm just so tired of it."

It was strange listening to a white woman talk that way. I hadn't met any white people who felt as she did. Everyone accepted segregation as a part of our lives. Everyone tolerated it, except Gregory. I didn't know white people like her existed. "Is there anywhere where segregation isn't a part of our lives?"

"I hear up north and out west. That's where I'm thinking of heading. Why does it have to be this way, white people over there, Negroes over here? We're all going to live in one heaven. There won't be a black side of heaven and white side of heaven."

Her statement stunned me. "You really think heaven will be

integrated?"

"Oh, heaven yes! There won't be a white side of heaven and a black side of heaven. We'll live as one body in the Lord—the way we should be living here."

I glanced at Timothy. He squirmed, pining for the chance to respond, but I shook my head.

Mrs. Broubaker folded her arms, staring off toward the hills. "Maybe I'll join a group called the freedom riders. Have you heard of them?"

I nodded. "I think it dangerous what freedom riders are doing?"

"Something has to be done to end segregation. Have you heard of the sit-ins?"

I nodded. A shudder rocked through me. I'd begged Gregory not to get involved with the freedom riders or sit-ins, especially around here and in Birmingham.

"Well, a group of people want to organize freedom rides through the South on buses and stage sit-ins at lunch counters to protest segregation. People from all different races will join the riders."

For a moment, I thought she was trying to recruit me for her cause. She peered at me as if waiting for an answer. "Sounds dangerous. You be careful."

"Probably is. But, something has to be done about these unjust laws. It's wrong. It's not Christian. With the cry of freedom comes danger, I suppose. But, if we can change things around here, it'll be worth facing the danger."

"I suppose."

Her gaze lingered on me for a moment. I hoped she didn't expect me to join those riders. I don't march with Gregory. I prefer to leave things alone and to be left alone. Things are fine with me — here in my paradise.

"Well, I'd better be heading back. Thanks for talking to me, Mrs. Smith. It was a real delight. I hope maybe one day to talk with you again. I'd love to share my heart with a fellow Christian — talk about things, life, the Lord, our faith. Believe it or not, I don't have a lot of friends. People shy away from me for believing that God made all men equal. They don't want to hear that kind of talk across the tracks. I love talking about the Lord, and if you love the Lord, then you're my sister. I don't care if you're white or black."

"I'd like that. I really would. Come by anytime. I'm usually here, except on Sundays."

She smiled. "I just might do that. I love talking about the Lord, and I love talking to God's people. I can tell you're a child of God." She looked as if she wanted to give me a hug, but she restrained herself. "Tim might as well stay home, since it is the end of the day. Tim, you have to do better."

"I'll speak to his daddy when he gets home."

She nodded, jumped into her truck, and drove off. I glared at Timothy. He huffed as if to force his case. "I don't want to hear it. I'll let your daddy deal with you. Go do your chores."

Meeting Miss Broubaker really blessed my soul. Her sincerity encouraged me in just the few minutes we'd talked. I didn't know there were white people who felt as she did. I wanted to know her, if that was possible.

What she said had surprised me. I had never considered if heaven were segregated. Things, as long I could remember, were separate. Negroes had always lived separately from whites. My daddy had told me it had been that way since slavery. Deep down, I guess, I assumed people would be segregated in heaven. In school, white teachers taught that

Negroes were inferior to whites, and that it wasn't natural for the races to mix together. Preachers preached that it wasn't God's will for Negroes and whites to live together. To do so would violate his will and the natural order. To hear this white woman proclaim that heaven will be integrated blew my mind.

I grabbed my Bible off the chair and sat to read. I was desperate to know what God's Word said about this place where skin color wouldn't matter. I pored through the pages, searching passages on heaven.

* * *

Two snorts rattled from my mouth, jolting me from my sleep. Gregory kissed my forehead and gave me a squeeze. I smiled, still reeling from the special time we'd shared. With the ruckus we'd kicked up, God had to have put the children into a deep sleep. The night was young—around midnight, I figured. I could go for another special time.

Thoughts of being with Gregory charged my anticipation, now that he was going to be home. Our days, I selfishly planned, would be filled with talks, walks, and special times. In between all that, he'd catch up on chores. I really looked forward to our new life together.

Peace and calm held the farm in perfect tranquility. Not so much as a whisper of a breeze. Beads of sweat dripped from my body, though I lay perfectly still. The moon colored the night with a bluish tint. Insects buzzed and whined. Frogs croaked. Owls hooted. It couldn't have been a more perfect end to the night. I was where I wanted to be, snuggled tight in my husband's arms. It couldn't have been more peaceful. Struggling to keep my eyelids open, I was fast disappearing into a blissful sleep.

An ominous roar crept through the window. My eyes snapped open.

Chapter Four

Gregory sprang to his feet and shot to the window. "Dear Lord, no."

Sitting up, I clutched the sheet against my chest. "Gregory, what is it?"

Gregory didn't look back. "Katie, stays in this room, and don't come out."

"You're scaring me. What are you looking at?"

"Dos what I say, and stays in this room."

"What about the children?"

Gregory whirled around with widened eyes. The dread on his face jarred whatever sense of security I had.

"Help us, Jesus." He threw his coveralls on with no shirt or shoes and rushed out of the bedroom. "Gets dressed!" he yelled back.

Stumbling out of bed, I paused for a moment then dragged myself to the window. Three sets of headlights stampeded toward the house in a single-file procession. I shuddered as my black flowered print dress slid over my body. "Please, Lord, don't let this be true."

I closed the window and lowered the shade. I don't know why I did that.

"Katie!" I flinched at the thunder of his voice. "Get out here."

Closing my eyes, I drew a long breath. My heart pounded so hard, my knees weakened. I walked into the living room, dazed and unable to think clearly. I lowered the window and shade and closed my eyes. *Please, let this be a bad dream.* When I opened my eyes, Edward and Timothy yawned, clueless about the danger. Maxine's eyes darted between Gregory and me. Ruby stared fixedly at Gregory with no expression on her face.

Gregory peeked out of the window. He turned around with that dreadful look on his face and huddled us as snug as he could. "Lord Jesus, please, keep my family safe from those evil men. I commit 'em to You."

Bright lights flounced across the window shade, casting a dim glow over the room. Gregory raised his head with furrowed brows and terror fixed in his eyes. This was the first time I'd ever seen fear in him. He wasn't afraid for himself but for us.

Car doors opened and slammed shut. Engines revved, horns blared, and voices jeered. Shadows bounced across the window.

"Come out here, Smith!" a voice hollered.

Gregory embraced each of the children. "I gots to go, y'all."

A shattering crash sent shards of broken window pane crashing to the floor. I screamed. The girls screamed. The boys jumped.

"Gregory Smith!" the voice yelled. "You get out here, now!"

"Yeah, nigger, get out here before we come in there and get ya," another voice shouted.

"Daddy, what's going on?" Maxine said.

Gregory peeked out the window again and shook his head. He reached for the door. His fingers trembled as they touched the latch.

Gregory, don't walk through that door. I wished to God I could say something to keep him in the house, but I couldn't utter the words. I couldn't move. It was as if an evil force had clamped around my entire body and held me tight in its clutches.

Ruby latched her arms around Gregory. "Daddy, don't go out there."

He reached around his back and gently grasped her hands. "Baby, I gotta go. You gotta be strong." Tears raced from his eyes as she squeezed tighter. Torment crinkled his face. He shook his head. "Katie, get this child." I wanted to respond, but I couldn't move. He peered into my eyes as he pried Ruby's hands from around his waist and held them firmly. He looked into her eyes. "I gotta go, Ruby." He leaned toward her cheek but shoved her away, hard and cruel. "Stay over there, baby." He stood upright, wiped his eyes, and unlatched the door. "Dear Lord, they's in Your hands now."

Gregory pulled the door open. A shaft of light poured into the room as he turned and looked at us. He held us with his eyes one more time and stepped into the light as if stepping into heaven's glory. I tried to will the strength to keep him inside. I tried to muster the power to hold him still. I closed my eyes to hold that image of him in my mind. I wanted to hear him say, "Everything will be all right." I wanted to feel his gentle breath brushing against my cheeks, whispering, "I love you." The door shut. I flinched. When I opened my eyes, Gregory was gone.

Chapter Five

Gregory's silhouette appeared against the window shade. Another shadow crept up behind him. Cradling my stomach, I tried to scream, but only groans sputtered out. *Watch out!* I was desperate to warn. The shadow crept closer. *Get away from him!* I hoped to ward the shadow away but fear shackled my tongue. The shadow raised its arms, holding a long something. *Look out!*

"What y'all…?" The shadow swung. There was a loud thud, an "Uuuh," and that was the last I heard from Gregory. His shadow disappeared from the shade. I squeezed my eyes shut as tight as I could hold them.

"Take that, you dirty, stinking nigger," someone yelled.

"Get 'em, boys." *The man with the Fedora.* There was no mistaking his voice.

The thudding echoed in my ears and didn't seem to stop. "Betcha he won't be agitating the darkies after we is done with him." That was a different voice, but one just as vicious.

Shots fired. My animals squealed, yelped, yowled, and yipped. I kept my eyes closed, straining to hear any sounds from Gregory. *Scream out, moan, or grunt, Gregory, anything to let me know you're all right.* I would even settle to hear him beg for his life. That would have meant he was alive.

I opened my eyes, unleashing a stream of tears down my cheeks. The horror etched on the children's faces pricked my heart. I wished I could shield them from the atrocity happening outside, but my strength had failed. Ruby eased over to the window and stared out. I wanted to cover her eyes. I could imagine the brutality she saw.

She yanked the door open and bolted out. A power I only can ascribe to God energized me. I darted after Ruby and grabbed her shoulders before she left the porch. Wrapping my arms around her, I held her still. Gregory lay on the ground, his limbs twisted and flung in every direction. His face was beaten, battered, and bloodied. I didn't recognize him. "Oh, Lord, please, let him be dead," I screamed.

The men stopped and looked intently at me with cold, callous stares. They had no mercy, compassion, or remorse. I looked down so as not to make eye contact, only glancing up momentarily. As if nothing had happened, they went back to savagely murdering my husband.

My gaze fell on Gregory. An agonizing pang sliced through my heart. His eyes were fixed open and empty. He was gone. *Thank God.* What were his thoughts in his last moments? Did he think about the children, the times they'd played together, the times he'd lectured them, the family talks on the porch? Did he think about us, our walks around the farm, or our special times together? Or, was he preoccupied with the mob's assault on his body?

Lord, give him peace and strength to pass through the river of death. A smile broke through my glower, as I envisioned the Lord Himself pulling Gregory from the dark, murky grave into his loving arms. I opened my eyes with that comforting image.

The man with the fedora straddled Gregory. "I told ya I was going to get ya if you didn't stop stirring the niggers. But you had to keep preaching your 'free the niggers' crap. We ain't never mixing with the likes of you." He stood, heaved, and spat on Gregory.

"Let's do it, Gus. Let's lynch this nigger," a short, stout man shouted. He had golden-blond bangs and a boyish face, almost innocent-looking, but his viciousness matched Gus's, if not more.

With a wicked grin plastered across his face, Gus looked toward the oak tree.

"Come on, let's do it," the stout man egged Gus on.

Gus kicked Gregory in his side and stomped his chest. Straightening his hat, he looked at a short, scrawny man wearing thick black glasses. "Lester, drag this boy over to that tree."

Lester licked his lips and watched Gus stomp away. "Hey, this is a big ol' coon. I can't carry him by myself."

Two young men emerged from the back of the house with rifles slung on their shoulders. One of them, the loud one, yelled at the short, stout man. "Orville, you shoulda seen how fast that barn went up. You shoulda seen those animals trying to run out of the barn faster than we could pick them off, but we got 'em all. Some of 'em fell a-blazin'."

The other man, the quiet one, was well-groomed with a thick mustache that reminded me of Hitler. He wore round wire-frame eyeglasses. He wasn't dressed like the others, in T-shirts and jeans. He wore a short-sleeved dress shirt tucked into dress slacks.

"Having fun yet, Deacon?" Orville said to the man with the Hitler mustache.

The deacon glowered.

"How come y'all not dragging this boy over to that tree?" Orville shouted.

Lester pointed. "They staring at us. I can't do this with them watching."

Orville looked at me, then back at Lester. "Get this boy over to that tree, so we can get this over with. I have to take my truck to the shop early in the morning. Don't pay them niggers any mind," he ordered and stormed away.

"I'll give you a hand, Lester," the deacon said.

Lester nodded, and they grabbed Gregory by his armpits and dragged him across the yard. One of the men hopped in his truck and parked with the bed facing the tree. Another man parked the other car with the headlights shining on the tree.

"Daddy, Daddy!" Ruby screamed, jerking away from me. By the time I looked up, she already had her hands around Gregory, clutching his body. "You leave my daddy alone."

Dropping Gregory, Lester looked back. "What the heck?"

Gus grabbed the rifle from Earl Ray and stormed over to Lester. "What's going on?"

"It's his kid. She came out of nowhere," Lester said. Gus looked down at Ruby.

"Please, Lord, help my baby."

He raised the butt of the rifle high above his head, but Lester grabbed his arm, "No, Gus, you'll crack her skull wide open if you hit her like that."

"Oh, Lord, please don't let this happen!" I yelled.

Gus jerked his arm away. "I don't give a crap about this little nigger. They're all animals to me." Gus took his foot and shoved Ruby off of her father. She rolled over, crouching on her hands and knees, squinting defiantly. "You a feisty little picaninny, ain't ya?" He leaned in. "You stay put, or we gon' string you up next to your daddy." He stood. "Get this nigger over to that tree. We've wasted enough time here. And you, stay put, you little monkey."

Looking up to heaven, I exhaled a silent, "Thank you,

Lord," as Gus stormed away. God's strength came over me, filling my soul. I walked as briskly as I could and with a single swoop scooped Ruby into my arms and walked back toward the porch.

"Mama, Daddy's dead. His eyes didn't move," Ruby whispered in my ear, resting her head on my shoulders.

I squeezed Ruby tight. "I know, baby. He's in heaven now with the Lord. They can't hurt your daddy anymore."

Setting Ruby on the porch and huddling the children behind me, I looked fixedly at the tree. "The Lord is our strength. He will see us through this." Ignoring their sniffles and wails, I continued, "Y'all look to the Lord. He's going take care of us now."

Earl Ray threw the noose over the branch while another man tied the other end of the rope to the back of his truck. Lester and the deacon threw Gregory in front of the tree.

"Throw that rope on that boy," Orville said.

Pacing back and forth with gritted teeth, Gus snatched the rope from Earl Ray and slapped the noose around Gregory's neck, jerking the slack tight. Staring into Gregory's eyes, he spat.

Orville looked at the deacon with an annoying smirk. "You want to say a prayer over 'em?" The deacon didn't respond. "Let 'er rip!" Orville yelled, slapping the back of the truck.

The engine revved. The truck lurched forward, jerking Gregory's body up in the air.

"Oh my God!" Maxine screamed and buried her head in my shoulder.

"Now, that's how you lynch a nigger," Orville yelled.

"Ooh wee, look at that boy dangle!" Earl Ray shouted.

Lester tied the rope around the tree while the deacon held the slack. Lester joined the jeering as the men slapped one another's back.

As I watched them, I wondered what Gus's thoughts were, now that he had murdered my husband. Was he coming for us next? As I peered toward the tree, Gregory's words came to mind. "Lord, forgive those men for the evil they do." I knew this was what God expected of me, but how could I truly forgive them from my heart?

Pacing back and forth, Gus fixed his gaze on Gregory. He stopped and reached into his coveralls pocket. He looked up and flung his arms.

Orville jerked his head. "Whatcha doing, Gus? What's that you're slinging, boy? You're getting it all over me."

Gus struck a match and flicked it. A bluish-yellow flame swirled up Gregory's legs and enveloped his body.

"Oh, my Lord, Mama, why are they doing this to Daddy," Maxine shouted.

"Whatcha go and do that for, Gus?" Orville said.

"We couldn't leave without barbecuing us a nigger, could we?"

Orville shook his head. "He was already dead, ya dang fool."

Gus laughed and slapped Orville's back. "Well, I wanted him good-n-dead. Now we can call it a night, boys."

He waved them on, following Orville, Earl Ray, and Lester.

"This nigger's blood is all over me," Orville said, feverishly wiping his clothes. "It looks like I'm wearing a red polka-dotted shirt. I gotta get this coon's filth off of me."

I moved in front of the children. Not that it would do any good. My small frame wouldn't stop them if they were coming for us. I looked directly at each man as they stood by the car, wondering how anyone could be so cruel and vicious.

Orville got into the car first, never acknowledging my presence. Earl Ray puffed his chest out, arrogantly displaying Gregory's blood on his T-shirt. He flashed a gloating grin and then slipped into the car. Lester looked my way. When our eyes met, guilt, remorse, and shame spilled from his soul. *What did my husband ever do to you, for you to take his life? What my children ever did to you to make them fatherless? What did I ever do to you to make me a widow?* That's what I wanted to ask him, but he turned his head and retreated to the backseat. He glided his tongue across his lips and stared the other way.

Gus looked toward the tree and glowered. He disappeared behind the car for a moment.

Orville looked around. "Come on, Gus, let's go. I gotta get up early."

Slamming the trunk with a maddening gaze and sickening grin, Gus waved a bottle stuffed with a rag, in front of me. I braced for the end. I even hoped this was the moment we would make our transition into the Lord's presence and be reunited with Gregory. Forever, we would be a family. Just the hope of that filled me with peace and charged me with anticipation. I wasn't afraid to die. I looked forward to seeing my Lord face-to-face.

Gus's menacing squint was meant to crush me. I resisted. He wanted my submission to his terror. I refused. Instead, it made me welcome death all the more. I looked fixedly into his eyes. His pupils dilated with a vicious scowl. He stepped out of my peripheral vision.

I winced at the smash of the window. A loud whoosh, pop, and crackling told me what I feared. My bedroom, where just an hour ago I'd lain in my husband's arms, ignited in flames.

Gus stood before me with a gloat in his eyes that demanded

I bow. I stood even taller. He waited for me to declare him the victor. I denied his triumph over me.

"Come on, Gus, for crying out loud, let's go!" Orville called.

God's presence saturated me with strength and assurance I couldn't explain. "My Father is the Creator of the universe. I have nothing to fear," I mumbled. "All this man can do to me is kill my body. He cannot destroy my soul. I belong to God. He is my Shepherd, my Savior, and my Redeemer. Who can separate me from my God's love? Not this man." Compassion filled my heart for this lost sinner. *I am free in Jesus. He is bound by hate and rage.* "God loves this fool."

Gus leaned toward me and grimaced.

I looked up toward heaven, smiled, and peered directly into his eyes. "Mister, Jesus loves you, and so do I. Jesus forgives you, and so do I."

Gus, his eyes shifting from side to side, opened his mouth, but my words had stifled his fury. He hurled a wad of spit that exploded all over my face. My stomach tightened. I wanted to wipe his vileness away, but I let it dribble off my chin. He squinted with a look of surprise. "You better keep your nigger mouth shut, or you'll be swinging dead like that husband of yours."

"Jesus loves you, and so do I."

Gus stared into my eyes, shook his head, and jumped into the car.

"You didn't have to burn them niggers out. We came here for Smith," Orville said.

The car sped off as soon as Gus slammed the door. "Segregation now, segregation tomorrow, segregation forever!" he shouted.

I wiped my face as I watched the trail of red lights

disappear into a haze of dust and vanish off of the land. *It's over.*
Everything that was my life here is over.

Chapter Six

An angry flame raged at us with a vicious crackling and popping. A blast of heat scorched my back. "Move!" I shouted.

Scrambling to get the children off the porch, I spun around as the roof collapsed, shooting bright orange embers in every direction. I threw my hands over my mouth, horrified by how fast the fire devoured our home. In a moment, everything that had been my life was gone. The stench of burnt wood filled the air. Smoke irritated my eyes.

"Why did they do this?" Maxine screamed.

There was no answer—not one that would make sense. There was no justification for this. These men didn't know us. They didn't know whether we were good or bad, saints or sinners. Only one evil could cause this. "Hate, baby. Hate did this."

Maxine tugged my arm. "Mama, we have to leave this place."

Hearing those words made me snap. At that moment, I lost all sense of reality. My world collapsed in on me. Nothing seemed real. "We're not going anywhere!" I shouted.

The children looked at one another, bewildered.

"Mama, everything is gone. There's nothing left here," Maxine pleaded.

"Y'all get into the car." I refused to let go, even though I knew everything I held dear had been violently taken away from me. I was desperate to cling to anything that was my life here: furniture, clothes, crinkled photos, familiar smells—something, anything that could keep me on this farm. "This is our home. We're not going anywhere. God gave us this land. He's going to keep us safe here, on this land."

Saying those words jarred me back into reality. They used to fill me with joy and peace. But now, watching what had once been my home fizzle into crackling embers, an agonizing pang tore through my soul. Where was God? How could He let this happen? Where was the strength that caused me to stand boldly in the face of those evil men? I no longer felt God's presence. I felt abandoned and destitute.

The children climbed into the car. I didn't know how to comfort them. They would ask why, just as I had asked. I didn't have the answer. And as I glanced up toward heaven, I knew only silence would reply. What would God say? What could He say? What answer He could give that would ease my pain?

I paced back and forth, shaking my fist. My head spun. I felt weak. As I bent over, I gagged, and my stomach released everything that was in it. I wiped my mouth and stared as the flames died out. I screamed at the top of my voice. I moaned, twisted, and jerked about, wanting someone, anyone, to yank me from this horrible nightmare. I wanted to wake up in the comfort of my home, with my family nestled close and Gregory holding me tenderly. Only God could make that happen, but He was nowhere to be found.

I looked toward the tree. The charred form hung straight as a plumb line and perfectly still. "Gregory. Oh, Gregory, what have they done to you?"

I squeezed my eyes shut, but the images of terror hounded me. Horns blared, and engines revved. I could hear the spiteful jeers, vile curses, and annoying snickers. Windows smashed, and gunfire popped everywhere. My animals yelped, and tires peeled. I recounted every horrible detail with vivid clarity. Gregory being dragged across the yard, violently jerked off of the ground, set on fire, and swinging like a burning rag doll played over and over in my mind. I screamed.

The flames had died out when I opened my eyes. A few embers flickered, and burnt wood crackled. That was all that was left of my home. The land reeked of charred animal flesh and burnt rubble. The air was deathly still. The moon, bright and full, illuminated the hillside with a soft light. Crickets chirped, frogs croaked, mosquitoes whined, but the owls didn't hoot. Raccoons and other varmints had fled the cursed place. I yearned for the peace that had once clothed the land.

I stood in the hot and stuffy air for two, maybe three hours; I didn't know. Time stood still. Sweat soaked my dress. Fatigue, exhaustion, and biting mosquitoes forced me into the car. *This shouldn't have happened here. Nothing bad or evil was ever supposed to happen on this land.*

God, why did You let evil come here? Was there something I could have done to stop this? Did I sin against You? Are You angry with me? You warned me all day. Why didn't I listen to You? Looking around at everything, what residue of hope I had left had vanished. "God has forsaken us."

I hated Gus. The more I looked around, the more those bitter feelings churned in my soul; it was the only way I could spite him. I despised his malicious stare, the nauseating sound of his voice, and the foul stench of his breath. Most of all, I loathed his evil, gloating smile. I hated Gus for destroying everything good in my life.

How am I going to make it without Gregory? I'm lost without him. I'll miss my friend, my soul mate, my lover. He was my husband, whom God gave to me. I glanced at the tree. *He was my companion God took away from me.* Oh, how my heart ached for my husband. I felt my sanity slipping away.

I wanted to hate, vent poisonous venom, afflict pain the way Gus hurt me. I felt helpless, with nowhere or no one to turn to. At that moment, I needed to hate someone, anyone, but I knew I'd get no satisfaction. Only hating Gus would bring me the resolve I deserved.

I thought to curse God, as Job's wife suggested. He'd allowed that monster to desolate my life. I knew it was foolish to think that way. I couldn't fight God. To what court would I plead my case? What charges would I bring against the Almighty? Despair consumed my soul.

"Cock-a-doodle-doo," rang out, announcing daybreak.

Whipping around, I desperately looked for my old friend. Hope filled my heart. "Thank God Ben made it," I whispered. "Maybe God isn't through with us yet." I lowered my head and wept.

Morning crept over the hills as if to taunt me. I wished it was night; darkness had been merciful, had masked the brutality. I did not see the horrors of the night, not its gory details. A black pile of burnt rubble lay where the house once stood. Everything was destroyed: furniture, clothes, dishes, buckets, everything. I hoped some of the animals might have survived as Ben had, but charred carcasses lay sprawled among the burnt rubble.

The outhouse was the only structure left standing. I chuckled. At least, we can use the bathroom. My eyes fell toward the tree. I snapped my head away, but it was too late. I closed my eyes and shook my head, trying to shake the horrific image from my mind. *It wasn't human. It was just a burnt, battered, mangled hunk of flesh.* The butchery and the brutality were more than I could bear. I hated that I had looked. *Daylight, you are so cruel.*

"Eddie, get me out of here, now!" I screamed, jolting the children from their sleep. "Take me from this place. I can't stay here anymore!"

Edward jumped, fiddling with the key and patting the pedal. Gasoline fumes filled the car. Coughing and gagging, we spilled out, gasping for air. I didn't know what to do. I lowered my head and cradled my stomach. When I looked up, Maxine's hand covered her mouth. She gawked with wide eyes. Ruby stared with no expression. Edward turned his head. Timothy squinted with pursed lips.

"Don't look at that!" I shouted. "Turn your heads. That's not your father."

Maxine took me in her arms. "Mama, it's going to be all right."

I jerked away. "No, it's not going to be all right. Eddie, get me out of here, now."

"Mama, the engine is flooded. The car won't start," Edward said.

I buried my head in Maxine's shoulder. "I just want to leave this place."

"It's going to be all right, Mama." Maxine held me as tenderly as she could, but it didn't help. "Eddie, try to start the car," she said.

The roar of an engine barreled over the hill. My head snapped up; my eyes fixed on the driveway. Terror seized me. Two people raced toward us.

"They're coming back to kill us!" Edward shouted.

I hadn't escaped death after all. This time, the children

would be brutally tortured and murdered before my eyes, in the full light of day. "Eddie, start the car, now!" I screamed.

Edward jumped into the car, frantically turning the key and stomping the gas pedal, but the more he stomped, the more the engine flooded.

Hopelessness and helplessness overwhelmed me. "Eddie, please start the car," I said barely above a whisper.

"Eddie!" Maxine shouted.

Lifting my head, I held Maxine and reached over and grabbed Ruby, pulling her in tight. I purposed not to shield the children from death. They would never have to experience terror again. They would never have to feel the pain of a loved one being ripped from their hearts. Yes, I welcomed death. I closed my eyes and prayed the end would come swiftly.

"It's Auntie Louise and Uncle Curly," Maxine shouted.

I kept my eyes closed, skeptical about what I'd heard. Maxine and Ruby broke away from me. I opened my eyes. Maxine pointed toward the black sedan. *It's over.* I softly sighed and bowed my head as a single tear fell from my eye. My elation was mixed with disappointment. I looked over at Gregory's form. *It'll be a while before I see you again, my darling.*

Louise jumped out of the car, looking around. "Oh, my sweet Lord. I can't believe what I'm seeing. I was just here yesterday." She looked toward the tree. "Curly, is that...?" Her eyes fell on Ruby and widened. "Curly, Ruby's hurt. She's bleeding. The girl has blood all over her." She grabbed Ruby and felt her chest, arms, and face. "Ruby, where are you hurt?"

Ruby stared, eyes blank—almost zombie-like.

Louise looked at me and turned to Curly. "She's not bleeding. This is Gregory's blood. Katie has his blood on her, too." She squeezed Ruby. "It's going to be all right, baby."

Ruby reached around Louise and squeezed. "They killed my daddy, Auntie Louise."

"I know, baby. We are here now, and no one is going to hurt you." She looked at the boys and reached out her hand. Timothy was the first to wrap his arms around her waist with a tight squeeze. "It's going to be all right, babies."

Edward found a spot and latched onto her, too. "I'm so glad you're here, Auntie Louise. It's been a horrible night."

It broke my heart that I couldn't comfort my children. I should have been their refuge. I should have been the one they found shelter in. But, I had nothing in me to give.

Louise shook her head. "I'm so sorry, babies, for what's happened to y'all."

She pried herself from their grip and nodded at Curly. He did the best he could not to cry. Curly was a thin man, bald in the middle of his head and shorter than Louise. He was timid like the reverend, but he was a tower of strength this morning. He thoroughly inspected each of the children and guided them to his car.

Louise grabbed Maxine's hand. Maxine nodded, her eyes puffy and tear filled. Slowly, Louise walked toward me. My knees buckled as I fell into her arms. "They killed him, Louise!" I screamed and buried my head in her chest. "They killed my Gregory. They strung him up like he was an animal."

"I know baby. I know. Everything is going to be all right."

That's a lie. Those men broke my heart and crushed my spirit. Nothing could ever change that—no apologies, explanations, or absolutions. No amount of justice would be enough to heal my heart and restore what was taken from me.

A train of cars, trucks and station wagons filed over the driveway as the sun broke over the hills. They parked wherever they found space. I stood perfectly still and stared at everyone as they poured from their cars. They were too late. Old Man Tank backed his station wagon as close to me as he could. Louise opened the rear door and sat me on the edge of the car. People streamed by, hugged, touched, and expressed their sorrow. Expressionless, I ignored them all.

Women attended to the children, wiping them clean and helping them change their clothes. Several women erected a wall of sheets around Ruby and me. One of the ladies removed my bloodstained dress and wiped the soot and smudges from my face. The lady's eyes drooped, and her mouth hung open. Expressionless, I stared ahead as if she weren't there. She helped me change into a clean dress and kept silent.

Another woman kept shaking her head, struggling to control her emotions. She removed Ruby's bloodstained gown, cleaned her body, and put a pair of pants and a shirt on her. I couldn't think of the women's names, though I knew them.

Reverend Sims clenched his jaw, but tears escaped his eyes. He pointed toward the car as he talked with Edward. He patted Edward's back and came and stooped in front of me. "Sister Smith, are you all right?" I couldn't respond. "We're going to remove him now." He grimaced and glanced at Louise. "Why didn't you leave in the truck?" I didn't answer. He nodded and patted my knee, then looked at Louise. "Do you know who called you and told you about this?"

Louise shook her head. "I got a call… I guess, thirty minutes ago. He said, 'That nigger's dead. We strung him up.' Then he hung up. Then I called you."

Reverend Sims looked around, baffled. "I felt something was wrong. That's why I called everyone and told them to come as fast as they could and bring whatever they could. I didn't know what to expect. I thought it was just a fire, nothing like this."

More people arrived and poured from their vehicles. Horror, dismay, and shock were plastered on their faces. Tears gushed from their eyes as they tried to express their condolences. Most of the people didn't know what to say to me, and I didn't want to be bothered. I wasn't in the mood to hear how sorry they were, how Gregory was a good man, or that emptiest of all promises: "If there's anything I can do, let me know." Could they bring my Gregory back? Could they take the pain out of my heart?

A gray '55 Chevy Impala charged over the hill and screeched to a halt. Mavis, my youngest sister, jumped out of her car, hair half in rollers, barely wearing her housecoat, screamed hysterically. Falling to my knees, she wailed, "Katie, Katie, what have they done to you?"

A loud, anguished howl made me look up to see Jonny, Gregory's brother, on his knee in front of the body. "They kilted my brother, man. I'm gonna get them for this." Henry tried to console him, but he jerked his shoulder away, refusing any consolation. Reverend Sims walked over and knelt beside him, patting his back. "Naw, Rev, they kilted my brother. He ain't never hurt nobody. He only did good for our peoples, and they kilted him for that."

The reverend looked around. People wandered aimlessly. He glanced at the children and me. Jonny's friends showed up and started murmuring about going to town. Reverend Sims ordered the deacons to remove the body from the tree.

Henry found Maxine and held her. She fell into his arms and wept. I was glad he attended to her. He was gentle and nurturing, something I couldn't give her at this moment. Louise and Curly took care of the other children.

While the deacons prepared to take the remains down, Louise gathered the children. "Katie, we're going to take y'all back to my house." Louise pulled me to my feet and held me on one side. Mavis held my other side. "Don't y'alls worry about nothing. We're going to rebuild this place brand-new."

I jerked away. "We're not building anything here ever again. This land is dead to me. Take me from this place. I'm never stepping foot on this land again."

Chapter Seven

The week leading up to the funeral was long and grueling and wore out every nerve I had. People pulled on me from every direction. Some wanted to talk. Others wanted to tell me how to grieve. There were those who told me what I should do about Gus, and there were those who had the nerves to tell me to move on from Gregory—marry and have more kids. A few wanted to hear the gory details about that night. I wanted to be left alone, so I locked myself away.

I kept the drapes drawn in my new surroundings, unaware the darkness nurtured my anguish, confusion, and bitterness of soul. The room sizzled. I perspired from every pore of my body, soaking my sheets with musk. The room reeked.

My self-imposed exile left me alone with my thoughts— mostly about what those men had done to me. I curled into the fetal position. I didn't consider the torture my imagination would afflict. When I closed my eyes, the horrors of that night played vividly in my mind. I could smell the stench of burnt flesh and rubbish. The sounds of screaming, yelping, and whooping animals blared in my ears. The charred, mangled form of my husband hanging caused an excruciating pang in every fiber of my being.

I got out of bed, wringing my hands, and paced back and forth. The room had lots of space, with an oak dresser, chest, and desk. The full-size bed was made up with thick quilts and stuffed with plenty of pillows. The décor was like something out of a furniture magazine. I couldn't enjoy its comfort, though, because Gregory wasn't here to take away the loneliness in my heart.

Louise's house was a two-story white frame with three bedrooms upstairs. My bedroom was on the first floor in the back, just off the kitchen. It was a guest bedroom for visiting ministers. I liked its isolation. The window looked out into a large yard enclosed by a white picket fence. I'd loved visiting here, but I'd never thought this would be my home. It didn't feel like home. I felt out of place.

I threw myself on the bed and sat against the headboard with my knees drawn up to my chin, yearning for happier times, yearning to do the things I'd used to do on my farm. I knew that part of my existence was over, but I refused to accept this new life. *Why, God? Why did You allow those men to destroy me?* Looking toward the door, I wished Gregory would burst through, sweep me into his arms, and take me back to our paradise. *Why, God? Why did You take my husband away from me?* They were questions that would never be answered. God's silence only strengthened my despondency.

Like a chain wrapped around my body, forging its links by the moment, despair latched onto me, dragging me further into its dark pit. My sanity was slipping away. I lost the ability to reason. I'd entered into a dangerous place with no will to fight.

A soft knock brought me back. Louise stuck her head in. "Katie, you awake?"

"Yes, I'm awake," I said, wishing she would go away.

"I know you don't want to be bothered, but there's someone here to see you. I think you should talk to her." As I raised my head to decline, Louise rushed over to fling open the drapes and raise the window. The harsh morning sun tore through the darkness, making me squint. A strong breeze pushed a whiff a fresh air into the room. She gave me a quick look-over to make sure I was presentable, but she couldn't do anything about the odor. She scooted to the door and waved her hand. "Come on in."

The young lady stepped in with a pleasant smile. I didn't recognize her at first. She wore a dark-blue dress and a matching hat. She sat on the bed with her ankles crossed, and her hands folded on her lap. She held her chin up. Her petite frame and proper, prim mannerisms made me remember her from the other day. She wasn't fazed by the stench. Louise must have warned her, or she really wanted to talk to me.

"Hello, Mrs. Smith. I'm sorry for your loss," she said. I stared at her with no expression. "You remember me, don't you? I'm Miss Broubaker, Timothy's teacher from school." I nodded. "You have to press charges against the men who did this. You have to fight against this evil system. I know it might be too soon to bring this up, but I just want you to know there are people who are ready to stand with you on this."

She reminded me of Gregory, full of zeal and vigor for the cause. Why was fighting for Negroes' rights so important to her? She was young and beautiful. She could have any life she wanted. I wondered what white folks thought about her work for civil rights — not too pleased I supposed. Was she ready to die for what she believed?

Taking her hand, I forced a smile. "Miss Broubaker, now is not the time to talk. I barely can think straight. On Saturday, I'm burying my husband...."

"I'm sorry, Mrs. Smith. I didn't mean to be insensitive. I just wanted you to know that there are white people who want to see you get justice."

"Do you love the Lord, Miss Broubaker?"

She furrowed her brow. "Why, yes. I believe I told you that the other day."

"Gregory believed that the civil rights movement and the Gospel were not the same."

Miss Broubaker squinted. "He did?"

"He questioned if God's will was being done in the movement. 'God has to change men's hearts first. Then you can stop prejudice. Only the Gospel can do that,' he said." Miss Broubaker's eyes shifted down as she considered what I said. "He was going to leave his work. But, I don't want to talk about it now—I can't. After this is over, I'll sit down with you and tell you his entire story." I left it at that and watched her stand.

"I'd like that, Mrs. Smith." She touched my hand and smiled. She stared at me with disappointment in her eyes. She wanted to hear about marches, sit-ins, arrests, and the great motivators of the movement, not doubts or questions if God was in the struggle. "I'll contact you sometime after the funeral. I'm very sorry for your loss, Mrs. Smith," she said and walked out of the room.

I lay back down to brood. I figured since I wasn't getting the answers I sought, I had the right to sulk in my sorrows. Life terrified me now. Men could just come on your land, destroy everything, and get away with it. It angered me that my Lord allowed that. People had told me God had a purpose in this. What purpose could He have that would allow evil to prevail? What good could come from taking everything from me?

* * *

I dragged myself to the edge of the bed and just sat. The

day I dreaded had finally come; it meant a final farewell. With all my heart, I didn't want to say goodbye. I had hidden in my room every day, all day, hoping somehow that would keep this day from coming. Maybe if I didn't get dressed this nightmare would go away.

Louise barged through the door and whisked the drapes open. This time, she didn't knock. "Katie, you have to get dressed. We have to be at the church by ten."

It was as if everyone came in on cue. Maxine brought the dress I would wear and laid it on the bed. Mavis set her makeup kit on the dresser. Ruby laid a bag with stockings and undergarments next to the dress. Edward and Timothy loomed outside the door. I think they just wanted to know I was all right. Seeing them did my heart good.

Louise pulled me to my feet and led me to the bathroom upstairs. When she was sure I was okay, she closed the door. Leaning on the sink, I stared into the mirror. This was the first time I'd seen my face since that night. The gaunt image bothered me. Red and swollen eyes stared at me. My collarbones bulged from my skin. My hair was tangled in a frizzy mess.

It took all the energy I could muster to wash up. My stomach growled. I hadn't eaten in days. I needed nourishment. It was time I got myself together. *Look at me. I'm the only one hurting.* I allowed myself to see only death and misery. I had blinded my eyes to the life I still had: my children, my health, and most of all my Lord. It was time I stopped blaming God. Those evil men destroyed my life; God didn't. They murdered Gregory; God didn't.

Lord, forgive me. Help me come out of this despair. I blamed You when I should have trusted You. I hid from You when I should have run into Your arms. Give me strength to go on.

I slipped back into my bedroom and sat on the edge of the bed. Mavis came in and stood by the chest. She peered at me with concern. I appreciated her presence. She had decided to move back home after living in Atlanta. Being the youngest, she was the prettiest of the Scotts girls, and the wildest. Even without makeup, men flocked to her as if she were a movie star. And she exploited her beauty. Her eye for fashion and skill in cosmetics were what I needed today.

"It's all right, Mavis," I said, squeezing her hand.

She disappeared and returned a moment later, pulling a comb from her bag. As gently as she could, she raked it through my kinks. She darted out of the room, returned with a hot comb in her hand, and started pulling through the long strands of my hair. The smell of burnt hair filled the room. She darted out and returned.

"I can go in the kitchen, Mavis. You don't have to keep running back and forth."

"I don't mind. I know you don't want to talk to anyone right now."

I reached behind me and squeezed her arm. When she was through with my hair, she did my makeup and helped me slip into a black, knee-length dress. I grabbed the black hat from the chest, emerged from the room, and walked toward the front door. All kinds of food were sprawled across the counter and table. I had no appetite, but I needed to eat. I took a spoon and wolfed down some eggs, a piece of bacon, and toast, forcing myself to drink some orange juice.

I walked out the front door, feeling a jolt of energy, and stood by the fence. The children watched me. Though I didn't smile, I gave them a look that said I was all right. The girls wore new black dresses, and Mavis had pressed their hair. Louise had bought the boys black suits, and Curly had trimmed and lined their hair.

Maxine held me a long time. "The Lord is gonna get us through this, Mama."

"I know, child. I know. It hurts so much, not having your father here."

We cried for a moment, and Maxine let go. I wiped my eyes and hugged Ruby, then the boys. Ruby looked at me with pleading eyes. I gave her another hug. Edward rubbed my back. I drew from his strength and squeezed his hand.

Henry parked his truck and stepped out wearing a black suit. He grabbed my hand and pulled me into an embrace. "The Lord bless you, Sister Smith. Be strong. Hold on to God's unchanging hand."

"I will, Deacon Scott."

Henry let go and held my hand for a moment. He took Maxine in his arms and held her. I stood back and retreated into myself. My thoughts went to Gregory. How would the service feel? Worse than my mother's funeral, I imagined. I hid my face behind the veil. I didn't want the children to see my anguish.

The wind had vanished, leaving the Saturday morning heat feeling as if it were high noon. I had just started to sweat underneath my dress when Old Man Tank parked his puke-green Ford station wagon in front of the gate. Everyone loaded in, not saying a word. The ride to the church was short, only two blocks. I wished I'd walked.

The churchyard filled with people who either stood on the grass or sat in wooden chairs. Louise and Curly locked both of my arms in theirs and plowed through the sea of people who expressed their condolences with drooped eyes and doleful frowns.

People packed the sweltering church. Two black pedestal fans, propped in the back of the sanctuary, battled the hot air in vain. Women, mostly the elderly, crammed the pews, fanning their heads with handheld cardboard fans. Men stood around the walls and filled the choir stand, blotting their necks and foreheads with handkerchiefs or face cloths.

All twelve of my brothers and sisters and their families filled the second and third rows on both sides of the church. To my surprise, Daddy stepped into the aisle and held his hands out until I walked into his embrace. He wrapped his arms around my back and held me for a long while. I threw my arms around him and wailed.

"I'm so very sorry, Kathleen," he said. "Gregory was a good man."

He pressed my hand in his, walked me to the front row, and refused to leave my side. Daddy looked thin and frail, but as always, he was dapper in his black suit. I froze, squeezing his hand. A large bouquet of flowers sat on top of the black pine casket. "Help me, Jesus. I don't want to do this," I mumbled.

Daddy's gentle squeeze calmed my soul. "It's all right, Kathleen." His words strengthened me, just what I needed at the moment. Gregory's coffin was more than his remains being interred. It reminded me that he was never coming back. Daddy slid his arm around my waist. "That's only his body. He's in heaven," he said and guided me to my seat.

I couldn't look at the coffin. My gaze fell on Gregory's brother. He sat between Louise and Curly, dressed in red double-knit slacks and a pullover dress jersey. His hair was slick and wavy, down his shoulders. He stared at the coffin with pure hatred and vengeance in his eyes. Two men, well-dressed

and well-groomed, sat next to Reverend Sims near the pulpit.
They must have been the friends Gregory worked with in the
movement. Surprisingly, a few white faces were sprinkled
throughout the crowd. Miss Broubaker stood in the back.

The choir sang an A and B selection. Gregory's friends
spoke of the times they'd spent with him. His two colleagues
praised his zeal. They had never seen someone so committed
to the movement. Henry spoke fondly of the impact his
mentor had on his life. I sneered at those who pretended to be
his friend, knowing they despised his work. Reverend Sims
struggled to contain his emotions during the eulogy. Several
times he broke down and had to regain his composure.

Immediately after the service, we headed out to the Negro
cemetery. The procession was slow due to the long train of cars
and trucks, and we were forbidden to travel through town.
Everyone gathered around the coffin as it lay over the open
grave. Reverend Sims was short in his remarks. The pallbearers
lowered the coffin.

I thrashed and flailed. I couldn't bear the sight of the casket
dropping into the ground. Daddy and Louise struggled to hold
me still, but I broke away. I shook my head in a crazed frenzy.
"Gregory, my Gregory, they've murdered you like you was a
dog!"

* * *

I had gotten out of bed, washed up, laid out my clothes,
and sat on the edge of the bed, wondering what I was going to
do with my life. How would I provide for my family? Where
would we live? I couldn't stay with Louise forever. Eventually,
I would have to get a job. I supposed I could clean white folks'

homes or work in the fields. Maybe I could get a job cooking for someone. I could move to Birmingham, but the thought repulsed me.

I pondered if I was going to put on the clothes I'd laid out. What would I do with myself, anyway? What chores would I perform? I missed my farm. There my days were filled with work unending. I never wondered what I'd do or when I'd do it, but those days were gone. It was hard to believe a month had passed since the funeral, and already I felt restless and useless. A knock at the door grabbed my attention. "Come in."

Louise stepped in and eased the door shut. She bent over, just inches from my face. "Katie, that lady is here, and she's brought the sheriff. They want to talk to you."

A nervous knot formed in my belly. "The sheriff? What does he want with me?"

"I don't know, but you'd better talk to him."

I quickly threw on my clothes and walked into the living room. Miss Broubaker stood next to a tall, burly man whose form overshadowed her. She barely came to his shoulders. His belly bulged so that the buttons strained to keep his shirt fastened. He wore a beige hat that had a silver emblem of the Confederate flag on the front. A bushy, sandy-blond beard nearly hid his face. He folded his arms and kept shooting an annoyed look at Miss Broubaker.

"Hello, Mrs. Smith. I brought the sheriff here so you can tell him what happened that night. I was appalled he hadn't spoken to you." The sheriff shifted his eyes and scowled. "You tell him what happened to you, so he can arrest the men who murdered your husband."

My body trembled at the mention of that night. I didn't know what to say. I'd never met or seen the sheriff. He'd never come out and talked to me. What if he took Gus's side against me? He seemed irritated, mostly at her. "What do you want to know?"

Miss Broubaker, undaunted by the sheriff's menacing posture, pointed her finger at him. "Tell him it was that Gus...."

"You wait just one minute, missy. Don't throw names around if you ain't got proof," the sheriff said. He glared at me. "Well, lady, do you know who attacked you that night?"

By then, everyone assembled in the living room. I shot a glance at Timothy. He kept quiet and watched. That nervous knot persisted. Answering his questions wouldn't accomplish anything. I wanted to leave it alone. Nothing would come of this. I had never heard of a white man going to jail for murdering a Negro.

"Sheriff, you know that good-for-nothing Gus and his band of degenerates did this," Miss Broubaker said.

"Hush up and let the lady talk for herself." He threw another glare her way and looked at me with furrowed brows. "Well, do you know who did this?"

"I don't know his name, but I know his face. He was tall and thin. He wore coveralls and no shirt. And he wore a brown hat."

"See, I told you, Sheriff. That's Gus. Now arrest him."

"You're not the sheriff, missy. Stay out of county business." He looked at me. "I'll look into this." He grunted, glancing at Miss Broubaker, and walked out of the house.

A smile came upon her face. "Thank you, Mrs. Smith. I told you, we're getting justice for your husband. I'll be in touch." She darted out of the house.

I eased over to the door and watched Mrs. Broubaker drive off, chasing after the sheriff. I knew that was the last time I'd see him. Nothing would be done to those men. This issue was as dead as my husband. It was time for me to get on with my life.

Chapter Eight

1962

I paced around the bedroom, pondering whether to go through with my plans for the day. I was a little nervous, but it was time I faced my fears. I brushed my hair into a neat ponytail that fell behind my shoulders. With my eyes fixed on the mirror, I tossed my head from side to side, looking for any wrinkles in my peach flowered dress. I swabbed a light coat of lipstick across my lips, then crowned my head with a peach Tam hat. A soft knock interrupted my primping. "Come in," I said, glancing over my shoulder.

Louise dropped into the chair, panting. "So, this is your big day, huh?"

I nodded.

"I know this is a big step for you. But, you're a different woman than the one that left the farm two years ago. That woman was insecure, reclusive, and afraid of the world."

"God has brought all of us a long way. It was rough at first, especially for the children," I said, glancing back.

"Thank God for bringing them through that storm."

Sitting on the edge of the bed, I shook my head. "Maxine jumped every time she heard a car drive past. Edward and Timothy tensed up every time they saw a crowd of white men, whether they were city workers or teachers. And Ruby — she worried me the most. She'd wake up screaming in a cold sweat every night."

"I used to hear her. Thank God that's all over."

"I still worry about them having to face that man at school every day. Who knows what he'll do? How are they supposed to learn anything with him looming around?" A shiver shot through my body. "Every day, I ask the Lord to protect them."

"Are you sure it's him? Was he there that night?"

"Eddie recognized that funny-looking mustache. He didn't say much, but I remember him. He didn't dress like the other men, either. He dressed rather well for the occasion."

Louise shook her head. "To think, he's a teacher...."

"And a deacon. Edward is sure the man doesn't recognize him. Thank God for that. It still bothers me that no one talks about that night. People go about as if Gregory's murder never happened. I hate that."

"Just leave it alone, Katie. Things are back to normal."

"You're right. I'm going to walk to town, pick up a few things for Maxi's wedding, and who knows? I might even get a little something to eat while I'm there."

Louise frowned. "You know you're not allowed to eat anywhere in town. Don't go meddling. You know how they are, and you know what they'll do to you. I'll have lunch ready for you when you get back."

"That was only wishful thinking. Don't worry about me. I'm not Gregory, looking to stage a sit-in. Anyway, I'm not going to let that spoil this day."

"Amen. You should get your driver's license, though. That way, you can get around on your own."

"I will. I know Curly is tired of taking me everywhere."

"He doesn't mind. You know that. I'm talking about you

being independent. We're here for you as long as you need us. You sure you don't want Curly to take you to town?"

I shook my head. "I want to do this myself. It's time I start doing things on my own." Standing, I slid my feet into my beige pumps. "It's hard to believe Maxi is getting married. Where'd the time go?"

"I know. Who knows, Edward might be next."

"Girl, he thinks he's too cute to settle down. He's talking about playing football for one of those colleges when he graduates." I gave myself a final look in the mirror and spun around. "Pray for me. I finally feel like that night is behind me." I grabbed my purse, walked out of the bedroom and through the living room, pushed the screen door open, and marched out. "Come on, Ruby."

Ruby caught up with me as I made my way down M Street along the dirt path that crossed over the tracks. The sun beamed on my neck and arms. A mild breeze passed through my dress with a cool, soothing feel. I thought to stretch my arms and enjoy the wind sweeping across my face. Front Street's line of brick storefronts reminded me that those days, times, and moments were gone. This was my life now, here on this street, in this city.

I grabbed Ruby's hand, but she jerked away. "Mama, I'm not a baby."

"You're my baby."

"I'm twelve and a half."

I smiled, amazed at how tall she'd grown and how much she filled out. She was herself again, bouncing around in a yellow sundress and yellow shoes. That was good to see. Two neatly braided pigtails pulled away from an even row of bangs covering her forehead. She'd combed her hair herself. I grabbed her hand again. "Look at my baby."

"Mama, I'm almost a teenager," she said, pulling her hand away.

"You must take after the women on your daddy side. They fill out young, too."

"Mama, please, you're embarrassing me."

We crossed the tracks. I exhaled and stepped onto the sidewalk on Front Street, relieved that downtown wasn't crowded. A few folks casually strolled in and out of stores. A car or truck periodically drifted past. I preferred it that way. It wasn't as daunting as I'd braced for.

"Come on, let's go in the Five and Dime store," I said.

"Mrs. Smith."

I turned to see who had called me. Miss Broubaker moved slowly with a limp. She needed a cane and winced with each step. She wore a sleeveless summer dress and dark sunglasses — none of which hid the bruises on her face and body. "Hello, Miss Broubaker." Normally, I would have kept my mouth shut, but the contusions on her arms and forehead alarmed me. "What happened to you?"

Both sides of her jaw were swollen. She spoke each word with effort. "Oh, I took part in the freedom rides. As you can see, it didn't turn out well."

"I thought you were headed out west somewhere to teach."

"I was. But, I chose to ride the freedom buses instead." Her voice trembled. "My plan was to spend the summer on the buses and then head out west."

"What happened to your face?"

"We were mobbed in Georgia, then again in Anniston. Anniston was worse. I was beaten so badly, I thought they broke every bone in my body. They didn't care if I was white or black. I was released from the hospital two weeks ago."

"That's terrible. I'm so sorry."

"I thought I was going to die that day."

"Are you going to ride those buses again?"

Miss Broubaker turned her head. Her spirit was crushed. "I don't know. The doctors said I should take time to heal." I couldn't help but think if they meant more than her body. "Can I buy you lunch, Mrs. Smith? I want to tell you about my experience."

"Well, I really have to...."

"Please, Mrs. Smith. I don't have anyone to talk to. Most people think of me as a race traitor, even Christians. I don't understand. We are all God's people, and yet we're so divided." She peered at me, desperate for an answer. "I won't keep you long. I promise."

My heart ached for her — that she felt that way. I coveted isolation. If I never talked to anyone ever again, that would suit me fine. She just wanted to fellowship with fellow Christians, and she didn't care who they were or what color they were. "Well," I said without thinking through my answer, "I guess we can have a quick lunch." A smile came on her face. I nudged Ruby, who furrowed her brows. "We'll finish shopping after lunch," I said to Ruby.

"We haven't started shopping, Mama."

I squinted at Ruby and followed Miss Broubaker to Charlie's Place. I hesitated when we came to the door. "No Niggers Allowed," said the sign in the window. She touched my arm. "It's all right, Mrs. Smith. We're just eating lunch."

"I don't think this is a good idea. I'm not allowed in there."

"You will be all right. You're with me," she said, tugging me into the café.

The room had about fifteen tables with four wooden chairs each. Several booths lined the walls and windows. It was small but neat and clean. The aroma of eggs, bacon, sausages, and hash browns made my stomach growl. Hank Williams's "Your Cheating Heart" crooned from the jukebox. I remembered the song from that evil Gus riding through colored town.

Elderly people owned the room, talking, playing cards, checkers, or just eating their meals. Everyone became quiet and stared at us when we walked in. Some squinted and frowned. Others stared, seemingly wondering if I had lost my mind. Some glanced toward the kitchen with dread in their eyes. I've should have left right then.

A blank expression came on Ruby's face. "Mama, let's go. I don't want to be here."

Miss Broubaker nodded and then led us to a table. But, before we could sit....

"What's that nigger doing in here?"

My heart dropped at the boom of his voice. I turned my head, and there he stood by the counter, wearing coveralls with no shirt and his brown fedora. He glared at me viciously. I grabbed Ruby's hand and turned to walk out. But it only took a few strides for him to get in my face.

He recognized me. When he looked at Ruby, he narrowed his eyes. "What are you doing in my place? I don't allow niggers in here! Now, you get your dirty, stinkin' hide out of my place before I throw yous out."

Ruby squeezed my hand.

"They have a right to eat here," Miss Broubaker said.

Gus balled his fists tight and glared at her. "You ain't learned yet? What's worse than a nigger is a nigger-lover. We don't tolerate nigger-lovers. You best mind your place.

You oughta have learned your lesson, wallowing with those agitators."

I yanked on Ruby's arm and rushed out of the café, walking as fast as I could toward Front Street. "Mrs. Smith!" She kept calling after me, but I kept walking. I wanted to get out of downtown. "Mrs. Smith, please wait up. I can't walk as fast."

I stopped and whirled around. Miss Broubaker limped toward me with a pained frown. She caught up with me outside of the Five and Dime store. "What is it, Miss Broubaker?"

"I just want to say I'm sorry. I didn't mean for you to go through that."

"What did you think would happen?" I didn't give her a chance to answer. "You know colored people aren't allowed in places like that. Oh, my Lord, it's worse that it's his place."

"I'm sorry."

"Sorry isn't good enough. You've put me and my daughter in danger. I know you mean well, but people don't see life as you do. You're white, Miss Broubaker. You can always walk away from this anytime you want. I can't. My skin is always black. I can't walk away from that." The hurt in her eyes touched my heart. I caressed her arm, something I wasn't supposed to do. "I know you mean well. It's just I don't have the grace you do. I can't walk in a place like that without some kind of retaliation. I have to go. I want to get away from here." I turned to walk away but spun back around. "I'd like to hear about your experiences—just not here."

She smiled. "Thank you, Mrs. Smith."

As we rounded the corner onto Front Street, I could see the tracks and thought, *Thank God, almost home.* "Come on, baby, we'll come back another time...."

"Mama!" Ruby screamed. "What are you doing?"

Fuzzy darkness with blots of orange engulfed my vision. Tiny, bright stars danced across my peripheral vision. I didn't know if I'd been punched, kicked, or what. I kept my eyes shut, trying to figure out what had happened. A loud snarling pierced through the confusion. I realized I was lying in the street.

"Let this be a reminder to stay in your place. Niggers ain't allowed in my place. I don't even want the dirt off the bottom of your shoes in my place. Next time, I won't be so nice."

That wicked voice—it could only be one person. I opened my eyes and sat up. "Why don't you leave us alone?"

His laughter reeked with callous mockery. Ruby tried to help me up, but I jerked my shoulder away and stared at Gus. Miss Broubaker limped from across the street.

Gus pointed his finger at me. "Nigger, you lay in the street like the animal you is."

"You are an evil man, evil!" Ruby screamed. "You are a murderer and an evil man!"

"Leave her alone, you animal!" Miss Broubaker shouted. "I'm going to get the sheriff."

Gus sneered and walked away. He stopped and turned around with his eyes locked on Ruby. "Still the feisty little picaninny, ain't ya?" He walked away, snickering.

Ruby scrambled around the street, grabbing the things that had spilled out of my purse. Miss Broubaker insisted on helping me up. I felt my forehead and looked around the street. White people walked past, staring at me. Some shook their heads. *Lord, I'm trying not to hate white people, but look at them.*

"I'm so sorry, Mrs. Smith. This is all my fault. I never meant to hurt you." She held onto my arm. "What can I do?"

I shook my head. "Nothing. You can't do nothing." Ruby

handed my hat to me. I trembled as I slipped the Tam across the top of my head and straightened my clothes. "Come on, baby, we're going home." Numbness made my feet wobble. I felt lightheaded. Dizziness threatened my consciousness. I tried to contain my frustration, but I couldn't. "This isn't my home!" I shouted and burst into a loud cry. "Lord, I can't take this anymore."

Miss Broubaker held me as tenderly as she could. Tears streamed down her face. "Don't feel that way, Mrs. Smith. I know things are hard now, but the Lord will bring us through." I snapped my head toward her. "I'm in this with you, not as a white woman or a freedom fighter, but as your sister in Christ. I'm not a Negro, but I'm a child of God, and you are, too. That makes us eternal sisters. I'm standing here with you because we both belong to God."

I wanted to stew in my anger, but her words melted the hate away and strengthened my soul. I couldn't hold malice against her if I wanted to. I couldn't even hate Gus, as evil as he was. He needed the Lord. Who knows what good he could do if he knew the Lord? I stared at her. She had to have seen that my heart had softened, because she smiled.

"Thank you, Miss Broubaker. God sent you to me for such a time as this. Your words have strengthened me to go on."

She wiped the tears from her eyes. "May I drive you home? Your knees are bruised up really badly. It would be no trouble."

"No, thank you. I walked here on my own, and I'll walk home on my own. Thank you for offering, but I'll be just fine."

I felt an eternal bond to her. She was my sister in the Lord. Glancing around to see if anyone was watching, I embraced her. Negroes weren't supposed to touch white people, especially in public. We held each other for a long while. At the moment, I didn't care who saw us or what the consequences would be. All of my fears melted away as I held her. She was my sister, and I was sharing this moment with her.

Chapter Nine

I hadn't walked into the house a second before Louise —
brow furrowed — ran up to me and lifted my head. "How did
you get that knot on your forehead?"

I sat in the chair with my head propped between my hands.
The throbbing in my temples pounded harder by the moment,
and the scrapes on my knees stung. "I don't want to talk about
it, Louise."

"You need that bump looked at. Curly, bring me some
peroxide."

Keeping my head down, I hoped she'd leave it alone. "No,
I'm fine."

Louise sighed. "Curly, hurry up."

Curly rushed into the room, holding the dark-brown bottle.
"What's wrong?"

"Something happened to her in town." She scooted a chair
next to me. Opening the bottle, she doused a washcloth and
blotted my knees. My muscles tensed from the stinging. "What
on earth happened to you?"

Wincing at each swipe, I surrendered all hope of avoiding
talking about Gus. "That man tripped me in the street and
mocked and cursed me some terrible, in front of Ruby."

"Oh, my Lord. Let me call the doctor, Katie."

"I'm not going to the doctor. I just want to forget this day
ever happened."

Louise grimaced. "That man is crazy, Curly. What are we

going to do?"

Pacing around the room, Curly stared at the floor. "We havta call the sheriff."

My head snapped up. "No, Curly. That would only make things worse. He did nothing to those men who killed Gregory. White folks did nothing. I don't trust them — none of them."

The screen door slammed.

"Mama, that boy went off to do something foolish!" Maxine yelled.

Louise turned toward Maxine. "Who?"

"Tim."

I cupped my hands over my mouth. "Oh, Lord Jesus."

"Curly, you gotta go get that boy before he do something stupid," Louise said.

Following Curly and Louise to the car, I trembled so badly, I thought my joints would come apart. The thought of Timothy in a confrontation with Gus sent my heart racing. I closed my eyes. *Jesus, Jesus, Jesus.* Curly sped across the railroad tracks and parked at an angle in front of Charlie's Place. My eyes widened. Dismayed, my mouth dropped open.

Gus had pinned Timothy against the brick wall with both hands around his throat. Timothy's arms flailed, and his eyes bulged and rolled to the back of his head. My fist clasped the front of my dress. I closed my eyes. I couldn't bear to look. *We're too late.* "Oh, Lord Jesus, help my baby."

A patrol car screeched to a halt in front of Curly with one wheel on the sidewalk. The Sheriff jumped out and rushed over to Gus. "Turn him loose."

Ignoring the sheriff, Gus, with a baleful smile, tightened his grip. "This nigger is mine."

"I said let him go." The sheriff whipped his baton out

and rapped Gus across his head. Gus released Timothy and stumbled back against the wall, holding his head. "What's the matter with you, you dang fool? You trying to kill this boy in broad daylight?"

Jumping out of the car, I grabbed Timothy as he gasped for air.

Gus pointed his finger at Timothy. "This nigger attacked me, Wally, a white man." He lunged toward Timothy, but the sheriff pushed Gus away. "He needs to be strung up. We can't be letting niggers go around attacking white people."

I grabbed the sheriff's arm. "Please, Sheriff, spare my baby. He doesn't know better. He's only a child."

Surprised, the Sheriff frowned and jerked his arm. As he studied me, his brow arched. "You're Smith's widow," he said. "Your boy dun attacked a white man, even if it is this idiot." He shook his head. "What was he thinking, hitting a white man?"

"He doesn't know no better, Sheriff. Please, don't take him to jail."

"He got more serious problems than going to jail. He dun attacked a white man."

"You're gonna swing from a tree, nigger. I promise you that!" Gus yelled.

The sheriff glowered and grabbed Gus by his shirt. "Let me handle this, Gus."

Gus stomped around in a circle, keeping his stare fixed on Timothy. Evil raged from his eyes, the same evil I'd seen that night. Timothy wasn't safe. *He's going to kill my son.*

The sheriff glowered at Gus and looked at me. I couldn't tell if it was pity or compassion in his eyes. "You take your boy home, and keep him away from here, if you know what I mean. You hear me?"

I nodded and glanced at Gus.

"Well, get him out of my sight, and remember what I told ya." I grabbed Timothy's arm and shoved him into the car. I glanced over my shoulder to see the sheriff grabbing Gus by his arm. "I told you to leave them people alone. I'm tired of cleaning up your mess. You and your daddy are nothing but trouble—always been. I ain't gonna cover for you this time. I don't care what the big wigs say. Let them clean up after you. I'm through."

I nodded for Louise and Curly to get us away from there as fast as they could. I looked back as Curly sped away. Gus flapped his arms, screaming at the sheriff.

The radio was off, the car engine purred quietly, and the wind gushed through the open windows. No one said a word. I was glad. I wasn't in the mood for anyone to tell me that everything would be all right. No matter what the sheriff said, Gus was coming for Timothy. Whether in broad daylight or the wee hours of the night, he was coming. Timothy had hit him, and in public. Gus would never let that go. Timothy pretended to be unfazed, but I knew he was shaken to his core. *Thank God. Maybe this will calm him down.*

I waited until everyone had left the house. It took that long to muster the courage to tell Louise the resolution I'd reached. She and Curly had been so good to us. They had taken us into their home unconditionally, but the image of Timothy swinging from a tree limb over-shadowed all the happy memories of living here. I had to leave Blount City.

Everyone had left for the evening, except Timothy, who had locked himself in his room. This was the perfect time to talk to Louise; she took advantage of the peacefulness by reading her Bible. I walked into the living room and looked out the window.

Peering up and down the street, I sighed with relief that Gus wasn't outside. I sat on the couch. "Louise."

She marked her place and set her Bible on the lamp table. "Yes, Katie."

"I have something to tell you." I swallowed. "I want to leave here."

Louise grimaced. "Why?"

Pow! I flinched.

"It's just a car backfiring," she assured me.

"I can't take it anymore. Timothy's got me worried sick. He stays in trouble at school. He won't stop preaching that militant stuff. The principle has threatened to expel him. But, what happened today—I know that man is coming for him. I can't bear to lose my son."

Louise stared off for a moment as if trying to think of an argument to keep me here. But a look of surrender appeared on her face. "I know, Katie. I don't know what to tell you. Where do you want to go? Birmingham, to live with Daddy?

"No."

"Where do you want to go, then? You've lived here all your life. It'll be hard to start over somewhere strange."

"I know, but I can't stay here. I have to leave. I have to leave the South."

Louise thought for a moment. "You can go to Washington, D.C." I shrugged. I hadn't talked to my brother since the funeral. That didn't feel right.

"I got it," Louise said. "Aunt Mae Bell lives in California."

My spirit roused. *That's it. That's the place.* "That sounds good, Louise."

"Tomorrow, we'll call and talk to her about you and the kids coming to California. You know, you two have something in common. Her husband was killed by the Klan in the thirties. That's why she moved to California."

"Wow, I didn't know that."

The next day, we made the call to California. Aunt Mae surprised both of us. She seemed to be expecting our call. God prepared her heart to receive us. I marveled at His grace. She even insisted on paying for our bus tickets and said she would wire the money later that week. She was more excited about me coming to California than I was.

* * *

The week flew by. I'm glad Maxine had the wedding after church. We did everything that day—celebrated and said our goodbyes. People streamed past the newlyweds and lavished them with hugs, kisses, and envelopes. Maxine looked beautiful in her white gown that swirled around her legs. Ruby, wearing a pink gown, stood behind Maxine, making sure her dress was always positioned right. Maxine's hair was perfect, flowing from under her veil down her back. Her eyes sparkled with the right touch of makeup, thanks to Mavis.

The sight of my baby, now a grown, married woman, did my heart good. I felt at peace, leaving Maxine in Henry's hands. He looked handsome in a white suit with white shoes. I mused, remembering my own wedding day, but I was ready to go.

People circled out of line and made their way over to me to say their goodbyes. They had only found out during the morning's church service that this was our last Sunday with them. Most of the people were shocked and sad to see us leave, but they understood my reasons. I was relieved because I didn't feel like explaining myself over and over. People told me they were just getting used to us living in town, and it seemed as if we were being snatched away.

* * *

Monday could not come fast enough. All night, an ominous feeling goaded me. I got out of bed by 4:00 a.m. I couldn't sleep. I wouldn't have peace until I was far from this city. I feared that Gus loomed nearby. I darted to the living room and peeked out of the window. I had to check. He wasn't there. I went back to the bedroom, grabbed my suitcases, and set them by the front door.

The loud rev of an engine paralyzed me. I closed my eyes to collect my thoughts. My fist clenched in a tight wad. When I pulled the curtain aside, a pair of headlights glared at me. The engine revved repeatedly. Whisking the drapes shut, I leaned against the wall with my eyes closed. The room spun. *Gus is here.*

My heart pounded as if it would crash through my chest. When I peeked out the window again, the string of headlights I saw that night flashed across my mind. I closed my eyes, trying to figure out what to do. Who could I call? Who would help me? Sadly, there was no one—not Curly, not Reverend Sims, and certainly not the sheriff. White folks would stand by Gus. He would get away with murdering my son just like he got away with murdering my husband.

The room faded into a dark blur of fuzzy colors, with crazy patterns floating across my peripheral vision. My knees wobbled. I leaned against the wall. How could this be happening? How could God allow this? If only I'd left for California when the money for the bus tickets had arrived, I wouldn't have had to face this evil man. Why had I let everyone talk me into staying? I would have been far from the reaches of my enemy. The engine revved again.

At any moment, Gus would kick the door open. He'd stare at me with those hateful eyes. He'd flash his evil smirk and kick each door open until he found Timothy. He'd drag Timothy by his neck and throw him into his trunk. They'd find his body hanging from a tree, in a field somewhere.

A soft knock made me flinch. I pulled the curtain aside and peeked out the window. Mr. Tate, my neighbor, stood at the door. *How silly of me. He always leaves at this time.* Grabbing my chest, relieved, I pulled the door open. "Good morning, Mr. Tate." My voice trembled.

"I saw you were up. I just wanted to say goodbye. I won't get a chance to see you later."

"Thank you for stopping by. I'm going to miss you."

"You all right, Katie? You're trembling."

"I'm fine. I thought you were someone else."

He peered at me for a moment. "Things gon' be all right, Katie."

I thanked him, shut the door, and rested against the wall for a moment while the pounding in my heart slowed. I was thankful it wasn't Gus. I sat on the couch for a few moments. I was tired of looking over my shoulder all the time, wondering if and when Gus would strike.

At 7:00 a.m., I walked out of Louise's house to a crowd of tearful faces. Reverend Sims and his wife, along with a few folks from the church, barraged the children and me with hugs and kisses. I scanned both ends of the street, making sure Gus wasn't there.

A big smile came on my face when Maxine and Henry

walked up. "I thought y'all was meeting us in the city."

Maxine fell into my arms. "We never went to the hotel. We stayed at Henry's house. We decided to go after y'all left." Maxine held me tight. "I'm gonna miss you, Mama."

"You're going to be all right, child. You're married now and have a new life with your husband. He's a good man."

I kissed Maxine's forehead and headed for the car. I waved, and after Louise and Maxine had made a long, drawn-out attempt to delay our departure, I got into Louise's car. The boys rode with Mavis, and Henry and Maxine drove their car. We headed south on Route 7.

Louise slowed the car and stopped. I glanced at her and looked straight ahead. A swarm of memories flooded my mind — good times on the farm. I glanced toward the driveway. It looked the same as I'd left it. Rutted paths, overgrown with weeds and shrubberies, disappeared over the hill. For an instant, I longed to look over the farm, but memories I'd desperately tried to forget surfaced. It was too painful to think about the life I'd had here.

After a moment, Louise drove away without saying a word. She had told me I should see the land before I left. Louise thought it would bring closure. I disagreed. She reached over and patted my hand. I glanced behind the car, relieved I didn't see the red Fury.

The bus driver loaded our luggage at 11:45 am. Reverend Sims handed me a couple of bags of food. He had surprised us by driving down. The children boarded the half-empty bus. I hugged and kissed everyone for the last time, then boarded. I didn't want to look out the window, but I felt compelled to wave as the bus left the depot. Maxine cried in Henry's arms. I hated to have their tearful faces as the last images of my hometown.

As I watched them grow smaller and smaller, I thought about how God had put them in my life. They were the ones who had stood by me and supported me in every way. They were the only reason I regretted leaving this place. When they vanished into the horizon, I turned around and faced the front. I looked behind again. I had to make sure I didn't see the red Fury. I faced the front and looked straight ahead as the scenery flew past me. *Hallelujah. I'm leaving Egypt, the land of my afflictions.*

My thoughts went to Miss Broubaker. I wished I could have spent more time with her. Had it not been for her kindness, I would have hated all white people. I told Maxine to get a hold of her and let her know I'd left. I was glad I'd gotten a chance to tell her about Gregory. It seemed to put balance in her perspective on the movement. She was a godly woman. She'd helped me to appreciate all of God's people and what he did for everyone.

My eyes opened as "You are leaving Alabama" flew by in bold black letters painted on a white metal sign. I sat up and gawked with anxiousness. The next sign read "You are entering the state of Mississippi."

I felt as if I were born again. It finally happened. I was free from my old life. And though I never doubted the depths Gus would go to exact vengeance, I no longer worried about him. But I couldn't help to look behind, just to be sure. It was silly. No way had he followed me. The red Fury wasn't there, nor was the man who wore the brown fedora.

Chapter Ten

The bus driver announced our descent into the Los Angeles basin, snapping me to full attention. I felt tiny as the bus wound its way down Highway 5. The lower we descended, the taller the hills swelled, and the harder my ears popped. A mixture of green and brown grass sprinkled with houses covered the mountains. The sun brushed a golden shine over the early-morning sky as a gray haze hovered over the valley. The city stretched westward past the horizon. More cars and trucks appeared on the road the closer we drew to the city. They came out of nowhere. I had never seen anything like it.

Thoughts of this place disquieted me. What kind of people lived here? I'd hoped not prejudiced ones. What if there were people like Gus here? What if they treated Negroes the way the South treated Negroes? What had I gotten myself into? I didn't know a single soul in California. Aunt Mae had left Blount City when I was a little girl. I didn't even remember how she looked.

The bus pulled into the station and parked at an angle between two other buses. The driver pulled the lever, and the door swished open. Sliding his hat on his head, he stood and briefly faced the back. "Los Angeles, final destination. Next stop, Pacific Ocean." He shot us a grin and stepped off. I waited for everyone else to leave the bus. I didn't see a colored lady looking for us. The sea of white faces made me nervous. I never had been around so many of them.

Stepping off of the bus, I took Ruby by her hand and

watched the driver pull luggage from the compartment. People pushed us aside, grabbing their suitcases with frowns, sneers, sighs, and grunts. I looked both ways and swiveled around. For a moment, Gus popped into my head. Frantically, I scanned the crowd, looking for his face. It was silly to think that. He was thousands of miles away, but, still, the absence of his face brought a huge relief to my mind.

No one spoke, greeted, or said hello. People bustled about in their own world. Negroes disembarked from other buses to meet relatives or friends and be whisked away with hugs and kisses. Aunt Mae was nowhere in sight. Suddenly, I felt alone, scared, and threatened by failure. How would I make it in this monstrous metropolis? I squeezed Ruby's hand and made sure the boys were close. A hand touched my shoulder. I jumped and whirled around.

A white lady, about my age, smiled at me. "Are you all right, Miss? You look lost."

Her smile was warm and friendly. That put me at ease. "I don't know where to go."

"Don't let this big city or the people scare you." The woman placed her hand on my shoulders and pointed toward the large opening. "Just walk that way, and that'll take you to the lobby. I'm sure the person you're looking for is through there."

"Thank you."

The lady smiled. "The Lord is with you. Don't be afraid."

I nodded, and she vanished into the crowd. *Thank you, Lord, for giving her words that put me at peace.*

Ruby turned my hand loose. "She was a nice lady, Mama."

"Yes, she was. Edward, Timothy, grab the luggage."

I followed a few people through the large opening that led into a lobby bustling with all kinds of activity. People stood in line buying tickets; others rushed to catch their buses, and some sat in the waiting area filled with wooden benches, reading, talking, or simply off by themselves.

A short, fair-skinned woman wearing a hat with flowers on the brim waited for us. "Kathleen, look at y'all," she said. This had to be Aunt Mae. "The last time I saw you… what, you had to be ten years old."

I wrapped my arms around her. "Aunt Mae, thank you for taking us in."

"Child, think nothing of it. I'm just glad to have family out here. Nobody ever comes out here to visit me. It's so far away. Come on, I'm parked outside." We followed Aunt Mae to the parking lot. "You're going to love it out here. It's warm all the time, just like back home. The kids are going to love the beaches. There's so much to do out here."

"Edward, Timothy, y'all load the suitcases into Aunt Mae's trunk."

"Here you go, boys," Aunt Mae said, lifting her hatch. "Y'all some handsome boys. The girls are going to go crazy over them, Katie."

We loaded into Aunt Mae's car and drove off. People filled the street. The buildings towered so high, I couldn't see the tops. Everything seemed to close in on me: the buildings, cars, buses, and the people.

Aunt Mae gave a quick tour around downtown. The streets were wide and paved. Cars bustled up and down the lanes and whizzed across intersections. Narrow, thin trees lined the streets like flag poles as we headed west.

"What kind of trees are those?" Ruby said.

"Those are palm trees. You're going to see them all around here," Aunt Mae said.

'HOLLYWOOD', in giant letters, stretched across a steep hill. The hill, it seemed, filled the entire valley. "What in the world is that?" I had to ask.

Aunt Mae chuckled. "You mean the Hollywood sign? That's been up there for years. You know, they make all the movies out here."

"Movies? I don't watch TV," I said, staring at the sign.

Edward pressed against the window. "Will we see movie stars?"

"You might," Aunt Mae said. "One day, I'll take y'all to see Hollywood Boulevard. You'll see the names of movie stars on the sidewalk."

The car turned on a street named La Brea. The road twisted and bent as we drove through steeper hills that seemed to close in on us. I wanted to hang my head out of the window and gawk like a young child seeing the world for the first time. Large homes appeared wedged in the side of the hills. How did they stay up there?

Aunt Mae turned into a neighborhood that had palm trees lining both sides of the street. They were paved with sidewalks and curbs. Every house was neat and clean. This had to be a white neighborhood. What were we doing here? Maybe Aunt Mae cleaned for one of the white women or was here to pick up laundry.

She pulled into 514 and looked at everyone. "Welcome to y'all new home." She jumped out and opened the trunk.

Stepping out of the car, I looked around, wondering if my auntie was playing a joke on us. Negroes didn't live in places like this. Across the street, a white couple walked along the sidewalk. They looked to be in their late fifties. He dressed in shorts and T-shirt. She wore a sleeveless shirt with Capri pants.

"Hey, Mae."

Aunt Mae waved. "Hello, Maggie." Aunt Mae rolled her eyes. "Hello, Nate."

Nate shot a mean glare that disturbed me. He reminded me of Gus. Aunt Mae led us into the house. I couldn't get that man out of my head. I peeked out the window and watched the couple walk down the street, the man especially. He kept looking over at us, squinting.

Aunt Mae waited for Edward to bring in the last of the bags. "Boys, y'all can take one bedroom. Ruby, you can take the other room with your mama. It shouldn't be so bad. We can talk about chores later."

Aunt Mae's house was immaculate. The furniture looked new and well-kept. I wondered how she would adjust to living with a bunch of rowdy kids. She only had one TV, in the living room. Her floors were polished. Compared to our old house, this was a palace.

"Thank you, Aunt Mae," I said. "Y'all get settled in y'all rooms." I drifted back toward the window and peeked out. Aunt Mae touched my shoulder. I jumped.

"Relax, baby. You've been jumpy ever since you've got here."

"That man...."

"What man, baby?"

"He was with that lady."

"You mean Nate. Listen, ain't nobody going to hurt you. People here don't like colored people moving to the city, but as more and more of us move in, their attitudes are changing. Maggie is one of the nice people. Nate is a mean cuss, but he won't do nothing more than give you a dirty look. You are perfectly safe here."

I nodded and looked back out the window. California definitely was a different world. Back in Alabama, things were simpler. Coloreds lived on one side of the tracks, whites on the other. They never mixed. Living around white people confused me — terrified me. "I don't know if I could ever feel safe."

Aunt Mae rubbed my back. "I felt the same way when I first came here. Imagine my shock when I moved into this neighborhood. They were a lot meaner back then. But, over the years, they got used to me living here."

"It's different, Aunt Mae."

"Give it time. I felt that way, too. They killed my man back in thirty-five. I thought I would never get over that, especially the fear of being around white people. It took me years to feel safe around them. Just trust the Lord."

"I wish I could believe that."

"I think God is doing a work in you, Katie — both of us."

"What do you mean?"

"Look at us. Two women from the south. Both our husbands murdered by white men, end up living in a mostly white town. God is doing something."

* * *

Aunt Mae had been urging me to get out of the house and experience southern California. I refused her invitation to run about town with her. She wasn't one to sit in the house. She went somewhere every day and was gone most of the day on Saturdays. After two weeks, I was bored, mostly because I was in strange surroundings. L.A. wasn't my farm.

Since I was a teenager, I'd never dwelled close to people. And for sure, I'd never seen white folks walking and driving up and down the streets I'd lived on. Aunt Mae had been here for years — that said something about this city. I decided to test the waters and take a walk around the block.

The children had gone with Aunt Mae — somewhere she called a Swap Meet. They loved being here and had already made friends. I wasn't surprised about Edward, but I worried about Timothy's attitude — though he had lightened up on his militant rants since his encounter with Gus. Ruby ran up and down the street every day with her new friends. They were nice girls, though they never came in the house.

I dressed earlier. Wearing pants had taken getting used to, but I loved the comfortable fit. Back home, I'd only worn dresses. I stepped outside. The morning felt good. The weather here confused me. In the day, it was hot, and at night it was cool. I didn't mind the variety. It beat the constant heat of Alabama. I made sure the door was locked. Aunt Mae often reminded me this wasn't Blount City and for sure this wasn't my farm. I'd never locked my door on the farm. In fact, we hadn't had locks on the door.

The street wasn't like streets I'd lived on. The houses had different colors: white, peach, beige, and brown. Strange-looking plants with large limbs decorated some of the lawns. The street was clean, smooth, with painted curbs and addresses painted in front of each house. Every driveway had a nice car parked in it. As I walked the next block, this street looked the same: neat and clean.

Rounding the corner, I lost my bearings and had to think which way to go. Seeing Maggie sweeping her sidewalk, I headed her way. I waved, walked up to the door, and twisted the knob. After turning and pulling for a moment, I remembered I had locked the door. I also remembered I'd left the key on my dresser. That was another thing Aunt Mae had told me: "Don't forget your key to the house."

Maggie must have seen the panic on my face, because she dropped her broom and came right over. "Katie, is there something wrong?"

"I'm locked out of the house, and I don't have my key."

"Well, if I know Mae, she'll be gone 'til late afternoon. She's religious about her shopping. Wednesdays are her Swap Meet days. Why don't you come over my house 'til she gets back?"

"I don't know…."

"Don't be silly. You can't stay outside in this heat."

I couldn't argue with that, but visiting in her house worried me. I had never stepped foot in a white person home before unless it was to clean or pick up laundry with my mother. Negroes didn't socialize with people on the other side of the tracks.

"Katie, we'll have lots of fun, you'll see."

The prospect of waiting all day in the hot sun convinced me to suppress my fears. "All right, if it's not too much of a bother."

Maggie waved her hand. "Don't be silly. I'm pleased to have you."

Stale cigarette odor and dog scent assaulted my nostrils as I followed Maggie through her door. Her house was just like ours except turned the opposite way. Orange and green shag carpet spread throughout the house; beige wooden tables faced a large, square, wooden TV in the corner of the room. The house looked cluttered for just the two of them.

Nate sat in the chair, wearing a white T-shirt, knee-length shorts, black socks, and house slippers. A half-smoked cigarette hung from his lips. He squinted, grunted, stood, and disappeared into the back of the house. A dog barked and scratched on a door somewhere in the back.

"Don't mind him. He's a mean ol' grouch but harmless — both Nate and our dog." She stretched her hand toward the couch. I sat with my hands on my lap. "I'll be right back." She disappeared and returned with two sets of yarn and knitting needles in her hand. She sat next to me and handed me a ball of yarn and a pair of the knitting needles. "I've been trying to get Mae to knit with me for years. It's relaxing. Let me show you how."

Maggie took her time and demonstrated stitching the yarn. She was right. I found knitting relaxing — so much so that I forgot all about Nate and that dog. He'd appear every so often and duck into the kitchen. Maggie passed the time by talking about her life. She touched my heart when she recalled the death of her son, Andy. He'd died in the Korean War.

Sharing her pain put me at ease to share mine. She hadn't asked, and I didn't know if Aunt Mae had told her why I had moved to California. I felt comfortable with Maggie. I told her about the night Gus came on the farm. She stopped knitting and covered her mouth.

"Oh, my Lord, Katie. I had no idea. How terrible. To go through something so horrible, I can't even imagine. I guess living out west has sheltered us. We have our bigots. Negroes complain about police brutality all the time. And there are those who are not ready for integration. I love my husband, but he refuses to accept change. But, to go through that...." She touched my arm. "Did they ever catch those men?"

"The South is different, Maggie. They never brought charges against those men."

"They knew who they were?"

I nodded. "Even if they would have gone to trial, they

would have gotten off. White men are never convicted for crimes against Negroes."

"Oh, my Lord, that's terrible." She stared off, thinking about what I'd said.

I couldn't tell if she was genuinely shocked. I'd assumed all white people knew that. Negroes sure did. I went back to knitting. We changed the subject and talked about the schools. I would have to enroll the children in the fall. I got better at knitting as time whizzed by. We talked about her upbringing. She'd lived in Inglewood all her life. Nate had lived next door in Hawthorn and had retired from a meat factory a year ago.

Maggie stood and looked out the window. "Mae has made it home."

"What am I going to do with my blanket? It isn't finished."

Maggie took my unfinished blanket, yarn, and needles and placed them in a large basket in the corner. "They'll be right here—tomorrow. I want you to be my knitting partner."

I stood and hugged Maggie. "I really enjoyed myself. I'd love to be your knitting partner."

"Same time tomorrow?"

I smiled. "Same time."

When I walked into the house, Aunt Mae had a dreadful look. "Where have you been? We came in the house and didn't see you. I was worried sick."

"I decided to take a walk, and when I returned, I'd forgotten my key. I've been across the street at Maggie's. We've been knitting."

Aunt Mae laughed. "Maggie has been trying to get me over her house to knit for years. I told her I'm no knitter. So, she's roped you in, huh?"

"I like knitting."

Aunt Mae smiled. "See, I told you, you were going to adjust here. It takes time, but you'll see this isn't a bad place. You're going to be fine."

"You're right, Aunt Mae. I like it here. I never thought I would, and I never thought I'd ever have a white friend, but I do."

1970

I walked across the street and stuck my key in the lock and unlocked the door. I turned and waved at Maggie. She always made sure I made it into the house. The phone rang. I closed the door and went to the kitchen. Was something wrong? Aunt Mae Bell was usually home from shopping by now. It wasn't like her to be this late. I picked up on the fifth ring. "Hello."

"Hey, Mama."

"Is everything all right, Maxine?"

"Everything is fine. Guess who came by here?"

I was relieved she didn't have bad news. "Who?"

"That man, Gus."

It was as if lightning had struck me. My body numbed from shock. It had been years since I'd heard Gus's name uttered out loud. "Did he hurt you, Maxine?"

"No, Mama, that's just it, he wanted to talk to you. He was nice and respectful. I think it's a ploy. He wanted to know where you had moved to, but I didn't tell him."

My heart dropped. This man is still looking for me. I grasped my chest and leaned against the counter—the thought that he may hurt Maxine and Henry to get to me made my legs wobble. "Did he threaten you?"

"No. He was very respectful. He was desperate to talk to you. He told me he had something to say that he could only say to you. I still wouldn't tell him anything. Henry talked to Reverend Sims about it. The Reverend talked to the sheriff. He told the Reverend we had nothing to worry about. Gus had left town—said he moved to Tennessee. I haven't seen or heard from him since."

I was relieved to hear that Gus had left town without making any trouble. I didn't have to worry about Maxine, but something in me wouldn't rest. I couldn't help but wonder if he was planning revenge. "How long ago was this?"

"He came by last week."

"Y'all be careful, Maxine. I know I'll be praying for God to protect y'all from that evil man." I hung the phone on the wall. I had to collect myself. I didn't know what to think about all this. "Lord, please protect us from that wicked man." I had to get off my feet before I collapsed. Sitting on the couch, tears gushed out of my eyes. "When will this end, Lord!"

Chapter Eleven

1975

The saints of West Florence Baptist Church knew how to celebrate a homegoing. They sang, preached, and shouted Aunt Mae Bell into heaven Holy Ghost style. The flowers were spectacular. Ushers stood at their posts in matching black suits, white pocket squares, and white gloves. She lay at peace in a rose casket with red roses embroidered on pink interior cloth bedding. She wore her favorite pink dress and hat with flowers around the brim. What a service. The burial was just as spectacular, and the repast had every kind of dish imaginable. I think Aunt Mae would have loved her sendoff.

The limousine dropped me off at the church, and Edward brought me home. He said he had somewhere to go—running the streets, chasing after young girls. I worried about that boy. I pulled my funeral clothes off, threw on my loungers, and sat in the living room. The house felt empty, even though Ruby and Maxine had stayed over. Ruby was going back to the valley tomorrow. She hated it up there, but that was her first teaching job. Maxine was leaving the day after tomorrow. She and Ruby were out somewhere.

I was mad at Timothy for not coming to the funeral. He said he couldn't get out of an important rally in New York. Knowing him, he was working some political angle to rise in the ranks of the Civil Right Movement. He could have come. Aunt Mae was too important not to pay his respects.

Patient, virtuous, and wise—that described my Aunt Mae. My eyes filled with tears. When I'd cowered in the house for fear of white people, she'd urged me to get out and experience the city, which I'd done. Aunt Mae nurtured the friendship between Maggie and me. Maggie was the first white person I'd ever opened my heart to. My entire world had changed because God had touched Aunt Mae's heart to take us into her home, which was now mine. I was her sole heir. She helped me put my past behind me. She helped me come out of my shell enough to feel comfortable around people.

All I knew about Los Angeles, Aunt Mae had taught me. She had introduced me to culture and had finally gotten me to go shopping with her. Now, I can't stay out of the stores. She took me to the parks, museums, Hollywood Boulevard, and other sites. Aunt Mae knew how to live, and when it came time for her to make her transition, she'd hugged me goodnight, gone to sleep, and never woken up.

It broke my heart that she would miss my graduation. She encouraged me to get my GED and my masters in psychology. I wanted her to see me walk across the stage and receive my degree. Everyone was coming. Edward said he'd hire a limousine to take me to the ceremony. Ruby had a dress tailored for me. I still wear a size six. Maxine and Timothy would fly in for my graduation party at the Beverly Wilshire Hotel. I owed a lot to Aunt Mae.

My taste buds screamed for a steaming cup of hazelnut coffee, but I was too tired to move. A truck with a long trailer whizzed past the window and screeched to a stop in front of the house. Puzzled, I willed myself the strength to get up and look out the window.

The truck backed into Maggie's driveway. Movers appeared and started wheeling furniture into the truck. I slipped on my house coat and shoes and walked across the street. *At least, she didn't move out in the middle of the night like the other neighbors.*

Maggie carried a lamp out of the house and set it on the lawn. "Katie, I've been meaning to come over and tell you we're moving. I just haven't had the time. I meant to tell you at the funeral, but you were so busy. Hold on." She darted into the house and appeared with an envelope in her hand. "This is for you. I was going to leave it in your mailbox, but...."

The last thing I wanted was an insincere sympathy card, but I took it to be cordial. "I can't believe you're moving. I'm going to miss you."

"The truth is, Nate is the one who wants to move. You know me. I don't see color. I see everybody the same. But, Nate is concerned with the number of blacks moving in."

My expression must have surprised her. She looked toward the door and leaned in. "You know I don't feel that way, but you know how he is."

My gut told me she was lying, but there was no use arguing with her. If she didn't feel the same as Nate, she would have never had agreed to leave. "Where are you moving?"

"Riverside. It's not that far away."

"I'm just surprised. Are you coming to my graduation? You said you were coming."

"I know, but... I'll try. Well, I'd better get back to packing. I'll write. I promise." Maggie touched my arm and walked into the house.

I turned, walked back home, shut and locked the door, and

tossed the envelope into the trash can. Once that truck drove away, that'd be the last time I'd see Maggie.

No matter how I tried to pretend, Maggie's moving away hurt my heart. It was another rejection, another slap in the face of my worth. We got close, I'd thought. I opened my heart in friendship. *White people are the same, here, down South. They all think the same.*

1980

It was one of those days. The bruises, welts, and broken leg on this child hit me hard. Abuse of little children always did. Alicia, my newest granddaughter, reminded me that children are a blessing. It saddened me to see other children treated this way. The number of abuse cases was rising, mostly due to drug addiction.

Children's Memorial had completed an extensive renovation of the pediatric wing. Neutral colors brightened the floor; state-of-the-art monitoring systems kept watch on the infants, and electronic locks controlled who entered the floor. All this meant nothing when I saw the marks and bruises on innocent children.

I tossed the file on the nursing counter. "I'll be back in the morning to take him to a foster home, Peggy."

Peggy shook her head. She was short, with long hair. "How is he?"

"Kids are something, trusting, forgiving. He's worried about being separated from his family. If his father shows up, call the police."

Peggy reached up and took the file. Strobes flashed, sirens blared with a piercing shrill. I covered my ears. Peggy jumped to her feet and leaned over the counter. "Katie, you have to exit the building!" she yelled.

I shook my head. "I'm not going anywhere."

"It's a fire alarm. You have to vacate when there's a fire alarm."

"It's a false alarm. I'm tired of walking down four flights of stairs every time we have a false alarm. If this is real, I'll help carry the babies out. But, we both know it's a false alarm."

Peggy darted to the nursery's door and pushed through. I held my hands over my ears. After another moment, the sirens stopped. I opened another file. Strobes flickered and flashed, irritating my eyes. "Why don't they turn those darn lights off?"

"They can't until they clear the floor," a smooth baritone voice uttered.

When I turned around, a tall, fair-skinned man wearing a dark-blue suit and blue striped tie smiled at me. He was well-groomed, with just the right touch of salt-and-pepper hair. I didn't know what kind of cologne he wore, but it smelled good. "Clear the floor of what?"

The man kept his eyes on me. "Once the fire system goes into alarm, it can't be cleared until someone resets the panel. Hospital protocols require every alarm must be checked out and verified that there is no fire before the panel is cleared. In fact, protocol requires everyone exit the floors until the all-clear is given."

"Well, somebody ought to fix this darn thing. It goes off every day, all through the day. I'm tired of running down the stairs every time this thing goes off. If we followed your darn protocols, we'd have to move a dozen babies every time this thing goes off. Can't they at least turn these irritating lights off?"

"I'm sure they'll have the system reset in no time."

"How about you tell whoever is ripping the hospital off millions of dollars to fix the system right in the first place?"

"We're working on it," he said with a wide grin. The strobes stopped flashing. "See, as I said. That's progress, isn't it?"

"It'll be better if they fix the thing right," I retorted and walked away.

Looking around the empty cafeteria, I spotted a table I could eat at in peace. It took me all morning to catch up on my work, so I took a late lunch. Setting my lunch tray on the table, I sat and pulled my Bible from my purse and set it next to the tray. Whispering grace, I opened my eye to see the man I'd talked to earlier standing in front of me, holding a lunch tray.

Gawking at me with a pleased grin, he motioned at his tray. "Mind if I sit?"

I shrugged and waved my hand.

He made a place, set his tray on the table, and sat. He bowed his head and shut his eyes for a moment. His lips moved repeatedly. That surprised me. He looked up and smiled. "Taking a late lunch, huh?"

"It's been a busy day."

"I'm Irvin Parker."

"Katie Smith."

"Really pleased to meet you, Katie."

"What do you do?"

"Irvin. That's my name."

I arched my brow and threw him a disapproving look. "What do you do, Irvin?"

"I'm vice president of operations for AD&T. We installed

the fire systems."

"So, you're responsible for my torment."

Irvin chuckled. "Guilty as charged. We have a few kinks to work out."

"Please, work them out, for my sanity's sake."

Irvin chuckled. "So, what do you do here, Katie? By the way, that's a lovely name."

His flirting took me by surprise. "I'm a social worker for Child Protective Services."

"Do you like your job?"

"It has its moments, but I love working with children."

"What about the bad cases? They ever get to you?"

"Yeah, but the children I help make the effort worth it. And, occasionally, I'm able to help one of the bad cases. Do you like installing fire safety systems?"

"Our company does more than fire systems. We do home and commercial security and monitoring. One day, our systems will be able to call you at work and let you know you have a problem at home."

"What kind of problem?"

"Fire, burglary, mechanical problems, broken pipe, power outage—it'll do it all."

"Yeah, right."

"You'll see. That's the wave of the future. I'd love to show you our office."

I sat back and folded my arms. "I bet you would."

"No, really, we have a state-of-the-art shop." He glanced down. "That's your Bible?"

He reached over and snatched my Bible. Several pages flew out and floated to the floor. "Do you mind?" I scooted my chair out.

"I'm sorry. I'll get those." Irvin grabbed the scattered pages from the floor and handed them to me. "You're a Christian?"

"Yes, I am. You?"

"With all my heart. Where do you fellowship?"

"West Florence Baptist Church."

"I know the church. How do you serve there?"

I glanced at Irvin. *Now he's just being noisy.* "I haven't been in a while," I said and scooped from my bowl of soup. I felt his eyes browsing over me. "The truth is, I'm looking for another church."

Irvin's expression remained the same; eyes glued to me. "I see."

"You see what? I'm tired of all the mess that goes on in churches. I just want to go to church and worship the Lord without the games they play."

"What games, Katie?"

The nerve of this man, prying into my life. Yet, there was a genuineness that drew me to him. In fact, he intrigued me. "Pastors are only out for themselves. They don't care about the people. They only care about their fame and offerings."

Irvin leaned back and peered at me. "You know all preachers aren't corrupt."

"Where do you go to church?"

"I don't have a church home, at present."

I folded my arms. "You don't go to church? All that preaching you just did."

Irvin grinned. "You don't understand. The church I went to, Westlake Baptist, folded."

"Folded?"

"The pastor just up and left." Irvine must have anticipated my next question. "Greener pastures, I guess."

"Isn't that church over by Marina Del Ray?"

Irvin nodded cautiously.

"That church is all white, isn't it?"

Irvin furrowed his brows. "Was. Not all white. I was there."

"You know what I mean."

"There were a few black people who attended."

"How can you go to an all-white church? Aren't there churches in our neighborhood you can attend?"

Irvin squinted as if thinking carefully what he wanted to say. "I don't attend a church based on race. I was drawn to that church because it teaches the Word of God. Like you, I'm tired of games churches play. I just wanted to serve God and learn His Word."

"At least it was a Baptist church. There's hope for you."

He returned my smirk with a smile. "Maybe we can have lunch on Sunday… or dinner… or coffee after church."

My first instinct was to brush him off. I was too old to think about courting. He was trying with all his heart. I wanted to say no, but more than his extremely good looks, good manners, and exquisite dress, I could see he was a godly man. I hadn't met a man with that kind of heart since Gregory.

"Maybe, but you'll have to go to church with me. I'm not going to a white church."

Irvin adjusted in his seat. "Katie, why are you so adamant not to go to a white church?"

His question surprised me. I hadn't realized I'd voiced my prejudices so graphically. I've just had bad experiences with white people. I prefer to worship with my own."

Irvin frowned. "Own what? We're all God's people, Katie."

For a moment, he sounded like Gregory. "I know. But, you don't understand what I've been through with them."

"I'd like to hear about it… over dinner?"

I pretended to be blasé, but I liked him more by the moment. And I began to sense that he was the man God had brought into my life. I was afraid of a close relationship, though. It had been a long time since Gregory. Irvin's multicultural worship troubled me a lot. I wasn't ready for that, either. It was wrong to think like that, but maybe he was the man to help me overcome my bigotry.

Chapter Twelve

1999

Irvin pulled into the church's parking lot and parked in one of the three visitor spaces marked by a cardboard sign. Cars were parked on poorly marked spaces, and other cars overflowed onto a dirt lot next to the property. The building looked old and shabby with stained, white stucco walls with blue trim. "South Bay Baptist," the old, worn sign read.

Irvin noticed my frown. "This is the place you want to visit?" I asked. Irvin turned the car off and looked ahead for a moment. "We could have stayed home."

He forced a smile. "We need to be in church, Katie."

"I agree, but look at this place. How did you find this church?"

"One of my clients attends here. They said it was a good church."

"At least it's Baptist," I said, tossing him a smirk.

Irvin shook his head. "This is a place where we can serve God. I don't care what denomination it is. West Florence was Baptist, wasn't it? I want to go somewhere where people serve the Lord in sincerity. I know you do, too."

I surrendered, knowing he was right. Pushing the door open, I threw him a look. "Let's go and get this over with."

Irvin walked around the car and extended his hand. He pulled me into his arms. "You know I love you more than life."

"Yes, I do. That's why I'm doing this—for you." I smirked. "I'm expecting something really special for our twenty-year anniversary."

Irvin smirked. "We could stay home—lock in and spend quiet time together—just me and you." I tossed him a look. "I'm taking you to Hawaii for two weeks of bliss in paradise." He kissed my lips.

"That makes me feel a lot better."

Before he opened the door, he turned to me. "There's one thing I need to tell you."

"What?"

"This is a mixed church."

Frowning, I let go of his hand. "What do you mean, 'mixed?'"

"It's multicultural—mostly white."

Stunned, I stepped back. "You should have told me, Irvin."

Irvin grabbed my hand. "There's no color in God's redemption. We're all one in Jesus."

"You still should have told me."

Irvin grimaced and coughed. I didn't like the way he'd been coughing lately.

"Are you all right?"

"Just some congestion that won't go away, I'm fine."

"You should go to the doctor. You'd been coughing like that for a while. And you still should have told me about this place. You know I'm uncomfortable around...."

"Shsssh." He put his finger on my lips. "God is in this, trust me."

The service had already begun. The music and singing were

different from what I was used to. But better than I expected. One man, playing an acoustic guitar, led two singers in contemporary worship songs. A projector displayed the words of the song on a white screen in the center of the stage. The people clapped, out of time, and some raised their hands, but a sweet presence permeated the room. We followed an usher to our seats.

The room filled with people, mostly white. Irvin was impressed by the diversity. I was more curious than anything. Mexicans, blacks, Asians—we didn't have this at West Florence. The man leading the worship finished after two songs and quietly left the stage. The pastor took the offering, which took all of five minutes, then gave a wonderful sermon. I was used to preaching, but his teaching made the Bible clear and easy to understand. He wore blue jeans with thick red suspenders over a blue argyle shirt. No one dressed up, except Irvin and me.

After the message, Irvin wanted to hang around, but I was ready to go. He introduced me to people he'd already met. He loved it here, and I knew this was going to be our church home. The pastor extended his hand to Irvin. "Hello, Irvin. I'm glad you've made it back."

"I am, too. This is my wife, Katie."

"Katie, I'm pleased to meet you. I'm Pastor Phil Capello. I hope you enjoyed yourself." I nodded. He turned toward Irvin. "You must come back. We have Bible study on Wednesdays, prayer on Fridays, and men's fellowship every Saturday. We get together and pray and have breakfast...."

I drifted over to a wall covered with pictures. The entire church's history was here: past and present members, the church at its various building stages, and a young-looking Pastor Phil. The pictures reminded me of a family reunion—

minus black faces. I looked around the lobby; people hugged and loved on each other as they left. This place wasn't so bad.

A lady who looked to be in her sixties approached me. She dressed impeccably in slacks and blouse with a matching jacket. She was the first person I'd seen who wore Sunday dress clothes. She had a well-kept hairstyle with a streak of silver in the middle. "Hello, my name is Claire."

"I'm Katie. Pleased to meet you, Claire."

"Did you enjoy the service?"

"I did. The sermon was good."

Claire took the time to tell me about herself and how she'd come to join the church. She was a widow of four years. Her job kept her on the road, but I could tell she wanted friendship. Most of the people were younger than us. Before I knew it, I had agreed to have lunch with her.

Irvin tapped me on the shoulder. "I'm ready to leave whenever you are."

"Honey, this is Claire. Claire, this is my husband, Irvin."

"Pleased to meet you, Claire."

"Likewise. Katie, I'll call you later this week to set a time for lunch."

"I look forward to it," Claire smiled and walked away. Irvin grinned at me. "What?"

"Lunch? You've already made a friend and are having lunch?" Irvin replaced his grin with a smirk. "You like it here, don't you?"

I looked away to keep from grinning. "It's growing on me — since I have to go here."

"I think God has placed us here, Katie. I think we can grow and serve God here."

I didn't argue with him. I had my reservations. I didn't

want to admit that I was uncomfortable around this many white people. But, these people, on my first visit, touched my heart by the kindness and love they showed. I sighed in surrender to the Lord's will.

* * *

Reaching for my phone to switch it to vibrate, I realized I'd left it at the hospital. In my rush to make it to church on time, I must have left it on my desk. I'd ended up being late anyway. The service had already started. I'd hoped to catch the end of worship. Irvin was going to fuss. I knew he'd been trying to call me. I told him I'd meet him there. He was probably already inside, though it was strange I didn't see his car outside. I looked forward to seeing him. I hadn't seen him since that morning, and we'd planned to grab a late dinner after the service.

When I rushed inside, the sight of Claire standing next Ruby and Edward surprised me. My stomach knotted. My first thought was that something had happened to Alicia. That girl had been on my heart. Drugs had gotten a hold of her and wouldn't turn her loose. I feared she'd end up dead. My heart pounded as I gazed at everyone. "What's wrong?" I said to Ruby.

Ruby grabbed me in her arms. "Mama, it's Irvin."

* * *

The funeral home did a nice job on the body. Irvin looked nice in his black Brooks Brothers suit, his favorite. Everyone was kind and supportive. His brothers and sisters gave their condolences. He had no children. He'd married me late in his life.

Ruby and Joseph did everything as far as the arrangements were concerned. Ruby was short, like me, but she had gotten plump. Joseph was short with a pot belly, but a good man. Ruby had dressed them both. Maxine and Henry matched in black Saint John's suits, Maxine's favorite. They always matched each other. That was Maxine's style. Timothy and his wife, Dorothy, made a grand entrance, wearing their elitist pride. Edward showed up with one of his baby mamas. I couldn't recall this one's name.

Seeing my grandkids made me glad. Timothy's two children looked like fish out of water. They always thought they were better than everyone, just like their parents. A few of Edward's kids showed up with a string of their kids. All of Maxine's children were well-mannered. When Alicia came in, I wanted to scream. She was back on crack. She hadn't even bothered to clean up—her clothes, hair, and face were a mess.

Shaking my head, I looked over at Irvin. He was a good man, but as much as I hated to admit it, he never measured up to Gregory. I felt guilty about that. I wondered if he'd known he didn't have my full heart. He'd given me his; I had no doubt about that. Gregory and Irvin couldn't have been more different: Gregory had been crude, uneducated, and zealous for civil rights; Irvin had been refined, educated, and more business-minded than socially conscious. Yet, both men loved the Lord with all their hearts.

Claire never left my side. Neither did Pastor Phil. South Bay Baptist parishioners filled the room, as well as people from West Florence Baptist. I'd decided that Pastor Phil would officiate. Timothy insisted on making remarks. Henry told me he didn't have to say anything. He was humble that way. But, the other ministers felt they needed to say something. I drew the line at Reverend Houston, my former pastor. I didn't want the service to drag on all day.

I was glad I had the repast at the funeral home. My first choice had been to have everything at South Bay, but the funeral director said he'd give the entire facility to me for the day. I guess no one else had died. As it turned out, the funeral home filled to capacity. We interred Irvin at Inglewood Park Cemetery and arrived back at the funeral home within two hours. I was relieved because I could leave here and go straight home to peace and quiet.

"How are you doing, Madea?" Alicia threw her arms around me. "I'm so sorry for Irvin. He was like a granddaddy to me."

"It's all right, child." Looking at her, I pressed my lips together. She'd made a complete mess of her life, yet she was the only grandchild who sincerely cared about me. "When are you going to get yourself together, child?"

"I'm doing fine. I have a job and my own place," she said, leaning against my chest.

I found what she said hard to believe. She didn't know Edward kept tabs on her. "You should stay with me ... until you get your life together."

"That would be a bad idea, Mama. She'd rob you blind," Ruby blurted out.

Alicia rolled her eyes and stormed away. I shook my head. "Ruby, you need to stop."

Ruby shrugged. "You know that girl ain't ready to change. Anyway, I'm going to wrap things up here to take the food to the house."

I nodded as she walked away. People streamed by to express their condolences and leave. I was ready to go. Claire gave me a gentle hug and said she was coming by the house. Pastor Phil said his goodbyes. I thanked him for his time. As he walked away, it occurred to me that I had joined South Bay's widows club.

I pulled into my usual space and turned the ignition off. It was hard being here without Irvin. Twice widowed, I found myself at the same crossroad of life. Irvin's death was different in many ways. I'd had no time to grieve over Gregory. I'd had the kids to occupy my mind. Irvin's death left a giant void in my soul. It seemed my entire life was empty and weighed down. I needed something to take my mind off of everything.

The dirty stucco walls bothered me to no end. I'd been coming to South Bay Baptist for almost a year. The parking lot, the lawn, the entire church needed a major makeover. "That's it." The epiphany hit me. *I'll speak to Pastor Phil about it. I've found my cause.*

Walking in the lobby, I was happy to see everyone waiting for me. I got bounced around from one warm embrace to another until Claire rescued me. I thanked them all for their love and support, and Claire whisked me into the sanctuary. Pastor Phil gave me a warm hug and delivered his message. After the sermon, he dismissed the service, forwent his usual meet-n-greet, and took me to his office.

He motioned for me to sit, and I did. He sat and watched me for a moment. "How're you doing?"

"I'm doing all right, Pastor. It's starting to hit home — the loneliness."

"After my Pat passed, it took a long while to get over not

having her around. Pastoring the church helped occupy the time, but I still ached for her."

"I understand. Speaking of occupying my time, I want to propose something to you."

"Sure, anything."

"I'd like to remodel the church. We need a makeover."

Pastor Phil's leaned back. "I don't know, Katie. We don't have the money in the budget to...."

"Leave that to me. I'll give you a budget you can live with. I need to do this."

Pastor Phil peered into my eyes. I wondered if he was searching for a gentle way to turn me down. "All right, Katie. You're right. We're way past due on remodeling. I'll speak to the elders and see what we can do for money."

Immediately, ideas flooded my mind. By the time the next service came, I had put together a full proposal and budget for the remodeling and had presented my bid to the church board. They were amazed by the efficiency and speed with which I put the budget together. Pastor Phil announced the project and enlisted volunteers to help. The response was miraculous. All hands went up to offer their talents in some way. I told everyone work would begin on Monday.

That night, I made out a schedule of what needed to be done and who would do what. I laid out the work according to availability and what skills or trade someone offered. The next day, we cleared the ground of weeds and dead trees, since the funds for the inside would take longer to come through. Tuesday we cleaned and prepped the walls, and the crew came behind us painting. I chose light beige—something neutral.

By the end of the week, we began work on the parking lot, filling in holes and smoothing out dips and humps. I worked right alongside the men, though they never allowed me to overexert myself or work too long in the sun. By the end of April, we finished outside. The funds came through for the interior. I was glad because I didn't want to work outside in the May heat.

In my daily meeting with Pastor Phil, he asked how long it would take to complete the work. Since all the labor was supplied by volunteers, I showed him my tentative schedule of how and when I'd used the various trades. So far, I told him, everyone had been pretty faithful to his or her commitments. I estimated that we would be finished by mid-June.

He and the board decided to move the congregation into a banquet hall temporarily while we finished the interior renovation. I was thrilled. That gave us unhindered time and space to work. We pulled out the old pews, removed the old light fixtures, outlet and switch covers, and painted the walls by the end of the first week. By the end of the second week, we had finished the lobby and restrooms, and by the end of the third week, we had finished the kids church, nursery, and multipurpose room. Now, we were only waiting for the new light fixtures and carpet. I went with white and olive for the lobby and white and dark olive for the sanctuary.

Pastor Phil pulled me away from my work and led me to his office. Once there, he pulled my chair out and motioned for me to sit. I braced for bad news—we had run out of money or some other snag. He sat in his chair and smiled.

"Is everything all right, Pastor? We haven't run out of money have we? The city code inspector isn't complaining, is he?"

Pastor Phil waved his hand. "No, nothing like that."

"What's wrong?"

"I just wanted to see how you were doing."

His concerned stunned me. "I'm all right."

"You've been working so hard since the funeral. I wanted to make sure you're okay."

"Truth is, Pastor, this project provided a welcomed distraction. I realize the best way to overcome your troubles is to serve others."

Pastor Phil smiled. "You're quite a lady, Katie. Thank the Lord He brought you to us."

* * *

The grand opening for the new church was ahead of schedule, as I'd hoped. We made our church a home. Everyone lent a hand. We did it as a family. I couldn't help but muse if heaven would be like this. I was most proud that blacks, whites, Hispanics, and Asians had worked side by side to build a safe haven for God's people.

Claire gave me a big hug and helped with the refreshments. Pastor Phil said a few words of dedication and prayed over the building and the people. Watching everyone mingle afterward really blessed my heart. I was home among my Christian family.

Chapter Thirteen

Pastor Phil, his face wrinkled with agony, labored through his sermon, wearing, of all things, an old brown polyester suit. He rambled on about new beginnings and hard changes and then dragged to a long, arduous close. The announcements and offering were brief. It felt more like a funeral than a church service. He nodded to Mark Zappa, the worship leader, and stepped off of the platform.

Mark and the three-member praise team softly sang, "Jesus, you're the rock of my faith," a cappella. The five-member band joined the three angelic voices in a contemporary beat that sent everyone to their feet, clapping hands and swaying side to side.

The music roared to a close, and people took their seats. Praise percolated in my soul. The joy of the Lord charged my spirit. Waving my hand above my head with my eyes shut, I couldn't help myself. "Hallelujah. Thank you, Jesus," I belted.

Claire slid her arm around my waist. "I don't know about you, Katie, but I needed that."

"Amen to that," I said, wrapping my arm around her shoulders.

We took our seats on the front row. A sharp pinch shot up my arm. These limbs were too old to wave like that, but it was worth it. I loved saying his name. I loved praising my Lord. I couldn't wait to experience heaven.

Pastor Phil took the podium. He looked down, fidgeting with his pen. He kept glancing toward the back of the sanctuary. I turned to see what held his attention.

The board of elders entered the sanctuary and filed onto the platform. The group of six stood behind Pastor Phil with clasped hands and stoic stares. The room became quiet, and suddenly my joy drained from my soul. *Please, don't let this be news of a scandal – one of the pastors or elders fallen into immorality, or someone caught pilfering church funds.* I had been through both situations at my last church. I hated these kinds of announcements.

Three associate pastors took the stage alongside the elders. *This is bad, really bad.*

Pastor Phil looked up, avoiding eye contact with anyone. He tugged on his tie and cleared his throat. "I have an announcement to make. After much prayer, we, the pastoral staff and the board of elders, have come to the decision to relocate the church." Pastor Phil waited for the murmurings to die down. "I know some of you are surprised—shocked even. South Bay Baptist has been in Carson since 1968. Many of you have been with us from the beginning. This wasn't an easy decision."

I glanced at Claire. Her eyes twinkled with excitement.

"Where are we moving?" someone yelled.

"Costa Mesa," Pastor Phil answered.

"Costa Mesa," echoed around the sanctuary.

"That's over thirty miles away!" someone else shouted. "When are we moving?"

Pastor Phil shot a glance at the men behind him. "The end

of the month."

Heads turned with baffled looks, snapped with shocked glances, and swiveled with stunned stares.

"I know you have questions and concerns. We'll address all of them. I know this transition will be hard for some of you, but once you see the new place, you'll see the Lord is in this move."

Pastor Phil and the elders fanned out along the front of the platform.

People rushed the podium. I refused to move. I didn't want to hear his prepared explanation or crafted comments. From time to time, he shot me a look. I didn't respond. Why now? I couldn't wrap my mind around this. Why so far away, and why Costa Mesa? It bothered me that they had already found a place and had made the decision to move without talking it over with the congregation.

Claire turned to me. "I have to leave. I'm flying out to Denver for that health conference I told you about. I'll be back on Wednesday. Let's do lunch. I know you'll want to talk about this. I'm excited. The timing is perfect. I've been planning to move out that way."

We stood and embraced for a long while. Her plans took me by surprise. "Have a good trip. I'll see you when you get back." Sitting back down, I stared toward the front.

Brother Mann walked away from Pastor Phil, shaking his head. "Hello, Katie. Do you believe this? It's hard enough taking two buses to get here on Sunday. There's no way I can get out to Costa Mesa." He shook his head and walked away.

Sister Nora wrapped her arms around Pastor Phil, squeezed for a moment, and walked away with tears streaming from her eyes. Pastor Phil wiped his eyes. Sister Nora stopped and looked at me. "Hi, Katie. What do you think about this?"

I shrugged.

She glanced toward the front. "Why Costa Mesa? Anyway, you look nice. You always look nice. What dress is that, Anne Kline or Taylor? I like the green color." She looked toward the front again. "I feel like I'm being abandoned. I'll talk to you later." She walked away.

Pastor Phil stood in front of me, straining a smile. "I know you want to talk. C'mon, let's go to my office. You must have a lot of thoughts on this. I can't wait to hear your input."

Winding through the narrow hall, I followed him to his office and sat. He was a simple man with simple taste, content with his vintage décor. He wasn't like the other pastors I'd known, who had extravagant furnishings and wore expensive suits and jewelry. Pastor Phil never wore clerical robes or collar. He preferred old jeans or corduroys, cotton button-down shirts, and suspenders. He never tried to hide his balding gray. I loved his down-to-earth approach. He didn't mind rolling up his sleeves and working in the trenches with the people. However, I didn't understand his thinking about this move.

"I'm glad that's over. You want a water or juice, Katie?"

I shook my head. "What's this about, Pastor?"

"I thought you'd be happy. ..."

"Why would you think that?"

He did a double-take. "New place, open doors," he said cautiously, pulling a bottle of water from his fridge and plopping into his chair. "We felt it was time to move. The Lord has opened a wonderful door for us in Costa Mesa. This move will help fulfill our vision."

"How will moving forty-five minutes away do that, exactly?"

"A Lutheran church was selling its property. It's smaller

than this building, but the land has growth potential."

"There are church buildings closer. What's the real reason you're moving?"

Pastor Phil lowered his head and rubbed his brow, letting the question dangled for a moment. "The truth is, a lot of people are concerned about the changes around here."

"What people, and what changes?"

"Carson has changed a lot over the years."

"How?"

Pastor Phil shifted in his chair, deliberating his answer. He wasn't one to beat around the bush, but his hesitancy bothered me. "People," he blurted.

"People? Carson is a middle-class suburb. It's one of the most diverse cities in California. Wait a minute. You're not moving the church because of black people, are you?"

"People want to feel safe, that's all. People are afraid to go to work, go shopping... come to church."

"Pastor, what crime has happened here? Are you telling me the white people in this church are uncomfortable around black people? That's who you're talking about, isn't it?"

"I know that sounds bad, but look at it from our point of view."

I bit my lip. "What point of view is that?"

"As pastor, I have to look out for the interest of the flock."

"The white flock?"

Pastor Phil stared at me. "All the flock."

"You sponsor missionaries to Africa, Haiti, and South America. You're fine with sending people overseas to live among black people. You gather food and clothing for the poor people in the inner city. You're even eager to drive to the ghetto to deliver those goods. But, when too many black people move too close, you want to pack up and move away? As long as we are over there, you're fine with us, but don't let us live next door to you?"

"Don't make this about race, Katie."

"What else could this be about?"

"Open doors for this congregation."

"Pastor, if some of your congregation harbor racial feelings, don't you think you should address it rather than move away? Wait a minute. Do you feel this way?"

Pastor Phil leaned back in his chair, his eyes down. "I have my concerns."

My head snapped at his words. How had I not seen this?

Pastor Phil leaned forward. "Don't look at me that way. You know I don't think that way of you. You have done great things with your life. You're educated, articulate. I respect that. You have impeccable taste. Because of your input, this church could be featured in *Architectural Digest*. I hope you'll lend your skills at the new place." He leaned back. "You're the most decent and honest person I know. This is not about you."

I would never have guessed that Pastor Phil, of all people, felt this way. There were people in the congregation who had problems with black people. I knew who they were. Some of the elders and one of the pastors kept their distance from me and other people of color. I ignored them. I was used to ignoring bigotry. But, Pastor Phil—how could I accept this? This was my pastor and my friend. He'd never shown any signs of prejudice. He made me feel welcomed and loved from the first moment I'd stepped through the church doors. Had the entire ten years at South Bay Baptist been a lie?

"What about the black members you're leaving behind?"

"We feel the people of this community are best served by

someone they can identify with. I've asked a black pastor, a good friend of mine, to take over the church. I've known him since seminary. He's a good man."

"A black pastor… not a pastor?"

Pastor Phil nodded with a forced smile. "Many church growth experts agree that indigenous people are best equipped to minister to the needs of their community."

"Where did they get that from?" I exhaled a loud sigh. "You grew up in Carson. Doesn't that make you indigenous?"

"I know this sounds terrible…." Pastor Phil said.

I stood, shaking my head. "What about the white people you're leaving?" His furrowed brows surprised me. "Yes, there are just as many white folks in Carson as blacks. Some of them are a part of this church and may not want to make the long drive to Costa Mesa. Have you considered them? Aren't you leaving them to the indigenous people? And, since there are just as many whites as black in this city, who are the indigenous people? Whom are you abandoning?"

Sullenness crinkled Pastor Phil's face. "I'm not abandoning anyone, Katie. Everyone is welcome to come with us."

I batted my eyelids to keep the tears from falling. "You know black people won't follow you all the way out there. That's why you asked your black friend to take over the church." I turned around and walked toward the door.

"Katie, don't leave like this."

Whirling around, I glared at him. "Pastor, you know my past. You know how afraid I was. You know what it took for me to come here, to finally feel comfortable around white people again."

"Katie."

"I thought you, of all people, didn't see race. I thought here, skin color didn't matter."

"This move doesn't change how I see you."

"Pastor, you're leaving me. That hurts." I turned and walked out.

* * *

Pecking out the last word on the keyboard, I yawned and stretched my arms. What had started out as a day at the library, grazing through a few magazines two weeks ago, had ended up as an exhausted research session on racism in the church. What I uncovered horrified me. Combing through the plethora of news articles, books, video clips, and audio tapes sparked a burning passion to respond.

I had no idea racial feelings ran so deep among Christians. Pastors and parishioners harboring such feelings disturbed me. *How could God's people be this way?* What did the cross of our Lord mean to them? I had to face my own feelings about how whites had treated me in past and the present. I still had bitter feelings against them.

I really hoped I'd found a church where the walls of prejudice didn't exist. I'd hoped at South Bay Baptist that people saw one another not just as equals, but as true brothers and sisters in the family of God. It grieved me that African Americans saw themselves as black Christians, not just Christians, that they felt isolated from whites in the same church. It saddened me that whites didn't feel the need to reach out to their brothers and sisters of color. It was not supposed to be like this in the body of our Lord. I tapped the keyboard, and the screen flickered on. I wanted to proof what I'd written one more time.

To the white churches

Why do you move away from your black Christian family members? We, black people, have survived the brutality of the segregated South. We understand its hate and cruelty. We've survived fire hoses, dogs, clubs, fists, kicking, spitting, shootings, and lynching the South afflicted on us. What we didn't survive was the pain of being devalued. You, white people, move away from us like we're filth. Your actions tell us you don't value us. Your actions, white churches, are nothing more than modern-day segregation minus the brutal hand of Jim Crow. You are our family. It's not supposed to be this way in the body of our Lord, Jesus Christ. Consider this:

God loved black people enough to include them in the same body of Christ that you're a part of.

The precious blood of Christ was shed for both black and white sins.

Blacks and whites will live together in the same heaven as one family.

You won't be able to flee to a white part of heaven because there won't be one.

What kind of witness does your self-imposed segregation display to the world?

And, most of all, have you considered how a divided family breaks the heart of our Heavenly Father?

My heart pounded hard in my chest, and my finger trembled. Once I pressed the key, this would forever be out there for the world to see. The man at the paper had told me if I got the letter to him tonight, he'd make sure it made the next Sunday's edition. Would sending the letter do any good? Were my motives right?

I hit send.

Chapter Fourteen

Chad Watson checked his GPS to make sure he had arrived at the correct address. He hated coming to this part of town. Every night, the news reported a carjacking, a liquor store robbery, or a drive-by shooting somewhere in L.A. He didn't see any other white people, and he feared becoming the news instead of reporting it. However, if he wanted to be a reporter, he had to go where the stories were.

He'd expected to venture deep into the jungles of the ghetto. At least, that was where his co-workers had teased he would be going. Yet, riffraff didn't run rampant here. Bums weren't standing on corners drinking malt liquor, smoking weed, and yelling curse words at each other. Old, tricked-out cars weren't cruising the streets, blasting gangsta rap music. Gangbangers with guns tucked in the back of their oversized jeans weren't roving as packs. There was no gunfire popping off, and there were no police cars speeding to crime scenes with sirens blaring. Still, being in this area gave him the jitters.

The drive up the 405 was long, but the traffic was light. It was a clear, brisk January day. The sky was crystal blue, and the wind pushed fresh air over the city. The view of the L.A. skyline surrounded by the snow-capped Santa Monica Mountains was a rare treat, but a delight to his eyes. Excitement over his first assignment took his mind off his apprehension of coming to the city. He was disappointed he hadn't landed a more prestigious assignment. Nevertheless, it felt good pounding the pavement, working a story.

Well-dressed and well-groomed people walked their dogs and pushed strollers, surprising him. Shrubberies posed like flawlessly sculptured art on dark-green lawns, without a speck of litter. The houses wore colors of white, beige, light brown, and a few muted colors, but they all blended with the décor of the neighborhood.

Late-model Fords, Buicks, and Chryslers perched in driveways represented the typical middle class. A few men meticulously washed and detailed their Cadillacs and Lexuses. The streets were smooth, without cracks, and clean. The sidewalks were evenly spaced and spotless. There was no difference between this part of Inglewood and his city. He grabbed his black leather carrying case, stepped out of the truck, and continued his surveillance. He aimed the remote toward his Dodge Ram, making sure he heard two chirps.

The house was light peach with a large, tinted picture window and tile shingles. Perfectly trimmed bushes and plants lined the front of the house, and the lawn was dark green with thick blades of grass. The black Mercedes 430 parked in the driveway told him she was a lady of some means.

Chad strode up the walkway and primped in front of the full-length glass door, making sure his blue polo shirt and beige Dockers were free of lint and wrinkles. He raked his fingers briskly through his blond bangs and nodded; his reflection was presentable enough to ring the doorbell. There were no bars on the windows. He scanned the street again and saw that none of the houses had bars or security gates.

The door was whisked open, and an elderly woman peeked out. She looked to be in her late sixties. Black, silky hair with strands of silver fell behind her back, highlighting her nearly wrinkle-free skin. She wore a linen slip dress with flower print that buttoned down the middle.

He pressed his ID against the door. "Chad Watson, from the *Orange County View*."

"Yes, come in." She unlocked the door and pushed it open. "I'm Kathleen Parker, but you may call me Katie."

He pulled the door open and walked in. "I'm pleased to meet you, Katie."

Chad did a quick glance around. There wasn't a speck of dust anywhere. The cozy Gaisbauer Austria furniture impressed him. The artwork and figurines testified to her exquisite taste. Every piece of furniture was in immaculate condition and was meticulously placed in the room. She loved plants, especially large ones, judging by how many crowded the house. Copies of *O*, *Ebony*, and *Woman's Health* spread across the coffee table in a neatly arranged pattern. She expressed her culture through African art displayed on the walls; especially prominent was a large portrait of a black Jesus. That piece intrigued Chad.

With a warm smile, Katie motioned toward a pair of armchairs, but he detected caution in her demeanor. Chad sat where he was directed. The room was warm. A hazelnut aroma permeated the house. His gaze fell on a large, black mug filled with steaming light brown coffee. Her Bible, old and worn, lay next to the cup. The black leather was cracked and frayed, and some of the pages lay loosely in the binding. He realized he'd imposed on whatever Saturday-morning routine she followed.

Chad finished his surveillance and discreetly ran his eyes up and down the aged lady. Katie's energy impressed him. She moved about with such vibrancy. He wanted to probe her for more information, but the house had already revealed a lot about her.

"Would you like something to drink? Coffee? I just made a fresh pot."

"No, thank you. You have a lovely home." Chad unzipped his bag. "Thank you for agreeing to talk to me."

Katie sat in her chair and sipped from her cup, never taking her eyes off of him.

"I apologize for being late. I misjudged how long it would take to drive here."

She nodded her acceptance.

He pulled a notepad from the bag and glanced at it. "Mrs. Parker...."

She sat her cup on the lamp table and swallowed. "Please, call me Katie."

"Katie, what made you write an op-ed on the front page of the *Los Angeles Times*?"

Katie threw a smirk at him. "Wasn't it self-explanatory?"

Chad blushed. "Right. Do you really think that all white people are racist?"

"All white people aren't racist. That's not what the letter said. But, racism is pervasive throughout the Christian world. I never knew how much until I experienced it myself."

"Meaning your church moving away? How was that racist?"

"They moved away from black people."

Chad's brow furrowed. "You know that for sure?"

Katie nodded.

"What did you expect from posting your op-ed?" Katie shifted in her chair. "Frankly, I didn't expect anything."

"I'm surprised, Mrs. Parker."

"I just wanted to let white churches know how we felt."

"We?"

"Black people, Mr. Watson."

A Basque green wall covered with pictures and awards caught Chad's eye. A large photo of Katie hung in the center of the wall. She sat in a large, red velvet throne chair with gold leaf frame, surrounded by dozens of people. She held her degree with a wide, proud smile. Above them, a banner declared, "Anything's possible at 50."

"You were in your fifties when you earned your degree?"

"Yes."

"What motivated you to go to school so late in life?"

"My father was disappointed that I had dropped out of high school. Education was very important to him. When my children left home, I went back to school and completed my education."

"May I ask what your degrees are in?"

"You want to know my life's story?" Katie stood by the wall and folded her arms. A smile came across her face as she gazed at the pictures. For a moment, she let her guard down. "This is my life's story, right here."

Chad stood beside her, studying the wall. "This is quite a spread."

"I like to start each day by giving thanks to the Lord for being so good to me. This wall is a memorial of the dark place He's brought me from."

Chad did a double-take. "What do you mean by dark place, Mrs. Parker?"

Katie rolled her eyes.

He knew he'd struck a nerve. "I mean, Katie."

"These are my children and grandchildren."

Chad pursed his lips. It annoyed him that Katie had sidestepped his question. To a reporter, that was like waving a juicy piece of meat in front of a hungry tiger. What was she avoiding? He studied the photos. What had he missed? His eyes widened.

"Mrs. Parker...."

She looked at him with raised brows.

"Katie, how old were you when you came to California?"

"I was thirty-five... no, thirty-seven."

"What year did you come here?"

"Nineteen-sixty. ..." Katie thought. "No, 1962."

"So, you're 85?"

"Manners aside, yes."

"I have to ask you. How do you have so much energy? And you look great for your...."

Katie waved her finger. "Stop while you're ahead. I try to eat right, and I make sure I walk every day. Mostly, I think God has blessed me with good genes. But, I move like an old woman, feel like an old woman, and look like an old woman."

Chad smiled and focused on a picture of Irvin. He held Katie in a tender embrace. "Tell me about your husband."

Her body relaxed as she gazed at the picture. "Irvin was a wonderful man. The Lord gave us twenty wonderful years together. He passed back in ninety-nine."

Chad arched his eyes. "How old is your oldest child?"

"Maxine is sixty-six."

"Tell me about your first husband."

Katie snapped her head toward him. "How did you know about him?"

"I didn't. I added up the years. I just assumed...."

Katie looked away. "I was a different woman back then."

The pain etched on her face told him he'd opened an old wound. "Tell me about her."

"I thought leaving Alabama would mend my heart, but it was too wounded. It had been that way ever since that night." Katie closed her eyes and shook her head repeatedly. "I couldn't be whole. No one ever could expect a person to be whole after such a horrible night like that."

So, there is another life. "What night, Katie? What happened to you?"

Katie sat with her head down. "Talk about something else."

"Maybe talking about that night will help you."

She wiped her eyes and looked at him. "This isn't about my wholeness."

"Telling your story might give you closure."

Katie chuckled. "So, this interview is about me getting closure?"

"All I'm saying is that you can share what happened to you in your own words."

"With whom?" Anger wrinkled her face. "I don't want to talk about this anymore."

Chad glanced at his notepad. "May I ask you a question?"

Katie nodded.

"Does your past have anything to do with how you feel about white people?"

Katie cut her eyes at Chad. "You don't know anything about my past."

"True, but... okay, let me ask this... do you think your past has anything to do with how you feel about your church moving away?" Frustrated that she wasn't answering his questions, he added, "Do you consider yourself a racist?"

Katie frowned. "What kind of question is that?"

"You asked white people why they are prejudiced, right? I mean, that's what your letter is asking, isn't it?"

"Your point?"

"Do you feel that all whites are prejudiced?"

"Since I don't know all white people, I can't possibly answer that, can I?"

"But your letter implies so."

"How old are you, Mr. Watson?"

"Thirty."

"You don't understand racism. You were born after the conflicts of the civil rights struggles and sheltered by your white society. Nowadays, people don't want to talk about the subject. They dismiss it as if it never happened. White people move away. That's how they deal with it. Your schools never talked about slavery or race issues outside a mere mention."

"Katie, with all due respect, you don't know anything about me. How can you say I don't understand the struggles you've been through? Aren't you stereotyping?"

"That's ridiculous."

"Is it? I know that whites served alongside of blacks in the fifties and sixties. They put their lives in jeopardy just as much as the black freedom fighters. Yet, their struggles in the Civil Rights Movement are minimized, if mentioned at all. I know for a fact that a lot of whites are just as angered by racism as blacks, but you never give us credit for that. Blacks can be just as prejudiced as whites."

Katie glared at him. "You have some nerve." She stood, walked over to the entry, and flung the door open. "This interview is over."

"What did I say?"

"Just leave."

Chad stood and slung his bag over his shoulder. "I'm sorry if I offended you, Katie. That wasn't my intention." He peered at Katie and then walked out of the house.

Chad felt he had blown his big opportunity. He traced his actions in his mind. Her abrupt change in demeanor surprised him. Where had he gone wrong? The mention of that night in Alabama was what had set her off. What happened there?

Chapter Fifteen

The response to the open letter overwhelmed me. I received hundreds of emails, and after a month, they numbered in the thousands. I hadn't realized people held so many different views on race. Opinions divided along racial lines. White people looked at race from a white point of view, and black people looked at race from a black point of view. This shouldn't have surprised me, but it did. What amazed me the most was that neither view was Christian.

Flashes of light bounced off the brass trim on the blinds. I looked up, glanced at my watch, logged off, and shut the computer down. *He's early this time.* I felt bad about the way I had snapped at Chad. I didn't know what came over me—why talking about that night had upset me so. I had called him and asked him to come over and finish his interview.

The front lock clicked, rattled, and the door whooshed open. Timothy came in with a wide smirk on his face, and a copy of the *Los Angeles Times* tucked under his arm. He wore casual slacks, a polo shirt, and suede shoes. Of course, his cologne dominated the room. Timothy sat on the loveseat and crossed his legs. "Why the surprised look?"

I got up and sat in my chair. "I was expecting someone else." I sipped from my cup. "Ugh. This coffee is cold." I looked at Timothy. "Go on. Say it."

Timothy's smirk morphed into a full-blown grin. "Say what, Mama?"

"Don't play with me, boy."

He raised the paper. "I wish you would have come to me first. I could have helped you with this and saved you a lot of money."

"It wasn't about the money. Despite the negative responses, contributions are pouring in—and, surprisingly, from white people. That's encouraging."

Timothy unfolded the paper and cleared his throat. "Quite a letter. I agree, though. White churches are no better than their secular counterparts. Remember, they were the bedrock of the Jim Crow South." Timothy shifted his body. "I can rally some people...."

"I'm not looking to start a movement."

"So, why did you publish this?"

"I wanted those churches to know how we feel."

"Who are 'we'?"   I didn't want to get into this with him. "The church I attended moved away because too many black people were moving to Carson."

Timothy chuckled. "Really?"

"Straight from the pastor's mouth."

"That's something I'd expect to hear down South. I don't know why you and Irvin joined that white church, anyway." Timothy shook his head. "Where did they move to?"

"Costa Mesa."

"That figures. Costa Mesa is all white."

"So, what's this Ruby told me about my grandbaby?"

"Same old story. I had to go down to county and get her. She got arrested for shoplifting—trying to get money to buy drugs."

"We need to help that child."

"She has to want it, Mama." He glanced down at the coffee

table and picked up a business card. "What's this?"

"That's the reporter who interviewed me the other day."

"Reporter?"

"He's from some paper called *The Orange County View*. I thought you were him."

Timothy squinted. "I know the paper. You sure you don't want me to handle this? I can speak to this reporter for you."

"No, thank you. I don't want you turning this into one of your civil rights crusades."

Timothy stood. "Church isn't my thing, anyway. Are you going back to West Florence? At least there you'll be around your own kind."

"No, I'm taking a break from church."

"I never thought I'd hear you say that."

"I still believe in God, and somehow I know He's going to sort all this out."

Timothy smirked. "Still hanging on to the white man's religion. White folks don't want you, Mama. When will you get it?" Timothy shook his head, kissed my cheek, and left.

The doorbell chimed. I opened the door. Chad had a curious stare about him—as if he didn't know what to expect. His case was strapped over his shoulder, and he wore business casual, the same as before. He pulled the screen door open. "Hello, Mrs. Parker. Thank you for calling me."

I motioned him in, and he went straight to the chair. He didn't look around as he had the last time. He sat when I sat in my chair. "Thank you for coming back. I'm sorry for blowing up at you. It was uncalled for. I want you to finish your interview. Can I get you something to drink?"

"I wouldn't want to bother you."

"Don't be silly. What would you have?"

"Well, I would love a cup of that coffee you had last time."

"It'll be my pleasure." I went to the kitchen and rinsed out the coffee pot. "Go ahead with your questions." I poured the water to the eight-cup mark and scooped the coffee into the filter. He stood by the wall, studying the pictures. "The coffee will be ready in few minutes."

"Thank you." He peered into my eyes. I could tell he was choosing his words carefully. After his last visit, I couldn't blame him. "Katie, you tell a wonderful story of your life with these pictures." He pointed at the wall. "But they only show your life in California. Tell me about your life before here."

Puzzled, I arched my eyebrows.

"You had a life before California… in Alabama. It's obvious it ended horribly. And, I think it's related to why you feel the way you do about white people. I think talking about your past would make a great story and help readers understand the impact of your op-ed." He sat in his chair and crossed his legs.

"You want to know about my past?" I stood by the window and stared out. I took a deep breath and looked directly at him. "Are you a Christian, Chad?"

"Why do you ask that?"

"As a reporter, you want all the juicy details about my life, and they are juicy. I've never shared my story before. It's too painful. I'm willing to consider that my testimony could help people, but not for the general public. So, I'll ask you again, are you a Christian?"

"I don't understand what this has to do with sharing your story."

"You haven't answered my question."

"Yes, I am, but…."

"Tell me what being a Christian means to you."

Chad frowned. "I'm not sure what you mean."

"It bothers me that Christians are prejudiced against fellow Christians. We're supposed to be examples of Jesus' love. So, I'll ask you again, what does Jesus mean to you?"

"I believe He is the Son of God, but I don't understand why you're asking me this."

I walked to the kitchen and poured his coffee. Peering at him, I handed him the mug and sat in my chair with my eyes fixed on him. "Tell me about Chad, the Christian."

"I grew up in the church. All of my life, I was the poster boy for home-grown Christianity. I can't even say that I've ever had my faith seriously challenged. But, I love the Lord with all of my heart. I believe He died for my sins on the cross, rose from the dead the third day, and is seated at the right hand of God."

"Then you're my brother." I stood by the window and stared out for a moment. "But you're naïve. You're right. You probably never had your faith tested." I faced him. "I've been through the fire. My faith has been tested. I can tell you a story that'll curl your hairs."

Chad leaned forward. "I want to know Katie, my sister in Christ."

I turned around. "All right, then, but I want to talk to Chad, my brother in Christ, not the reporter, and not the world."

"I'd like that."

"Good, then I'll share my heart with you." I folded my arms and gazed out the window. "That day… it was a sizzling, hot day...."

Chad scribbled feverishly without looking up. He'd turned his recorder on, but he told me he liked it better when he wrote his thoughts out by hand. I'd given him a lot to digest. His open mind impressed me. He showed a genuine concern for what I'd been through in Alabama. He asked a few questions, listened to the answers, and always allowed me to get my thoughts out. At times, he stopped writing and just listened, shocked by the gory details. He surprised me by how much he knew about black history.

He hadn't noticed an hour had passed. I gave him a few more minutes to catch up with his thoughts. I liked Chad. I was glad I told him my story. I felt a bond with him. "Would you like some more coffee?"

Chad didn't answer. He looked up and stared at me curiously. "So, Katie, your second husband passed away before you joined South Bay Baptist?"

"He died three months after we joined."

Chad furrowed his brows. "You praised the church for how wonderful they treated you. How could they be racist?"

"I was completely blindsided when the pastor told me he was moving the church away. He and the people didn't care to reach out to those they were running away from."

Chad leaned back; his eyes bored into mine. "Is it possible, Katie, that they were just plain scared instead of racist? I'm not excusing or defending their actions. I think they were insensitive. I'm not sure they were racist."

Clenching my jaw, I tensed up. I hated that he could be right. "I never considered that."

"Would you consider that they might be good-hearted people who did an insensitive thing? Their actions may be wrong, but their hearts are right."

"I suppose you could be right."

A smirk etched Chad's face. "Katie, I think you should

consider your feelings about white people, whether they're racially based or Christ-based."

"What do you mean?"

"White people have done you wrong, no doubt about that. But, if you are to move forward, don't you have to face your resentment of us? Shouldn't you see us as God's people, who need grace, mercy, and forgiveness?"

"I wouldn't call it resentment." I looked away from his frown. "Okay, I guess you're right. But, I do see them as God's people. That's what hurts so much. I'm rejected by the people who should embrace me. I hold no bitterness toward white people. I'm just hurt is all."

Chad's eyes dropped to the floor. He looked up and peered into my eyes. "It's going to take God to heal you, Katie. And the way you're going to overcome your hurt is to love those who have hurt you."

"You're right."

Chad scribbled, then looked up. "Why did it hurt you when the church moved away?"

"After what happened to me in Alabama, it was hard to trust white people. It took me years to feel comfortable enough to be around them."

"That's understandable."

"This neighborhood was all white when I came here. I was terrified of the people. One lady became my friend. When she moved away, I felt like discarded trash. I wasn't good enough to be around."

Chad tilted his head. "She moved away because…?"

"Like everyone else, the neighborhood was changing."

"Other whites had moved away. Why did this neighbor moving away hurt you?"

"I guess she was the first white person I'd ever opened up to. We'd developed a friendship, I thought. Her husband was a mean ol' racist. It turned out she shared his feelings — maybe not as bad, but she, too, was uncomfortable with the growing number of black faces. She moved away from me. I wasn't good enough for her to stay."

"Because you are black?"

I nodded. "You have to understand how it feels to be discarded. That's what white people do when they pack up and move away. Living through segregation was an awful time. White people saw us as filth, trash, and refuse. Every time I took a drink from a colored water fountain, I wanted to vomit. Every time I was forced to use the Negro restrooms, I felt like waste. The food we received from the back door of a café tasted like garbage. That's why I loved living on my farm. I didn't have to deal with all that.

"Even out here, whites acted the same way as whites in the South. They moved away from us as if we are animals. Black people won't admit it, but it hurts them to be thought of and treated that way. South Bay Baptist moving away felt like the same old stuff: moving away because of the color of our skin, like we're trash."

"This has been quite enlightening. I mean it, Katie. I've been sheltered from the harsh realities of race. In many ways, people like me have turned a blind eye to those realities. I've never had a reason to face them as you have had to. I want to do a more comprehensive story on this, if this is all right with you."

"I appreciate your heart, Chad. You are the third white person I've opened my heart to. I don't say that lightly."

"I'm honored. But it shouldn't be that way."

"I guess the Lord is working in me."

"I have some research to do." Chad stood and grabbed his bag. "I'll call you when I have my research together?"

Katie opened her arms. "Give me a hug, my brother." He gave me a tight squeeze. "Call me when you're ready."

"Thank you, Katie."

Chad pulled the door open. "I have to confess something. I was terrified to come here. I was surprised that this neighborhood was so well-kept. We both have to stop pre-judging each other, huh?"

"I guess we do, my brother."

Chapter Sixteen

Alicia Williams stomped around the living room of her on-and-off-again- boyfriend's apartment, stepping over and around people to get to her stuff. Searching through cabinets, digging under cushions, and peeking behind the entertainment center, she couldn't find it. Someone stole her stash. She went from person to person, searching pockets and jackets. Nothing. Scratching her arms and chin, she frantically scanned the room.

People came and went from Derrick's apartment at all times during the day, selling and buying the stuff she craved, mostly buying. She moved from one room to another, looking for anyone who had a bag, hit, or taste.

The apartment was dark, cramped, filthy, and putrid. People sprawled around wherever they could find a spot to shoot up or enjoy their high. Women traded sexual favors for fixes — a few in front of their children. Alicia was willing to trade such favors, but for some reason strange to her, no one had what she craved.

Derrick sat up, scratching his chin. He was thin with matted hair and a scrubby face. He stared at Alicia with a glaze in his eyes. "You jonesing?"

"Where's the stuff, nigga?" she shouted.

Derrick shrugged. "I'm out, shorty."

Agitated, she rushed out of the apartment without looking back. Hopping into her rusted, white Corolla, she turned the key repeatedly. Pounding the steering wheel, she cursed the car for not starting. After several coughs, the car burped a big puff of blue smoke, and she puttered west on Century Boulevard toward her usual spot.

She parked on a side street just east of the airport, where a strip of seedy bars and motels accommodated out-of-towners inconspicuously looking for quick gratification. She didn't like to walk the streets—it was too easy to be spotted by the police.

She ran the comb through her short, nappy hair; rubbed cocoa butter over her ashy face, and swiped a layer of lip gloss across her chapped lips without looking at the mirror. She paced the streets, ducking in and out of doorways, avoiding the police. She marked a john coming out of a strip bar tucked away at the back end of the lot. She hiked up her short shorts and tugged her black tube top down.

The john looked late-fortyish and wore jeans and a T-shirt. He looked around nervously. She knew what he wanted. Their eyes locked on each other. She threw her hips in motion and darted across the street, wasting no time leading him to his rented Chrysler 300, doing her deed quickly and collecting her fifty dollars. She spotted another john and enticed him for another fifty. She spotted a third john, but her cravings forced her to score.

Alicia woke up the next day in Derrick's bed, reeling from her high. He was definitely her on-again boyfriend since she had scored crack. Shielding her eyes from the beaming sun, she jumped out of bed, threw on her top and shorts, and rushed to the door. "I gotta go. My Mama gonna snap, big time."

Derrick sat up, rubbed his eyes, and stretched out with a wide yawn. "Hey, shorty, let me hold your EBT card. I'm out of food."

"Come on now, Derrick. You do this every month. You

spend all the money on your card, and now you want to spend up mine."

"You know the county cut me off, shorty."

Alicia sighed. "Here, nigga, but don't spend it all up. I hate going to the welfare office. They act like they better than everybody else. They won't give me another one 'til next month. That's for me and my son." She tossed the card on the bed and rushed out of the house.

Jumping in her car, she drove west toward home, formulating the lie she would tell her parents. Three-day binges were always hard to explain. Her father would be easy, but no way would her mother buy her story. A wave of conviction swept over her. That hadn't happened in a while. Getting high had always drowned out that nagging inner voice, but not this time. She wiped her eyes, but the tears kept streaming down her cheeks.

She hadn't always been this way. She'd once been a music video model. She'd strived to be the number-one vixen. She had the build for it, thick and voluptuous. At first, it was fun—the attention, hanging out with famous rappers, working on music sets at different locations, dancing, partying all day long. She'd loved all of it. She'd loved the money; she loved the opulence, or what she'd thought was opulent. Rappers poured bottles of Cristal like water and tossed around hundreds and fifties dollar bills like Monopoly money. She'd been enticed by it all.

Her dreams had disintegrated when a video director told her she was too dark-skinned ever to have a starring role in a video. From that time, she'd given in to depravity, but the truth was she loved to party. Before long, her reveling had enslaved her to drugs. She stopped doing video shoots, blew through the money she earned, and ran the streets.

This binge was one of the better ones, but, as always, it left her empty. Drugs never gave her the peace she sought. She felt good for the moment, but after the high wore off she had to face the awful reality of her wretchedness. No amount of drugs could erase that from her mind. Depression fell on her heavy. She despised herself for what she had become. She flipped the mirror away, disgusted by her loathsome reflection.

She parked in front of her house and took a deep breath. Trying to make a stealthy entrance, she tiptoed through the kitchen, hoping to make it to her bedroom.

"Where have you been, Alicia?" Ruby demanded.

Alicia froze in place. *Dang*. Ruby walked from the living room, wearing her housecoat and matching scarf. Alicia threw her stare toward the floor. "Out with friends, Mama."

"For three days? Do you think I'm stupid?"

"I don't know what you want, Mama."

"I want you to get yourself together. I want you to stop running the streets like a dog in heat. I want you to be a mother to your son. You do remember you have a son, don't you?"

Alicia rolled her eyes. "Okay, Mama."

"Don't roll your eyes at me. You're twenty-nine and act like a child who needs her diaper changed every five minutes. When are you going to grow up? When are you going to be a mother to Deshon? That boy calls me Mama, and I don't blame him."

Alicia rolls her eyes. "He knows I'm his mama."

"The boy is confused. After all, you're never here. I'm the one who feeds him, clothes him and takes him to school. I'm the one who has to explain to your son why his crackhead, whore mama isn't in his life."

Alicia fixed her eyes on Ruby. "You've got some nerve. You're not a real mother. You're just a fill-in. That's all you've ever been." She looked off. "Sorry."

"Sorry won't cut it this time, Alicia. You've gone too far. You're out of control, and you won't let anyone help you."

"Mama, you are making a big deal out of nothing."

"I want you out of my house."

Alicia's mouth dropped opened. "Mama."

"You heard me. I want you to leave, today."

"You can't be serious."

"As a heart attack."

Alicia visibly trembled. Ruby stared at her as if she were having a withdrawal episode. Alicia looked at Ruby with pleading eyes. "You can't put us out. We have nowhere to go."

"I'm not putting Deshon out. I'm putting you out."

Alicia frowned. "You can't take my son from me."

"You don't think I'm gonna let him roam the streets with a crackhead, do you?"

"I won't let you take my son away from me."

"We can do this the easy way or the hard way. The easy way is for you to get up and walk out of this house. The hard way is I pick up the phone and call Child Protective Services. Who do you think they're going to leave Deshon with, his crackhead mother or me? Either way, I'm keeping Deshon here. I won't have him living in the streets like a dog. Here, at least, he'll be in a loving, stable, home."

"Mama," Alicia said, barely above a whisper. "I have nowhere to go."

"Look, you get yourself together. Deshon will be here. I'm sorry it has to come to this, but you leave me no choice." Ruby swallowed. "Go on. I want you to leave, now."

Ruby walked to the kitchen. Alicia's eyes drooped. She felt defeated. Her entire life was one big failure. Her father walked with her son, Deshon. He looked at Alicia with compassion and glared at Ruby. He was short, stocky. He loved his casual dress, and his cologne dominated the room. She looked at her father with pleading eyes, hoping he'd stand up for her.

Ruby walked from the kitchen with her arms folded. Deshon tried to run to Alicia, but Joseph clenched his shoulders. Deshon wore the striped shirt and shorts Ruby had bought him last Christmas. Alicia hated the way she dressed him.

"Mommy, where are you going? I want to go with you."

Alicia peered at Deshon. "Mommy has to go away to get better."

Joseph glared at Ruby. He reached into his pocket and pulled out a thick wad of bills covered by a hundred-dollar bill. He glowered at Ruby and handed the wad to Alicia. Ruby rolled her eyes and looked away.

Alicia wiped her eyes. "Bye, baby." She ran out the house.

* * *

"You shouldn't have given her that money. She'll spend it on drugs," Ruby said.

Joseph shook his head and walked into the living room. He looked out the window. Deshon pressed his hands on the window with a blank stare.

Alicia looked toward the house. Her soul looked empty, self-loathing, and no value of life. Ruby wanted to run out the house and stop Alicia from leaving. She wanted to take her child in her arms and make all the bad go away. She was tempted to give Alicia another chance. But Ruby resisted, knowing that would turn into another and another and another chance. This was the time for tough love. Alicia got into her car and drove away.

Ruby followed the trail of blue smoke until it had disappeared over the hill and out of sight. Panic gripped her heart. What had she done? She thought about the dangers Alicia would face living on the streets and the dreaded call that could come from the police.

Joseph grimaced, took Deshon by his hand, and walked outside. Ruby went into the kitchen and put on a pot of coffee. She went to her bedroom and ran her agenda for the day through her mind: cook Joseph's breakfast, pay some bills, go to the grocery store, and take her mother shopping—but first, spar with Joseph. She sat on her bed, thinking this wasn't how her life was supposed to have turned out.

She was supposed to have gone to UC Berkley, earned her degree in education, traveled the world, worked as a teacher in an elementary school, married the man of her dreams, and had three kids and a whole lot of grandkids, in that order. She hadn't traveled the world, and she'd married Joseph in her second year of teaching. Alicia had come after her third miscarriage, which had nearly killed her, and Deshon was the result of one of Alicia's drug binges. Thank God he wasn't a crack baby.

She had done everything by the book. She had given Alicia everything she wanted. She raised her the right way, in church, in a safe neighborhood, in a loving home. *What more could I have done?* Walking into the kitchen, Ruby poured a cup of coffee just as Joseph and Deshon walked in. *Here we go.*

"Did you *have* to throw the girl out today? She was trying, Ruby."

"Don't start, Joe. That girl is spoiled, and you spoiled her, spoiled her to no good."

"*I've* spoiled her?"

"You know you did."

"You drove her away with your overbearing, nagging mouth. That's what drove her away. She wanted to get away from you."

Ruby snapped her head. "Joe, that was spiteful and hurtful."

"It's the truth, Ruby. I should have stopped you years ago. I have been telling you forever to ease off of that girl, but you wouldn't. You kept laying it on her."

Leaning back on her feet, Ruby folded her hands. "Laying *what* on her?"

"Your high-and-mighty attitude. You kept pushing her to be Little Miss Perfect. Her only escape was drugs. She needs help."

"I don't think we can help her."

"Really?" He waved his hand toward the window. "And you think the streets can?"

"I got to go. I'm taking Mama shopping."

Ruby stormed to the bedroom and slammed the door. Sitting on the edge of the bed, she shook her head. It had started when Alicia was fourteen, her rebellion—little things at first: not cleaning her room, skipping school, hanging out with the wrong crowd. She'd always attracted thugs. That year, she'd run away from home—not far, only three blocks to her grandmother's.

At fifteen, she started drinking and smoking weed. She ran away again, but that time she'd been gone for over a week. The police brought her back. She kept getting into trouble at home, in school, and with the law. When Alicia was eighteen, Ruby had put her out of the house. From time to time, she'd come back home, mostly at the behest of Joseph and Katie. Alicia got pregnant at twenty-three. That seemed to sober her up, but her sobriety had been short-lived.

She'd stolen to support her habit: cell phones, jewelry, clothes, the TV in her bedroom, and her radio. Then she nabbed Deshon's things: his bike, toys, PlayStation, anything of value she could sell or pawn to get a few dollars. She looted the house: her mother's jewelry, china, paintings. She'd stolen her father's gold jewelry, golf clubs, and tools. She'd stolen from stores and burglarized homes. She'd been arrested for armed robbery. "I did all I could do for that girl. She's in Your hands, Lord." Ruby stood to get dressed.

* * *

Alicia pulled into Derrick's apartment complex. The image of Deshon in the window crying reminded her of the mess she'd made of her life. Her mother was right. At least there he'd be in a stable home. All she would give him was a hard life on the streets. She didn't want that for him. She didn't want to be like the crack-hos hanging out in Derrick's house, tricking for a fix in front of their kids.

It was time to put all of that drama out of her mind, and there was only one way she could do that. For a moment, she felt relieved. She was free to live her life, with no one criticizing her every action. She ran up the steps to the second floor and pounded on the door. "I know this nigga here," she mumbled, peeking in the window. "Derrick, open up, nigga!" she yelled, pounding the door again.

The door opened halfway. Derrick peeked out, rubbing his eyes, yawning, and wearing only his jeans. "What up, shorty?"

"'Bout time, nigga. What took you so long?" She tried to

walk in, but he moved his hips in front of the door, blocking her way. "What's the matter with you? Let me in. My mama put me out. I need to stay with you. You got some stuff? Cuz I need some bad."

Derrick kept shifting his eyes to the ground. "Yeah, look here, shorty, come back in the morning, and I'll hook you up."

"Come back tomorrow? Nigga, I need a place to stay *now*." Alicia stepped back, studying him. "What's up with you? Why you acting like this?" She tried to push her way through, but he blocked her with his hip. "You got a trick up in there?"

"Stop trippin', shorty. Come back tomorrow. I told you, I'll hook you up then."

"You a dog, Derrick," she said, pointing her finger at his face. "Come out here, trick. I know you in there! She screamed. "You know what, I ain't even gon' trip. You a dog, Derrick." She waved the wad of cash her father had given her in his face. "Do she got this?"

Derrick's eyes lit up. He tried to grab Alicia's hand. "Hold up, shorty."

Alicia ran to her car and drove off with nowhere to go, frustrated and angry — at herself, mostly. "I should have gotten my EBT card from that nigga. He just like all the niggas in my life. All they do is use me and throw me away."

Alicia drove around L.A. with nowhere to go, sleeping in her car, copping from wherever and whomever she could. She had run through the money her father had given her, and it didn't take long before her cravings forced her toward the airport.

Chapter Seventeen

I whisked the blinds open and stepped back, admiring God's awesome handiwork. Giant, puffy, white clouds decorated the crystal-blue sky. The neighborhood was quiet and calm. I opened the front door, leaving the glass security door locked. Sitting in my chair, I took a sip from my cup and swished the hazelnut and cinnamon taste around my mouth. "Umm, this is a good brew, if I say so myself." I grabbed my Bible, but the doorbell chimed.

I stood and grimaced. Alicia's wretched form decimated the picturesque scene I'd been enjoying. When I unlocked the door, she dragged herself past me, avoiding eye contact. Sitting back in my chair, I couldn't help running my eyes up and down her emaciated body.

Alicia bent over and hugged me, still avoiding eye contact. "Hey, Madea."

"Good morning, child. I wish you'd come by more often."

"I've been busy, Madea."

I raised my brow, and she looked away. "Remember who you're talking to, child."

"You know what I mean."

Sipping my coffee, I didn't even bother to hide my disgust. I'd hoped the hazelnut aroma would mask the fetor, but the stench overpowered the room. It was the kind of odor that saturated everything, lingering in clothes, couches, and in your nostrils long after the person was gone. I covered my nose, but queasiness churned in my stomach. I glanced at the wall.

The picture of Alicia didn't help. She wore micro braids with long extensions and a gold diamond piercings over her right eye, in her nose, under her bottom lip, and in her tongue. Her face was fuller, her body thick and voluptuous, her skin dark, smooth, and flawless. She wore a green striped tank top with an inappropriate amount of cleavage showing. Her low-cut jeans exposed her black thong. She'd been on some video shoot and a hot mess, but at least she'd been healthy.

But, looking at her now, I had to take a sip. Dark spots blotted her face where her piercings had used to be. No doubt, she had sold or pawned them. I glanced at another picture of her. We were at Disneyland, posing with Mickey Mouse; she had to have been eight or nine. She wore a plaid jumpsuit. Her hair was braided into pigtails with bangs covering her forehead. As I looked at her now, the sight grieved my heart. How had she come to this?

"Baby, don't you think it's time to get right with the Lord? He loves you so much."

Staring down for a moment, she looked up with tears in her eyes. "I know, Madea. I am so tired of my life. I know I need to change."

Goose bumps tingled all over my body. I clenched my jaw to stifle my elation. Normally, Alicia would brush off my preaching. This was the first time she had shown any cracks in her stony heart. *Lord, let it be so,* I prayed.

Alicia grabbed her bag. "Can I borrow fifty dollars, Madea?"

I arched my brows. She knew better than to ask. She kissed my cheek. "I guess not. I got to go. I'll see you later."

Alicia walked out of the house. I let out a long exhale and

raised my hand toward heaven. "Thank You, Lord, for working in my baby's heart. Keep doing your work, Lord."

* * *

"You did *what*?" Katie shouted from her bedroom.

Just about what I suspected. Ruby regretted shouting the news as she came into the house. She should have waited until they were on their way. She wasn't thinking. She'd left in a hurry after her tiff with Joseph.

Katie stormed into the living room, wearing only her slip, with her nostrils flaring and her eyes glaring. "She was just here and didn't say a word about that. I wish you would have called me before you threw her out on the streets like a dog. She could have stayed with me. I don't like the idea of my baby being out on the street like that."

"Mama, she gave me no choice." Ruby looked away. "Deshon, stop playing on the couch. Besides, you don't want her living with you in the condition she's in. She'd only cause you a lot of grief. You can't trust her."

"I didn't even get a chance to talk to her. Where is she living?"

"She didn't leave a forwarding address."

"Don't get smart with me. I'm still your mother."

"I don't know, and I don't care."

"You *should* care. She's your child, your only child." Katie walked to the window. "I can't help but imagine that child sprawled out in an alley somewhere, fighting rats for food." She shook her head. "You pushed that girl away."

"Mama," Ruby squalled. "What is this, 'beat up on Ruby' day?"

"For years, I've warned you that you were driving her away."

"That's not fair. She's a grown woman. She has to take responsibility for her own life. You can't blame me for her choices."

"I blame you for driving her to the streets." Katie spun around. "Nothing she did was ever good enough for you, and you made sure she knew it."

"So, I'm the reason she got on drugs? It's *my* fault she ran the streets? Yeah, I was hard on her, because she kept rebelling. She kept getting into trouble. Joe never disciplined her. All you did was spoil her with your gifts. You only saw your perfect little angel. Well, she was only that way when she was around you. You didn't want to see the devil in that girl." Katie folded her hands and clenched her jaw.

"So, I made the tough decisions. I disciplined her. I was the bad guy." Ruby sighed. "What else was I supposed to do?"

"Did you ever tell her you loved her? I'm not criticizing you for disciplining her. I know she needed that. But, you never told that girl you loved her. She always thought you hated her. She thought she was a mistake, a burden. She never felt wanted. She needed your love way more than your discipline."

Ruby had no defense. She turned her head, feeling beaten up. *I should take Deshon and go down south. Get away from this mess.*

"Don't think you can run down south and hide, either … and don't think you can relive your motherhood through Deshon. He has a mama."

* * *

This is the most popular shopping spot in Southern California? I wasn't impressed. Ruby had pestered me to come with her to Orange Grove Mall. I'd finally given in, but I regretted my decision. The fifty-mile drive was long and grueling, even for a Saturday. After exiting the 405, we'd crawled along Orange Boulevard for another thirty minutes. It took another fifteen minutes to find a parking space.

She dragged me from one end of the mall to the other, and that was only on the first level. The mall had three. Everything was new and modern: marble tiles, plants, artwork, sculptures, large plasma monitors, and state-of-the-art equipment. But I was tired.

"Ruby, I have to rest. We've been walking around this place all day."

Ruby looked for a seat and pointed to a set of yellow iron benches by a waterfall. She set the bags on the floor. "Mama, I'm going to run in this store to check out their sales."

I leaned back, tempted to shut my eyes.

"Katie, is that you?"

When I looked up, Claire stood before me, wearing a white summer dress. "It's good to see you."

This was awkward. I hadn't seen Claire since she'd moved down here. We'd talked a few times, promised to get together, but never set anything definite. I didn't know what to say to her. The few times we talked, I sensed hesitation in her; maybe she felt uncomfortable talking about the church, especially Pastor Phil. I couldn't blame her for her apprehension. I was extremely critical of South Bay Baptist every time we'd talked. I regretted being so harsh. A smile crossed my face; I stood and embraced her. "I'm glad to see you, Claire."

We sat on the bench, holding hands. "Katie, I didn't know

you shop down here."

"I don't. I came here with my daughter."

Looking fixedly at me, Claire seemed to be sizing me up. "I don't live far from here. And the church is not far from here, either."

"It's nice down here—a bit crowded, but nice."

"I want you to see my house. Maybe one Saturday you can spend the night. We could go to the church and afterward, get some lunch. It's not the same without you."

"I can't. I'm not ready."

Claire forced a smile. "We're always here for you, Katie." She stood and touched my hand. "I have to get going. Call me when you're ready. Let's stay in touch."

I nodded and watched her disappear into the crowd. Ruby came out of the store with more bags in both hands and a look that told me she wasn't through. "They had a great sale in there. I got several eight-hundred-count sheets for seventy percent off. Who was that?"

"An old friend from South Bay. Ruby, I'm ready to go. I'm really tired."

Glancing up at the second and third level, she looked at me with pleading eyes. "There's so much more of the mall we haven't explored. There's so much to see, buy...."

"All of this will be here next week."

"All right, Mama," she said in surrender. "I'll pull the car up, so you won't have to walk in the heat." With that, Ruby disappeared.

I waited a few minutes and stood. "That girl left all of these bags."

As I struggled to grab hold of all the bags, a tall, burly man with a long, bushy, white beard smiled at me. He wore cowboy boots, jeans, shirt, and a wide-brimmed, cowboy hat.

"Ma'am, could I help you?" He asked in a strong Southern twang.

His accent was definitely from somewhere in the South. A large lump formed in my throat. I didn't trust him—especially a white Southerner. "I think I have it under control."

He smiled. "Ma'am, you would bless me if you would allow me to help you."

His pleasant disposition disarmed me. I smiled, and he grabbed the rest of the bags and led the way. "I guess I can do that. I'm supposed to meet my daughter by the west door."

"I'm Jerry Adams."

"I'm Katie… Katie Parker."

Jerry made small talk as he led me to the door, mostly telling me about the mall and the city of Orange Grove. "Wait here, Katie, and I'll see if your ride is here." He put the bags down and looked out the door. As I watched him, I wanted to keep him at bay, but I found myself overwhelmed by his kindness. He stepped back inside. "I don't see a car outside."

"You don't have to wait with me, Jerry. I'll be fine."

"I don't mind. I'm sure she'll be right along shortly, and I'll load the bags in your trunk. Besides, I love talking to you."

"You do? You don't know me."

Jerry chuckled. "I can read people well. And I think you're a good Christian woman."

"I know the Lord, that's for sure. How about you?"

"Yes, I do. Katie, you're going to havta visit our church, Grace Chapel. I'm formally giving you an invite."

"What kind of church do you attend? I'm a diehard Baptist—Baptist-born, Baptist-raised, and Baptist I'll die."

Jerry laughed. "Well, Grace Chapel is just a simple church

that loves the Lord, teaches His Word, verse by verse through the entire Bible, and welcomes any and all people, even if you're a Baptist."

I laughed. "I'll consider that. Maybe one Sunday I'll visit your church."

"Not only do I hope you'll visit us, but I'm gonna pray that God makes a way."

Ruby walked in the door and looked at me, then Jerry. "I'm ready, Mama."

Jerry smiled. "Hello." He tipped his hat, "Katie, I'll be praying I'll see you soon."

Ruby squinted as Jerry walked away. "Who was that?"

"A nice man—a nice, Christian man."

Chapter Eighteen

Jerry Adams traced his finger around Kristen's youthful face. Her dark-brown hair streaked around her dark-brown Sicilian eyes, highlighting the warm smile that always filled him with joy… and she always smiled her special smile for him. She stood out in a squad of twenty, in her blue and gold uniform, posing only for him. He smiled as tears filled his eyes and overflowed down his cheeks, soaking his beard. That was his little girl.

She had been full of life. When she wasn't playing tennis, she swam; when she wasn't swimming, she cheered; when she wasn't cheering, she ran; when she wasn't running, she traveled. She had earned her master's degree that year and had hit every continent at least once. She had completed a missionary trip to South America and had taken a position at the church as Director of Missions. She'd fallen sick that same year.

Jerry would see his only child again. He figured, at seventy-two, it wouldn't be long before their heavenly reunion. That didn't ease the pain. A smile etched his face. He mused about the day when he would be ushered into the Lord's presence. *She'll probably meet me at the gates and show me all the heavenly points of interest, knowing her.* Jerry kissed her picture and placed it back in its treasured place on the mantle.

He straightened his Stetson hat, wiped his face, blew into his handkerchief, and picked up his bag of stuff to take back to the apartment. He glanced around his darkened living room and stepped outside. He tried pulling the side door shut without looking toward the carport, but he couldn't help himself. He had to look. He always had to look. He had bought the car as a gift when she'd taken the position at the church. She'd been thrilled when she received it. She'd driven it less than a year. It had been parked under the carport since she'd fallen ill.

So young, he thought, *so innocent.* His heart ached. *Why didn't God take me?*

He stood by his truck and couldn't resist another look. Twenty-nine was too young to go home, especially like that. His heart demanded an answer, but he humbled himself. *God does as He pleases.* He held up the remote, and his F-350 Super-Duty with a double cab started with a quiet purr. Had his youthful sins come home to roost? He choked back his tears and climbed into the truck.

He drove the seven-minute trek across Orange Grove toward his café, enjoying the cool California air caressing his face. He loved the early-morning hours for their peace, quiet, and lack of traffic. He loved the fall because it prepared him for winter, his favorite season. He flashed his hi-beams at a squad car perched in the 7-Eleven parking lot. The squad car flashed back.

Kitchen and bath lights flickered on. The morning routines began; coffee pots brewed, toasters popped out toast and bagels; showers and baths spiked the city's water demand, and aerosol cans eroded the ozone. In an hour, Orange Boulevard would swell with commuters cramming the 405. Jerry thanked the Lord he wasn't one of them.

He turned onto Main Street, which took him to the center of

the old business district. A mixture of deep South and southern California architecture, the old district was like stepping into another time and place. The buildings had either wood-frame or stucco exteriors, with assorted bright colors. The district reminded him of an early nineteenth-century setting, with vintage lanterns lining both sides of the streets.

He drove to the back parking lot of the Country Café and parked in his space. The café had a dark wooden exterior with vintage lights mounted on the wall for both decoration and night lighting. Grabbing the bag he had brought from the house, he decided to walk across the street, sit on one of the benches, and enjoy the morning as it crept over the Santa Ana Mountains.

Life had been good to Jerry. He'd formed an investment group and built Orange Grove Mall, which he regretted. It had made him millions. People came from all over just to shop there. Unfortunately, undesirable people discovered their hidden paradise. Gridlock made entering and leaving the mall unbearable. Crime hit the city like a plague. Burglaries, carjacking, and arm robberies were now common where once people left the doors to their homes and cars unlocked. Police patrols were unheard of, now cop cars occupied the streets. He had ruined their paradise.

All of his investments had done well. He used some of his money to revitalize the old district, his apology for the mall. Still, he would have given it all up if he could have his Kristen back. But, she was gone forever. That was one deal he knew he'd never negotiate. He gazed up at the second floor. The bedroom light came on. Nancy was up. He'd settle for having his wife back in her right mind.

* * *

The Country Café bustled with its usual Saturday rush. Hostesses corralled diners to their tables. Waitresses served food among a monotonous chatter of family and friends fraternizing with one another. Silverware and dishes clanked as busboys scooped dirty plates, utensils, and glasses into gray dishtubs and then hurriedly cleaned the tables. Cooks whipped up tasty Southern dishes that sent out enticing aromas to eagerly waiting customers.

The interior had a country décor, with walnut wall panels and flooring and vintage light fixtures that softly illuminated the rooms. The entrance led to a large waiting area that was sprinkled with country trinkets and pictures of cowboys, horses, and cattle grazing in fields. The aroma of cinnamon saturated the lobby as Christian country music softly played.

Jerry read his Bible in his private space, which he nicknamed *The Sanctified Booth*. He'd stockpiled an arsenal of soul-winning tools and weapons. Reaching over, he straightened pocket New Testaments, tracts, church CDs, and other pamphlets; he loved the right presentation. He loved sharing his faith with people. He had the perfect lure — breakfast or lunch on the house — while they heard the Gospel. Jerry glanced around the room, hoping the Lord would send him a soul to talk to.

Nancy, his wife, came from the kitchen and dragged past the booth, lethargic. It pained Jerry to see her like that, and it was painful that the Lord hadn't returned her to him yet. He yearned to see the old Nancy, the way she'd greeted people with her warm smile, melted their hearts with her tender embrace, and always uplifted them with her comforting words. They all appreciated her genuine concern for their welfare. He missed that Nancy.

She was just a couple of years younger than Jerry but looked ten years older. Her face furrowed with deep wrinkles and thick bags under her eyes, without a shade of makeup. Her hair was pulled back into a silver-streaked ponytail, and her clothes looked old and thrifty. With an empty stare, she counted twenties, tens, fives, and ones and recorded them on the cash report sheets, only looking up to cash a customer out.

"Lord, take away the pain in her heart." Jerry closed his Bible and walked over to the cashier's booth.

"Dave hadn't come by for his coffee," Nancy said without looking up.

"I'm sure he'll be by." Jerry debated whether to ask. It would be wonderful if she said yes. "You know, we can go by the house later if you want."

She didn't raise her head. "You know I'm not ready."

Jerry shook his head. Her words sliced into his heart with a stinging pang. He'd really hoped that this time she'd, at least, consider going to the house. It hurt him that she acted as if there wasn't anything to live for. He was worth living for.

Jerry decided to go outside and sweep up the grounds to clear his head. As he walked toward the back, he realized he had forgotten his broom and dustpan. He was about to turn and go back inside when he noticed a white Toyota Corolla selfishly hogging two spaces in the corner of the lot. He wondered why he hadn't seen the car earlier and wondered why customers hadn't complained about it. Parking was scarce on Saturday mornings.

Peering into the back window, he clenched his jaw. A girl was curled in the fetal position in the backseat among clothes, empty bottles, paper wrappers, needles, foil, tiny plastic sacks, and used tourniquets. She slept, dead to the world. He had never seen such a pathetic sight. A knot tightened in his heart. How had this lost soul come to be here? "Oh, Lord, please give me the words to reach this precious soul You've sent me."

He gave a couple of raps on the rear passenger window — no response. He knocked again, a little harder. Still no response. He pounded the roof, startling the girl out of her sleep. Her emaciated frame jolted his nerves. Her hair was disheveled, eyes bloodshot, lips badly chapped, and her clothes wrinkled. Jerry fanned his nose and turned away.

She sat up, rubbing her eyes. "All right, all right. You don't have to call the police. I'll leave. I don't want to go to jail."

Her eyes told a sad tale. Her hopes, dreams, and value of life had been stripped away from her. She had been reduced to nothing, and she had no choice but to surrender. Jerry restrained his emotions with all of his strength. Compassion for this child of misfortune overwhelmed his heart. He had to do something; whether her plight was self-inflicted or not, this was a precious soul for whom the Lord had given His life. She was precious to Him, and He had deposited her on Jerry's doorstep.

"I'm not calling the police. I just want to help you."

She looked at him with an empty stare. "Why...why would you help me?"

Jerry smiled. "Because you need help."

"Nah, I'm straight. Just don't call the police. I'll be out of your way, and I promise I won't come back here."

Frustrated, Jerry stepped to the side. He desperately wanted to help her, but she had put her defenses up. He wished that there was some way he could stop her from leaving. He waved her on. She climbed over the front seat and turned the key. The car gave a rattle and click, but the engine didn't turn over. Jerry bit his lip to quench his elation. She tried again. This time, there wasn't even a tick. Jerry walked around to the driver's side and gave the window a rap. "Pop the hood. I'll take a look."

She looked at Jerry for a moment and pulled the lever until she heard a pop. Jerry raised the hood, but it slammed shut. She slid a long stick through the cracked window. "Here, you got to use this."

Jerry grabbed the cut-off broomstick and propped open the hood, wondering if divine intervention prevented her from leaving. A moment later, he emerged with the dipstick in his hand; for sure, God had intervened. "Little lady, you ain't got a lick of oil in your engine."

"What that mean?"

"It means your engine is dead."

"Can we fix it?"

"No, you have to get a whole new engine."

Pounding the steering wheel and flailing her arms, she unleashed a string of vile expletives that made Jerry take a step back. She kicked the front door so hard it flung open and snapped closed. She kicked the door again and jumped out, cursing everything within the sound of her voice.

"Calm down, little lady. It's going to be all right," Jerry said, then waited until her outburst had subsided to heavy huffing. "I'll tell you what, why don't we get you inside, out of this heat? This is my place. Have lunch on me. Then we can figure out what you're going to do about your car. What's your name?"

She stared at the ground. "Alicia."

"Alicia, it'll be all right. Don't you worry."

"Worry? I don't got no choice. I'm stranded here with no way to get home. What else could go wrong?" A black-and-white patrol car pulled into the lot. She threw up her arms and rolled her eyes. "That's great. You didn't have to call the police.

I told you I'd leave."

Jerry rapped the hood twice. "Everything will be all right. You just stay put." He waved his arm as the officer got out of the car. "Everything is fine, Tom."

Tom propped his arm on the door. "You're sure, Jer?"

Alicia snapped her head, rolled her eyes, and looked off with her hands folded.

"I saw this car earlier," Tom said.

"She's my guest."

Tom, eyes glued on Alicia, slid into the car. "All right. I'll be around if you need me."

Snapping her head, Alicia rolled her eyes. "I'm sure you will."

Jerry tossed Alicia a disapproving glance and waved Tom on. He hesitated and backed out. Jerry turned around and motioned with his hand. He chuckled as Alicia locked the car door. "By the way, my name is Jerry."

He led Alicia into the café and quickly maneuvered her toward his booth. People covered their noses and looked around with frowns. Some gagged. Alicia scowled at the crowd, but Jerry placed his hand on her shoulder and guided her into the booth. He glanced quickly around the dining area. A couple of people got up and left. A few more followed them. Jerry figured he'd lose more patrons.

A waitress, in her twenties and slightly overweight, appeared. She discreetly covered her nose, darting her eyes between Alicia and Jerry. He nodded. She handed Alicia a menu with a forced smile. Alicia smirked and snatched the menu.

"Order anything you want, Alicia," Jerry said.

The waitress stepped away and exhaled as if she gasped for her very life. Jerry knew this was hard for the staff and customers, but Alicia needed the Lord. He'd make sure he'd give the staff a nice bonus for today's labor of love. He'd never witnessed to anyone who'd smelled so bad or been as raw as Alicia. Jerry prayed that God would touch her with His love.

"I'm ready," Alicia said.

Jerry waved to the waitress, and she promptly came.

"I want a triple Texas burger, large fries, and a large chocolate shake."

The waitress looked at Jerry. He waved his hand. His stomach couldn't take it. The waitress took Alicia's menu and quickly disappeared into the kitchen.

Alicia fidgeted, scratching her arms and chin and looking around erratically. "So, this is your place, huh? What you call it?"

"The Country Café. I opened it in the eighties."

"You like country and Western?"

Jerry chuckled. "Why do you ask that?"

"This place looks like a country kitchen, and you dress and talk like a cowboy."

"I like the country atmosphere and, well, I just like dressing in Western clothes."

Alicia shrugged. "Whatever is your thang. It's good marketing, though."

Alicia's nostrils flared every time a waitress carried a tray of hamburgers, fries, grilled chicken, onion rings, and other lunch food from the kitchen. Jerry wondered when she'd last eaten. Alicia frowned as she looked around the café. People stared and pointed their fingers.

Alicia jumped to her feet. "What y'all looking at? Y'all ain't better than nobody."

Jerry's brows rose, surprised at the outburst. Alicia stormed out of the café. Jerry chased after her. "Alicia, wait." Jerry caught her outside as she dashed into the street.

"Those folks don't want me in there. I see the way they look at me. I see them talking about me. They don't want me here because I'm black. I ain't got to take that."

Jerry was surprised at her pride. Where would she go? She'd forgotten she didn't have a car. Jerry didn't want to say that he understood why the patrons were bothered. Her odor was unbearable. Her attitude was abrasive. But Jerry knew the Lord had sent her to hear the gospel.

"Alicia, don't pay them any mind. Come back in and eat your lunch."

Alicia squinted and sighed.

"Come on. I know you're hungry. You'll at least get a free meal. And don't forget we have to figure out what to do about your car."

Jerry prayed within himself that God would touch Alicia's heart.

Chapter Nineteen

Alicia shifted her eyes back and forth, huffing and puffing. Jerry held out his hand. "Come back inside. Get out of this heat."

She walked past Jerry with pursed lips. Jerry chuckled and escorted her back into the café. People looked away as if they didn't notice her, but they did. They scowled and covered their noses. She tensed up, but Jerry placed his hand on her back and guided her into the booth. Alicia fidgeted with a fork and feverishly scratched her chin.

He sat and peered at her. "Alicia, the Lord loves you …"

Alicia perked up and gawked as the waitress set her plate in front of her. She immediately devoured the large Texas-style burger. Jerry extended his hand to pray, but she was too busy chomping away at her burger. He prayed anyway.

After nearly all the burger had been eaten, her eyes came up from the plate. She looked up at the King James Bible and the other tracts and pamphlets. "You saved?"

"Why do you ask that?" She nodded toward the Bible with her mouth full of food. This was the open door he'd hoped for. "Yes, I am. How about you? Are you saved?"

She chuckled. "Do I look like I'm saved? God don't want nothing to do with me."

"Why do you say that?"

"I done things you wouldn't believe. Trust me."

"I've done things you wouldn't believe, Alicia. We've all

done things that are unacceptable to God. We are all sinners before him."

"Not like me," she said, shoving several fries into her mouth.

Jerry preached the Gospel as if he'd been standing before a packed stadium. Alicia stopped chewing and fixed her stare on him. Jerry didn't know how to read her face. Did she reject the Gospel, or was her heart open? He prayed that God would soften her heart.

Alicia shook her head. "How can God forgive someone like me? I've done so many terrible things and hurt so many people."

"Grace, Alicia. Grace is God giving you mercy and favor simply because He loves you. It's hard to explain, because, in our minds, we receive good based on how good we think we are, how much we think we deserved it, or how many good deeds we think we've done to earn favor. But you can't do enough good to earn God's grace. To receive favor from someone simply because they want to do good to you doesn't compute to our minds. God doesn't give grace because we deserve it. If that were the case, not one single person would be saved."

"Then why does He give us grace?"

"Because God loves you."

"Plenty of men have told me they loved me."

"But none of those men have ever laid their lives down for you, have they?"

She shrugged. "Never. I was just a place for them to stick… anyway, no."

"God proved He loved you by giving His Son to die on the cross for you. Think about this, Alicia. God gave the most valuable thing He could give for you—His Son. He could give no greater gift. That's how much He values you—as much as He values his Son. Jesus died to bear your sins and to receive God's wrath for you. On the cross, He was punished for all of the bad things you've done in your life. That's why you can stand before Him clean and without fear of any punishment. God demonstrated His love by dying in your place. And the best part of His love is that when you put your faith in Him, He makes you a new creation."

Alicia's eyes lit up. "New creation?"

"That's right. Not only are your sins forgiven and wiped away forever, but God makes you a new person inside. You won't be the same old Alicia. I know, because many years ago, He made me a new person. I was a hateful person. He took all that hate away and made me new."

Alicia stared off. "Wow, to be a new person. I want that more than anything."

"God sees you through the perfect sacrifice that Jesus offered on the cross, which was Himself. He did all of that because He loves you."

Alicia's eyes filled with tears. "That blows my mind. To think He loves me that way."

"Would you like to pray and ask the Lord for His forgiveness?"

"Here, now? Don't you have to walk down the church aisle or sit on a bench or something?"

"The Lord is here, Alicia. You don't have to wait for Sunday to pray to Him. He's always near you. He's always been."

She blinked, sending two streams of tears racing down her face. She buried her head in her hands and sobbed. A hand reached past Jerry and gently rubbed Alicia's back. Jerry's eyes widened, pleasantly surprised to see Nancy's warm smile.

Nancy handed Alicia a napkin and slid in next to her. "You don't have to be afraid, honey. Just ask the Lord. He will forgive you." Alicia fell into Nancy's arms and wept even louder. She looked into Nancy's eyes, and without asking who she was, she just folded into her embrace. "He loves you so much."

Jerry could barely contain his joy. God's grace never ceased to amaze him.

With joy beaming from her face, Alicia tearfully bowed her head and prayed. "Uh, Lord, I don't know how to say this. I've done so many bad things. I guess You know all that. Forgive me, Lord. Make me a new person." She opened her eyes with a dumbfounded look. "That's it?"

"That's it," Jerry said, smiling. "Remember, Alicia, it's by faith that you are saved, not by feelings. Now, you have to grow in your faith." He turned to Nancy and smiled. He wanted to ask her what had brought her out of her shell. There was a lot he wanted to say to her, but he focused on the ministry at hand. "Honey, this is Alicia. Alicia, this is my wife, Nancy."

"Pleased to meet you, Nancy, I really am." Alicia looked at them, unable to stop crying and smiling. "I feel like a giant weight has been lifted off of me. I can't believe it was this simple. All of these years, I resisted the Lord. All of this time, I could have been free."

Nancy, staring at Jerry, rubbed Alicia's back. "Most of us never realize how close the Lord is to us. He's been watching over you your entire life."

Is this really happening? Do I really have my Nancy back? My dear Lord, I know You answer prayer, but I never could have imagined it would have happened this quick and in this way. Thank You, Lord, for bringing Nancy out of her depression.

Jerry leaned back and propped both arms on the back of the bench as Nancy took over the conversation. Who was this strange woman bursting with life? Who was this woman ministering with bold confidence? She was more than what he had prayed for. She was a different Nancy whom only the Lord could have brought forth. At that moment, it was all he could do to keep from grabbing her in his arms and squeezing her as tightly as he could.

Jerry felt doubly blessed. Alicia had found the Lord, and he had his Nancy back. They talked well into the evening. Night started to fall. Realizing the lateness of the day, Jerry checked his watch. "Oh, my, it's evening already."

He and Alicia exchanged a look.

"What? What's the matter?" Nancy said.

Jerry explained Alicia's predicament.

"Well, Jerry, you're going to have to take her home. That's all there is to it."

"It's more complicated than that." Jerry scooted out and walked to the cashier's booth. He made a call to a friend, hoping he could take Alicia tonight. Jerry returned to his seat with a somber stare. "Alicia, are you ready to deal with your addiction?" He waited for her nod. "I know a place that'll take you tonight, but you have to go right now," he said firmly.

"I'm ready," Alicia answered. "I'm tired of my life. I'm more than ready."

Nancy grabbed Alicia's hand. "We're going to be with you all of the way. You won't go through this alone."

"Thank you, Nancy. Rehab has never worked on me."

"This is a Christian place, with spiritual weapons. You have God's help now," Jerry said.

Nancy squeezed Alicia's hand. "And we won't be far from

you, Alicia; I promise you."

Jerry stood and waved Alicia toward the door. "Let's go."

Alicia stood and peered at him. "I have to call someone first."

Jerry furrowed his brow. He had worked with addicts enough to know that when it came time to commit to rehab, they always found a way to stall. "I don't think that's a good idea. We should get you to the place right away."

Nancy slid her arm around her shoulders. "Whom do you want to call, Alicia?"

"Madea."

"Who is Madea?"

"She's my grandmother. I know she's going to be so happy I've found the Lord. She's the one who always told me to get right with Him. She loved me when no one else did. I have to call her and tell her the good news."

Chapter Twenty

Jerry made the change from the 405 to the 73 freeway. He watched Alicia through the rearview mirror while listening to Nancy talk nonstop. Alicia was running out of time. She twitched and clenched her teeth. Her silence alarmed him. He knew she craved a fix.

Nancy stopped talking, looked at Jerry, then turned around and grabbed Alicia's hand. "Are you all right, Alicia?"

She shook her head. "I have a bad headache. I need an aspirin. Do you have any?"

"I'll see." Nancy unzipped her bag and rummaged through her purse.

Jerry grabbed Nancy's hand and shook his head. "We'll be at the place in a few minutes, Alicia. Hang on. It won't be long."

"Where is this place?" Alicia asked. "Will they have something for my headache?"

Jerry glanced at Nancy. "It's in the foothills east of Escondido. It's called The Covering. It's a Christian rehab house. Though it's not required that an addict be a Christian, most of the addicts are referrals from local churches. You ever been to Escondido?"

Alicia shook her head and stared out the window, scratching her chin.

It was just after ten when Jerry parked in front of The Covering, a large, white Victorian house with black trim and a black wrought-iron fence around the yard. Jerry helped Alicia out of the truck maintaining a firm grip on her arm. Alicia looked at the house and hesitated for a moment. Jerry pushed the button. The gate buzzed and clicked as it unlocked. Jerry, with Alicia in tow, pushed through the gate and walked up the steps.

Sammy and Jackie Willoughby met them with the door open and waved them in. Sammy was a big man with a silvery ponytail. Jackie was tall and slim with frizzy silver hair down her shoulders. Both wore T-shirts, jeans, and gym shoes. Two men stood quietly by the stairs. They wore T-shirts, jeans, and were medium height, and fit.

"Jerry, Nancy, how are you guys? This must be Alicia," Sammy said. "Alicia, we're going to get started." Sammy nodded, and the two men escorted Alicia upstairs.

Jackie gently edged Jerry and Nancy out of the door. "It's for Alicia's best. You can see her in a week."

The door shut, and the light turned off.

* * *

Jerry sped down the freeway as fast as he was allowed. He received the call from Jackie at nine and been on the road by nine-fifteen. He was thankful they had missed the morning rush hour, but traffic was still heavy. He reached over and patted Nancy's hand. She'd been a mess ever since he had told her Jackie had called.

It had been six days since he had dropped Alicia off. He hadn't call to check on her, or despite his desire, driven to visit her. Sammy told him not to contact her for a week. He'd assumed everything was going well. How could something like this have happened?

"Hurry, Jerry," Nancy said. "I should have followed my heart and never left Alicia alone." As they pulled up to The Covering, Nancy's face crinkled with a dreadful look. "Why are the police here?" She jumped out as the truck came to a stop. Jackie was in her robe and house shoes, talking to a police officer. "Jackie, what happened?"

Jerry grabbed Nancy's hand. "Honey, calm down."

The officer glanced at Jerry and back at Jackie. "We'll have patrols looking for her. We'll contact you when we find her."

Jackie waited until the officers left to address Nancy and Jerry." She ran away again."

"Again?" Nancy said, flustered. "How did this happen?"

"She's determined to score." Jackie looked at Jerry. "She's stolen money and jewelry from staff and other residents. When we got up this morning, she was gone. No one has run away from the house this many times."

Jerry took her hand. "Where's Sam?"

"He went to look for her."

Jerry patted Nancy's back and headed for the truck.

"Where are you going?" Nancy yelled.

Jerry turned around. "You stay here with Jackie, just in case Alicia shows up. I'm going to look for her. The Lord will work it out." He looked at Jackie. "Everything is going to be all right. We'll find her. She can only be one place."

Jerry sped away with his cell phone plastered to his ear. His first call was to Sammy. His second call was to a friend at the sheriff's office. Jerry didn't have a clue where to look; he didn't know where the crack houses were in this area. Jerry rendezvoused with Sammy, and by the time Sammy had jumped into the truck, Jerry had received the location of a crack house where Alicia would most likely have gone.

"I know the place," Sammy said. "It's on the other side of Escondido, not far from The Covering. Many of our people have scored there."

It took only a few minutes to reach the address Jerry's friend had given him. The quiet, well-kept street surprised Jerry. He stepped out and cased the two-story home. The lawn was neat and trimmed, with two Harleys parked in the driveway. Druggies weren't streaming in and out of the cul-de-sac buying meth, and drug paraphernalia didn't litter the lawn.

Sammy pulled a long, silver-barreled pistol from his pocket and checked the chamber. He glanced at Jerry. "A .500 S&W Magnum, the most powerful gun in the world." He tucked the gun in his pants.

Jerry frowned. "Sam, you know how I feel about guns."

"It's only for protection if we need it. You never know what you're going to face. Most of the time, all I have to do is lift my shirt, and they'll get the message."

"Let's pray." Grabbing Sam's hand, Jerry didn't wait for his answer. "Lord, You, watch over us and protect us by Your grace, in Jesus' name. Now we're ready."

Sammy brandished a collapsible wand and slid it into his pocket. "No, now we're ready. It's not that I don't trust the Lord. I do. I trust Him and the tools he's given me." Sammy slapped Jerry's back, laughing.

A large man with a big belly opened the door on the first knock. He wore jeans, a black T-shirt, black leather vest, and black leather boots. A silver chain was clipped to his belt with the other end tucked in his back pocket. His hair was combed back behind his ears, and his voice was deep and raspy. "What do you want?"

"We're looking for someone," Jerry said, "a girl."

"This isn't the lost and found. Beat it," he said and tried to slam the door. He raised his brow when Sammy wedged his boot in the door. "Move it, or I'll break it."

"I don't think so," Sammy said. He shoved the door hard, sending the man to the floor. A tall, scruffy man ran from the back of the house, yelling, "I got them, Chuck!"

Sammy spun around and with one swift stroke whipped out his wand and hit the man in his shins. He went down hard and fast, writhing and screaming. "Stay down, partner."

"Sam," Jerry said.

Sammy shrugged. "What?"

"Christlike."

Sammy held up his hands. "I am. I didn't shoot him." He turned to Chuck. "You don't want to have this conversation outside. Now, just take it easy, and we'll be gone in no time."

Jerry clenched his jaw, silently praying. The house was clean and quiet. There were no other people around that he could see. The living room had no furniture, and the family room had a pool table in the center of the room. There were no chairs, couches, or pictures. A large flat screen hung on the wall, and there was a door that must have led to the garage.

Chuck stood and pulled his shirt up, revealing the butt of a pistol.

Sammy laughed.

Chuck frowned. "What's so funny?"

"This is." Sammy lifted his shirt and pulled his gun, just enough to reveal the long barrel. "Now, there are two ways we can do this: one, we have an old-fashioned gunfight. That would be bad for business and your cash flow, and I think for you. Besides, you wouldn't want the police camped out here in your nice cul-de-sac, would you? Let us conduct our business, and we'll be out of your hair in a few minutes."

Chuck grimaced and looked at Jerry. "What do you want?"

"We're looking for a girl… late twenties."

"I'm sure she's not here."

Jerry's brows rose. "Well, I'm sure the girl we're looking for won't be hard to spot."

"Everyone here is regulars. I know them all."

"Everyone?" Sammy grunted.

"She's black, dark-skinned," Jerry said.

Chuck shook his head, pointing across the family room. "I knew she'd be trouble."

"You think?" Sammy said and nudged Jerry.

Sammy walked across the family room and opened the door. He looked at Jerry and walked in. His nostrils assaulted by the stench, Jerry breathed through his mouth. The garage had been converted into a large room with couches and loveseats around the walls. One mounted light fixture dimly lit the room. There were a couple of people sprawled on the couch. A man stuck a needle in his arms in a zombie-like trance, and a woman sat on the loveseat staring toward the ceiling, spaced out. Alicia sat on one of the other couches with her head slouched down. A couple of strips of clothes scantly covered her body.

Jerry grimaced and stormed out. Grabbing Chuck by his shirt, he shoved him against the wall. "You made her hook for her drugs?"

Chuck shoved Jerry off of him and reached for his gun.

Sammy grabbed Jerry with his gun drawn. "Easy, partner."

"I thought you said this would be easy, man," Chuck said.

Sammy eased his gun up. "Just answer the man's question, and we'll be on our way."

"It was her idea. She showed up here, begging to score. She didn't have any money. She said she'd do anything... anything. It was her idea. Nobody forced her to do anything."

Sammy tugged Jerry's arm. "Come on, Jerry, let's go."

"I don't get it, man. Why do you care about a no-good, black crack whore?"

Jerry looked at Sam, touched his arm, and turned toward Chuck. He moved in close to his face. "She's someone Christ died for. She means something to Him."

Sam grabbed Jerry's arm. "Come on, Jer."

Jerry grabbed a sheet from one of the couches and wrapped Alicia with it. He carried her out and slid her in the backseat of the truck. Alicia looked at him with glazed eyes.

"Hey, Jerry, what are you doing here? I'm higher than a kite." She laughed and plopped her head back. Jerry shook his head and strapped her in.

* * *

Nancy and Jackie rushed the truck as Jerry drove up. Jerry followed Sammy as he carried Alicia into the house. Nancy held Alicia's hand, crying and fussing at her. Sammy carried her upstairs and disappeared into the bedroom. Jackie pulled Nancy from the stairs and into the living room. "We have to strap her in."

Nancy frowned. "What?"

"She ran away three times, Nancy. She's stolen from us and others. She gained the trust of one of the other residents. You can imagine how. He helped her get out of the house. It's going to take stronger measures to get the drugs out of her system and to get her mind strong enough to resist the urges. That's what's driving her, the cravings."

Jerry put his arm around Nancy and nodded. Jackie shot up the stairs. They heard a door close. Jerry squeezed Nancy's waist. "We have to let them do their job, honey."

Nancy rested her head on Jerry's chest. "What are we going to do?"

"We're going to pray. We're going to camp right here and pray with her, for her, around the clock."

Sammy walked down the stairs. "She's strapped in."

Nancy turned her head. "Sedated?"

"No, we're doing it cold turkey. It's the only way. It's going to be a rough ride. You should go home."

Jackie followed Sammy. "There's nothing you can do for her here." She looked at Nancy. "It's going to get ugly, real ugly."

Jerry took Nancy's hand. "We're not leaving. There is something we can do, Jackie. We can pray for her. And when her head is clear enough, we're gonna change her thoughts with the Word of God."

Sammy looked at Jackie and nodded. "Let's get to work, then."

* * *

Alicia thrashed and screamed at the top of her voice. The ten days since Jerry and Sammy had brought her back to The Covering had been unbearable. Alicia's head throbbed; sweat drenched her sheets, and all the muscles in her body tensed so tight they felt as if they were ready to snap apart. She begged. She pleaded. She fought to get loose from the hospital bed Sammy had strapped her to. The room was large with white walls. A large window looked out at a full view of the mountains. Alicia felt as if she were caged in a cell.

She gritted her teeth. Her body trembled. She clenched her fists so tight her veins bulged in her arms. She darted her eyes toward Nancy and then Jerry. It was as if thousands of pins stuck and jabbed all over her body. "Let me go, Jerry."

He touched her hand. "Alicia."

"I have to get out of here. Let me go."

"You have to stay here to get better." Jerry stiffened his jaw.

"I can't take it… I don't want to be here anymore."

"Alicia…."

"You can't hold me against my will!" Her voice crackled.

Nancy woke up and rushed to the bed's side. "Alicia, be strong."

"Let me go!" Alicia screamed, thrashed, and yanked her restraints. "I want to get out of here. Let me go now!"

Alicia screamed for drugs. She felt raw, vile, and vicious. She cursed Jerry and Nancy with everything in her being. She cursed Sammy and Jackie. She was desperate to get loose. She'd do anything and say anything to be free. But, they were loving. They wouldn't yield to her pleas. She hated them for that. She cursed their prayers. She scorned their love. The withdrawals retaliated, torturing her with throbbing pain all over her body. She demanded to be let go. She screamed to be set free. She begged for a hit—of anything.

She cursed her life. She cursed the day she was born. She cursed her low-down, drug-dealing boyfriend who'd given her that first hit, her first taste of smack. He'd given her all the drugs she'd wanted, at first, when he thought the loving was good—until she'd gotten hooked. Then he'd made her pay for every hit. Eventually, he'd turned her out on the streets to make his money. When she no longer could earn him money, he'd thrown her away. She screamed and cursed him.

She cursed her mother for putting her out of the house, which had led to her suffering in this place. She cursed her father for going easy on her growing up. The withdrawals hit, hard and painful. Every inch of her body ached and throbbed as if someone poked, jabbed, or burned her skin. She cried out only for a taste, only to smell the smoke from some weed. She'd settle for an aspirin, coffee, soda, anything that had a stimulant in it. She shivered, quaked, and demanded to be released. They refused to give her any medicine.

"I can't take this pain anymore!" she screamed.

It got worse, the pain. She cursed. She pulled her hair out. Blood oozed from the cracks of her lips. Her skin stung from the sweat running over the open scratches on her face. She tried to run when they let her go to the bathroom, but Sammy was right there to restrain her. The pain was severe, worse than she had ever felt. She blanked out.

* * *

Alicia opened her eyes. A crystal blue sky with puffy, white clouds stretched over the mountains. It was a beautiful sight. It was morning, she guessed. She didn't know the time, but she felt free. That demonic hold was broken. She was finally clean. It had been a hard fifteen days. She didn't feel sick anymore.

"Good morning," Jerry said, smiling at her.

Alicia sat up and leaned against the bed rail. Nancy grabbed her hand. "How are you feeling?"

Her restraints were gone. She shrugged. "Better. Much better." Alicia looked down. "The things I said… I'm sorry. I'm sorry for running away, for stealing. I'm sorry."

Nancy squeezed her hand. "It was the drugs talking."

"I don't think I can win this, Nancy. Every time I try to kick the habit, I fall right back into the same rut. I thank you for what you've done for me. You tried, but it's no use. I can't beat this thing." She closed her eyes and shook her head. "I'm not worth the time."

"That's enough of that kind of talk," Jerry said. He pulled a Bible from a bag. "What you have this time that you never had before is the Lord's grace." He held up the Bible. "And His Word to strengthen you."

Nancy patted her hand. "And we're going to be here night and day, praying with you."

Jerry sat on the edge of the bed. "Kicking the habit, that was the easy part. Walking the walk and staying off drugs is the hard part."

"I can't do it, Jerry."

Jerry frowned. "Don't talk like that."

"I can't help it. I've tried before, and every time I fall back into this life. Each time, it gets worse."

"Like I said, you didn't have the spiritual weapons you have now. Now, we're going to pray and study His Word until you get built up in your mind. That's very important, to get built up on His Word. You have to change the way you think. God's Word will change your thoughts and empower you to stand against the temptation of drugs. You must get the Word into you. Then you'll be strong enough to resist the cravings." Jerry grabbed her hand. "And never forget, Alicia, the Lord is always with you, and He will strengthen you to win. He will never forsake you. He loves you, even when you fall. You can never exhaust His love. Don't ever forget that."

Alicia rested her head on the pillow and stared out the

window. How long would it take for her to relapse from this rehab—a day, a week, or a month? She really wanted to stay clean this time. "I hope so, Jerry."

Chapter Twenty-one

Jerry held Nancy's hand as they walked into The Covering. He loved having his wife back. He loved everything about her: her round Sicilian eyes, the way her gray hair streaked around her face, and the way her yellow summer dress hugged her body. He'd forgotten how fit she was. He loved the way she walked, talked, and smiled at him. He valued her wisdom, friendship, and companionship. He treasured the gift God had given him. Jerry reached his arm around her waist and kissed her cheek.

Sammy walked down the stairs, chuckling. "Okay, you two, this is a respectable house."

Jerry laughed. "Where's our girl?"

Sammy pointed upstairs.

Jerry looked forward to taking Alicia to church. She had really worked hard to stay clean. Jerry made sure he or Nancy came by at least every other day to see her. They talked, studied the Bible, and prayed. Jerry was pleased that Alicia had grown in her faith. He wanted to get her out with other believers in a church setting.

Headed up the stairs, he pulled Nancy along. He knocked and walked in. Alicia sat in the chair, staring out the window. She wore knee-length shorts and a T-shirt.

Nancy wrapped her arms around Alicia and squeezed. "How are you doing?"

"I'm fine. I was just looking at the mountains."

"How would you like a field trip?" Jerry asked.

"Where?"

"To church."

Alicia squinted. "Church? I don't know if I'm ready to go to church yet. I'm nervous about being around people, and I look a mess."

"Hogwash," Jerry said. "I know you're hungry for the Word. And nothing would be better to quench your hunger than a good sermon and fellowship with other believers. And, I know you're stir-crazy, being cooped up in here day in and day out."

Alicia smiled. "You're right. I'd love to get out of here, if only for a day."

Nancy pulled Alicia to her feet. "I think I can help in the looks department. Jerry, wait downstairs."

Twenty minutes later, Nancy and Alicia walked down stairs. Alicia looked at Jerry as if she were a shy little girl being introduced to the world for the first time. He thought of her as his little girl, if only in a spiritual sense. She wore a plain pair of jeans, a white T-shirt, and white gym shoes. Her hair was short and frizzy, but neatly combed. Her face was a little ashy, but clean. She wore no makeup or jewelry. There were dark marks on her face where her piercings had been. Jerry hoped he wasn't pushing her out too soon.

They arrived at church just before the service started. Normally, Jerry would drop Nancy off at the front door and park the truck. But, he wouldn't dare let Alicia out of his sight, especially since he had told Sammy he would be personally responsible for bringing her back.

Alicia seemed overwhelmed by the energetic, happy crowd bustling around the lobby. She fidgeted and jumped as people streamed by; some smiled, but most scurried toward the sanctuary. Nancy stepped away to talk to someone.

Jerry guided Alicia to the side by one of the large windows. "Alicia, I'm stepping right over there to the information booth to get a bulletin."

Alicia nodded, and Jerry darted over to the booth. A man grabbed Alicia's hand. "Welcome to Grace Chapel," he said, attempting to hug her.

Alicia shoved him away, shouting curse words. "Don't you ever put your hands on me again!"

Nancy rushed over and grabbed Alicia, trying to calm her. People halted, looking with wide eyes.

Jerry nodded, waved at everyone, and grabbed the stunned man, pulling him aside. "Don't mind her, Brother, she's new here. Don't take what she said to heart."

The man glanced at Alicia nervously, nodded, and walked away.

Jerry placed his hand on Alicia's shoulder. "He was just trying to welcome you."

"I know. He took me by surprise. I'm sorry."

Jerry smiled. "Are you ready to go in?"

Alicia nodded.

Nancy squeezed her hand and walked into the sanctuary. They sat in the back. After her blow up, Jerry thought that was best. As the service progressed, Alicia relaxed and got into the worship. She leaned forward and listened as if she had an unquenchable appetite. She seemed to pull every word out of the pastor's mouth. He talked about the woman who was brought to Jesus, caught in adultery. Her eyes widened with a hopeful gleam. Tears streamed down her face when Dave talked about how Jesus told the women that He didn't condemn her but that she should go and sin no more.

After the service, Jerry introduced Dave. He was of medium height, wearing casual clothes. Dave reached out his hand. "Hello, Alicia. I'm glad you could fellowship with us."

Alicia, shifting her eyes from side to side, shook his hand. "Me, too."

Dave looked at Jerry. "Well, I have to get going. Nice to meet you, Alicia. Please visit us again," he said and hurried away.

Nancy rubbed Alicia's back. "So, how did you like the service?"

Alicia smiled. "I liked it. I'd like to come back. I like the way he teaches."

Jerry smiled. "I think I can arrange that."

* * *

Alicia heard a knock, and the door opened.

Jackie peeked in with a smirk on her face. "Could you come downstairs?"

At least she knocked. Alicia nodded and watched the door shut. She was thankful for Jackie and Sammy and the care they had given her, but she hated the intrusion on her privacy. Every time she'd go to the bathroom, she was monitored. Every time she went outside, she was monitored. She was monitored when she ate and when she left the table. She was checked for food, drugs, or anything she could make into drugs. They searched her room several times a day, and she had frequent surprise searches.

Alicia was tempted to react the way the old Alicia would have, but she purposed to show them that she had changed.

She purposed to prove she could be trusted. She understood why they had to take such measures with her; she had a rough beginning. She learned to fight her urges by praying, quoting and reading Scriptures, and going to Jackie or Sammy for prayer when the cravings overwhelmed her. It was still tough at times — the urges.

She felt like a wretch for having such desires. She thought God would have removed her craving for the stuff. It was hard fighting her sexual appetite. She was ashamed she'd seduced her fellow resident the last time she'd escaped. Her actions caused him to relapse. She felt dirty when those urges came, as she had when she'd been on the streets. When those urges overwhelmed her, she felt as if she'd never changed.

She loathed the grittiness of that life. The putrid smells of her debauchery were enough to make her vomit. She considered those actions worse than living like an animal. She'd gone beyond reckless abandonment, sharing needles, drugs, and lewd sex, lots of sex with lots of men. "Thank God I didn't get AIDS," she grunted.

She knew plenty of people who had contracted the deadly virus. During that time, she never had considered how dangerously she had lived. She'd seen a lot, and she'd experienced a lot. She prayed that the Lord wouldn't allow her to fall back into that life. That was her greatest fear, falling back into that disgusting habit. But, she was growing stronger in her faith that God would keep her from falling.

At times, she thought God grew tired of her constant pleas for mercy, that He was frustrated with her constant cravings for sex, urges for drugs, and desires to party. She wondered how many times God would forgive her for those awful thoughts and feelings. She knew that if she weren't at The Covering, under Sammy and Jackie's care, she would be somewhere doing all of those awful things. That was what scared her the most.

Yet, she had also learned to rest in the knowledge that she was secure in the love of God, despite her weaknesses. And she grew strong in the confidence that nothing or no one could snatch her out of her Savior's hand. That gave her peace.

She stood. "We walk by faith, not by sight," she whispered. She walked down the stairs and burst into a deep wail. "Madea! Daddy! I'm so glad to see you."

Katie extended her arms, and Alicia rushed right into them. "It's so good to see you, child." Katie squeezed Alicia and held her for a moment. "Let me look at you."

Alicia let go and wiped her eyes. She reached over and grabbed her father. "Daddy, I'm so glad to see you. You're a sight for my sore eyes."

Joseph squeezed Alicia until he lifted her off of her feet. "I'm so glad to see you, baby. You look good."

Alicia couldn't stop smiling. "Let's go in here."

Jackie smiled and walked into the kitchen.

Alicia led them to the parlor. It was a large room, nicely decorated with pastel colors. A sixty-inch plasma TV and pictures of serene countryside scenes were bolted to the wall. The furniture was made of cherry wood frames with bright floral print cushions. Katie and Joseph sat on a couch, and Alicia sat in a chair.

Alicia looked toward the door. "Where's Mama? She refused to come, didn't she?"

Joseph reached over and patted her knee. "You know your mother."

"I wish I could have seen Deshon." Alicia looked at Katie. "Bu, it's good he doesn't see me here. I don't want him to see me like this."

Katie nodded. "How are you doing, child?"

"I'm doing better. At first, it was hard. The withdrawals nearly killed me. But, the Lord brought me through and set me free. Now, it's just the daily challenge of staying clean. It was a struggle not to think about getting high. Then, it was a bigger struggle not wanting to get high. I had to learn how to resist the urges. It's a day-by-day walk. It's not so bad now."

"How do you cope?" Joseph asked.

"Daily prayer and Bible study. I went to church for the first time three months ago. I go every Sunday now. We have prayer and Bible study here, but...."

Katie clasped her fingers together. "But what, child? What's wrong?"

"Don't get me wrong, I appreciate what God has done for me here... but I'm tired of the mundane routine."

"What do you mean, baby?" Joseph said.

"Daddy, all I do is read, go to devotion, group discussion, and that's it. If it wasn't for going to church on Sundays, I'd die of boredom. The last six months... it feels good to be free from drugs, but they are the most boring in my life. There's only one TV in the house. I don't like the kinds of programs everyone else watches. I don't like the games they play, though I'm learning how to play Ping-Pong. I spend most of my free time reading my Bible."

"Child, maybe you should think of ways you can serve."

"What do you mean, Madea?"

"The best way to take your mind off of your boredom is to serve others. That's what helped me when Irvin died. I filled my time with remodeling the church. You should think of serving here somehow."

"How?"

"However, wherever you can. The Scriptures say, 'Whatever your hand finds to do, do it with all your heart,'" Katie said.

Alicia's eyes brightened. "You have made my day. This has helped a lot."

"I'll be glad when you leave here," Katie said.

"Me, too, but I have a few months to go before I'm through. But, you really helped me."

Katie smiled. "I'm glad, child."

"I hope to see Deshon soon."

Joseph grabbed Alicia's hand. "Let me work on that, baby. You know how stubborn your mother can be." He squeezed her arm. "I'll handle her."

Alicia smiled. "Thank you, Daddy."

Two weeks flew by as if they were just a few moments. Alicia thanked God she had taken her grandmother's advice to help out around The Covering. She cleaned the downstairs rooms and bathrooms, did the laundry and helped outside by grooming the yard. She helped new residents acclimate to the program. She hadn't realized how effective she was until Sammy and Jackie had her orientate all new residents. She'd found her gift.

Madea was right. It was wonderful to serve others. Alicia hoped that one day she'd be allowed to teach a group Bible study. Jerry's Bible studies had helped her, and she wanted to help others in their spiritual growth. Still, one thing troubled her heart. No matter how many people she helped, she couldn't plug the giant hole in her heart.

It had started with her grandmother and father's visit.

It sparked a yearning in her heart to be with her family. She missed them terribly. She wanted to have the fun times she remembered from when she was younger: the barbecues, birthday parties, Christmas, Thanksgiving, Easter, the Fourth of July, and all the holidays. Going over to her uncle's house and playing with her cousins, swimming in his pool, was always fun.

The biggest pain was not having her son. She wanted to see him, hold him and kiss his puffy cheeks. It was as if God had given her new maternal instincts, and they were stronger than ever. Being reunited with her son was the hope she lived for now. Staying clean wasn't an option; she had to, for her son.

Chapter Twenty-two

Jerry closed his Bible, prayed, and dismissed the class earlier than usual. He had just completed a long and exhaustive study of the letter to the Galatians and looked forward to teaching the book of Ephesians. He loved explaining each verse, chapter, and book, breaking words down in Greek, and giving historical details on biblical passages. It took him three months to go through Galatians.

More than his love for teaching the Bible, he loved the power of the Word to change people's lives. He glanced at Alicia. She sat on the front row with her Bible open, writing in her journal. *Now, there's a living testimony to the life-changing power of the Word of God.*

Jerry spent the rest of the evening answering questions from the few people who stayed after, about everything from Galatians, prophecy, marriage, heaven and hell, to angels, demons, and other subjects. At one point, he wondered if the people loved the Q and A sessions more than the Bible study. There were a few visitors to Grace Chapel who stayed behind to listen. Alicia, as usual, had her queries. Jerry patiently answered every question.

After an hour, the last of the people left the sanctuary. Alicia rested her head on the back of the chair and stared at the ceiling. Jerry plopped down next to her, leaned his head back, and blew a long sigh. "Boy, I'm tired. Did you see where Nancy went?"

Nancy walked out of the side door by the stage, buttoning

her sweater. "Jerry, I'm ready. We'd better get going. You have to get Alicia back to The Covering tonight."

Alicia stood up with her Bible and journal in hand. "Guys, could you give me a few minutes? I have to see Julie about my schedule in the nursery."

Jerry lazily waved her on. "I wish I didn't have to drive you back tonight."

Nancy furrowed her brow and turned to Alicia. "All the more reason to hurry before he gets too tired to drive you back."

"I won't be long," Alicia said and dashed off.

Nancy smiled and sat next to Jerry. "Alicia has changed a lot. It's hard to believe she's the same person who wandered into the parking lot eight months ago."

"She'll be done with rehab next month. Jackie has asked her to stay on as a counselor."

"She has really matured. She'll do well there."

"Not to sound selfish, but I hope she doesn't stay on."

"Jerry, that's not nice."

Jerry chuckled. "It's a long drive to Escondido."

Nancy shook her head and stood. "I'm going to check on Alicia, so we can get out of here. You definitely need to get some rest, and I hate driving your truck."

Jerry shut his eyes and felt himself slipping into a deep sleep.

"Where's Nancy, Jerry?"

Jerry kept his eyes shut. "She went looking for you." He felt Alicia sit next to him. "You ready to go?"

A moment passed.

With his eyes still closed, he asked, "Something on your mind?"

"I was just thinking."

"'Bout what?"

"I'm leaving The Covering next month, and I don't have anywhere to go. I know I can't go back home. My mother would never let me back in the house."

"Maybe when your mother sees how much you've changed, she'll change her mind."

"My father and my grandmother have visited me. My mother hasn't, and she won't let me see my son. I might be able to stay at my grandmother's. Truthfully, I'm afraid to ask her."

"Why?"

"I've stolen from her. I've stolen from a lot of people. I've burnt a lot of bridges. I don't think any of my other relatives would take me in." She paused for a moment. "Maybe my auntie down South will let me live with her, but I really don't want to go there."

"Do you want to go back home?"

"Not really."

"You don't want to stay on at The Covering? I know they won't pay much, but as least you'll have a roof over your head, and you'll be doing what you love."

"I don't want to stay at The Covering. When I'm done with rehab, I want to leave. I wouldn't mind going back to teach or help counsel, but I don't want to live there."

Her answer surprised Jerry. "Where would you like to go?"

"I would love to stay in this area. I love going to church here. I don't know where I'm going to go to church when I leave The Covering. I'll ask Pastor Dave if he knows of a church where I can attend. I have to find a place to live first. I really don't want to go back to L.A."

Jerry sensed a real panic in her voice. He opened his eyes and sat up. "Alicia, is there something else bothering you?"

Alicia shrugged.

"Alicia, what's wrong?"

A deep sadness poured from her eyes. "I'm terrified, Jerry."

"Of what?"

"What am I going to do once I leave The Covering? I have no skills. I squandered my college years on the streets. Where will I work?"

Jerry swung his arm around and patted her shoulder. "Don't worry. God will provide."

Alicia sighed. "I know."

"What are you so afraid of?"

"The streets. Living at The Covering is great. I love Sammy and Jackie. They've been good to me. But I won't have them or The Covering as a shelter when I leave."

"You'll be all right, Alicia."

"Will I? I won't have you and Sammy rescuing me from a drug house."

"Is that what's bothering you — the possibility of falling back into drugs?"

Alicia nodded. "This feels so good… being free. I don't want that life anymore. I don't want to lose what I have."

"I don't think you have anything to worry about."

"Jerry, you know the life I've lived, or at least some of it. I've robbed, fought, and even stabbed someone over something as silly as taking a hit from a joint. I have to confess that sometimes I feel those same urges that kept me in the gutter. I can see myself on the streets again, hooking, using, and living like an animal."

"All right, Alicia, I've heard enough. Haven't you learned anything these past few months? The Lord did not save you, get you off of drugs, place you in a nurturing home and church, and surround you with godly people who love and support you, just to let you fail. You should have learned, more than anything, that God loves you, and He won't let you fall."

"I know, Jerry, but...."

"No buts. You have to settle it in your mind that God is with you every step of the way. You have to trust that God has you in the palm of His hand, and He's never letting you go."

Alicia nodded and smiled. "I talked to Madea today. She really wants to meet you."

"I want to meet her, too. Every time she and your father have visited you, we were busy. I sure want to meet the woman who planted the seeds of God's word in your heart."

Alicia stared ahead with a somber look. "You're right, Jerry. God has my life in His hand. He's protected me from people and situations I know should have destroyed me. I know God has protected me. I should be dead right now. I know a few people who have been murdered, killed in car accidents, or OD'd on the very drugs I used. In some cases, I was using drugs with them when they OD'd. God has been good to me."

"See, God has a plan for you. Trust in that." Jerry patted her hand. "Just worry about completing your rehab. God will provide for all of your needs."

* * *

Jerry smiled like a proud papa on graduation day. Alicia had made it all of the way. She looked stoic and downright scared as she went from room to room, saying her goodbyes. Sammy and Jackie walked her down the stairs. Jerry followed, carrying her one bag of clothes and personals. Nancy waited by the entryway.

Jackie grabbed Alicia and held her in a long embrace. She looked into Alicia's eyes with a tender smile. "I'm so proud of you. You have done remarkably. The Lord has blessed your walk. It's truly been a blessing having you here."

Sammy took his turn and grabbed a hug. "Normally, I would load you down with exhortations about not falling into your old habits. But I don't have to do that with you. Just stay in your walk with the Lord, and you'll be fine."

"Thank you, guys. Thank you for obeying God in opening this place. This was the place God used to set me free from that life of drugs."

Alicia gave Sammy and Jackie a final hug. She looked up at the residents lined on the stairs and waved. Then Nancy walked Alicia to the truck with her arms around her waist. Jerry glanced through his rearview mirror as they drove away. Alicia leaned back and stared out of the window, apathetic. Jerry knew she worried about where she was going to live.

It took Jerry over an hour to drive from Escondido to Orange Grove, testing his patience to the max. The traffic was horrible. He led Nancy and Alicia up to the second-floor apartment and sat in a chair. Alicia sat on the couch and stared at Jerry.

Alicia folded her arms. "Jerry, why do you have a smirk on your face?"

Jerry shrugged. "Honey, maybe we should decorate the place." The apartment was small, plain, and bland—no artwork, no personal touches at all, just plain white walls and simple furniture. "Spruce the place up, now that we have a guest."

Nancy threw him a peevish glare.

Alicia stood and looked out the window. Jerry knew the

scene she watched. Many nights, he'd stood in the very spot and admired the view. Green grass, flowers, shrubberies, bushes and large trees covered the park. At night, vintage street lamps cast a soft light that made you feel as if you were in another time and place, one of peacefulness, serenity, and innocence. Alicia's gaze told him she wanted that life.

Over these past nine months, God had bonded them together. He couldn't see himself without Alicia in his life. In a way, she filled the void left in his heart by Kristen's death.

Jerry looked at Nancy and smiled. "So, Alicia, are you ready to go home?"

Nancy frowned. "Jerry, that wasn't nice."

Alicia scowled at him. "Yeah, Jerry, that was cruel."

Jerry laughed. "All right," he said. "Alicia, when you told me you would like to stay in this area, I talked with Nancy about you living with us. We have plenty of room, and you can stay here for as long as you want."

Alicia's mouth dropped open.

Nancy glanced at Jerry and back at Alicia. "What do you say?"

With no expression on her face, she said, "Yes."

"Are you sure?" Nancy asked.

Alicia, with a stupefied stare, said, "I just don't know if this is real. A moment ago, I didn't know what I was going to do. I was asking the Lord where I was going to live. I thought I was going to end up at a shelter." She wiped the tears streaming down her cheeks. "Thank you, guys. This means a lot to me, more than you could know."

Nancy wiped her eyes. "You're our family, Alicia. We wouldn't have any other way."

"Well, it gets better," Jerry said. "I want you to work

downstairs at the café."

Alicia's eyes widened. "You want me to work for you?"

"Unless you have a better offer, yes. You'll have to start at the bottom."

"I'll start anywhere you put me." Alicia shook her head. "I can't believe how good God is. He's provided me a place to live and a job, all in the same day."

Jerry pointed his finger toward heaven. "Grace, Alicia."

* * *

Jerry sat in his booth, looking around at everything that was his life. He couldn't believe how blessed he was. Nancy sat across the booth, enjoying a cup of tea. The café bustled with the normal lunch crowd. Alicia helped a busboy prepare a table for a waiting guest. It amazed Jerry how quickly she had mastered her job. In just two months Alicia had demonstrated management potential and was learning the restaurant business faster than he could teach her.

He felt awed by the grace of God, which had suddenly turned his life around. He had reconnected with Nancy in a way that made him feel youthfully vibrant, like when he had first courted her. Because Alicia performed her job so well, she took over Nancy's day-to-day duties, giving Nancy more free time to spend with Jerry. The two of them would disappear like teenagers ditching class.

It thrilled Jerry to be discovering his love for Nancy afresh. He enjoyed thinking of ways to bring a smile to her face. It was always the simple things—a touch, a word, a hug, and mostly just being in each other's company. He brought out his original 1937 Jaguar SS100 Roadster and had it cleaned, detailed, and tuned up. He loved driving Nancy down the Pacific Coast Highway with the top down. Sometimes, he'd surprise her by getting a room at a vintage bed and breakfast with an ocean view and spend the night. He was truly blessed.

Alicia seated the guests at the table and went back to the hostess booth. She checked to see who was next to be seated and stared off. Jerry noticed the change in her demeanor and wondered what bothered her.

"I'm really proud of her," Nancy said.

"Remember when she cursed out that brother the first time she came to church? Poor fella didn't know what had hit him." Jerry laughed. "I marvel at her hunger for the Bible."

"I know." Nancy blushed. "I have to admit, she puts me to shame, dragging me to Bible study every week. She knows stuff about the Bible that I don't even know."

"I remember the first time I saw her in the parking lot. She smelled awful. I have to confess that when Tom showed up, I wanted him to take her with him."

"Jerry, that was mean."

"Thank the Lord, she's put on at least twenty pounds."

"Don't you dare tell her that," Nancy smirked.

"It's a good gain. She looks healthier."

"She has blossomed into a lovely young lady."   Jerry gazed at Alicia with a tender smile. "She sure has."

Nancy's brow furrowed. "Excuse me, honey." She slid out of the booth and walked over to the cashier's station. She said some words to Alicia. Alicia stopped working and said something back to Nancy with a saddened stare. Nancy came back and sat in the booth shaking her head. "I feel terrible."

"Why?" Jerry asked.

"Alicia misses her son. She hasn't seen him in months. How

could we not have considered her feelings? It's only natural for her to yearn for her son. I feel awful."

Jerry frowned. "We have to do something about this." He thought a moment and whispered in her ear. He straightened and rubbed her back. "But you're going to have to take a step of faith, honey, and face your grief."

She looked at Jerry with her brow arched and walked over to the cashier's station. "We have a surprise for you, Alicia." Alicia stopped writing and looked up. "What is it?"

Chapter Twenty-three

Alicia watched the tender way Jerry squeezed, patted, and caressed Nancy's hand during the entire drive. He was caring and protective of her. He was just as protective of Alicia. No other man had cared for and protected her as Jerry had done, not even her father. No other man had looked out for her as Jerry had done. She loved him for that. All of her life, she had come to disregard the word love. People used it in many ways — mostly men before they abused her body, stole her drugs or made her walk the streets for their money — but never how it was meant to be used.

When Jerry told her God loved her, she hadn't had anything to compare His love with. But, over the past ten months, Jerry had modeled God's love in a pure, unconditional way. She was grateful to the Lord for giving her a living example of the way people were supposed to love each other. In her heart, she purposed to love her son by the same example.

"Are you all right?" Jerry asked as he pulled into the driveway.

Nancy nodded.

"Whose house is this?" Alicia said.

Nancy glanced over her shoulder. "It's ours."

Alicia drew her brows in and looked toward the front of the truck. She didn't know what surprised her most, that they had never mentioned having a house or that they had one and lived in a two-bedroom apartment above the café. With all the money they had, why weren't they living a more lavish life?

"I thought the apartment was your home."

Neither Jerry nor Nancy responded.

Nancy closed her eyes as the truck came to a stop. She flashed a grin at Jerry, jumped out of the truck, and opened the rear door. Her jaw clenched, and her lips quivered. She couldn't hide the deep sadness in her eyes. Alicia stepped out of the truck, wondering why it was so painful for her to be here.

Alicia gazed up and down the street, admiring the neighborhood. The ranch-style homes had low, sloped tile roofs, bright colors, and neatly trimmed lawns. Jerry's house was the largest one on the block, with a wood shingle roof, beige stucco walls, and large windows. The bushes and trees needed trimming, and the lawn needed edging. The grass was brown, starved for water, and a few weeds sprouted between the cracks of the concrete.

Jerry opened the side door, but Nancy grabbed his arm. "Alicia, you go inside and make yourself at home. The living room is straight ahead. I'll be in momentarily." She motioned toward the door. "Honey, can I talk to you for a moment?"

Alicia felt her way through the darkened kitchen. She heard Jerry say, "That's a great idea. I'll do it now. It'll be clean and spiffy."

Modest for millionaires, Alicia noted, easing into the living room. Pictures of Jerry, Nancy, and a girl drew her to the mantle. The girl was pretty, with long, brown hair and a great figure. She dominated every picture and seemed to have the ideal life: a beautiful home, family, friends, and plenty of nurturing. *This is their daughter.*

She looked happy in every picture: birthday parties, vacation Bible schools, and missionary trips. There were no photos of her with boys or at nightclubs, just ones with her friends and family. She posed in native garb in Mexico, the Bahamas, Japan, Paris, and London. Alicia wished she was that girl.

Questions swirled through Alicia's mind. She rubbed her arms, and a sharp, tingling feeling shot through her gut. The room echoed with hollowness as she moved about. Dust coated the high-end furniture. She walked past the awards, certificates, and degrees hanging neatly on the wall. It reminded her of her grandmother's wall. Alicia ventured down the hallway, looking for the bathroom.

Opening the door on the right, she peeked in. The room had a cold, stale, and eerie feel to it. A hospital bed sat in the center with no sheets. Two IV stands stood beside the wall, and the dresser and chest were piled with all kinds of medical supplies: bandages, pills, needles, rubber gloves, and other items.

Alicia closed that door, opened the door across the hall, and turned on the light. Three curling irons lay on the counter, plugged into the outlet but switched off. A hairbrush with strands of brown hair in its teeth lay in the sink.

She clicked off the light, closed the door, and walked back to the living room. Throwing her hand on her hip, she looked around the room. Curiosity urging her, she peeked out the window. An abandoned inground pool, half-filled with green, slimy water, surprised her. A torn blue cover draped sloppily off the edge of the deep end, telling her no one had swum there in a while. She wished she had a pool like that; she'd swim every day.

What had happened here, and why was the bedroom empty except for hospital equipment? It occurred to Alicia that, in the past year she'd known the Adamses, she knew very little about their life. She stared at the photos again. They had never talked about what had happened to their daughter, and Alicia had never thought to bring it up.

"Her name was Kristen," Nancy said, startling Alicia.

"She died?" Alicia blurted out, biting her lip.

Nancy nodded. "A year and a half ago. She would have been thirty."

"I'm sorry, Nancy."

Nancy wiped her eyes. "It's been hard, but the Lord has been seeing me through this."

"What happened to her?"

"We were getting ready for church when her heart gave out. The doctors don't know why. It was unrelated to her illness."

"What was she sick from?"

"Leukemia."

Alicia squeezed Nancy with a gentle hug. "I'm so sorry, Nancy."

"I'm doing better now."

"I can't imagine what you must have gone through."

"This is the first time I've been in this house since that day." Nancy wiped her eyes and smiled. "God used you to help me come back here."

Alicia's brows furrowed. "Me? How did He do that?"

"The first time I saw you in the café, I came alive. I felt an instant bond to you." Nancy glanced around the room. "The funny thing is, I never wanted to come back here, ever. We brought you here to show you the house. We were going to move back here so you could feel like you had a home. But, when Jerry pulled into the driveway, I suddenly missed my home."

"It's time for you to come home, Nancy."

Nancy thought for a moment. "Yes. It's time to stop running away from my life. Kristen is with the Lord, and I'll see her again one day. I've been hiding in the café far too long. It's time I start… restart my life. I have a wonderful husband, church family, and friends… a wonderful new daughter," she smiled and touched Alicia's arms. "I have a wonderful life that I'm squandering on grief."

"I have an idea," Alicia said.

"What?"

"Let's clean this place up. Make it a home again."

Nancy did a double-take. "That's a wonderful idea." Walking to the utility closet in the kitchen, she pulled out cleaning supplies. "Alicia, the vacuum cleaner is in the hall closet, so I remember."

"By the way, where is Jerry, and what is this surprise?"

"He's taking care of something, and you'll see when he gets back. Let's get to work. Jerry is going to be so happy when he sees the house all cleaned up."

Alicia slid a pair of yellow cleaning gloves on and carried a spray bottle, sponge, rags, and a bucket filled with soap and water into the kitchen, where she started wiping down the cabinets and counters. Nancy started dusting in the living room. Alicia thought nothing of deep cleaning. Her mother had often made her clean the house as punishment. Alicia chatted with Nancy as they cleaned, and before they knew it, a couple of hours had flown by.

She finished cleaning the kitchen at the same time Nancy finished vacuuming the living room. Alicia followed her to the bathroom. Nancy opened the door and turned the light on. She picked up the hairbrush and held it firmly with an empty stare.

Alicia came up from behind her and slowly eased the brush

from her hand. Nancy looked at Alicia and released the brush. "This is where Kristen collapsed. She thought she was strong enough to dress and go to church—but she wasn't."

Alicia nodded, took the brush and three curling irons, and hid them in the kitchen trash can. She came back, and they cleaned the bathroom quietly, not saying a word. They finished and went into Kristen's bedroom. Nancy stared at the bed. Alicia reached out to take Nancy's hand, but she rushed out. Alicia heard Nancy whimpering and wondered if she should go to her.

Nancy walked back into the room, composed, and resumed cleaning. Alicia boxed the medical supplies and stacked them by the bed, not saying a word. When they were done, Nancy closed the door, walked into the living room, and sat on the couch.

Whipping out a handkerchief, she blew her nose, staring toward the mantle. "That's enough cleaning for now, Alicia. I'll finish my bedroom later, and I'll have someone remove the bed and supplies next week."

Alicia sat on the couch. "Nancy, how come you or Jerry never talk about your daughter? I mean, you've only mentioned her a few times."

Nancy looked at Alicia as if wondering what to say. "I don't know. It hurts so much to think about her. I haven't talked much about that day. I tried to block it out."

"How could you?"

"I couldn't. The more I tried not thinking about her illness and death, the more I turned into myself and shut everyone else out. I became an empty shell."

"How did Jerry take Kristen's death?"

"He took it harder than I did. He just didn't show it."

"What do you mean? Did he cry?"

"Jerry will cry at the drop of a hat. He cried over Kristen, a lot. But, he went on with life. Me? I shut everyone out."

Alicia mused. "So, really, Jerry is just a big softy at heart."

"He doesn't like to admit it. You know, being the tough, rugged cowboy—but yeah, he's way more sentimental than I am. That's why I know Kristen's death hurt him more than he's willing to show. Jerry cherishes his family more than anything in this world. He wasn't raised in a loving home. He did everything in his power to make sure Kristen was loved. Watching her suffer like that really tore him up—nearly destroyed both of us. It was just as hard watching Jerry lose his precious angel as it was watching Kristen go through her ordeal."

"I didn't know that."

Nancy looked around the room. "The house feels like home."

"Nancy?"

Nancy turned toward Alicia.

"How come you don't live in a bigger house, or drive a fancier car, or travel more? You have the money."

"We bought this house right after we got married. We've added on over the years. We never wanted to move. We love the house, the neighborhood, the city. We love the people the most. We could live in Newport Beach, Yorba Linda, or Laguna Beach, but we decided we wanted to raise Kristen in modest surroundings. We never liked being around phony rich people. We never felt we had to display our wealth or impress people by what we have. Jerry always said he knows how wealthy he is, and he can spend his money any time he wants.

"Don't get me wrong, we spend plenty. The refurbishing of

the Old District—we were the largest investors, ninety percent. The Covering, we put all the money up for that. We sponsor dozens of missionaries each year, so we give more than our fair share. And we pamper ourselves plenty. We're content knowing that we can buy whatever we want, whenever we want. We chose to be frugal. Besides, what would I do with a fifty or forty-room house? You can only use one toilet at a time, and when you have to go, it doesn't matter if the toilet is gold or porcelain."

Alicia laughed.

Nancy thought for a moment. "We wanted to instill godly values in Kristen." She smiled. "I think we did that."

"I wished I could live in Newport Beach or Yorba Linda. They have it made."

Nancy frowned. "Alicia, I can have that life. I don't want it. All they care about is their status, and what they have or don't have. I thank God for what I have right here."

"But still, to live in those houses… a girl can dream."

"Well, I think you'll love living here."

Alicia raised her brow. "Nancy, what are you saying?"

Nancy giggled. "This is part of the surprise. Jerry is going to be mad at me for telling you, but yes, this will be our new home, and yours, too, if you want to live here."

Alicia heard a car outside.

Nancy jumped up. "That's Jerry with your other surprise."

"Other surprise? Nancy, you're driving me crazy. What is it?"

Jerry beamed with surprise and wonder when he came through the door.

"Surprise!" Nancy said and kissed his cheeks.

"What's all this?" Jerry whiffed. "The house is so clean and bright. Smells like peach."

"Well, Alicia and I decided it's time I stop moping around like I don't have anything to live for." She reached up and kissed him again. "I have everything to live for."

Jerry grabbed Nancy and squeezed her tight. "I love you so much."

"Hey, what about me?" Alicia said, stretching out her hands. "I need some love, too."

Jerry and Nancy sandwiched her with a hug. "Thank you, Alicia," Jerry said.

"For what?"

"For letting God use you. Many days, I prayed for this moment."

Tears flooded Alicia's eyes. The thought that God had used her messed-up life to touch someone this way was overwhelming. She had always been the one needing help, the mess that needed cleaning up. "I couldn't have imagined God would ever think of using me for anything good. I'm just grateful for His forgiveness."

"It doesn't take much for God to use you. He only needs willing vessels," Jerry said.

"All right, time for the other surprise," Nancy said, pushing them out of the door. She stood next to Jerry with a giddy smile. Nancy and Jerry grinned like parents watching their children open gifts on Christmas morning. Nancy nodded toward the car. "Surprise."

Alicia raised an eyebrow. Nancy nodded, and Alicia looked toward the Chevy Malibu. It had been moved from the carport and had been washed and waxed.

"It's yours!" Nancy blurted out.

Alicia looked at Jerry and then Nancy. "What?"

"We're giving you the car," Jerry said, wiping his eyes.

"Alicia, we would be blessed if you would take it. You need a car, and this one was just sitting here not being used," Nancy said. "So, what do you say?"

"Yes. Thank you, guys. Thank You, Lord." She walked around the car. She loved the maroon color and mag rims. The shine was perfect. Opening the door, she sat in the seat, running her fingers over the tan leather. She played with the power locks, windows, and the moon roof. She inhaled the new car scent. Jerry handed her the keys, and she turned the ignition. The engine started with a quiet purr. She read five thousand miles on the odometer, and when she looked out the rear window, she was relieved there wasn't a trail of blue smoke billowing from behind. "Thank You, Lord," she kept saying.

"We'll change the title over tomorrow. You should be okay until then," Jerry said.

"Thank you, guys. You really don't know how much of a blessing this is to me."

"Alicia, it is our pleasure," Nancy said, wiping her eyes. "Now, you can visit your family anytime you want."

Alicia looked up at them and smiled.

"Go ahead, Alicia. Take her for a ride. Get the feel for her. I've filled the tank," Jerry said.

Alicia nodded as she began backing out of the driveway.

"Hey, Alicia!" Jerry called out. She stopped the car. "Don't forget to check the oil."

She laughed. "I sure won't."

"Alicia!" Nancy yelled. Alicia leaned out of the window. "When you come back, come here to our new home."

Chapter Twenty-four

Alicia pushed autoseek, and the radio scrolled through stations, mostly the ones she didn't like. Contemporary Christian; *better than Old-Time Gospel.* Classical; *boring.* Rock; *that was never my style.* Spanish; *never understood the language.* The eighties; *too young and a lot of bad hairstyles.* Alternative; *weird.* Smooth Jazz; *nice, but too slow.* Country. Alicia chuckled. "I bet Jerry has this station programmed in his truck."

She relished the envy people would lavish on her, especially Derrick and the old crew she'd gotten high with. She couldn't wait to flaunt her good fortunes, the money she had, the clothes she wore, and how she looked. She couldn't wait to see the regret on Derrick's face for how he had treated her. He'd beg and plead to get back together, and when he'd groveled enough, she'd walk away from him. It felt good just thinking about it.

Jay-Z caught her ear. "That's my song!" She whooped, throwing the volume up. She rolled the windows down, slumped on the door, and bobbed her head. She couldn't wait to hook flat screens on the back of both seats and one giant screen in the front, lodge eight-inch speakers in the trunk, tint the windows all around, and slap twenty-two-inch rims on all four tires. *I can't wait to see Derrick's face.* "That nig…." She caught herself.

A wave of conviction flooded Alicia's heart. She sat up and turned off the music, chiding herself for her pride, for boasting about what she had rather than showing Christ in her life. Fear swept over her soul at how quickly she had fallen. She hadn't even driven a mile from Jerry's house. This was a cold reminder of her wretched nature and just how much she needed the Lord's grace. She turned around and drove back home.

* * *

Alicia spent the next week getting acquainted with her new neighborhood. She loved living in Orange Grove. She loved working and earning her own money. She had become a normal fixture around the Old District, and she loved the people for accepting her. She loved walking to the beach on her lunch breaks and after work. She loved shopping at the mall and at the shops around the Old District. Life was good, and she felt as if she really belonged.

She wore the kinds of clothes she wanted, though she'd gone up a size since rehab. She'd even found a hair salon that did micro braids. She had to drive to Santa Ana, but it was worth the drive. She wore long-sleeved shirts until she could find a place to remove her tattoos. *The foolishness of depravity*, she thought every time she looked at the mirror.

Alicia drove into the driveway and parked in the carport. She locked her car, even though she didn't have to—a habit from living in the city. Walking in the house, she heard Jerry and Nancy laughing and talking in the living room.

"Alicia, is that you?" Nancy shouted.

"Yeah, it's me." Alicia plopped on the loveseat. "Hi, guys."

Nancy, giggled, trying to tickle Jerry. "How was Bible study?"

Alicia fiddled with her keys, looking down. "It was fine."

"Just fine?" Nancy sat up. "What's wrong?"

"Nothing."

"Don't give me that. Usually, you're bursting at the seams telling us how good Bible study was, what revelation you received, what you'd learned from the questions-and-answer time. So, what's bothering you?"

"I'm bummed out about Deshon."

"Why don't you drive up to see him?" Jerry said.

"I don't want to just visit him. He should be with me."

"You have to start somewhere. Start with visiting him. That way, your family will see how much you've changed," Nancy said.

"You have to remember, Alicia; you were an addict the last time they saw you," Jerry said. "Why don't you take the day off tomorrow and go see your family?"

Alicia smiled at that suggestion. "I think I will."

"But remember, it's going to take time. Be patient. Let's pray that God will restore your son to you," Jerry said.

Nancy squeezed her hand. "God promised to restore what the cankerworm destroyed."

* * *

I walked into the kitchen just as Ruby walked through the front door.

"Mama, I'm here," she called.

"Be right there." Stepping into the living room, I glanced around and sat in the chair. "Where's Deshon?"

"Joe took him fishing."

"Alicia called me last night. She might come by today."

Ruby rummaged through her purse. "What scam is she

pulling now?"

"Why won't you give the girl a chance?"

Ruby flashed a doubtful stare. "Haven't we been down this road with her?"

"Maybe if you would talk to her, you'd see that she's changed."

"She's played this same game before. And before you know it, she disappears with money or valuables."

"I believe the Lord has changed her."

Ruby huffed. "I'll believe it when I see it."

"Have you been praying for her?"

"Mama, you know I have."

"Then why wouldn't you believe that God would answer your prayers? Why wouldn't you trust that God has changed her heart? You haven't seen her in over a year, and yet you reject any notion that she's changed."

"Okay, Mama, I'll hold off judgment until I see her. But, I'll be handing you a big terry cloth towel to wipe the egg off of your face when she turns out to be the same old Alicia."

"You should reach out to her. Don't wait until it's too late. I did that with your grandfather. I wish I could have spent more time with him before he died."

"You could have. No one stopped you from going to Alabama to visit him."

I hadn't realized I'd frowned.

"You know I'm right," Ruby continued. "You could have visited Granddaddy before he died."

I stood and walked to the window. "You know I don't like going to Alabama."

"Practice what you preach. You tell me to let the past go. You should do the same," Ruby said, then walked out of the room.

"Whose car is this? You know anyone who drives a maroon Malibu?"

"No," Ruby shouted.

"Oh, my Lord, it's my baby."

Alicia walked in with a big smile on her face. I hugged her for a long while. Stepping back, I couldn't stop gawking at her. "I'm so glad to see you, child. My, my, you're beautiful."

"Hey, Madea. I've missed you so much."

I thought I was looking at a different woman. Alicia wore beige slacks and shoes with a beige shirt. Her hair was cut in a neat, feathered bob, and she wore very little makeup. Her skin was smooth and flushed. I could barely see any of the marks left over from the piercings. She looked as if she had put on a few pounds, but I was glad for that. I grabbed Alicia and hugged her again.

Alicia smiled as she took my hand. "Why are you crying, Madea?"

"I'm so happy to see you. And I'm thrilled at what the Lord has done in your life. It's so evident that no one can deny it."

Ruby walked from the back. When she saw Alicia, her face went blank.

"Hello, Mama."

Ruby ran her eyes swiftly up and down Alicia. "Hi."

I wondered if Ruby could deny the Lord's grace in Alicia's life. She surprised me. She didn't smile, hug, or show any affection to her child. Her stare was stiff and cold. Her stubbornness and hardness of heart infuriated me.

"I would have called you sooner, but I...."

"It doesn't matter."

"Ruby, stop being evil."

Alicia glanced around nervously. "Where's Deshon?"

"He's fishing with your daddy."

"I'd like to see him, Mama."

"I'll think about it. I'm not convinced, as others are, of this so-called new you." She picked up her purse and started for the door. "I'll see you later, Mama."

Ruby walked out before I could respond. Alicia cleared her throat and sat on the couch, struggling not to cry.

I shut the door and grunted. "Are you all right, child?"

Alicia wiped her eyes and nodded. "I'm okay. She just needs time."

"She's being stubborn. She sees what the Lord has done in your life."

"I don't know, Madea… I was hoping… I want to see Deshon."

I thought for a moment. "I'll talk to her. She's grown attached to him."

"I know Mama doesn't want to give Deshon to me, but I'm ready, Madea. I'm ready to be a mother to my son. I miss him so much." Alicia stared at the floor. "I just feel so lost without him."

"Be patient, child. Look where the Lord has brought you from. It took time to get you here, remember? The Lord will finish what He's started in your life."

"I know," Alicia said, still staring at the floor. She perked up and beamed a proud smile. "So, Madea, are you coming to my baptism Sunday?"

"I wouldn't miss it for the world. And I'm dragging your stubborn mama by her nappy head if I have to."

"That's the same thing Daddy said when I talked to him last night. And you know he's scared of Mama."

"So, tell me about these people you live with, child."

"They've been such a blessing to me. Not only did Jerry lead me to the Lord, but he and Nancy stood with me through my rehab."

I forced a smile. I'm not one to be jealous, but I found myself fighting strong feelings of envy. Why had they gotten to share those moments with Alicia and not me? That fact they were white added more salt to that wound. I was surprised and ashamed that I harbored such feelings. "That's real nice, child."

"I live with them. They gave me that car, and I work at their restaurant."

"Work?"

"Yeah, Madea. I have a full-time job. I even have a little money saved up."

"I'm really proud of you, child." I leaned back and smiled. "So, tell me about this church you go to, and tell me about this plush neighborhood you live in now."

"It's not so plush, but it's nice. The church is wonderful, Madea. They're a church-planting church."

"What does that mean?"

"They put sister churches all around L.A. What I most like about it is learning the Bible. I go to Bible study most nights, and I help out in the nursery. The people are wonderful, and I've made friends. God has been so good to me."

Alicia's testimony brought joy to my soul, but I still resented that strangers had gotten to share in her transformation. I felt left out. I had prayed hard and long for Alicia. I felt cheated that I couldn't be by her side to comfort her through her trials and to rejoice with her in her triumphs. In some ways, I felt I deserved it. *Lord, forgive me.*

"So, Alicia, these people just gave you the car?"

Alicia smiled. "Yes, Madea, they just gave it to me. It was their daughter's. She passed away."

"I'm sorry to hear that."

"In a way, they're like second parents to me. After Mama kicked me out, I drove around for weeks, with nowhere to go. I don't even know why I drove to Orange County that day. I was tired of living on the streets. I found Jerry's place because I was dodging the police."

"Dodging the police? Why in the world were you doing that?"

"Madea, I was parked at a 7-Eleven, plotting to rob the store. I saw a lady sit a little girl on the counter. I was moved by the way she played with her daughter, laughing and tickling her. After that, I couldn't go through with it. That's when I saw a police drive by. I know he saw me. I got out of there before he swung back around. I ducked into the first place I thought was out of sight. I was so tired when I parked in Jerry's parking lot, I don't even remember turning the car off. The next thing I knew, he was pounding on the window. He took me inside and fed me. I was so hungry. I hadn't eaten in days. He shared the Gospel and prayed with me, and that night he took me to rehab."

Listening to Alicia, I felt silly for being jealous of Jerry. However Alicia had gotten to this place of blessedness, I only had God to thank. A year ago, I'd prayed that God would send someone to help my baby. The Lord answered my prayers in the most wonderful way. I didn't think He'd send a white man as an answer, but I was glad He did. I was foolish to allow such feelings. If by God's sovereign will, he chose Jerry, a white man, as His instrument to reach my baby, who was I to complain?

"But, Madea, with all that God has done for me, I still feel empty without Deshon."

I took Alicia's hands. "Be patient, child. After listening to your testimony, I have no doubts that God will reunite you with Deshon. Just let Him do His work."

Chapter Twenty-five

I stepped out of Ruby's car and stood on the main walkway of Grace Chapel Community Church, impressed by its size and beauty. People got out of their cars under a large canopy that extended over the main drive. I appreciated not standing in the sun. The white stucco exterior had large tinted windows and doors. The building didn't look like a church at all. It resembled more a spruced-up corporate center.

The sidewalks and grounds were lined with shrubberies and tall, slim palm trees. I was amazed at how spread out everything was. It reminded me of a small college campus. The parking lot was massive, packed with cars. Each parking aisle was color-coded and labeled with Scripture verses. Safety personnel scooted around the parking lot in green and white golf carts, ferrying people from the far end of the lot.

Walking into the lobby, I thought I had stepped inside of a mall. The church was spacious and elegant, with plenty of plants, flowers, and small trees. Large plasma monitors were spaced throughout the lobby, broadcasting church announcements, events, and directions around the building. Information booths were spaced throughout the lobby. I noticed three larger booths, one for missions, one for children's church, and a general information booth.

"Welcome to Grace Chapel." A casually dressed woman greeted me with a pleasant smile. She handed me a church bulletin and continued greeting others.

The bulletin had an eye-catching graphic on the front and was a few pages thick. People smiled and waved as they streamed into the sanctuary. Everyone I saw carried a Bible. Parents tugged their children through a wide arched gate with "Welcome to Kiddy Kingdom" lit up in flashing blue, yellow, orange, and green. Underneath the sign, a Scripture read, "Forbid them not, for of such is the Kingdom of God."

I was overdressed in my peach Ann Taylor button-down dress with white buttons and a matching peach hat. I'd worn my pearls for the special event.

Alicia jogged over, wearing long shorts, a pullover top, and pink crocs. She hugged everyone with a jolly grin. "Hey, guys, I'm so happy you came." She turned toward Ruby. "Thanks for coming, Mama,"

Ruby responded with a cold shrug.

Sammy and Jackie, holding hands, walked over wearing warm smiles with their khaki shorts, T-shirts, and sandals. Sammy wrapped his arms around Alicia. "You look fabulous."

Alicia wiped her eyes. "Thank you, Sammy. Thanks for coming. You guys put up with a lot of stuff from me. I thank God for The Covering."

"The pleasure is all ours. To see what the Lord has done in your life was worth it all. And now, we get to witness your baptism. We're so excited for you," Jackie said.

Ruby fixed her eyes on the couple. She leaned over and whispered to me, "Alicia sure sounds white, doesn't she?"

I frowned and turned away.

Alicia squeezed Jackie's hands. "Guys, this is my mother, Ruby... you know my father and grandmother. Mama, these are the people who brought me through rehab." Ruby gave Jackie a quick hug, barely moving her arms. Alicia grabbed Deshon up in her arms. "And this is my heart, my son, Deshon."

"I'm pleased to meet you all. Katie, it's good to see you and Joseph again. Alicia, we'll see you inside," Sammy said and walked away, holding Jackie's hand.

Joseph shook his head and grabbed Alicia's hands. "Baby, you look so beautiful." He leaned in and whispered, "See, I told you I was going to get your mama here."

"Thank you, Daddy." She kissed Deshon's cheeks. "Mama misses you so much."

"I missed you, Mommy." Deshon squeezed her neck and blew a slobbering kiss on her mouth and cheeks. "Mommy, you look pretty."

Alicia squeezed Deshon even harder. "Thank you, baby, and you look very handsome."

"You smell nice, Mommy."

Alicia laughed, holding Deshon tight. "Thank you, baby."

"Hey, y'all."

Alicia swung around. "Aunt Maxine! I wasn't expecting you."

Maxine sashayed over and wrapped her arms around Alicia. "Me either," She gave me a peck on the cheek. "Hey, Mama."

"This is a surprise," I said.

"I was in San Francisco helping Deidra settle into her apartment. I decided to hop a plane and fly down." She turned and cradled Alicia in her arms. "I'm proud of you."

"Thank you, Auntie. This means a lot to me. Look at you — you're gorgeous."

Maxine twirled around, showcasing her black St. John suit with her black, wide-brimmed hat. "Well, thank you, my dear."

"So, what do you think of my church?"

"It's big," I said.

"Well, you'll have to get used to the music, and they don't know how to clap in time," Alicia warned.

I chuckled. "I know what you mean. They were the same way at South Bay."

A large man with a long, bushy beard and a wide smile stretched across his face approached us. There was something familiar about him and his cowboy garb. He held the hand of a casually dressed woman with a jovial twinkle in her eyes.

"Hey, everyone, I'm Jerry. You must be Madea. Alicia talks about you all the time."

I reached out my hand.

"I'm not shaking your hand." Jerry leaned over and wrapped his arms around me. "You must be Ruby and Joseph. I know all of y'all. Alicia talks about y'all non-stop. Except this lovely lady—I believe I don't know… wait, don't tell me your name, but I bet you're the auntie from down south."

"Jerry, Nancy, this is my aunt Maxine," Alicia said, turning to Nancy. "This is Nancy, Jerry's wife, and my employer."

Jerry grabbed Nancy's hand. "I want to say on the behalf of Grace Chapel, welcome."

"Jerry is the senior elder here, and he teaches a Tuesday-night Bible study," Alicia said.

Jerry tipped his hat. "Hope y'all get to sit in on a Tuesday night study sometime. We go through the entire Bible. Right now, we're going through the book of Ephesians."

I nodded, impressed. I could see why Alicia was excited about this church. Everyone exhibited the same excitement. I could tell by the way people hurried about. Parents quickly dropped their children off in Kiddy Kingdom and rushed to the service. Men rushed in from the parking lot, rendezvousing with their wives. Stragglers rushed in with teenagers and elementary kids, dispersing from each other once they hit the lobby. Everyone—parents, children, and singles—scurried to his or her destination with great enthusiasm.

Ruby fixed her eyes on Jerry. "I know you."

"Brother Jerry!" I shouted. "I met you at the mall. You carried my bags."

Jerry lit up with a wide smile. "That's right. I remember." Jerry looked at Alicia and me. "My, my, my, look at how the Lord works. I told you I was gonna pray that the Lord brings you here. Look at how He got you here. I had no idea you and Alicia were related. See how God works."

Music roared from the sanctuary. Jerry motioned his hand and escorted everyone inside. I followed Jerry to our seats on the front row, amazed by the thousands who crammed into every seat. I was used to worshiping in a crowd of three hundred.

Words scrolled across two giant monitors on either side of the stage. Three men and three women, dressed casually, sang in front of a full orchestra. They held their hands toward heaven and harmonized beautifully. A young man stood out front, playing guitar, leading the worship. The contemporary music was just like the songs at South Bay.

The sanctuary was semicircular, with a balcony jammed with people. The walls were white, the pews violet, and the carpet dark purple. The sound system was crystal clear, like surround sound. The church was well-thought-out: the aisles were wide and accessible for the handicapped, and some of the rows had special places for wheelchairs. There was an enclosed room with tinted glass along the back wall, where mothers watched the service while holding their babies.

The voices tapered off, and the music came to a soft stop. A middle-aged man took the podium. Children stampeded down every aisle and out of the auditorium before he could dismiss them.

I was blessed by how thoughtful and helpful everyone was. There was always someone who gave directions, answered questions, or just loved on people. I felt loved and welcomed. I hadn't felt that way in a long time.

The man on the stage announced upcoming events, Bible studies, small group meetings, and other support group meetings. The pastor took the stage and, after introducing himself as Dave, reminded the congregation of Alicia's baptism following the message. He prayed for the offering and took his seat while the worship team sang. The ushers passed the offering buckets. I closed my eyes and enjoyed the song.

He took the stage, welcomed the visitors, highlighted a couple of announcements, and directed all to open their Bibles. Dave's message moved me, but I was bothered by Ruby's constant squinting and glaring at the way Nancy hugged Alicia. There was a real mother and daughter bond between them.

From time to time, Ruby glanced over at Jerry with a puzzling gaze. I nudged her to stop, hoping Jerry didn't take offense.

After Dave finished the sermon, Alicia quietly got up and left. Dave prayed and quickly disappeared offstage while the music played and the worship team sang. It seemed only moments passed before the large drapes slid open at the back of the stage. Alicia appeared by the baptismal pool. She wore a white, knee-length T-shirt covering another T-shirt and black tights. Dave wore a black wetsuit.

He turned toward the congregation. "I'm honored to

celebrate our sister's acknowledgment of her faith. The Lord has brought her a long way. We've seen her growth these past few months. Some of us remember all too well, don't we?" He waited for the chuckles to die down and handed Alicia the microphone.

"I want to thank the Lord for having so many people pray for me. He sent Jerry to me that day in his parking lot to share Jesus. He and Nancy have mentored me—patiently, I may add. They have seen me through rough times, really rough times. I thank God for His grace and the people He had helping me." She handed the microphone to Dave.

Ruby leaned over and whispered, "You'd think she was hatched from an egg, the way she tells it."

"Hush up, Ruby," I said.

"She acts like she had no life until she came down here."

"I said hush up. I'm trying to listen."

"Alicia, I baptize you in the name of the Father, and the Son, and the Holy Spirit."

Dave placed his hand on Alicia's back and his other hand on her shoulder. Alicia folded her arms over her chest and fell back into the water until she was fully immersed. A moment later, she emerged with her hands raised toward heaven as the water cascaded off of her face. The music roared, and everyone erupted into applause.

I followed a line of people into the multipurpose room and took a seat along the wall. It was a large, open area with white walls and purple carpet. A few ladies wearing white aprons placed trays of snacks on the tables. Besides the family, a few people filed in.

Alicia walked in, drying her hair with a towel, joy radiating from her face. I stood to walk over to her, but Nancy grabbed her and rocked her in her arms.

Ruby glared at Nancy. "She's hogging Alicia as if she were her child. I was the one who labored twelve hours and twenty-nine years with that girl, not that woman."

"You need to quit. I've never seen you so jealous. You should be thanking God that she's turned her life around. Instead, all you can do is gripe about the love she's receiving."

Pastor Dave walked in. He had changed into slacks and a T-shirt.

I managed to squeeze between people hugging and wishing Alicia well and took my hug. "How are you doing, child?"

"Wonderful, Madea. I'm glad you came."

"I'm glad I came, too."

"I really want Mama to see that I've changed."

"I told you to trust in the Lord. She sees the change in your life. She knows you're not the crackhead she threw out."

Alicia smiled and squeezed Deshon. "I'm going to block out all the negative vibes and concentrate on my little man."

"Amen, child."

Dave walked over and hugged me. "Katie, I'm sorry I've been so busy that I haven't had the chance to talk to you."

"That's all right, Pastor."

"Sometime in the future, I'd love to sit and get to know you."

"Anytime, Pastor, anytime."

Pastor Dave chatted with Ruby and Joseph, mostly Joseph. I looked at the people God had touched through Dave's ministry. What an awesome work of grace He was doing. I was ashamed to admit it, but I had been away from church too long.

* * *

Jerry smiled at the way Alicia beamed with joy. She was elated that her family was here to share what God had done in her life. Jerry was happy for her. God did a wonderful work in her life. He hoped Deshon could come home with her.

Nancy gave Alicia another hug. "We're very proud of Alicia."

"We are, too," Ruby retorted. "You're not the only ones who had input in this girl's life. We raised her, long before y'all came along."

Stunned, Nancy glanced at Jerry. "That's not what we're saying, Ruby."

"Well, that's how y'all act."

"Ruby, I don't know why you're so angry," Jerry said.

"Because y'all act like y'all the only ones who had an impact on this girl."

"Mama, it's not like that," Alicia said. "I'm sorry, you guys...."

"Don't apologize for me. I don't need you to defend me."

"Ruby, stop it," Katie said.

"No, Mama, I'm not going to walk on eggshells because she thinks she's better than us." Ruby glared at Alicia. "Remember, we know where you came from. You may have them fooled, but we know the real you."

Jerry looked directly into Ruby's eyes. He had it with her attitude. Ever since she'd shown up, she'd thrown daggers at everyone, him especially. If it were a fight she wanted, then he'd give her a fight—but not the one she'd expect. "I want you to know that I love you, and there is nothing you can do about it."

Ruby rolled her eyes, folded her arms, and squinted.

Jerry smiled the kindest smile he could stretch across his face and prayed that the love of Jesus would radiate through his lips and melt her cold, stony heart.

Ruby shifted on her feet and returned his gesture with a contemptuous glare.

Jerry wasn't moved by her disdain. Love was winning. He saw it in her eyes. His weapon overpowered her bitterness. He had made his stand, throwing all the gentleness he could muster at her. "Ruby, I know you can't deny the grace of God you see in Alicia, no matter how you try. Only someone who has been touched by the love of God can be filled with such joy. She's not acting. Her life has truly changed by the power of God. Stop kicking against the pricks. You know what you see in Alicia is real. You know God's love in your life—and you see it in hers."

Tears filled Ruby's eyes. She blinked and quickly turned away, pressing her lips tight. She turned and looked Jerry in the face. Suddenly, her brows drew in with puzzlement.

Love conquered. Jerry could hardly contain his joy. Her hard shell had fractured.

Ruby moved closer, studying his face. Her eyes widened with a look of horror, then glared with rage. She looked as if she wanted to slap him.

Jerry wanted to step out of arm's reach. He braced himself and determined that if she slapped him, the love of Jesus would gush from every pore of his skin. He smiled all the more. The more she studied him, the more her face contorted. He tried to stretch his smile more.

Ruby's finger trembled as she pointed it just inches from his nose. "You murdered my father," she said, her lips quivering. "You are an evil man… murderer."

No one moved. Now one said a word.

"Ruby, you don't know what you are saying!" Nancy shouted.

Ruby snapped at Nancy with a vicious scowl, "And you don't know your husband. Tell them who you are, Gus. You didn't think I'd forget that evil grin, did you? You hid your hideous face under that beard. You masked that evil smile with your fake Christian act. You almost had me fooled, but that smile gave you away."

Nancy moved between Jerry and Ruby. "Stop it, Ruby. You're being mean and spiteful. I've never met a person as bitter as you."

Jerry looked into Alicia's eyes. She returned his stare with no expression. Jerry wanted to say something, anything. He didn't know what to say. He didn't know if he should say anything. He moved Nancy out of Ruby's way; he would bear the full brunt of her rage.

"Tell them, Jerry, Gus, or whatever your name is. Tell them how you terrorized us. You and your gang killed my father. Gregory Byron Smith. That's my father's name. You beat him so badly, you couldn't recognize his face. You didn't stay around to see what you and your mob had done. You left him hanging on that tree, beaten and burnt beyond recognition. You set fire to his dead corpse and kicked it, and then you burnt our home to the ground. You even burnt our barn and animals to death." Ruby whirled around. "That's your husband."

Nancy's eyes widened. She covered her mouth with her hands. She glanced at Jerry, but he kept his stare on Ruby.

Alicia shook her head. "Mama."

Ruby glared at Alicia. "And you call this man your mentor." Ruby's face furrowed with rage. She trembled uncontrollably and then collapsed.

"Mama!" Alicia screamed.

"Someone call the nurse!" a man shouted.

Nancy tugged Jerry's arm. "Honey, tell them she's wrong."

Chapter Twenty-six

Pacing in a small circle in the corner of the lobby, I tried to bring my thoughts and emotions under control. I desperately wanted to leave, and Ruby was taking too long. She had been ushered into the nurse's office after she'd fainted. I was furious at her. Ruby had provoked a malicious confrontation that had brought up the horror I had long tried to forget. I stood aloof from everyone. I just wanted to think and make sense of everything.

People bustled around the lobby in complete confusion. Joseph had gone into the office with Ruby. Maxine, her phone glued to her ear, walked around just outside the doors. She'd been on the phone ever since we left the multipurpose room.

Dave walked over and didn't say a word. He glanced around the lobby as if searching for the right words to say. What could he say?

I stopped pacing to be cordial. I wondered how much Dave knew of Jerry's past, how much anyone knew—the church, Nancy, the people of Orange Grove. I felt as I had in 1960, that the entire town was in on the cover-up. This was far worse than what had happened at South Bay.

"Katie."

I looked at Dave with no expression. It was all I could do to be civil.

"I don't know what to say. I can't even wrap my head around this. I know this sounds trite, but if there is anything I can do, please don't hesitate to let me know."

"Thank you, Dave." I hoped he'd leave. I couldn't stomach platitudes right now.

Dave pursed his lips and walked away. I went back to pacing. It was all surreal. I didn't know how to feel or what to think. I didn't even know why I was angry at Ruby. After all, it was Jerry who had murdered my husband, destroyed my life, and relentlessly badgered me until I'd been forced to flee my home state. How could I not have recognized him, even after all these years? His face was obviously evident now.

Maxine marched over, phone still glued to her ear. "Mama, are you all right?"

I waved her away.

Alicia walked over, holding Deshon's hand. Her eyes were puffy and red.

"Child, this must be very hard for you."

"Madea, I don't know what to think about any of this. How are you doing?"

I shook my head. "I don't know, child."

"I want to go back to your house tonight. I want to be with you."

I stroked Alicia's cheeks. "Of course you can, child. Just as soon as Ruby comes, I'll be ready to go. Here she comes now."

As if on cue, people parted to create a path for Ruby as she stomped toward me. "I'm ready to go. I can't stand to be here another second. It makes me sick to my stomach to be in this place." Ruby shot Alicia a look. Her glower lingered a moment. "I knew this was a mistake, coming down here."

"Ruby, I don't want to hear you ranting; not now," I said.

"I'm not ranting. We just found out the man who murdered Daddy is sitting in that office. That's not my fault. Alicia brought him into our lives, not me."

I turned to Alicia. "Did you drive your car?" She nodded. "I'm riding with you. I can't take Ruby now. I'll end up choking her."

"Let me tell Nancy I'm leaving."

I nodded.

Ruby eyed Alicia as she walked away. Ruby yanked Deshon's hand. "Well, if you're riding with her, I'm leaving now." Ruby stormed away with Deshon. "Come on, Joe."

Joseph and Maxine followed. Joseph glanced back and shrugged.

Alicia turned toward me.

I nodded. "There's Nancy."

Nancy had stepped into the lobby and was making her way toward me. Alicia met her and said what she wanted to say. Nancy nodded, hugged Alicia, wiped her eyes, and watched her walk away.

"I'm ready, Madea. Is Aunt Maxine coming with us?"

I shook my head.

Alicia must have read the expression on my face, because she didn't say a word after that, which was fine with me. I just wanted to think. This encounter with Gus perplexed me. Whenever he'd confronted me in the past, he'd always left me terror-stricken. Instead, seeing Jerry as Gus infuriated me. I wasn't afraid or terrified. I was angry.

I'd always imagined coming face-to-face with Gus would be just as dreadful as it had always been. Back then, the encounter had always left me terrified. I didn't feel terror now. I didn't feel love. I was ashamed to admit it, but hatred raged in my soul. But, how could I hate my brother? How could I hate the man who'd led my granddaughter to the Lord?

* * *

The shock of Ruby's revelation had worn off, but the anguish over what he had done tore through his heart. It was all Jerry could do to sit still. In an instant, the viciousness of his sin came alive in his mind. The hatred he felt was just as malicious. The words he'd spoke felt as venomous as when he spewed them that night. He had destroyed their lives with no mercy and had relished in it. It was as real as if it had just happened today.

He thought about the disdain he had felt toward Katie in 1960 when she had looked into his eyes and told him she loved him. Back then, those words infuriated him. He hadn't realized until later that those were the very words that had melted his heart. Katie had planted the seeds of life in his soul. He'd wanted that kind of love; the kind he had never received as a child.

He grimaced, slightly shaking his head. The moment he had dreaded had finally come, and he was relieved. He had often wondered how this day would unfold, but this was not as he had imagined. He had rehearsed what he would say or do a million times, but when the moment had come, he hadn't been able to utter a word. He knew he was a new man in Christ and that his past was dead and buried by the cross, but the guilt of that night was always with him.

He checked his watch. An hour passed in an instant. He sat in Dave's office, plowing through his thoughts. He wanted to talk to Alicia and Katie, but he had been rushed out of the multipurpose room, though not before the nurse had given Ruby a clean bill of health. She had fainted in the heat of the moment. He thanked God that she was okay.

Nancy had come and gone out of the office several times. She sat next to Jerry and held his hand in silence. She stared at the floor, occasionally looking his way. He didn't answer the question he imagined she was thinking.

She turned toward him. Her face wrinkled with deep anguish. "Is it true?"

The heartbreak in her eyes drove him to the edge of a breakdown. She had never looked this distraught, not even when Kristen died. At that moment, he wished there was something he could do to take away the pain. There were no words that could soothe her anguish. If there were, he'd speak them. Would she accept what he had to say? Did she think differently of him? Was he the same man she'd fallen in love with? He hoped so.

"Is it true, Jerry? Were you that Gus Ruby talked about?"

"Yes, it is true," he said somberly. "All of it is true. I was that man."

An awkward silence fell between them. Nancy bowed her head and stared at the floor. He thought about what he would say to Katie. He had to go to her. He had waited many years. He had a million things he could say to her and a million ways to say them, but only two words burned in his soul, yearning to be spoken: *forgive me*.

He'd always imagined the perfect setting, with lots of Christians gathered around, prayerfully supporting the both of them while he mended their wounds. He'd even been silly enough to imagine Christian music softly playing in the background—country music, preferably. And when all the hurts were voiced and the wounds healed, they'd hug and go their merry ways. As he thought about Ruby's outburst, he realized his notions had been just crazy fantasies.

When Ruby said that Jerry was the man who murdered her father, the look in Katie's eyes sent wrenching pangs through his heart. Her eyes had been filled with heartache. He felt as if he had destroyed the peace she'd worked so hard to gain. He was certain she had put the pain of that awful time behind her, only to have him resurrect her anguish after all these years. Would asking for forgiveness be sufficient? Would saying "I'm sorry" be enough to heal her heart?

The look in Alicia's eyes tormented him. She had stared at him as if she didn't know who he was. *Lord, I pray I haven't destroyed what You had forged between us.* If he had, he had only himself to blame.

How many times had he taught people that their pasts would catch up with them? "Be sure your sin will find you out." He'd preached that a lot. "What's done in secret will surely come to the light." He loved whipping that one on people. Those Scriptures stung now that they applied to him. He felt wretched. He felt as if everyone had turned against him, and who could blame them? He felt that God, as if playing some big cosmic joke, had waited until things were just perfect in his life, only to snatch all the good away from him.

"Why haven't you told me about your past?" Nancy said. "Every time I've asked you about your childhood, you always managed to avoid answering. Why, Jerry? Why would you shut me out of that part of your life? I'd never pushed you to open up, but I never would have thought you would have kept something like this from me. I don't know who you are."

Jerry snapped his head toward her. "What do you mean you don't know me? After all these years, you can look me in the face and say you don't know me?"

She looked away. "You know what I mean."

"No, I don't."

"This was a lot to take, Jerry. I find out you have this dark side you've kept from me. Who was that man?"

"That man is dead, has been for many years. I'm sorry I didn't tell you. That time in my life was so ugly. When I came to Christ, I put the past in the grave, where it belonged."

"Well, I want to know about Gus."

Jerry shook his head. "Nancy, I don't want to bring him up. He was a horrible person."

"I have a right to know who you are... were."

He looked at the floor and shook his head. "It was pretty much as Ruby said. I was a mean, hateful cuss. One night, I murdered a good man for no other reason than I hated him. He spoke out against my racist ways, and I hated him for it. So, that night, my friends and I went to his farm, forced him out of his house, brutally beat him to death, and lynched him. I wasn't satisfied with that, so I lit him on fire. I wasn't satisfied with that, so I burned their home to the ground. And the worst thing about that whole ordeal was that when I had left them completely destitute, I felt nothing about it, no guilt, remorse, or shame."

Nancy clenched her fist. "Why weren't you prosecuted?"

"No white man ever worried about being prosecuted for any crime against a black man back then. The morning after the murder, the sheriff pulled all of us into his office and told us to disappear, just get out of sight until it all blew over. I later found out that the town's leaders had ordered the sheriff to make the incident go away quietly. Not that they cared for me or justice, or the lack thereof. They just didn't want the attention."

Nancy cringed. "Oh, my Lord, that's terrible."

"Yes, it was a terrible time, and I'm ashamed that I was a part of that evil system."

"Is that what made you come to the Lord?"

"Not at all. I went on with my life. A few years after that night, an old, white Pentecostal preacher came to town, running a revival on the black side of town, of all places. One day, he came to the café I owned and invited me to his revival. Of course, I wouldn't be caught dead in a black church, so he preached Christ to me in the back room of the café where I used to party. He laid hands on me, and I accepted Jesus."

"Was that the first time you heard the Gospel?"

"Not at all. I was taught about God. Heck, church was a part of the culture. On Sundays, practically the whole town was at church, except me and my friends. The funny thing is, after I came to the Lord, no one wanted to associate with me. The blacks didn't trust me—not that you could have blamed them—and the whites rejected me as a race traitor, so eventually I left Blount City."

"Did you try to find Katie?"

"Yeah, but Katie's relatives wouldn't tell me where she'd moved."

"What would you have said to her if you had found her?"

"I would have begged for her forgiveness. I would have begged the kids for their forgiveness." He stared off for a moment, then looked at her. "I wanted to tell Katie that her words had gotten through, and that I was a new man in Christ."

"Why was that so important to you?"

"After we lynched him, I was so full of rage... Katie stood on the porch, looking fearless, her kids crying for their daddy. I wanted to afflict pain. When I looked into her eyes, she said that she loved me and that Jesus loved me. I have never forgotten those words. Even after I lit their house on fire, I looked into her eyes. I wanted her to hurt. But, she stared directly at me and said, 'Jesus loves you and forgives you, and so do I.' I never forgot that." Jerry turned to Nancy and looked directly into her eyes. "I'm going to go to Katie and make it right with her."

"What do you mean?"

"I'm driving to L.A., tonight, to Katie's house, and I'll beg for her forgiveness."

Nancy raised an eyebrow. "Are you sure you want to do that?"

Jerry nodded.

"Do you know where Katie lives?"

"I'll ask Alicia where she lives. I have to make things right."

"But do you have to do it there?"

"I never thought I'd get this chance to ask for her forgiveness. I feel God has opened the door to make things right with her."

"I don't know if you can, honey. I mean, if it were me, I couldn't forgive like that."

"Sure you could. You have Christ in you."

Nancy looked away. Her brow furrowed as she shook her head. "I hoped it wasn't true. I wanted you to scream your innocence. I wanted you to denounce Ruby for the lies she was spreading. I felt awful when you didn't answer her."

"There was no answer to give. I was shocked, stunned, but mostly I was relieved."

She turned toward him with surprise in her eyes. "Why relieved?"

"Because, after all of these years, I can finally bring this to an end."

Nancy smiled and squeezed his hand. "I'm with you,

whatever you want to do."

"Let's pray for the Lord's strength and guidance."

"And His divine protection," she added.

Dave walked in, flopped in his chair, and leaned back. "It has finally calmed down out there. I know you heard the news. Ruby is fine." He glanced down for a moment, then looked at Jerry. "The family went home. Alicia left with them."

Jerry stared down. "That's good." He looked up. "How was the meeting?"

Dave leaned forward, fiddling with his ink pen. "Are you sure you want to know?"

Jerry nodded. "Of course, I do."

"Most of the guys had already heard by the time they made it back — social media. They're pretty much split on the issue. Some of the elders think you should step down."

"Why?" Nancy asked.

"They feel Jerry would be a distraction to the church."

Nancy frowned. "In other words, they're afraid the offerings will dwindle."

"It's a valid point, Nancy… about the church, not the money," Dave said.

"Does loyalty count for anything? Jerry has served this church faithfully for over thirty-five years. That ought to count for something."

Jerry squeezed her hand. "Honey, they're just looking out for the church's interest."

"How about they look out for your interest? You're a child of God. Jesus still loves you. Have they thought about that?"

"Nancy, they have a right to point out what's best for the church." Dave stood and walked around to sit on the edge of his desk. "Jerry, you're my oldest and dearest friend. I won't allow them to throw you to the wolves."

Jerry smiled. "Thank you, Dave." He looked at Nancy and back at Dave. "The time might come when you might have to. You'll have to protect the church."

Dave sat back in his chair. "We'll cross that bridge when we come to it."

Jerry squeezed Nancy's hand. "You'll cross that bridge sooner than you think. Once this gets out to the news, I'm sure Alicia's family will want some kind of retribution."

Chapter Twenty-seven

It was dark when Alicia pulled into the driveway. The drive back had been eerily quiet. I appreciated that she'd left me to my thoughts. Timothy's Mercedes, Ruby's Cadillac, and Edward's Chevy Avalanche lined the street in front of the house. I shook my head. *They're in the house, stirring each other into a mad frenzy.*

I frowned when I stepped inside. "Who moved my furniture around?"

Everyone stopped talking. "Mama," Ruby said, "we just made room for everyone."

"Never mind," I huffed and found my chair.

Pacing back and forth, Edward kept muttering. "Gus... I can't believe he's here."

Maxine pushed the button on her headset and threw her iPhone into her purse. "That was Henry. He wanted to catch the next flight here, but I told him not to come." She folded her arms and shook her head. "I'd always wondered where that man went. A few years after y'all left, he came around asking about you, Mama. Where you went, how he could reach you. No one told him anything. I'd heard he went to Arkansas or Tennessee somewhere."

Timothy pranced around the living room as if in a trance. "All of this time, that pig has been living under our noses."

Dorothy, his wife, rubbed his arm. She was tall, gorgeous, perfectly groomed, and dressed in an Anne Klein pantsuit. Her hair was thick, long, and silky black. Her ears, neck, wrists, and fingers shimmered with gold and sparkled with diamonds. "Try to be calm, baby. Remember your blood pressure."

Timothy jerked his arm. "All of these years, he could have been in jail."

"I'll tell you what we should do. We should go down to Orange County and take care of him ourselves." Edward pounded his fists together. "He ain't going to jail under this white man's system."

"Are we sure it's him?" Maxine asked. "It's been so long, and he looks so different."

"It's him. There's no doubt about that," Ruby said. "I'll never forget that hideous grin. It's burned into my mind."

"He didn't deny it, that's for sure," Maxine said.

Edward hunched his shoulders. "So, what do we do about him?"

"We bring that monster to justice!" Timothy shouted. "We bring charges against him."

"How do we do that? A black man can't get justice in this system. Ya'll know that," Edward said.

"Don't be silly, boy. They've been bringing white people to trial for crimes they committed back in those days. Many of them have gone to jail, too," Maxine said.

Edward sighed. "I still say we go down there and take care of him ourselves. I can get my boys to...."

"Stop being silly. Don't go and do something stupid, because for sure they'll throw *your* silly behind in jail," Maxine retorted.

"She's right. You have to be smart about this. You bring criminal charges first, and then a civil case. You sue for wrongful death and take all of his money. Just like they did to

O.J." Timothy faced me. "I'll look into the civil case, but Mama, you will have to bring criminal charges against him."

Ruby frowned. "Why does *she* have to bring charges?"

"Because she saw his face up close. We know who he is, but none of us got a good look at his face. Now, we'll back up what you saw."

Alicia stood. "What about forgiveness?"

Timothy looked around, befuddled. "What?"

Alicia swallowed. "If we are all Christians, shouldn't we forgive, as Christ forgave?"

"What are you talking about?" Edward said. "This is the man who killed…."

"Murdered!" Timothy barked.

Edward rolled his eyes. "Murdered our father, your grandfather—whom you never met, thanks to this man. You want us to forgive him?"

"I know what he did was wrong."

"Wrong?" Timothy glowered. "He murdered our father in front of us. I was twelve. Your mama was ten. That man spat in my mama's face and burned our house to the ground."

Ruby leaned forward. "He terrorized us for two years after he murdered Daddy. He was relentless. He never hid the fact that he murdered Daddy, either. In fact, he rubbed our noses in it every chance he got. He threatened to do the same to us."

"Mama, all I'm saying…."

Ruby interrupted. "No, you listen to me. One day, we were in town—you remember, Mama—back then, you couldn't eat in white restaurants. He tripped Mama in retaliation for walking into his place. She fell flat on her face. He ridiculed her viciously while she lay, humiliated, in the middle of the street. And you want us to forgive that?"

"You're not understanding what I'm saying...."

"What are you saying?" Ruby snapped. "You've gotten religion and all of a sudden you're an authority on God. We've been in church all of our lives. You don't get to tell us how to live, not after how you have lived your life."

"Mama, all of us have done bad things, and the Lord has forgiven us for all of them. Yes, I've done terrible things, and I've hurt a lot of people, but I know God has forgiven me."

Edward's eyes widened. "You want us to forgive him for *murder*?"

"Jesus forgives you for all of your sins, Uncle Ed, and He commands you to forgive those who have wronged you. I know the Lord has forgiven Jerry and changed his life, just as He has changed mine. God used him to bring me to Jesus. He's mentored me in my faith. He was there with me, the entire time, through my rehab."

"That wasn't our fault." I looked at Alicia. "We never knew where you were until after you called us. We would have been there for you. We weren't asked."

Tears filled Alicia's eyes. Her stare lingered on me for a moment. I was ashamed of my outburst. "That wasn't a conscious decision, Madea. I had to leave for rehab that night."

Abashed, I nodded.

"When God works in your life, it's awesome and wondrous. I am grateful for God's mercy. We all deserve mercy. That's what I'm trying to say."

"What about justice? Isn't God a God of justice?" Timothy snarled. "For too many years, we have been denied justice. White folks have enslaved us, tortured us, beaten us, lynched us, and murdered us. They always get away with it. When do we get justice?" Timothy turned to Alicia. "You're a Bible-thumper now. What does God say about justice? Aren't there stories in the Bible about God exacting justice? How does that Scripture go, 'He by no means clears the guilty?' Isn't your man guilty of murder? Is God a God of justice?"

Alicia glanced at me and turned to Timothy. "Yes... He is a God of justice, but...."

"Your man is guilty of brutally murdering my father right in front of me. Is God going to give me justice?"

"The Bible also says mercy triumphs over judgment," Alicia said firmly.

"What does that mean?"

"It means that we all deserve His judgment, but He freely gives us His mercy."

"Enough of this mercy nonsense. Now, this is how it's going to be. Mama, you are going to talk to the DA...."

"Timothy, stop talking like a fool," I said. Everyone became quiet. I folded my hands in my lap, poised and dignified. I was proud of Alicia. She spoke the truth. I should have stood up for her. Timothy annoyed me, posturing as if he were Martin Luther King delivering a call to march. The confusion and turmoil on everyone's face let me know it was time to end this silliness. I knew what his motives were and wanted no part of it.

I chided myself for blowing up at Alicia. I knew better. I was ashamed of being jealous. God used Jerry to bring Alicia to the faith instead of me. I felt childish and stupid. "I will not be a part of your schemes to get back into the political spotlight."

"Mama, this is about justice for Daddy. That's what he would have wanted."

"You don't know what your father would have wanted. You're too blinded by your own ambition. But you *should* know—all of you should know. You were all there that night."

"Mama, what are you talking about?" Maxine asked.

"That day, your father came home earlier than normal, remember? He talked about God's will—about trusting in Him. But most of all, he talked to us about forgiving our enemies. He said, 'Y'all has to forgive. It's the Lord's way.'"

Timothy threw his hands up. "What's this got to do with us today, Mama?"

"It has *everything* to do with us today. We are children of God, and we should act like it. Like this child said." I paused, smiling at Alicia. "I almost forgot how it feels, those joyous days when you first come to the Lord. How alive you feel, how clearly you see. You have shown us something, child, by your example. The Lord commands us to forgive, and if the Lord has changed Jerry's heart, that makes him our brother. And as he is our brother, I will treat him as family."

Timothy grimaced. "That man will never be family."

The doorbell chimed several times. Alicia peeked out the window and slipped outside. I wondered who was at the door, but Timothy's ranting distracted me.

* * *

Alicia stepped outside and pulled the door shut. Her smile melted Jerry's agony away. He was desperate to know how she felt, what she thought, and what she was going to do. Would she move back to Inglewood and stay with her family? Would she leave Grace Chapel? He was desperate to know if he had destroyed their relationship.

She hugged Jerry and Nancy. "I'm glad to see you guys, but what are you doing here?"

"I had to come here, Alicia, to make things right. First, with you," Jerry said. "I didn't get a chance to talk, you... you know, with all that's happened. I didn't know what you thought about everything... about me."

"We all have a past we'd like to forget. God knows I do. Thank the Lord, our past is forgotten in Christ."

Jerry squeezed Alicia's hand. "I'm glad to hear you say that."

"I don't know the man my family remembers. I only know the man God sent to me that day in the parking lot of the Country Café. That man led me to Christ, took me to rehab, and stood by me while I went through that horrible ordeal. Gus? I don't know him."

Nancy wrapped her arms around her. "Oh, Alicia, you are wise beyond your years."

"Now, I have to make amends to your grandmother," Jerry said, wiping his eyes.

"You don't want to go in there. Everybody is in there—my uncles and aunts—and they're not going to be happy to see you," Alicia said.

Jerry glanced at the door. "Your uncles and aunts are in there?"

"Yeah, and they just so happen to be talking about you, Jerry. And it's not so edifying."

"Everyone is here. This is wonderful," Jerry mumbled. "Thank You, Lord, for this opportunity."

Nancy squeezed Alicia's hand. "I couldn't talk him out of coming here, and I don't think you will be able to prevent him from going inside."

"I've been waiting a long time for this moment. I feel like the Lord is giving me a chance to finally make things right."

"You realize my uncle wants to throw you in jail and throw

away the key—literally."

"I'm not worried about what happens to me."

Nancy nudged his arm. "*I'm* worried about what happens to you."

"I have to make things right. God has given me this opportunity to do it in front of everyone. I sinned in front of everyone. I'll make it right in front of everyone."

"All right, but it's rough in there," Alicia said, reaching for the door. "Hey, what's the story with the name Gus?"

"My full name is Jerry Gus Adams."

"I can't imagine you as Gus," Nancy said.

"Well, I was, and he was worse than you could imagine. Let's go in and face the lions."

* * *

I tried my best to ignore Timothy, but he badgered me to bring charges against Jerry. It was clear to me what God's will was, and I wasn't moved by Timothy's or anyone else's opinion.

Timothy's eyes widened as the door opened and Jerry followed Alicia into the house. "What's *he* doing here?"

Everyone snapped his or her head toward the front door. The room fell silent.

Timothy glowered. "You got a lot of nerve, coming here."

Jerry fixed his gaze on me. I leaped to my feet as if pulled up by an unseen force.

"I mean it. You don't...."

I thrust up my hand, silencing Timothy.

Slowly, Jerry moved toward me. With each step, his body cowered, and his eyes drooped with humility. "Katie, I am the man who caused the death of your husband, Gregory Smith."

His words were soft and full of meekness, but they resounded loudly. Slowly, he gazed around the room, his eyes landing on each of the children. "Your father." Then he turned back to me, looking directly into my eyes. "Katie, I've already asked the Lord to forgive me many years ago, and now I am asking you to forgive me."

"You got to be kidding me!" Timothy screamed. "If you think that's all it takes, you're sadly mistaken! I will never forgive you for murdering my father! I will spend the rest of my life making sure you pay for what you did! I'll see to it that you die in jail!" Timothy pointed his finger in Jerry's face. "I know you hear me!"

Jerry kept his stare on me. Tears poured down his cheeks.

I reached out and grasped Jerry's hand gently in both of my hands. Blocking everyone out of my vision, I peered into his eyes, as I had that night. "I forgive you, my brother." I made sure my voice was clear and loud enough for everyone to hear. I stretched out my arms, and Jerry fell into them, sobbing uncontrollably. "I forgive you with all of my heart."

I held him as if cradling a big baby. He wept loud and long. Edward turned his head and sniffled. Maxine cried. Nancy found her way over to Alicia and cried in her arms. Joseph held Ruby. She returned Joseph's embrace with no expression. I smiled as I looked at everyone. *How awesome is God to touch everyone with His grace?* I closed my eyes and held Jerry.

"Have ya'll forgotten what he did to Daddy? I haven't forgotten, nor will I forget." Timothy waved his hand for Dorothy to head towards the door. "You're going to pay for what you did, Gus. I promise you that." Timothy glared at Jerry and stormed out of the house.

Dorothy slowly stood, her eyes intently fixed on Jerry as

if she were unable to remove her gaze. Bewilderment was etched on her face. She eased toward the door and cast another lingering stare.   I nodded, wishing I could explain the bond between Jerry and me.

"Dorothy, come on!" Timothy yelled from the street.

Chapter Twenty-eight

I moaned each time Alicia's ten fingers made slow, soft, wide, circles on my scalp. Her massage took my attention away from the hectic chaos of last night. "Don't stop," I pleaded.

"I could put your hair in braids, Madea."

"You know me better than that—don't stop. This is so precious, to be fellowshipping with my baby. Remember when you used to spend the night when you were little?"

Alicia laughed. "I'd snap barrettes on the sloppily braided pigtails I'd twisted together. We talked, played games, and watched TV into the wee hours of the night. You'd take me shopping everywhere. That was a lot of fun."

"Yet, this moment is more precious to me, because we share an eternal bond that will never be broken."

"That's so true, Madea. I never thought about that."

"This was fun, cooking all this food. I haven't cooked like that in years."

"Ooh-wee, I love your biscuits."

I chuckled as she rubbed her belly. "I haven't made biscuits since I lived in Alabama."

"I feel like a stuffed pig." Alicia sprawled out on the floor in front of the couch. "Look at all of this food we're wasting. I'm going to get so fat."

I kicked off my house shoes and rested my feet on the center table. "I'm glad you slept over and didn't drive back to Orange Grove."

"I'm glad I listened to you. I was so tired. Nancy gave me a few days off."

"I'm glad she let you off. I wanted to spend some time with you."

Alicia nodded. "Breakfast was good. Everything was good – spending the night, sitting around in our pajamas, cooking and talking. I missed this."

"You think you might move back here? You can always stay with me."

Alicia stared at the floor for a moment. "I like where I am. I like the church. I like living with Jerry and Nancy. Eventually, I want my own place. I know Jerry would buy me a house or condo if I asked him, but I want to get it on my own. That's what I'm working toward, getting my own apartment and moving Deshon in with me. But, I have a car now, so I can visit you when I'm not working."

"You'd better." I chuckled.

"I'm glad you talked Mama into letting Deshon spend the night. Speaking of, is he still sleep?"

"Let him sleep. He'll wake up when he's ready."

"I hope Mama don't come and get him. It would be just like her… just to spite me." Alicia tossed her head up and smiled. "I'm not letting Mama spoil this moment."

I laughed. "No, don't. You have all day with him, so enjoy it."

"So, what did you think about last night?"

"It was powerful. I never thought I'd have a moment like that, that's for sure."

"Do you think Uncle Tim was right?"

"Child, please. He's so preoccupied with his political ambition, he can't see anything else. One thing is for sure; even he can't deny that everyone was touched by what the Lord had done. Even Edward, with his big-headed self, was moved to tears. He didn't think anyone saw him crying like a baby. I think God is really doing something with this situation that will bring Him glory."

"You think so?"

"He already has, child. He already has. Just look what God has done so far. The Lord took your messed-up life and brought about an event fifty years in the making. What were the chances of us running into Gus, let alone recognizing him? But, God brought Jerry and me together the way He wanted it to happen. Had I recognized him at the mall, only God knows how that might have turned out."

"Or Mama."

"Child, you know that's right. Instead, God did it His way — and His way is better."

"So, you think God had a purpose in all this?"

"I think God is just starting His awesome work. Only He knows the lives He'll touch."

Alicia smiled as she nodded. "God is so good."

"All because he used your life, child. Even I've changed."

"How?"

"For years, I harbored bad feelings about white people. I wouldn't call it hate, but that's what it was."

"Was it really hate?"

I nodded. "It wasn't just what Gus had done to me, but everyone who stood by and did nothing. Everyone from the people of Blount City, my so-called friend across the street who moved away, my church, my best friend at church, they all nursed my hate. My deep resentment of white people grew because of how I saw and interpreted their actions. I assumed every action was racial. That's how I took my last church moving away."

"How did you feel about Jerry being Gus?"

"I loved your grandfather so much. When Gus murdered him, I hated him for what he had taken from me. I struggled with forgiving him. Many nights, on my knees, I asked the Lord why I had to forgive him. I shed many tears resisting what I knew was right. Finally, the Lord healed my heart."

"How did the Lord take away your resentment?"

"A reporter interviewed me about the open letter I put in the paper."

"Letter? What letter?"

"Child, you were out on the streets when I did that. Chad said I was prejudiced against all white people."

Alicia frowned. "He had his nerve."

"But he was right. I did see all white people as prejudiced. I had to search my heart and ask God to forgive me. He did and took away the hate in my heart against white people. When I saw Jerry last night, that hatred I'd felt for Gus fifty years ago tried to surface. But the love of Jesus filled my soul, as it did that night in 1960. I had to forgive him."

"But, Madea, this isn't like forgiving someone for lying or stealing from you. He murdered the love of your life."

"When we see people how God sees them, we'll accept them as He does, washed in the blood of Jesus. If they are washed in the blood of Jesus, they're not only washed, but they're forgiven, too." I paused to think about that. It comforted me to know I'd done the right thing before God, despite what anyone thought—Timothy, especially. "That's how I see Jerry— washed in Jesus' blood. What do you think about all of this?"

Alicia leaned against the couch with her arms spread out on

the cushions. "I have a different perspective. See, I never knew the man who did those things. The man I know brought me to God, got me off of drugs, gave me a place to live and a job. To me, he's a godly man with an ungodly past that was wiped away by the blood of Jesus."

"That's a good perspective, child."

Alicia smiled. "Where's Aunt Maxine?"

"Tim came by early this morning and took her somewhere." I peered at Alicia, moved by her answer. She was right to think that way. No doubt Nancy, Dave, and the Grace Chapel family would have their perspective, too. They knew a different man than the one who had destroyed my life. I struggled to reconcile the Jerry I'd met at the mall with the Gus I'd encountered in Alabama. That man had been out of my life for fifty years. The man I had come to know mentored my granddaughter. That was Jerry. I, too, no longer knew Gus. He had died in Christ. "What are you thinking about, child?"

Alicia looked off for a moment. "Madea, tell me about my grandfather."

Fond reflections of Gregory made me smile. "He'd be real proud of you, child, real proud."

* * *

Maxine leaned back in her chair and watched the twenty-something, former *Jet* beauty walk out of the office with a sultry stride. She wore a draped mini dress, long black hair, no weave, all of which emphasized her perfect features and figure. Maxine turned and shot Timothy a glare through squinted eyes.

Timothy swiveled in a large, high-back leather chair, facing the wall-length window that looked out at the northbound traffic on Crenshaw Boulevard. His office was large and spacious. Two large plasma monitors, expensive artwork, pictures of Civil Rights icons, marches, conflicts, and confrontations lined the walls. Maxine chuckled at the red, green, and black Afro-American flag draped lazily on a brass flagpole in the corner.

He had promised Maxine breakfast, but she'd been cooped in his office for over an hour. Maxine was glad to see what he had done to the former Department of Water and Power building. She was especially impressed that the community center thrived with children's activities and programs.

Maxine leaned forward. "I'm ready to eat," she whispered.

Timothy swiveled around and hung up the phone. "I'm tired of waiting for her."

"Tim, why is your mistress working here?"

"She's not my mistress… anymore."

"You know, you are wrong for how you're treating your wife."

"Look, I broke it off, but I can't fire her. She can sue me for wrongful termination."

Maxine grimaced and shook her head. "I thought you were taking me to breakfast."

"I am. I had to take care of something. Besides, I thought you'd like to see the place."

"Miss Thing gave me the tour."

The phone rang. He held up his finger. "Hold on, I've been waiting for this call. Sarah, how are you doing?" He leaned forward. "Sarah, hold on, I'm putting you on speaker with my sister, Maxine. She was there that night." Timothy pushed the button on the phone. "Go ahead."

"Tim, what can I do for you?" Sarah's voice resounded,

crisp and clear.

"Did you get my brief?"

"Yeah… but I don't know what you want from me. Alabama has to bring charges. I have no jurisdiction, you know that. Are you sure he's the right man?"

"He murdered my father, Sarah. I was there. My sister was there, too. She'll tell you. I was hoping you could help get the wheels turning with the Alabama DA."

"Tim, you know how it works. You'll have to call Alabama. If they decide to open an investigation and find enough probable cause for an indictment, then they'll contact us for an arrest and extradition. Look, I understand what you want, but you know my hands are tied."

"That man is guilty of cold-blooded, first-degree murder."

"What proof do you have? You need more than your passion. No one was ever arrested. No charges were ever filed. Was a police report ever made out? You don't even know if the sheriff in Alabama is still alive. From what I can see, this incident never happened. You have no eyewitnesses and can you say you got a good look at his face that night?"

"My mother saw him up close."

"Will she testify to what she saw? From what I read, she won't. For Pete's sake, Tim, she had a love fest with the guy in her home. This guy's lawyer will have a field day with that alone. You need a lot more than what you have. Sorry, Tim."

Timothy placed the phone on the receiver. "There's more than one way to skin a cat."

Maxine scowled. "What was that, Tim?"

"I'm pushing to have that pig prosecuted. I got to get Mama to testify."

"You know Mama won't do that."

Timothy sprang out of his chair and grabbed his keys. "Come on. Let's go."

Maxine stood with her hands on her hips. "Where are we going? I'm hungry."

* * *

Maxine read *Orange County View* on the three-story modern office building with brown stucco walls and large mirrored windows. The growl in her belly made her glare at Timothy. She looked around the street, hoping to spot a fast-food place. "Tim, I'm hungry. I haven't eaten breakfast or lunch."

"I'll get you something to eat. I promise."

"Why are we here?"

"To see an old friend."

"You're here to see a reporter?"

He nodded.

"Why?"

"He'll help us with our story."

"Our story? What story?"

"Come on, this will only take a few minutes." Maxine followed Timothy into the building, fuming that she'd allowed herself to get roped into his shenanigans. Timothy checked in with the receptionist. A middle-aged man appeared and greeted Timothy. He was short and thin, with balding gray hair and a neatly trimmed beard. He wore casual slacks and shirt, and he rubbed his chin as they talked.

Timothy waved Maxine over. "Maxi, this is Aaron Starks."

The man kept his stare on Maxine. "Pleased to meet you, very pleased."

"So, how do you like your cushy job here?" Timothy turned

to Maxine. "He took this job to occupy his time after he retired from the *L.A. Times* a few years ago. I bet you don't get the juicy stories you used to get at the *Times*."

The man, his gaze locked on Maxine, replied, "It's all right. We get a few, domestics, drug busts, and a political scandal every now and then."

Timothy frowned and glanced at Maxine. "My sister is a pastor's wife, man," he said, rolling his eyes. "So, what can you do for me?"

Aaron focused. "I've heard of Jerry Adams. He's well-known around here. He's like Mother Theresa. Everybody loves this guy. It'll be hard for people to want to believe he's a racist, let alone a murderer. I can run a series of stories exposing his past. It's not quite the bite you're looking for, but it will sting a little. I'll have to run it by my editor. I'll be in touch." He began to walk away but stopped and turned around. "Hey, Tim."

Aaron spoke a few words to him. Timothy nodded and waved Maxine over. With her stomach still growling, she followed Aaron to a small conference room with wall-length windows that looked out toward the office. Aaron disappeared after directing them to sit.

Aaron returned with another man and sat across the table. He was middle-aged, neatly groomed and dressed. He kept shifting his eyes between Maxine and Timothy.

"Timothy, Maxine, this is the senior editor, Gary Duncan. Gary, Timothy, and his sister were there that night. It was their father who was murdered," Aaron said.

Gary listened as Aaron laid out the story he wanted to run; Gary's look told Maxine he wanted nothing to do with it. "I don't know, Aaron."

Aaron furrowed his brows. "I don't understand your

hesitation."

Gary shook his head. "I have to think about this. I'll get back to you."

Aaron glanced at Timothy. "Get back? Why? This story is ready to go."

Gary rubbed his forehead. "I want to look into the facts myself. We're talking about destroying a good man with a flawless reputation. He's a pillar of the community… a good Christian man."

"Is his past flawless?" Timothy asked.

Gary's brow arched. "I don't know. That's why I want to look into this myself."

Timothy bore his eyes into Gary. "What if everything that Aaron has told you is true? Will you run the story?"

Gary didn't respond.

"You're supposed to print the news objectively… unless you have some bias."

"Now, just wait one minute. No one is racist here, certainly not me. Aaron, you of all people know that. Remember, I was the one who hired you."

"I'm curious to know your reservations," Aaron said.

"I just want to know all the facts before I print a story that'll ruin a good man."

Timothy leaned forward. "Do you have a connection with Jerry Adams?"

Gary held Timothy's gaze for a moment then looked at Aaron. "I'll get back to you after I look into this myself." With that, he stood and left the room.

Aaron shook his head. "I don't know what that was about, but I'm going to get to the bottom of this."

"Are you going to run the story?"

"You bet I am."

Maxine blew out a deep sigh and stormed out.

Chapter Twenty-nine

The scent of cinnamon oatmeal, maple sausages, and freshly ground Columbian coffee woke Maxine. Throwing her house robe on, she followed the aromas into the kitchen, grabbed a magazine, sat at the table, and flipped through the pages nonchalantly. She looked forward to running around with Ruby after breakfast. Maxine wanted to spend time with Ruby and their mother before she left to go back to Alabama, but Katie had already told her she had other plans. "Morning, girl."

"Morning," Ruby, said, bustling around the kitchen.

"Good morning, Auntie," Deshon said, then slipped back into his playful world.

"Where are my manners? Good morning, sweetie."

Ruby set a cup on the table. "Deshon, eat your food."

Maxine looked around. "I like your new kitchen."

"Next year, I'm remodeling the entire house."

"Umm, the food smells good. I'm still hungry from yesterday." She grunted. "Fooling around with Timothy."

Ruby chuckled. "The food will be ready in a minute."

"He made me so mad yesterday."

"I can't believe you let yourself get sucked into his games."

Maxine sipped from the cup. "He took me all the way to… where does Alicia go to church?"

"Orange County. Why did he take you there?"

"He took me to some newspaper. He's obsessed with prosecuting Jerry. He doesn't care about anything else. This coffee tastes good, Ruby."

Ruby set a plate of eggs, sausage, and toast in front of Maxine. A moment later, she set a bowl of oatmeal next to the plate, then sat down, whispered grace, and started eating from her own plate. "You know how he is. Anything he sets his mind to, he goes at like it's the end of the world."

"This is different, Ruby. I don't think he's purely motivated by ambition."

Ruby's eyes came up from her plate. "What do you think it is?"

"I think he truly wants to see this man locked away for what he did. Remember, he almost killed Tim."

"I'd forgotten all about that. You may be right, girl."

"I saw Miss Thing at the office. Tim said he won't fire her because he's afraid she'll sue him for wrongful termination."

Ruby laughed. "He told you that, too? At least, this one can speak in complete sentences."

Maxine rolled her eyes. "Why does Dorothy put up with him?"

"It's not for love, that's for sure."

Maxine laughed. "I thought Alicia was taking Deshon to live with her."

"She is."

"You don't seem too happy about it."

"Nah, I'm fine with it. She seems to be on the right track this time."

Maxine set down her cup. "How do you feel about what happened Sunday night?"

"I don't know. I have mixed feelings. On the one hand, I know Mama is right, but… he killed Daddy, right before my eyes. I can see Tim's point."

"You know, Tim is so obsessed with getting Mama to press charges that he's overlooked the obvious."

"What?"

"You," Maxine said. "Besides Mama, you were the only one who saw his face up close. I saw him, too, but in all the confusion, a lawyer could raise doubt. That's why Tim isn't asking the rest of us to press charges. But, sooner or later, he'll remember that you were an eyewitness. Will you testify?"

"I don't know. Part of me wants to hate Jerry and see him suffer. I know the Lord isn't pleased with how I feel, but it's the truth. That's what I'm conflicted over. I'm torn between justice and forgiveness. It would be so much easier to hate him if he were the same cruel animal — not Alicia's mentor. What about you?"

"It's hard. But, after seeing how Mama forgave him, that strengthened my faith. I think I can forgive him. I want to because it's the Lord's will." Maxine glanced to the side. "Maybe forgiveness will be the right step toward your wholeness."

"What are you talking about?"

"The resentment you feel toward your daughter."

"Oh, that. I'm working on it."

"And the nightmares you have. Forgiveness might be your deliverance, girl."

"I know. Don't mention this to Tim. I don't need him hounding me." Ruby frowned and looked at the door. "What's all that ruckus?"

Maxine grimaced and turned toward the door.

"No, Dorothy. I won't stop until I nail that pig. I won't let him get away this time," Timothy fussed, walking into the house.

"Honey, you're letting this man consume your life. Hi, everyone," Dorothy said, walking behind him. "Maybe you should forgive him like Mama did. I've been thinking. Maybe you should turn him over to Jesus."

Timothy arched an eyebrow. "What? Jesus? You don't even believe in God."

"I never said I didn't believe in a higher power. I just never have seen any evidence of Him… until…."

"Until what?" Timothy asked.

"Hello, this is my house, you two," Ruby said. "What are you arguing about?"

Timothy held up his hand. "Just one second. I want to hear this. You saw what?"

"What are you two discussing?" Maxine asked.

Dorothy glanced at Maxine and back at Timothy. "What I saw the other night was powerful. The way Mama forgave him. I never saw anything like that before."

Timothy frowned. "Mama is a fool."

Maxine stood, holding her housecoat in place. "Timothy, watch what you say. That's our mother you're disrespecting."

Timothy flung his arms. "Well, she is. I can't believe that circus Sunday."

"You have to admit that something was at work over there. I don't know what it was. Call it God, Jesus, or whatever, but he was at work in your mother and in Jerry," Dorothy said.

"Jerry!" he shouted. "That man is the devil incarnate! He's pure evil."

"That's not what I saw," Dorothy said.

Timothy folded his arms. "Oh, yeah, what are you saying?"

"I saw a Christian. I saw what Mama always said a Christian should be."

Timothy scowled, strode into the living room, and stared out of the window.

Wow, Maxine thought. *That's quite some perspective for Dorothy.* She wasn't only a snob, but she was arrogant, especially against Christians. She thought those who believed in Jesus were weak-minded fools, idiots, mindless dolts. She considered all Christians intellectually starved. But, it wasn't a cleverly crafted argument that had gotten Dorothy thinking; it was a simple display of God's love between two people who should otherwise have hated each other.

Katie and Alicia walked into the house. Timothy turned and folded his hands, fixing his stare on Katie.

"Mama, why are you up and about so early?" Ruby asked.

"I'm going someplace this morning," Katie said.

"Where?" Ruby asked. "Who is taking you?"

Katie looked at Alicia with a smile. "My baby is driving me."

Ruby's face went blank. "Oh, that's nice."

Maxine hugged Katie. "Good morning, Mama. We were just having a spirited conversation."

Katie rolled her eyes. "I can imagine."

"Mommy!" Deshon shouted.

Alicia grabbed Deshon and whisked him out of the kitchen.

Maxine found a chair and sat, wondering how long would it take for Timothy to start badgering Katie?

Katie sat at the table and chuckled. "Still reeling from yesterday?"

Maxine smacked her lips. "I wasted all day running around with that fool."

Timothy walked into the kitchen. "I heard that."

"Well, you did drag me all over southern California. I didn't appreciate it."

"I'm just trying to get justice for us. You know I'm right."

"You're out of your mind," Maxine said. "You're trying to get your face in the papers."

"I have aspirations. I'll admit it. I don't see anything wrong with that. But this is different. I'm talking about the man who murdered Daddy. That should mean something to all of us. That man took everything from us. I don't understand why you don't feel the same."

"We just think differently about this situation than you do. It doesn't mean we care any less about Daddy than you," Maxine said.

"Let me ask you something, Mama. You don't think that man deserves to be brought to justice?"

Katie didn't respond.

"Well, I do. And it boggles my mind that you don't. The fact that this man hasn't answered for his crimes is an injustice in itself."

Katie pursed her lips. "It's not that I don't think he shouldn't be prosecuted."

"I don't get it, then. Why won't you press charges?"

"Tim, I have been over this with you. I don't think you're going to understand my reasons, because I think you have your own political agenda."

Timothy grimaced. "You're wrong about this, Mama. Even God agrees with me."

"Don't invoke God in your lame argument. But, since you brought Him into the discussion, let's talk about what God really wants. You've been taught the Gospel. You know what Jesus came into the world to do for all men. Yet, you act like you don't have a clue what redemption is about. If you want God to be fair and just, He'll start with you and your long list of sins. Do you want Him to judge you? You won't like that outcome."

"It's not right that he gets away with murder, and you know it," Timothy said.

Katie shook her head. "You refuse to see what God has done in Jerry's life. Look at his fruit. Alicia is a living example of God using Jerry to touch lives. But, you're too blind to see that. All kinds of people who have done all kinds of evil have received God's forgiveness. I pray that you'll see that you, like everyone else, need God's mercy."

"He deserves to be punished for murdering my father."

"Then let God exact His justice, not you. You keep going down this path, and you'll find yourself an enemy of God."

Timothy frowned. "So, you're saying God would take that murderer's side over me?"

"Yes," Katie said firmly.

Timothy's eyes widened. "I haven't murdered anyone."

"Yes, you have."

"No, I haven't."

Katie's eyes narrowed. "The Bible says when you hate, you are a murderer. It's evident you hate Jerry, with a passion. This hatred goes far beyond justice."

Timothy didn't answer. Dorothy looked on in amazement.

Katie looked fixedly at Timothy. "And, as far as God taking sides is concerned, He's not taking anyone's side. The difference between you and Jerry is that he accepted God's gift. You haven't. That's the reason you'll go to hell and he won't."

"You're telling me that God will send me to hell and let that murderer into heaven? I can't accept that."

"That's your problem. You fail to understand God's terms. Jerry did. He admitted he was a sinner and had done evil, including murdering your father. But, he also trusted in God's provision for justice, forgiveness, and mercy that Jesus provided by His death. Jerry accepted God's gift of salvation. And for that, he'll enjoy eternity, free of guilt and condemnation."

"Maybe he'll enjoy heaven, but down here, he gots to pay for what he did," Timothy said. "I'm going to make sure he experiences all the hell I can give him."

Katie stood and touched his arm. "Son, please let this go, for your own sake. If you don't, bitterness will rot your soul like gangrene. You'll never be satisfied or happy."

"That's where you're wrong, Mama. I'll be very happy the day the prison doors slam shut on that murderer forever."

"I'll be praying for you, son, just like I prayed for Gus. I pray that you'll find God peace and the strength to forgive."

"You'd better pray for your so-called brother, 'cause when I'm through with him, he'll think hell is a step up." He looked around. "Let's go, Dorothy."

He stormed out of the house, and Dorothy followed him, looking at Katie.

Chapter Thirty

Jerry held his eyes closed as tight as he could as he prayed. He hoped he wasn't squeezing Katie's hand too tightly. He hoped he wasn't babbling like an idiot. He had dreamed of this moment for years. He had pictured the scene: the two of them brought together by the peace of the Lord and bonded by the Father's love. The room would be tranquil, and calmness would rule everyone's spirit. It would be perfect, as only God could make it. He'd be strong and uplifting. He'd strengthen Katie and assure her.

He'd never felt more cowardly. He wanted this to be perfect, but chaos wreaked havoc in his soul. He'd rehearsed what he'd say and how he'd say it a million times. He sounded like a fool, stumbling through his prayer. Wiping the sweat with his other hand, he cracked his eye and sneaked a peek. Her head was bowed, and her eyes closed. Just as his anxiety was about to overwhelm him, Katie squeezed his hand and gave him a peace that calmed his soul.

He closed his prayer and let his gaze linger. "Would you like some lunch, Katie?"

"No, thank you, Jerry. I'm not hungry." She scanned the room and fixed her eyes on him. "I was surprised to receive your call last night."

"I meant to call earlier. It wasn't too late, was it?"

"Nah. These days, it seems, I get a lot of late-night calls."

"I would have driven up to Inglewood."

"I know. But, the way Alicia raves about this place, I wanted to see it for myself. When I got your call last night, I told Alicia I wanted to see where she works."

"Tuesdays are usually slow. You'd normally see Alicia bustling around here, running the place. She has really flourished—beyond expectations."

Katie nodded. A long and awkward silence fell between them. "I'd always imagined facing you in a hostile setting, like on the streets, or in a courtroom, but never in a place like this, with you praying and us talking amicably."

"I never knew how our meeting would unfold, either, though I prayed I'd get the chance to talk to you. I have to admit, I'm nervous."

"Don't be."

He smiled and nodded. "Are you sure you're not hungry? Guests of The Sanctified Booth always eat on the house. You can order anything you want."

"Sanctified booth?"

"That's what I call this booth." Jerry waved his hand. A waitress appeared with an order pad in hand. "Tell her what you want."

"Do you have hazelnut coffee and hazelnut creamer?" Katie smiled at the waitress's nod. "Jerry, you have to let me make a mix for you. I promise you, you'll love it."

He arched his brows. "I'll make a deal with you. I'll try your coffee if you try my special muffins. I use an old Southern recipe I made up years ago."

"It's a deal."

They jotted their orders on the waitress's pad and handed them to her. She read their orders with a curious smile, nodded, and whisked off to the kitchen.

A middle-aged woman approached the booth. She was well-dressed and wore signature eyeglasses. "Excuse me, Jerry. I want to introduce myself to your guest."

"Of course. Katie, this is Connie Baker. She's a member of our church."

Connie took Katie's hand. "I didn't get a chance to meet you last Sunday. I had to skip out early."

"I'm pleased to meet you, Connie."

"I hope you'll visit us again."

"Thank you. Maybe I will."

Connie smiled and walked away.

"She's nice." Katie looked around. "I take it word has gotten out about us?"

Jerry looked around. "Curious minds want to know."

"It seems to me that some of these folk are more than curious — the way they're staring and whispering."

"I think they're wondering what's going on here."

"Maybe."

Jerry opened his mouth to say something, but the waitress placed their orders on the table. "Here you go, ma'am, and here you go, Jerry."

Katie spooned sugar, cinnamon, and hazelnut creamer into her cup. "Here you go, Jerry. I want you to know…." She raised an eyebrow, handing him the cup. "I haven't shared this special blend with anyone. It's much too intimate. I drink this brew with just me and the Lord in my morning devotions."

"I want you to know I'm not a flavored coffee drinker." He smiled and held the cup to his nose, whiffed, and took a sip. He nodded and took another sip. "Katie, this is good. I mean it. If I were a flavored coffee drinker, I'd like this. Nancy would love this."

"Well, thank you, sir."

He spread a thick slice of butter over the raisin muffin and slid it before Katie. "Here you go. I only serve these on special occasions."

Katie picked up the saucer and watched as the butter melted between the cracks. She laughed. "I used to do this for Gregory with the biscuits I made him."

Jerry didn't know how to respond. "Sounds like you used to have a lot of fun together."

She pinched off a small piece of the muffin and slid it in her mouth. "Mm-mm-mm, Jerry, this is so good. It's so moist and soft; it just melts in your mouth. You should sell these."

He nodded, took a sip, and placed the cup down and looked into her eyes. His smile was gone. "Katie...."

"You know, this here...." She pointed to their snacks. "Reminds me of communion. I mean, us sharing a love meal like the early church used to do. I don't mean it in a literal sense of the Holy Communion...."

Jerry smiled. "I know what you mean."

Katie pinched off a piece of her muffin and glanced at him. "Interesting setup you have here. I like this Sanctified booth. Whatever made you think of this?"

"I don't know. I just wanted a place where I could talk to people about the Lord, somewhere secluded."

"This is secluded, all right. Do you win a lot of people to the Lord?"

"A few, as the Lord sends them to me."

Katie pulled the basket from the corner and flipped through the stacks of Gospel tracts.

"This is where Alicia found the Lord."

Katie stopped and flashed a wide smile. "That really blesses my heart to know that."

"Katie, I wanted to talk to you face-to-face about that night. That time in my life, I wasn't with the Lord. I want you to know that."

"Jerry, I was there, remember?"

He glanced around the café. Nancy and Alicia peered out of the swinging doors that led to the kitchen. He flashed them a smile and looked at Katie. "I searched for you after I had found the Lord, but you had already left town. I wanted to say I was sorry."

As he looked into Katie's eyes, he saw nothing but love. There was no judgment or condemnation. He could have gone on with his life, without ever mentioning that night, without ever apologizing for what he'd done, without ever asking for her forgiveness, and she would have loved him the same. He knew the Lord's mercy in an immeasurable way, but to have this woman whose life he'd destroyed show him this kind of love made God more real to him than he had ever experienced.

"I'd seen your husband earlier that day. He was preaching in the town square. That's what set my rage off. By the time I'd looked into his eyes that night, he was already gone. But, I insisted on lynching him. I can't explain the hate that raged in me. When I couldn't vent my hate on your husband, I vented it toward you. I wanted you to feel my fury. Really, I wanted your husband to feel it, but he was gone, and you were the closest person to him. I guess I thought in a twisted way, if I could afflict hurt on you, I would be afflicting hurt on him." Jerry shook his head, tormented by the shame of what he'd done. "The words you spoke to me that night never left me. Do you remember what you said?"

Katie just stared at Jerry.

"It was right after we lynched your husband. We walked back to the house to leave. I just couldn't let it go. The truth was, I had no peace, no satisfaction. I thought killing your husband would make me happy, but instead, it left me empty and dissatisfied."

Tears streamed from Katie's eyes. "I remember feeling so destitute. I wanted to leave this world. I wanted to go to heaven, but God had other plans for my life."

"I have never forgotten the words you said to me. You said, 'I forgive you, and so does Jesus.' You said, 'I love you, and Jesus does, too.' It was only after I came to the Lord that I understood what you said and why you said those words."

"You know, I remember that night vividly as if it were yesterday." She closed her eyes. "I used to have terrible nightmares. I'd wake up drenched in sweat and screaming at the top of my voice."

"Katie, I'm so...."

Katie held up her hand. "It used to be that whenever I came into your presence, I'd have tremors, shakes, or anxieties. I can close my eyes and see every detail of that night and our encounters on the street. I remember every vile word, every putrid smell, and every hateful look. I can feel the anguish that tore through my heart. Yet, there is no terror now. In a strange way, talking about that day is actually giving me closure. Your words are, once and for all, releasing my soul from the horrors of that night. After all of these years, I'm finally free." Katie threw her hands over her face and wept loudly.

"Are you all right, Katie?"

She took a moment. "I'm fine. It's just listening to you talk about that night, strange as it may seem, is giving me peace. After all of these years of praying to the Lord to take those tormenting memories, it is your testimony in the Lord that's finally setting me free."

Jerry could no longer hold his tears back. He cried with a loud wail.

Katie waited for Jerry to compose himself. "Don't misunderstand me. The Lord gave me peace back then. But, the terror of that night was always with me, taunting or haunting me in some way. Now, listening to you, I feel like the terror of that night is finally gone."

Jerry wiped his eyes and blew his nose. "It's funny. I always thought Pentecostals were a funny bunch of people, but God used a white Pentecostal preacher to preach His word to me. He was running revival at the black Baptist church in town."

"That's my son-in-law's church."

Jerry's brows furrowed. "I didn't know that. I still wouldn't have gone there. It was a black church. That preacher came to my café and shared Christ with me. God had begun to open my heart. He invited me to come to his revival, but I told him I'd never go to a church full of—I used the N-word. He kept coming to the café. He must have seen me as a challenge or something. He seemed to ignore my racist remarks and slurs. He kept preaching Christ, and that's what I saw.

"One day he asked if I wanted to pray with him. I said yes. After I prayed, the Lord took all of that rage and hate from me and replaced it with love, love for you and for your family, love for black people—heck, love for everyone."

"Did you ever go to his revival meeting?"

"Once, but my presence was too much of a distraction. In fact, after I came to the Lord, both whites and blacks kept their distance from me. That's why I left Blount City. But, Katie, your words were the seed God planted in me. I never forgot them. I so badly wanted to tell you that I was a changed man. I desperately wanted to share my faith with you."

"That really moves me, Jerry. That's quite a story."

"I wanted you to know that I was a changed man."

Katie grabbed his hands and looked into his eyes. "Are you finished?" She didn't allow him to answer. "I know the Lord has changed your heart. I knew the moment you walked into my house that you knew the Lord. I knew it when I met you at the mall."

"Thank you, Katie. You don't know what that means to me."

"Our work has just begun, brother."

"What do you mean?"

"I'm glad the Lord has changed your life, and I can finally put that horrible chapter of my life to rest. And I'm glad to have you as my brother. But now, we have to show the body of Christ this bond we share. Sadly, so many Christians, black and white, harbor racial feelings, prejudices, and in some cases, hate."

Jerry looked at Katie, bewildered. "What makes you say that?"

"Looking around here, I can see that there are some people who are uncomfortable with me being here, especially with you. That bothers me. Alicia has told me that there are people at y'all church that act awkward around her. And you know how my son feels about you. I haven't been to church in over a year because my old church moved away because of the color of my skin. I harbored resentment against white people for that. I see that was wrong. This problem of race is rampant in the Christian community. How can we say to the world that God is love when we don't love each other? I believe the Lord has called us to change that."

"How are we going to do that?"

"We show them how God's grace has bonded us together in an eternal bond."

"And we will show them by...."

Katie's face brightened. "Love, my brother. We will show them by the love we show each other."

Jerry nodded, smiling. "I hear you." He took the Bible from the shelf and opened to the Gospel of John. "Listen to this verse: John 13: 34-35. I love this Scripture," he said, dragging his finger across the page. "'A new commandment I give to you, that you love one another; as I have loved you, that you also love one another. By this, all will know that you are My disciples if you have love for one another.' It's by our love that we'll show 'em."

"Amen, my brother."

Jerry stared to the side for a moment, then looked at Katie.

She peered at him, "What's on your heart?"

"A thought just occurred to me," he said, unsure of whether she'd accept his suggestion.

"Just say it, Jerry, dag."

"We should go back home."

"To Alabama?"

Jerry nodded.

"I can count the times on one hand that I've been back home. But, I guess, since the reason I never went home is sitting before me a changed man, I have no reason not to go back home."

Jerry smiled. "I think it would be great for people to see in us God's forgiveness and reconciliation."

Katie nodded. "You're right, Jerry. What better place to demonstrate this than in Alabama?"

Chapter Thirty-one

Alicia kept her eyes glued on Dave. This was one Sunday morning she wished she had stayed home. She tried to focus on the message but was distracted. Everyone blamed her for Grace Chapel's being thrown into the spotlight: her uncle leading marchers in front of the church, the media painting the members as a cult of racists, and reporters pummeling the congregation with questions about Jerry. They were disquieted because of her. That was what the stares, whispers, and pointing fingers told her.

Had she known it would be like this, she wouldn't have come back so soon. Last Sunday was supposed to have been her baptism celebration. No one even remembered. She felt her old self trying to surface, but mostly she was hurt. For the first time since she'd started attending Grace Chapel, she didn't feel welcome. She didn't feel she belonged.

After the service, Alicia rushed out of the sanctuary and fled to the restroom at the far end of the building. Not too many people used this restroom, other than children's workers. She sat in one of the stalls to collect her thoughts. She couldn't stay for long, because she had ridden with Jerry and Nancy.

Her perfect little world had crashed all around her. Maybe she was naïve and had blinded herself to the realities her mother and uncle had chided her about—that she was just a black girl pretending to fit in a white world, and when it was all said and done, she was just black. Maybe she should move back to Inglewood. At least there, she would be accepted.

She walked out of the stall and made herself presentable, though she couldn't hide the puffiness in her eyes. She walked around the back hallway and emerged in the front lobby. Dave greeted people, as he normally did after each service. Alicia tried to ease out, unnoticed.

"Alicia!" Dave called to her.

She pursed her lips, walked over, and shook his hand. "Hey, Pastor Dave."

"I just wanted to say hi and see how you are doing."

"I'm doing all right." She looked toward the floor. "No, I'm not," she blurted out. "Some of the people are getting to me, you know, with their stares and stuff."

Dave frowned. "I'm sure they don't mean any harm. Everyone is just trying to understand everything that has happened; that's all."

"People look at me like I'm to blame for everything that's happened."

"It'll be all right. I promise you."

"It hurts, Pastor Dave. They made me feel like an outsider. I don't feel like family."

"Don't feel that way, Alicia. You *are* family. Don't let the attitudes of a few taint your view of all of us. Remember what the Lord has done in your life here."

"You're right, Pastor."

"I wanted to talk to you about getting more involved in the church."

"How so? I'm already helping out in the children's ministry."

"I know, and you're doing a wonderful job. I would like for you to get involved with the young adult ministry."

"I don't know, Pastor Dave… with all that's going on with Jerry…."

"The youth would benefit greatly from your life's experience, and *especially* with everything that's going on with Jerry. The young people need living examples of what God can do in their lives. I can think of no better example than you. Just think about it, please."

"All right, Pastor, I will."

"Let me know what you decide."

Alicia nodded and walked away not feeling any better. She headed out of the lobby to wait by Jerry's truck. Before she could get there, a woman touched her arm. Alicia turned and smiled at her walk-in buddy. They greeted each other as they walked into the church on Wednesday nights. She was in her forties, moderately dressed with slacks and a shirt.

"Hi, Ingra."

"Hello, Alicia. How are you doing?"

Alicia shrugged.

"Your emotions must be going up and down like a roller coaster. If there is anything I can do, please, don't hesitate to ask. I'll be praying for you and your family."

"Thank you." Alicia smiled and turned to walk away.

"Alicia," Julie Gucciani called.

Alicia stopped and turned around.

Julie squeezed Alicia with a one-arm hug, and her two-year-old daughter clipped to her hip. She was short with dark, thick, long hair, and wore black tights and a long, stained T-shirt. "Alicia, I missed you today in nursery."

"I just didn't feel up to it. You know, with all that's going on."

"How are you doing?"

"Okay."

"You want to come over to my house and hang out?"

Alicia smiled. "No, thank you, but thanks for asking."

Julie gave Alicia a look as if she wanted to push her, but she held her peace. "I gotta get this girl home. I ran out of Pampers. Call me if you want to hang out, girl, anytime."

Julie smiled and walked away. Alicia felt encouraged. God had sent two angels to cheer her up. Their good gestures alone made her feel better.

Alicia's phone buzzed. She read the message. "Julie, wait up!" Alicia shouted.

Julie stopped and turned around.

"Is that offer to hang out still on?"

Julie smiled. "Of course, it is. I have a house full of kids, and my entire family comes over for Sunday dinner. Not only will you have a good time, but you're going to get stuffed with a full-course Italian meal."

"That sounds wonderful. Can I ride with you? I came with Jerry and Nancy. She just texted me that they have some meeting to go to."

"Sure. I have plenty of room, if you don't mind a minivan full of kids."

"Not at all."

"Come on. Hal is waiting for me."

"Thank you for inviting me."

"Girl, I've tried to get you to come over for months. You're always welcome."

* * *

Jerry could not bring himself to leave the church as he'd

been told to do. It had been forty-five minutes since Dave had dismissed the service and ten since he had disappeared out of the lobby. Jerry decided to crash the meeting he'd been barred from. He felt he had something to say, and he was tired of sitting on the sidelines while other people decided his fate. He grabbed Nancy's hand and marched into the conference room next to Dave's office.

The room was spacious, with a contemporary décor. The tempest raging in the room surprised Jerry. The pastors, elders, and executive board vigorously argued and bickered with each other. The group of twenty quieted down and stared at him with surprise.

Dave raised his brow. "Jerry, you shouldn't be here."

"Why not, my friend? There is no bylaw that says I can't attend. I think my place is here. I want to plead my case among my friends. I'll abide by whatever y'all decide."

Dave nodded. "Of course. Have a seat."

One of the men yielded his chair to Nancy. She sat and folded her hands in her lap.

Jerry stood behind her and glanced at the headlines. "RACIST PAST CATCHES UP TO PROMINENT ORANGE GROVE MAN." Another headline grabbed his attention: "LOCAL MAN TIED TO MURDER OF CIVIL RIGHTS ACTIVIST IN THE '60s." Copies of the *Orange County View* were sprawled on the table. Jerry looked at Gary Duncan.

Gary shrugged. "There was nothing I could do."

Jerry looked into the faces of the men he knew, trusted, and loved. He tried to look directly into each of their eyes, but they turned away, hung their heads, or glanced at the table. He had mentored some of these men and had endorsed them for their positions. Now, some of his friends wouldn't even look his way.

"Jerry, if you want to stay, fine, but I don't think Nancy should be here," Dave said.

Jerry patted Nancy's shoulders. "Don't worry about her. You know she's a tough old gal. Now, let's get down to business."

Frank Fisk waved a copy of the paper. "What are we going to do about this?"

"We'll have to get a handle on this before it gets out of hand," Gary said.

"People are protesting outside, the media is all over us, and the members are nervous. It's already out of hand." Frank looked at Jerry. "You should step down."

Gary leaned back with his hands folded. "The media scrutiny will get a lot worse. I've recused myself as editor because of the obvious conflict of interest, so I don't have any input as to what the paper prints. This story is going national. Do we want that kind of attention?"

"Let's not worry about that now," Dave said. "I want to know how we can help our brother. Frank, you're the lawyer. Give us your take."

Frank cleared his throat. "Well, California won't press charges or arrest Jerry. It'll have to be in the state where the alleged crime took place. But, if Alabama decides to indict, Jerry could be charged with first-degree murder, manslaughter, conspiracy, kidnapping, accessory, accessory after the fact, and they can top it off with a hate crime. There are no statutes of limitation on murder. But, since the incident happened so long ago, the case seems weak. It will depend on what evidence and witnesses the state has."

Gary glanced at Jerry, then the board. "Timothy Smith will keep the pressure on. He came to us to run the story. I tried to squash it, but Smith did an end run around me and got the story printed. I know he's been pressuring the DA to bring charges against you, Jer, and I suspect he'll do the same in Alabama."

The room fell silent.

Jerry squeezed Nancy's shoulder. "Listen, I'm not worried about going to jail. There might come a time when you may have to make a decision to protect the church." He looked at Dave. "Who knows how far Timothy will go to get me? I think he'll bring down anyone he can—my family, friends, my business, and this church, if he thinks it'll hurt me."

"We'll deal with that when we have to, Jerry," Dave said.

"Jerry is right. We must take steps to protect the church. That's why you should step down," Frank said.

Dave tossed a glare toward Frank. "That's enough, Frank. We're not throwing our brother to the wolves."

"Dave, if the DA charges me, I won't allow the church to be dragged into my mess."

Dave squinted and bit his lip. "I won't let it come to that."

* * *

Alicia stepped out of Dave's Ford Explorer and watched him slide into the narrow parking space. She had reluctantly come after pleading with him that this was a bad idea. Dave had insisted he needed her support. Alicia wished she'd been more forceful with her refusal. This was a bad idea.

Dave locked the door and looked toward the Krispy Kreme in the same lot. "Want a donut and coffee, my treat? We have thirty minutes to kill."

"Sure." Alicia chuckled at the way Dave fidgeted and looked around with nervous eyes as they strolled through the parking lot. He couldn't have stood out more if he had hung a sign around his neck that read, "Nervous white boy." They grabbed their orders and sat on a graffiti-decorated wall that was hip-high on the corner of Crenshaw and Martin Luther King Jr. Boulevard. "Don't worry, Dave. This isn't the hood." She pointed. "It's a couple miles that way."

Dave shrugged and bit his donut.

"In fact, Crenshaw Boulevard divides the upper-middle-class from the middle and lower- class neighborhoods. My uncle lives at the top of those hills." She pointed. "Many black professionals, business owners, athletes, and movie stars live up there."

Dave looked at the hills. "I didn't know that."

"Not too far from here, about a mile south, is the famous Crenshaw High School. Several movies were shot there. This area is not as bad as people think." Alicia looked around and sipped from her cup. "I don't see his car."

Dave checked his watch. "I confirmed our appointment this morning."

"Knowing him, he'll probably be late on purpose." Alicia bit her donut.

Dave stood and tossed his cup into a trash can. "Let's go inside and wait for him."

"Why are you doing this, Pastor Dave?"

"I know I'm going to make a fool out of myself, but I have to try to get him to reconsider what he's doing. I don't mean to be indifferent to you or your family's feelings. I know Jerry did a horrible thing, and he deserves to pay for his actions. But, he's found the Lord. He's lived a good life all of these years. Doesn't that count for anything?"

"You're preaching to the choir, Pastor."

"I have to get Timothy to see that Jerry has spent his entire Christian life in service to the Lord, his family, and community. Timothy has to see that means something."

"I commend your heart in this, Pastor. I really do. But, my uncle will not see it that way. He sees the man who murdered his father. Did you know that Jerry almost strangled him to death?"

Dave furrowed. "No, I didn't."

"It happened after Jerry had killed my grandfather. One day, Jerry tripped Madea in the middle of the street. Uncle Tim attacked Jerry—Gus, then. He was only fourteen at the time. Jerry grabbed him by his throat. If the sheriff hadn't happened by, Jerry would have killed him." Dave looked away and shook his head. "I still have to try." He sighed. "Who knows? God might work a miracle."

"It's going to take a miracle, Pastor, a big one. Let's get this over with."

The smirk on Timothy's face when he walked in twenty minutes past their scheduled time told Alicia he was late for no good reason other than to be antagonistic. He frowned when he saw her. "I'm surprised to see you here with him."

"I asked her to come with me. I hope you don't mind," Dave said.

Timothy motioned to a set of chairs by his desk. "What can I do for you, Reverend?"

"Please, call me Dave. Thank you for seeing me." Dave cleared his throat. "I can't imagine how you must feel."

"No, you can't." Timothy cut him off with a sharpness that surprised Alicia. "You can't in your wildest dreams know how I feel, unless you've witnessed your father savagely murdered, hung on a tree, and lit on fire in front of your eyes, only to find out that the killer has been living under your nose for the past fifty years. So, no, you don't know how I feel.

"You can't know how I feel, because you're not black. You are going to get into your car and drive back to your *white* life, where everything is so nice, like sugar and spice. No, you don't know how I feel."

Dave shifted in his chair. "No, I don't. But, people change by God's grace."

Timothy leaped to his feet. "I see. You're here to plead for your friend's freedom. You know what really infuriates me? White people like you, who always come to the defense of some murdering, hateful devil. You white people never come to the defense of millions of black people who have wrongly suffered at the hands of evil men, like your friend! I can't even enumerate the atrocities that black people have endured from good-hearted, well-meaning, white folk. Why don't you ever plead for the black people who have been hurt by the hands of people like your friend?"

"I didn't mean to imply…."

"No, you didn't mean it. You never consider how the loved ones of the victims feel…." Timothy sat and looked directly at Dave with tear-filled, bitter eyes. "What we go through, how our lives suffer, and what we have to live with after we bury our loved ones. But, you sure are quick to come to the defense of a guilty white man." He leaned back in his chair, pressing his fingers together, and looked at Alicia. "You ought to know better."

Dave stood. His face flushed deep red, and his eyes were glassy and blank. "Thank you for seeing me." He nodded at Alicia and walked out.

Alicia stood and shook her head. "That was cold, Uncle

Tim."

"I know that man and Adams have helped you, but that doesn't erase his guilt."

"It does before God, and that's all that matters," Alicia said.

Timothy smirked. "We'll see about that."

Alicia walked out and found Dave brooding by the truck. "Are you all right?"

"I couldn't defend my friend."

"You weren't supposed to. God didn't call you to defend him before my uncle. Jesus has already done that. Remember, Romans 8:33: 'Who shall bring a charge against God's elect? God is the one who justifies.' Let God deal with my uncle."

Dave smiled. "Yeah, you're right. Let's go home."

Chapter Thirty-two

Chad read the file as he walked across the office to his cubical. He was thrilled at what he had found. Katie lived not fifty miles from the hotbed of the civil rights struggle in Alabama. The stories were horrific, but the courage people showed—black and white—inspired him. He looked up, casually, toward the conference room. He dropped the file on his desk and eased closer to get a better look. His brows drew in, in disbelief.

He was surprised to see his senior editor, Brian Duncan, escorting District Attorney Sarah Cooper into the small room. The wall-height glass window gave him a full view. His jaw dropped opened when Timothy Smith pranced in and dominated the room. Clearly, he was in charge, and Brian and Sarah nodded their heads listening to whatever he was saying. Chad knew he had to find out what that was about.

* * *

Checking all the doors before I bedded down for the night, I sat in my chair, thinking about everything that had happened and how God had worked his grace, especially in me. I had asked the Lord to help me with my trust issues with white people, and boy, had He, and in a manner I could never have conceived. God used the murderer of my husband not only to witness to my granddaughter but also as the instrument to break me free from my prejudices.

The phone rang. I braced for bad news. Late-night calls usually meant trouble. "Hello."

"Hello, Mama, this is Dorothy."

"Is everything all right?"

"Yes. Can I come over and talk to you? I know it's late, but this is important."

There goes my plan for a good night's sleep. "Sure, come over. I'll be waiting."

"Thanks, Mama. I really need to talk to you. I'll see you in a few minutes."

Laying the receiver on the base, I wondered what she wanted to talk about. Maybe she finally decided to divorce Timothy. I loved my son, but it's about time she did something about him. Lord knows, she'd put up with a lot of his mess. I could tell God was revealing Himself to her, but she had that analytical mind—always had to think things out—analyzing, deliberating, and investigating all aspects of theology. I just hoped her reasoning led her to a simple faith in Jesus.

The phone rang. *Who in the world is this?* I sighed, reaching for the phone. "Hello."

"Hello, Madea, guess what?"

"Slow down, child. What is it?"

"I'm picking Deshon up tomorrow. Mama is letting me take him."

"I know. She already told me."

"I can't believe it's really happening. God is so good. I doubted this moment would ever happen."

"Like I told you, child, you have to trust the Lord and be patient. The Lord knows how to soften a person's heart. You'll get some use out of those parenting classes you took at church.

You thought they were a waste of time. The preparations have paid off, haven't they?"

"Yes, they have."

"What are you going to do about his school?"

"I've been checking out the schools around here, public and Christian. Practically every church has a grade school, some up to twelfth grade. I've found a daycare, too. A lady from the church runs one out of her house."

"Good thing you started looking."

"I never thought it would happen so fast."

"God works as He pleases."

"Yes, He does. I'll stop by tomorrow after I pick Deshon up."

"Okay, child, I'll see you tomorrow."

After I had hung up the phone, my hands shot up toward heaven. "Lord, You have made her into a virtuous woman. Maybe You can send her a husband — just a thought."

Dorothy's Mercedes pulled into the driveway, interrupting my musing. She came in, collapsed her umbrella, and set it by the door. We both sat on the couch.

"What's on your mind, Dorothy?"

"I've been thinking about what happened between you and Jerry. In fact, I can't get it out of my head — how you just forgave that man."

"It was the love of Jesus that compelled me to forgive him."

"I don't understand how you can just simply let go of what he did to you."

"It wasn't that simple. But, Jerry is someone whom Christ died for."

"I don't understand it, but it got me thinking. My life is so messed up. Most of the time, I sit on my balcony alone, listening to my music or watching my cooking shows, trying to drown out my loneliness with bottle after bottle of wine. But, if God can change Jerry, couldn't He change Timothy? Couldn't He save my marriage?"

"Yes, He can. Jerry is proof of that. But the Lord is concerned about changing you."

Dorothy shook her head. "I don't understand."

"All have sinned before the Lord—even you, Dorothy."

"I'm not a bad person. I go to church... sometimes. I try to do the right thing. I've never done anything as bad as Jerry."

"Your problem, like so many others, is that you compare yourselves to other people instead of to God's standards of goodness. That's why a person like Jerry can humble himself before God and find forgiveness. Why do you go to church?"

Dorothy leaned back. "Truthfully, the only reason I ever went to church was for Timothy's career. I've always questioned the existence of God. My experiences with churches have always been from a black civil rights perspective. Jesus was defined in terms of black liberation theology, though I never saw anyone liberated. Those people were just like me, unhappy with their lives. The preachers just told us to live the best lives we could, which meant supporting social causes, which made sense to me. Though I questioned a God that allowed needless suffering, I believed in doing good for the needy.

"Church was just a formality, a meeting place for political and social networking. I pretended to be the supportive wife. I'm tired of acting. I want something real in my life. What am I supposed to do?"

That question made me smile. I spent the next hour explaining the Gospel in as simple terms as I could, which always turned out to be profound when you thought about it.

"Mama, I want to know the man who affected the entire world."

"Pastor Dave called earlier and invited me to come to their Easter service on Sunday. Why don't you come with me?"

Dorothy nodded.

"Let's pray."

* * *

Alicia grabbed her purse from the front seat and locked the car. She took Deshon's hand and walked toward the church lobby. Cars streamed in and out of the parking lot. She was glad she'd come to the late service. It was easier to get a good parking spot from those leaving the 8 a.m. service. Glancing both ways, she crossed the main drive. Deshon took off.

"Deshon!" Alicia shouted. She darted after him and grabbed his hand. "Don't run off like that. There are too many cars around here."

"Come on, Mommy. I want to go to church."

"You like Children's Church, don't you?" Reaching for the glass door, she turned around and frowned. "What in the world?"

Six black coach buses roared in front of the church and screeched to a halt. An army of protestors — old, young, male, female, and even children — filed out, peacefully, carrying signs labeled, "Justice for Gregory Smith." They chanted, "No justice, no peace."

Timothy stepped off the bus with a look in his eyes as if he were Moses leading the children of Israel through the Red Sea. He stepped out of line as Alicia walked toward him. "What do you want?"

"Why are you doing this, Uncle Tim?"

"Because that man you call your spiritual daddy should be rotting in a prison cell."

"Your wife is in there."

Timothy's brows went up as he glanced toward the church. "Dorothy's in there?"

"Yes. She's in there, worshiping the Lord. That's the good that has come out of all of this. People are discovering the love of the Lord."

"That doesn't change anything. My father is still dead. Adams still has to pay for his crime." Timothy postured as if he would head for the door. "You know what, I think I'm going to march in there and scream out to everyone what kind of man he is. I think people should know they have a murderer in their midst. What do you think about that?"

Alicia grabbed Deshon's hand. "On judgment day, everybody is going to reckon with God, including you, Uncle Tim. You won't be able to point to Jerry, accusing him of his sins. God is going to hold you accountable for your sins. And what are you going to do on that day? I'll tell you what I'm going to do, what Jerry and every other Christian is going to do."

"What's that?"

"Thank God that mercy triumphs over justice," she said and walked away.

* * *

I followed the usher down the side aisle to the front of the sanctuary. I had called Alicia and told her that we were at the church. She'd told me she just arrived, and she'd meet us in the sanctuary. Dorothy, Ruby, and Joseph followed me to our seats. I'd decided to make the eleven o'clock service, because I didn't want to rush to make the early service. I was surprised to see Maxine.

"What are you doing here on an Easter morning?" I said, giving her a big hug.

"I felt the Lord really wanted me to be here this morning."

She squeezed my hand. Jerry walked in the side door and embraced me for a good while. Nancy followed and gave me a warm hug, just as long.

The sanctuary fell silent as Dave took the podium. He looked around for a moment, walked over and whispered to the worship leader, and took his seat. The worship leader played his guitar softly. Members of the worship team trickled back onto the stage and softly harmonized, "Shout to the Lord." The orchestra joined the chorus, and the sanctuary erupted in a sweet, angelic worship that swept me into the presence of the Lord. I shut my eyes and basked in the peace, joy, and the love of my Heavenly Father. I glanced over and smiled; Dorothy had her hands raised, singing to the Lord.

Alicia slid next to me and whispered, "Uncle Tim is outside with a lot of people, protesting. I think he's planning on disrupting the service."

I smiled and gave her a gentle squeeze. "It's going to be all right. The Lord has everything under control, even that fool. Enjoy the worship."

The song ended, and everyone took his or her seats. The energy in the auditorium charged my anticipation. I looked forward to hearing what Dave had to say. He stood behind the podium with a solemn stare. The room quieted to a dead silence.

I returned Dave's nod with a smile. He tapped his iPad and looked across the auditorium. Grabbing both sides of the podium, he stared down for a moment. He looked around, smiling at some, winking at others, and nodding to most. He folded the iPad in the leather case.

"The title of today's message is 'The Color of Redemption.'" He pursed his lips. "What color is redemption?" He let out a long sigh. "Our perfect little world has been unsettled, hasn't it? The revelation of Jerry's past has shaken all of us. I've heard from many of you over these past few weeks. Some of you resent that we have been dragged into a race situation not of our doing. The reality is racism is a problem, and sadly, it's a problem in the church of our Lord. I think it's time we have an honest, non-partisan talk about race."

Dave looked toward the back of the room and nodded. I turned my head. Timothy stood along the back wall, squinting, with his hands folded. A troubling feeling settled deep in the pit of my stomach. I turned around and fixed my gaze on Dave.

"I have to start by confessing my own feelings on race. They've not always been Christian. We are a family of diverse people. How can we be prejudiced against one another, when we all have the same depraved nature? How can we continue to be prejudiced when we are born of the same heavenly Father? This notion that the races shouldn't mix is not only absurd, but it is just plain stupid. Think about it. We are exalting one skin color over another. God condemns all flesh as evil. 'Flesh and blood will not enter the kingdom of God.'

"When we hold to prejudices or racist views, we fail to recognize the work of the cross." Dave thought for a moment. "Communion is about our oneness in Christ, not our differences. Jerry, Katie, could both of you step up here, please?"

Dave motioned, and an usher rushed over with a shiny brass communion plate and cup.

Baffled, I took Jerry's hand and rose from my seat. Dave took the tray, placed it on the communion table in front of the podium, and uncovered a large loaf of bread. He took a brass picture and poured grape juice into the brass cup.

Directing us to the side of the communion table, he held out the platter holding the loaf of bread. "Jerry, could you take a piece?" Jerry took the platter, pulled a piece from the loaf, and held the bread out to me, waiting until I had broken off a piece. "This loaf represents the body of Jesus, which was broken for our sins. We all know this. But it also represents the common bond we all share through His body. He took a piece. "Please, eat."

I slid the piece of bread into my mouth, realizing what Dave was demonstrating. Dave took the cup and motioned for Jerry to drink. He took a big swallow and handed the cup to me. I drank, handed the cup back to Dave, and received Jerry's embrace. I felt an eternal bond to Jerry like never before.

"Now, if we had to eat from the same body and drink the same blood to be saved, then are we not one? Are we not the same family? Thank you," Dave said.

Jerry escorted me back to my seat and sat beside me. I grabbed his hand and held it with a gentle grip.

"If we had to eat and drink from the same source, Jesus, to be accepted by God, then how can we be prejudiced against someone of a different color who ate from the same bread? John tells us in his letter, 'Whoever believes that Jesus is the Christ is born of God, and everyone who loves Him who begot also loves Him who is begotten of Him.' How can we not love whoever is born of God, whether they are white, black, red, or yellow? If they come from the same heart of our Heavenly Father, how can we not accept them? To see your black brothers any differently begs the question: 'How do you see God?' I think you get my point.

"Racial reconciliation starts with us, the church. Heck, we should be leading the world by our example of unity. Sadly, we haven't—we've followed the world on race and have been poor examples of God's love. But, if we model the kind of love and forgiveness we've seen between these two, what an incredible witness for our Lord that will be to the world. Let's pray."

I looked around but didn't see Timothy. I'd hoped the message would have opened his eyes. I'd hoped the strong presence of love and peace here would have touched his heart. But, as I glanced at Dorothy, I was grateful for the lives God had touched.

Dave finished praying and nodded. An army of ushers filed down the aisles, carrying communion trays. "Let's share communion together."

Chapter Thirty-three

The plane began its descent into Birmingham International Airport. Jerry pulled a handkerchief from his pocket, wiped the sweat from his hands, and blotted his forehead. He'd faced tougher situations than this one. Why was he so nervous? He was used to being in control. Here he was anything but in control. He was out of his element in many ways.

Nancy stared at him as if she had met him for the first time. "I can't get over how smooth your face is," she said, rubbing his cheeks. "This is the first time I've ever seen you without your beard." She stroked his face. "What's wrong?"

"I wish I'd kept the reservations at the hotel. I'd feel better staying in Birmingham."

"Maxine insisted we stay at her house, but we can stay at the hotel if you want."

"No, that's okay." Jerry took Nancy's hand and squeezed. "It's funny."

"What?"

"It's awkward staying in the neighborhood I once terrorized. How will they receive me after all these years—especially after all the things I used to do to them?"

"You'll be fine. I trust they'll see the Lord in you."

Jerry shook his head.

"Katie said the farm was breathtaking."

"I wouldn't know. It was dark the last time I was there."

"Well, this time, you might get to see it in the daylight. I'm looking forward to it."

Jerry stared out the window, grimaced, and turned to Nancy.

"What? What's wrong, Jerry?"

He leaned in. "I didn't plan it this way, but this is the first day of June."

"Why does that matter?"

"This is the anniversary of… you know… the very day."

"Oh, my," Nancy said. She leaned back and stared ahead. "Oh, my Lord."

The plane touched down softly and, unlike LAX, taxied right up to the gate. He couldn't stall his fate. He corralled everyone through the baggage area and out the door to a waiting black stretch Hummer. A crew of skycaps trailed behind them, pushing several carts of luggage. The Hummer took a short tour through the city at Nancy's request. Birmingham's skyline was small, with only a few modern buildings. He'd forgotten how small the city was.

"Look at how narrow the freeway is—only four lanes," Alicia said to Nancy. "I'm so used to the eight-lane freeways in California."

The metropolitan landscape quickly gave way to the rural scenery of Route 7. Jerry had forgotten the beauty of the Alabamian countryside. Fields drifted by in a quiet, scenic view. People waved from the porches of their meager ranch-style houses or old mobile homes sparsely spaced apart. Children stopped their play and waved. Seniors rocked in their chairs and stared as the Hummer drove by.

Larger homes sat far off the road on large plots of land, some of them too far back to make out any details. Alicia and Nancy snapped pictures of the occasional barn and silo and gawked at cows and horses lazily grazing in the fields. The forty-five-minute drive from Birmingham to Blount City passed slowly for Jerry.

A foul stench seeped in. Alicia covered her nose. "Ugh, what's that smell?"

Jerry laughed. "We've must have passed a pig farm."

Katie looked around with surprise. "Did we pass the land?"

Ruby nodded. She knocked on the window, "Driver, turn here."

The Hummer turned on M Street and made a slow trek through the black part of town.

Katie stoically looked around. "Not much has changed here. I can't believe these same dilapidated houses are standing, and people are still living in them. They need to tear them down. They're an eyesore." She turned to Ruby. "People still doing the same things they did when I was here, sitting on their porches like they have nothing better to do. There are a few brick homes, and at least the streets are paved, but they still need sidewalks." The Hummer stopped in front of a white, two-story frame house with brown trim and a white picket fence. The lawn and bushes were neat and trimmed. "The house looks good."

Alicia leaned toward the window. "Whose house is this?"

"It was your great Aunt Louise's," Ruby answered. "Do you want to go in, Mama?"

"Maybe later," Katie answered.

Alicia sat back. "Who lives here now?"

"No one," Ruby said. "It's a guest house for Maxine's church—for when guest ministers visit. Driver, you can drive on."

Jerry squinted with surprise. He glanced at Nancy.

Nancy leaned forward. "Katie, I thought we were staying at

your daughter's place?"

"We are. She lives five miles out of town—on the farm we used to live on."

Nancy sat back. Jerry squeezed her hand. A deep-pitted feeling lodged in his stomach. How could he stay at the place he'd decimated, let alone sleep there? How would Katie feel? He could pretty much guess how Ruby felt. He shook as they drove over the railroad tracks.

"They still haven't smoothed the tracks out," Katie said.

Nancy's eyes widened. "It's so different—the two sides of the tracks."

Ruby chuckled. "Welcome to the South."

"It's like two different worlds," Nancy said.

"Yeah, and they have sidewalks over here, too," Ruby said, chuckling.

"Downtown looks the same," Jerry commented to Katie. "The bank is new."

"The City Hall complex was built within the last ten years," Ruby said.

Nancy looked at Jerry and glanced out the window. "Is that the café you owned?"

Jerry nodded. "Driver, stop here, please."

"Yes, sir," rang from the front.

The Hummer came to a soft stop. Jerry stepped out and gazed up and down the street. His eyes fell on the sign with a wary stare. *Charlie's Place.* It brought up many memories of his childhood, ones he'd rather forget. The building was old, and the brick painted white. The front of the café had a light-green awning and dark-green windowsills and door frames.

Nancy squeezed his hand. "It's quaint but nice."

"That's the name my father gave it."

"Charlie's Place?"

Jerry nodded.

Alicia filed out of the Hummer. "It looks so small."

"I want to see it. Let's go inside." Nancy took pictures with her camera phone like a giddy tourist. "Come on, Jerry. I want to see the inside."

Alicia peeked in the Hummer. "Come on, don't you want to see the café?" She asked the others. She straightened up and shrugged why they didn't budge.

Jerry leaned into the Hummer. "You want to come in?"

Katie shook her head. "That's all right, Jerry. We'll stay in the car—too many bad memories."

He nodded and walked in.

The café had bright colors and modern tables and chairs. Historic pictures of the town and notable people hung all around the café's walls. A mixed group, white and black, young and old, filled the café. They sat mostly segregated, whites with whites and blacks with blacks. The seniors owned the room. Some ate and talked; others played checkers or cards; a few women knitted and gossiped. The food smelled delicious, just as he remembered it.

An old pair of eyes studied Jerry. "Gus, is that you?"

Jerry turned and stared at the elderly man. He didn't recognize him. He stood five-two, with thinning, white hair, his black-framed glasses resting on his deeply wrinkled face. The man glided his tongue across his dried lips. He wore a tan shirt with brown stripes tucked into brown, double-knit slacks that were held up by brown suspenders.

Jerry opened his mouth with a wide grin. "Lester, you old son-of-a-gun."

"Gus, it's really you. How have you been? How long has it

been?"

Jerry gave him a quick hug. "Over thirty years—more than that. So, tell me, what's been going on with you and the old gang?"

"Most of 'em is dead. A black gal runs this place now. It was hard to take at first, but she lets us old folks hang out here. Yep, things sure has changed around here," Lester said, studying his face. "You've hardly changed."

"Thank the Lord," Jerry said.

Lester squinted. "That's right. You haven't seen the changes around here since you found religion and left. Well, some things changed for the good, and some things changed for the worse, if you know what I mean. Say, where'd you go after you left here?"

"California. I set up a place just like this one."

"Well, what do ya say about that?" Lester fell silent. "You remember that night?" The question surprised Jerry. They had vowed never to bring it up. Lester had the roughest time coping with what they had done. Guilt had driven him to drink, and his face bore the marks. "The Lord has forgiven me for that night. Let him forgive you."

"I go to church every Sunday. I try to do good, you know, be a good Christian. I don't bother the Negras anymore. Nobody bothers them people these days. Like I said, a lot of things has changed around here."

"That's not enough, Lester. You have to be born again, washed by the blood of Jesus."

"Same old Gus."

"I'm not that hateful man anymore. The Lord has changed me."

"You preached that born-again stuff after you got religion.

Was that how you coped?"

"Yes, the Lord gave me peace in knowing I was forgiven. And, Lester, a wonderful thing has happened since then...."

"Honey," Nancy interrupted.

"Honey, this is an old running buddy of mine, Lester. Lester, this is Nancy, my wife."

Lester's eyes widened. "Wife? I'd never thought you'd get married, Gus."

Alicia chuckled. "Gus."

Nancy, seeing how Lester glared at Alicia, smiled and grabbed his hand. "It's a pleasure to meet you, Lester. I'd sure like to hear some old stories about Jerry."

Lester laughed. "Oh, I could tell you a lot about this ol' boy here."

"That won't be necessary," Jerry protested.

"I'd like to hear some of those stories, too," Alicia chimed in.

Lester looked at Alicia and then looked at Jerry.

"Oh, I'm sorry, Lester." Jerry hesitated, conflicted about whether he should tell Lester who Alicia was. Lester needed to know the reconciliation the Lord had brought about and its fruit. "Lester, this here is Smith's granddaughter." Lester's face flushed red. "That's the wonderful thing I was gonna tell you. In fact, Smith's widow is out in the car. Would you like to speak to her? It would do your soul good."

Lester's jaw tightened, and his eyes shifted from side to side. His tongue grazed across his lips. His eyes fixed open as if he'd seen a ghost. "Smith's widow... here?"

"Yeah, she's out in the car. About a year ago, the Lord brought us together, and she forgave me, Lester. She forgave me with the pure love of the Lord. She'll forgive you, too."

"I gotta go. It's been good seeing you." Lester grabbed his cane and limped out of the café as fast as he could.

Alicia touched Jerry's back. "What was that all about?"

"A man wrestling with his soul," Jerry said.

Nancy whispered, "Was he with you that night?"

Jerry nodded.

"Thank God Ruby didn't see him."

Jerry watched Lester walk away, "Yeah, thank God. I've seen enough. Let's go."

Chapter Thirty-four

I had been true to my word, a vow I held as solemn as my commitment to the Lord—never to set foot on my farm again. I deeply regretted that now. As the Hummer turned onto Route 7, the desire to look upon my land overwhelmed me. It would only be a few minutes until we arrived at the driveway, but I yearned to see the two dirt ruts that led up the steep incline overgrown with weeds and shrubberies.

The Hummer slowed and turned onto a concrete drive. I looked at Ruby and smiled. A pair of tall, oyster-white brick posts with a black wrought-iron gate guided us through. It wasn't as steep as I'd remembered, and it was twice as wide, lined with neatly trimmed shrubberies, bushes, and oyster brick light posts spaced every thirty feet along both sides of the drive.

I wasn't disappointed. The land still boasted its spectacular beauty. Acres and acres of knee-high green grass, sprinkled with clusters of white azaleas and pink geraniums were just as I remembered—just as God had clothed them. *I feel like You arranged all of this especially for me, Lord.* "Oh, how I miss this land," I softly whispered.

A large, oyster-white brick home covered the very spot of my old house. The drive circled around in front of a three-car attached garage and had a sculpted waterfall in the center. Neatly trimmed trees and shrubberies decorated the well-groomed green lawn. *Exquisite.*

The Hummer crept by a line of cars parked in the driveway,

two deep. When the truck came to a soft stop, a crowd awaited us by the old oak tree. I couldn't take my eyes off of the small memorial park. A large tombstone enclosed by a black chain amazed me. "You were right, Ruby. It's a beautiful tribute to your father."

"I told you, you should have come sooner." Ruby smiled and stepped out of the Hummer.

Alicia followed with Deshon. Nancy kissed Jerry on the cheek and exited the car.

Looking at Jerry's face made think of the monster fifty years ago. "I don't know whether to like or hate that you've shaved your beard. Why did you shave your beard off?"

"I just felt it was time for a change. I didn't realize people would be so bothered."

"Thank God I know you're saved," I said, then chuckled. "Are you ready to do this?"

He looked over at the gravesite. "The last time I was here, I was full of hate. This time, I'll stand under that tree as a tribute to God's love and grace."

Patting his hand, I stepped out. Thunderous applause greeted me. White faces blended among the crowd, to my surprise. A white man dressed in a black suit and white clerical collar stood next to Henry. The crowd of whites and blacks seemed comfortable with each other. Everyone dressed in suits, dresses, and hats as if they were attending an outdoor Sunday service.

Maxine, dressed in an olive dress and hat, hugged me with a jubilant smile. "Thank you, Lord. You brought my mama home," she shouted with a gush of tears pouring from her eyes. "I know you didn't want a lot of fanfare, but I couldn't resist throwing a little something for you. After all, it's been fifty years."

I smirked and hugged Maxine.

The applause abruptly stopped when Jerry stepped out of the Hummer. Aghast, people stared and whispered to one another. Faces went from curious to dismayed. I was amazed they knew who he was after all these years.

Henry stood by the gravestone, poised, holding a yellow notepad. He wore a black suit with a white clerical collar. He stared at Jerry with gritted teeth and then looked down with pursed lips. "This is a mixed blessing." He spoke in a strong Alabamian twang. "I thank God we're celebrating Mother Smith's homecoming instead of her homegoing."

He paused and looked at Jerry. "I have to confess; I'm having trouble with this... with him... with you. God sho' know how to test us, don't He? I was fine with the notion of Mother Smith forgiving you, just as long as you was twenty-five hundred miles away.

"Deacon Smith was my mentor and my friend. But, if we believe that Jesus died for all men, then that means He died for this man." Henry cast his eyes at Jerry. "Paul said, 'God was in Jesus, reconciling the world to Himself, not counting our sins against us.' Paul himself beat, tortured, and jailed saints. But God had mercy on him and saved him. So, maybe God saved this man, too. And we're just going to have to accept it."

"He did save this man. I can testify to that," I proclaimed.

"Amen, Mother Smith. If God can forgive him, so should we... I do." He walked over and shook Jerry's hand.

Henry nodded, and I stepped forward. "I swore before God that I'd never set foot on this land. Nonetheless, under the very tree my Gregory was lynched from...." My lips quivered, trying to choke back the grief overtaking me. The memories—all of them—rushed my mind. Suddenly, I was thrust back to that day.

"Take your time, Mother Smith," rang out from the crowd.

"I imagine in heaven we are going to meet all kinds of saints who have committed all kinds of unspeakable acts." I paused and looked at the gravestone. "God had shown Gregory that He had to change men's hearts before society could change. Looking at y'all, he was right. Y'all are examples of that change."

Jerry stepped to me, wrapped his arm around me, and let out a loud, joyous wail. He wiped his eyes. "I apologize for losing my composure, but every time I think of the unconditional love this lady has shown me, I can't help but break down and cry. God is so merciful."

I patted Jerry's back. "It's all right, brother."

Jerry adjusted his hat. "I hated all of you. That's how I was raised—to hate anyone not white. The way I overcame hate was by God's love. This is the kind of love the world needs to see. But it starts with *us*—God's people, white, black, red, and yellow." Jerry stepped back and hugged Nancy.

Henry wiped his eyes and stepped forward. "What can you say after that? I want to acknowledge Reverend Zachery Jeffers and the saints of Pleasant Grove Southern Baptist Church for coming out to support us. Reverend Jeffers, say a few words?"

Reverend Jeffers waved his hand. "I'm just glad to be here to support y'all. I'm blessed to see what God is doing with your mama. Jerry, you was before my time by a few years. I know about the old you, but I'm really glad to see the new Jerry."

Henry hugged the reverend and turned toward the crowd. "There's plenty of food in the house. Stay around and stuff yourselves, and fellowship with one another. Go in God's grace and peace and love."

The crowd dispersed toward the house. A few people lingered around the gravesite for a few minutes, hugging, crying, and rejoicing with one another, and one by one they moved into the house for the repast. I stayed behind with Jerry and Nancy, talking to people who were anxious to talk to us.

I rejoiced at the work of grace the Lord had done in the hearts of everyone. That's what I'd prayed for the most, that people would be touched by God's love. Looking toward the house, thoughts of happier times, of times with Gregory, flooded my mind.

Henry touched my back. "Is everything all right, Mama?"

"I was just thinking."

"What about?"

I came here thinking I was going to show y'all something about reconciliation. But, God is already doing his work."

"Maybe that's what the Lord wanted you to see — what He had shown Deacon Smith many years ago. We started this fellowship about five years ago. Pastor Jeffers had it on his heart to reach out to black folks. He and his congregation come to our church regularly. But you and Jerry's reconciliation testifies of the Lord's grace in a big way. People's faith was strengthened by what they saw in y'all."

"I wish I'd come back here sooner. I don't know why I couldn't bring myself to come here. It's funny."

"What?"

"It took the Lord bringing Jerry back into my life to get me back on this land. He was the reason I'd vowed never to come back here."

"For sure, the Lord works in mysterious ways."

I shot Henry a smile. "Let's go inside. I'm ready to eat."

I stepped into the foyer, amazed. A wide staircase with cherry oak banisters led up to a second floor. A large crystal chandelier hung from the second-floor ceiling. The living room had contemporary furniture and a white carpet that led into the dining room, which had a large oak table with matching chairs for twelve; another chandelier hung from the center.

The aromas of smoked turkey, ham, fried chicken, dressing, macaroni and cheese, sweet potatoes, cranberry sauce, and greens enticed my taste buds. Someone had even cooked some smelly chitterlings. The ladies of the church had outdone themselves. Nancy went from table to table and sampled every dish, including the chitterlings.

I looked at Henry and shook my head. "All of this food got me hungry."

Henry rubbed my back. "Well, let's get you fed."

The sun had changed into its evening orange and descended behind the hills, dropping the temperature into the eighties. I walked out to the gravesite and sat on the bench, staring at my husband's grave.

"Katie," Jerry said softly.

I looked up and reached out my arm. He grabbed my hand, and I pulled him down next to me. "The last time I was here, there was junk sprawled all around the yard... back there," I said, pointing toward the house. "The chicken pen was back there. Ben—that's my rooster—woke me up every morning. He made it. That's what I said the following morning when I heard his crow. I was so happy he'd made it. He was the first sign of hope that everything was going to be all right." As I looked at the land and the hills, my heart overflowed with joy. My gaze came back to the house. "Maxi truly turned this place into a paradise."

"She sure has," Jerry said, looking around.

"I was sure surprised to see Reverend Jeffers and his church here."

"I was, too—pleasantly."

"It's good to see blacks and whites fellowshipping like that, especially in this town. I wish that'll happen back home."

"God is doing more than we can imagine, Katie, even if we don't see it," Jerry said.

Somberness came over me. "Timothy will never stop until he sees you in jail."

"I'm resolved to accept whatever the Lord's will is for me, even if it's jail."

"Well, I hope it doesn't come to that. You got work to do, and I don't think the Lord is finished with you, Jerry." I squeezed his hand. "You know, I might just stay down here for a while. I really miss this place. It's good to be here."

* * *

Alicia counted twenties, tens, fives, and one-dollar bills and stacked them neatly. She filled out the cash sheet, stuffed the money in the money bag, zipped the bag closed and put it in her purse. She looked around the café and headed for the kitchen. She was glad the day was over. The café was quiet except for the *cling-clank* of dishes and glasses and Jerry's Country music playing.

It was one of those days. They'd run out of ground beef at the height of the lunch rush. She had ordered only a third of what she should have. Jerry had to rush out to buy more meat at the retail cost. Frustrated, many customers refused to wait and ate somewhere else.

She strapped her purse over her shoulder and pushed the kitchen door open. "Nancy, I'm going to the bank." She stepped outside. Jerry was sweeping the front sidewalk. He'd come out to clear his head. He seemed preoccupied—he took long swipes, gazing at the ground. "I'm sorry for screwing up the order, Jerry. I wrote down the wrong figure. I missed one zero …"

"Things like this happens. Stop beating up yourself about it. I've made worse mistakes."

Alicia felt better, but it still stung that she had messed up like that. Jerry went back to his thoughts, taking long swipes with the broom.

"What's on your mind?"

He looked up and smiled. "Oh, I was thinking about my old friend, Lester. I wish he'd have opened his heart to the Lord. How did you like the trip?"

"I loved it. That was my first time down south. That was the first time I've traveled anywhere. I loved meeting everyone."

"I appreciate Maxine and Henry. They're godly people. The way they accepted me touched my heart."

"I'm jealous of Madea—taking her long extended vacation. She said she doesn't know when she's coming back. She's trying to make up for all the years she'd stayed away."

Jerry chuckled. "I'm glad."

"How come you didn't see your old house? Don't you want to see your relatives?"

Jerry shook his head. "Both my parents passed away years ago. The house I grew up in sits abandoned on a large plot of land outside of town. It's been so long—no, I don't have a desire to go back. I'll go back to visit Henry and Maxine's church, but there's nothing there for me."

The hum of engines made Alicia snap her head toward

the street. Six Orange Grove squad cars parked in front of the café, with lights flashing. Seven officers stepped out of the cars and took flanking positions. They wore brown pants and beige shirts with brown hats. Their sidearms were clearly visible but holstered. Jerry watched them with no expression.

Tom Sullivan stepped out of the lead squad car. He glanced at Alicia and squinted and walked up to Jerry. He shifted his eyes and pursed his lips.

Jerry looked over Tom's shoulder and peered at him. "What can I do for you, Tom?"

Nancy ran out of the café and wrapped her arm around Jerry's waist. "Honey, what's happening? What's going on?"

Alicia's jaw dropped opened. A black Mercedes Benz parked behind the squad cars in the middle of the street. Timothy stepped out wearing a black suit as if he'd dressed for the Oscars. He leaned against his car with a sinister gloat plastered on his face.

Tom looked back and rolled his eyes. He shook his head, slightly. "Jer, I'm here to arrest you." Tom nodded toward Timothy. "For the murder of his father."

Nancy stepped in front of Jerry. "Tom, what are you doing?"

"Nancy, I need you to step aside. I'm sorry. I have to do my job."

Jerry grabbed Nancy by her shoulders. "Honey, call Larry. Be strong."

Alicia took Nancy by the arm and pulled her away from Jerry. They held each other. Tom motioned, and Jerry turned around. Tom placed silver handcuffs on Jerry's wrist and marched him to his squad car. He guided Jerry into the back seat and shut the door. Timothy got into his car and drove away with satisfaction etched on his face.

Tom opened his door and looked at Nancy. "You can see him at the station. I'm sorry, Nancy."

Alicia watched Tom get into his car and lead the other squad cars down the street. She remembered Madea telling her how she felt the night Jerry—Gus—led his gang unto her farm and afflicted the slaughter that ended with beating and lynching her grandfather, whom she had never met.

That had been fifty years ago when Gus drove off of the land leaving Madea destitute. Alicia felt sadness because now it was her Christian brother being hauled away in cuffs, and it was her family who'd afflicted the pain.

She grieved for Nancy and the pain she felt. How could Timothy be so hardened? Did he even realize the hurt he caused? Could Alicia ever forgive Timothy?

Chapter Thirty-five

Alicia pulled inside the large parking structure adjacent to the Orange County Jail. She mouthed "thank you, Jesus," and grinned at Nancy, catching a car backing out of a space on the first level. Nancy stared as if she was a zombie. She had been that way since Jerry's arrest.

Alicia grabbed her hand and gently squeezed. "Are you going to be okay, Nancy?" Nancy nodded and got out the car. Alicia popped the trunk and stepped out of the car. She slipped off her watch, rings, bracelets, and necklace and put them into her purse and then put her purse in the trunk. "Nancy, put your jewelry and stuff in the trunk."

Nancy, still dazed, answered, "Why?"

"They'll make you go through a metal detector and search your purse. The more stuff you have, the longer it'll take to go through the line. I just take my ID with me, so I can pass through the line quickly. I have experience with jails." Nancy nodded and stripped her jewelry and gave them to Alicia. She put them in the trunk. Alicia slid her ID into her pocket and slammed the trunk shut.

Nancy's eyes welled up. "I know this is negative, but I'm afraid for Jerry."

"What are you afraid of?"

"It's been three months, and they won't grant Jerry bail. Your uncle is making sure of that. I'm afraid if they find out what Jerry is charged with, they might harm him."

Alicia took Nancy's hand. "You have to trust God to keep Jerry safe. You have to be strong so you can encourage him. Besides, most of the inmates are either white or Hispanic."

Nancy nodded. "You're right, Alicia."

They walked in the lobby and got in the line that passed through a metal detector. The detector buzzed and beeped as some women walked through with jewelry on, and as children carried their toys through. Alicia was relieved when they finally made it through. Orange County sheriffs checked their IDs, patted them down from head to toe, and asked the same irritating questions. "Who are you here to see? Do you have any contraband, drugs, or weapons? Has anyone contacted you to sneak drugs or contraband into the jail?"

Alicia submitted to every procedure with a deadpan face. Nancy pressed her lips tight, loathing the process.

The sheriffs directed them to the waiting area. Nancy fidgeted as if she needed a bath. "I detested strange hands probing my body." She paced back and forth, constantly looking toward the door to the side of the check-in desk.

Alicia chuckled, and they sat. "You might as well relax, Nancy."

"Why is it taking so long?"

"You know they take their sweet time."

A sheriff emerged from the back room and stood in the center of the lobby. He was tall, fit, dressed in a brown and beige uniform without a gun. "May I have your attention?" He waited for the room to quiet. "Visiting hours have been canceled for today." He turned and walked toward the door.

Nancy had rushed to the officer before he left the lobby. "Excuse me, Officer."

He stopped and turned around, annoyed.

"Why are they canceling visiting hours?"

"There was a fight in one of the cell blocks. We're on lockdown until further notice. That's all I know," he said and walked away.

Nancy walked back to the waiting area. "I hope nothing has happened to Jerry."

"I'm sure he's all right. We'll see him tomorrow," Alicia said.

Nancy tried to put on a brave face, but her eyes drooped and welled up. She kept looking toward the door the officer had gone through. "I hope Jerry wasn't in that fight."

Alicia rubbed her back. As they started to leave, the same officer emerged from the door. "Attention, everyone. Visiting is back on." He looked at a sheet of paper and shouted names. "Adams."

Nancy spun around. Alicia grabbed her hand and led her toward the officer. Others lined up, single file, and walked through the door.

"What happened?" Nancy asked the officer.

"I don't know, but visiting is back on," he said, nodding toward the door.

Nancy stretched a wide smile across her face. "Thank God for His intervention."

Alicia and Nancy walked into a large room. It was the size of a school cafeteria, with three large windows on one wall covered with thick metal bars. The interior walls were white cinder blocks, and the doors and window frames were blue. The floors had white tiles with blue diamond patterns spaced throughout. The tables and chairs were painted blue and bolted to the floor. The loud clash of doors slamming shut was a jolting reminder of where they were.

Chatter rose as the room filled with mothers, children, and friends waiting to see loved ones. Alicia and Nancy stood by a table. Jerry walked toward them. His hair was pure white, and his face was speckled with white stubble. His age had caught up with him. He wore an orange jumpsuit that hung on his body like clothes on a hanger.

Jerry held Nancy for a long while. He hugged Alicia. "You two make my day."

"Watch it, Adams," a voice shouted.

Alicia glanced the officer's way. They sat at the table. She fixed her stare on Jerry. "How are you doing?"

"I've been under the weather—nothing serious."

Nancy grabbed his hand. "I know it's been hard, but Larry is working on getting you out. He's doing all he can."

Jerry shrugged. "The DA and Timothy made sure they used whatever legal loophole they could to keep me in here." He peered at both of them. "Who's looking after the café?"

"Honey, don't worry about that now."

"Nancy, I'm going to be here a while. We have to face the reality that my past has caught up with me."

Nancy frowned. "Jerry, I don't want to talk about this."

Jerry turned to Alicia. "You have to look after the café. She has a lot on her mind."

"I'm sitting right here. Don't treat me like an invalid," Nancy retorted.

Jerry squeezed her hand. "That's not what I'm doing. But we have to face the fact that I may never get out of here. I've instructed Larry to set my affairs in order—just in case."

"I'm not just rolling over and giving up. I'm not crazy. I know you can go to jail for the rest of your life ..." Nancy glanced away, sniffling. "I'm praying ... trusting God."

"Adams, I won't tell you again."

Jerry withdrew his hands. "That's what makes this place unbearable—not being able to touch you, hug you, and kiss you." Jerry smiled. "You're right. Let's pray."

* * *

I waited under the canopy outside of the arrival lane at Los Angeles International Airport. I'd told Ruby not to park, since I brought only a carry-on bag. I kept a full wardrobe at Maxine's. Timothy occupied my thoughts while I waited for Ruby to circle around. I knew I had to find it in my heart to reconcile with him. I hadn't spoken to him since Alicia told me what he had done. He had tried to call me, but I refused to talk to him. Though I was furious at his actions, he was my son. I still loved him.

Political ambition no longer drove Timothy. Hate stirred his passion, to his destruction. He didn't care whom he hurt or the lives he destroyed. He'd use any means necessary to bring Jerry down.

A horn tooted twice. Ruby had nudged her Cadillac between two other cars in the taxi lane. I didn't have much time. The safety patrol officer was already heading our way.

I jumped in the car, and Ruby sped away before the officer slapped a ticket on the windshield. Thank God, I lived ten minutes away. My plan was to go home and rest, take care of a few things, and then midweek head out to Orange Grove. I didn't know what I was going to do, but I had to do something to help Jerry.

"How was your flight, Mama?"

"Fine. I would have stayed longer if I didn't have to deal

with this mess. I'm so mad at Tim, I don't know what to do. Did you know he was going to do this?"

"No, Mama."

"He should have talked to me first. He should have talked to all of us. Don't you agree?"

"What do you want me to say?"

"What he did involves all of us."

Ruby stared ahead as she drove. "Tim has a point. After all, that man did murder Daddy."

"But Jerry has changed, Ruby. I would think you'd acknowledge what God had done?"

"I do … but I also see Tim's point. A man can't kill someone, find God, and live happy ever after. Is that right?"

Ruby's response surprised me. I was so caught up in Jerry's redemption I failed to consider how others felt. The cold reality was not everyone thought Jerry should have a second chance. A lot of people, more than I wanted to believe, felt the same way as Tim.

My cell phone chimed. I tapped the screen.

"Hello … Chad, how are you doing, my brother? You're calling to talk about my book, I presumed … you're not … hold on; I'm putting you on speaker." I tapped the screen. "Go ahead, Chad, Ruby is in the car."

"Could you meet me at the *Orange County View* at noon tomorrow? I have something to show you concerning Jerry Adams's case."

I glanced at Ruby. "What is it?"

"I rather tell you in person. Trust me, you'll want to hear and see this, Katie."

"What could be that important?"

"We don't have much time. They're preparing to extradite

Jerry to Alabama."

Ruby looked at me. "I'll take you, Mama."

"I'll see you tomorrow at noon, Chad."

* * *

I followed Chad into a conference room on the second floor of the *Orange County View.* I kept glancing at Ruby. We both wondered what Chad had to tell us about Jerry. The building was small. I was expecting the grandeur of the LA Times, not a small suburban paper. Alicia and Nancy were sitting at the table.

Alicia jumped to her feet and hugged me. "Madea, I'm glad you're back." Alicia gave an awkward hug to Ruby. "Mama, I'm glad to see you."

"Where's Deshon?"

Alicia dropped her arms. "He's at school. He doesn't get out until three."

Nancy hugged me. "Hello, Katie. It's good to see you."

"How are you doing, Nancy?"

"I have to ask the Lord for strength every day."

I padded her hand. "Just trust in Him. He's going to work it all out."

Ruby sat. "Chad, what's this about?"

Chad stood at the head of the table. The room was spacious with a glass table that sat twelve. Chad wore a Hawaiian print shirt, khakis shorts, and leather sandals. He certainly wasn't dressed for work. He had a calm, peaceful demeanor, as if a burden had been lifted from his shoulders.

He looked at the clock on the wall. "Please, have a seat." He waited until we sat. "I've asked you here because you should know what the DA is up to. I stumbled upon a meeting a while ago. At the time, I didn't pay it much attention, though I thought it was odd who was at this meeting. When I heard of the arrest of Jerry Adams, I put two and two together."

Nancy sighed. "What are you talking about, Chad?"

"That day I saw my Senior Editor, Brian Duncan and District Attorney Sarah Cooper in a meeting with ..." Chad paused and gazed at me. "Timothy Smith."

My face must have deeply furrowed because Chad raised his brow in surprise. "Why would Timothy meet with the DA?"

Chad held up a large vanilla envelope. "I asked the same question. So I did some digging." Chad slid the envelope in front of me. "Timothy and Sarah forged your name on an affidavit that says you're pressing charges against Jerry. That's why they arrested him. They also contacted the Alabama Attorney General. They're preparing to extradite Jerry to Birmingham for trial."

Nancy gasped. "Oh my, God."

"Madea, what are we going to do? We can't let that happen."

"I know, Alicia. Chad, when are they taking Jerry to Alabama?"

"They're meeting today at one to hash out the details."

Nancy frowned. "What details?"

"I'd imagine press releases. They want this broadcasted on every available news outlet. See, this is a win for all of them. Our paper gets the scoop. DA gets the case of the century, and Timothy gets the justice he seeks—and as an added bonus, this raises his political profile. For sure, he'll be the next Al Sharpton."

Closing my eyes, I shook my head back and forth. A

distasteful sigh blew out my mouth. I stood and gazed out the window, vexed in my soul. "DA, reporters, and my son conspiring together. The last time I saw something like this was fifty years ago. Blount City had ordered the sheriff not to press charges against Gus for murdering my husband. But this is different. This is family, my flesh and blood who is using my good name to bring down a good man."

"How do you know all this?" Ruby asked Chad.

I whirled around and peered at Chad.

He pointed at the envelope. "Everything I said is documented. You have all the proof you need." Chad smiled with satisfaction. "They're meeting here at one."

I looked at the clock. It read 12:50. "Timothy is coming here at one?" He nodded. "I want to crash this meeting."

"I thought you would."

Chad left the room. I sat and pulled the documents from the envelope. My eyes widened as I read in disbelief: the fake affidavit, emails, phone logs, and court petitions. It was all here. Timothy went too far this time. I had evidence that'll end his law career. The irony is he could go to jail for trying to get the justice he sought for his father.

Ruby shook her head. "I can't believe Timothy did this. I want justice, but I won't be a party to this. What was he thinking?"

"What does this mean?" Nancy said, looking at everyone, baffled.

I took Nancy's hand. "They fabricated the entire case against Jerry."

Chad appeared at the door. "They're here."

We followed him to the elevator. No one said anything as we rode up to the fourth floor. Chad walked us around what

I thought was a long way to the conference room. I could see Timothy, across the rows of cubicles, sitting with his back against the glass wall. I couldn't hear what he was saying, but he did most of the talking. Chad huddled us to the side of the door where they couldn't see us. But I could see and hear them.

"I want you to hear them for yourself," Chad whispered.

The DA leafed through papers as Timothy talked. The other man, Chad's editor, listened and jotted notes on an iPad.

Timothy leaned back. "Brian, I want to see Adams being hauled away in cuffs on every news channel, and I want his mug shot splattered on the front page of every newspaper."

Brian nodded. "Just as long as I get my exclusive ... Sarah..."

Sarah looked up. "I'll perp walk him out in his orange jail suit with chains on his hands, around his waist, and clamped to ankles. It'll be a spectacular scene. I'll give my statement on the steps of the courthouse. I've called for a full-court press."

Chad touched my shoulder. "Heard enough?"

I nodded. Chad walked into the room.

Brian looked at him, baffled, maybe wondering why he was dressed so casual. "Chad, what are you doing? We're in a meeting."

"I know. There's someone who has something to say to you."

I walked in. Ruby, Alicia, and Nancy slid in behind me. Timothy and Brian raised their brows, surprised. Sarah stopped leafing through her papers and shifted her eyes between Timothy and Brian.

"What's going on here, Brian?" Sarah said.

Timothy leaned forward. "Mama, what are you doing here?"

I glared at Timothy. "Stopping this miscarriage of Justice. Mrs. DA, I know the three of you have conspired to frame Jerry. I have proof. I never signed my name to any affidavit, stating I wanted charges brought against Jerry Adams."

Timothy scowled. "Mama, you need to leave. You're going to ruin everything."

"You're so blinded by your hate you can't see you've become just as evil as the men who murdered your father. You have manufactured evidence and lied." Shaking my head, I looked at each one of them. "Now, this is what going to happen. Mr. Editor, you're killing any stories and press releases about Jerry. Mrs. DA, you're dropping all charges against Jerry, and he's to be released today."

Timothy pounded the table. "You'll do that? You'll take the side of a murderer over family? You're willing to let that man walk the streets free while my father's bones lay cold in his grave?"

Katie narrowed her eyes. "Lower your voice when you talk to me, Timothy. You're ending your crusade against Jerry." I glared at each of them, making sure they had my attention. "If you don't stop what you're doing, I'll go to the press with what I know. I'll go to the Justice Department and give them my proof—your emails, documents, and texts."

Ruby shook her head and walked out. Nancy and Alicia followed her. Chad touched my back. As I started to leave, I caught Brian's glare at Chad.

Chad had a slight smug on his face. "Consider this my resignation." He guided me out and led me to the lobby where everyone waited for me. "That felt good."

"I don't know how to thank you for what you'd done. I feel bad you've lost your job. What will you do now?" I asked.

Chad smiled. "Journalism was never my passion. Brian only hired me as a favor to my father. I'm going to finish your story and catch up on surfing."

"Give me a hug my brother," I said holding him tight. "Anything you need. Call me when you're ready to finish my book." Chad walked out the building, not bothering to take any personal belongings.

I looked at Nancy. "Let's go get my brother out of jail."

Chapter Thirty-six

Jerry walked into the conference room precisely at nine for his scheduled meeting with Dave and the board of elders. His appetite had returned, but his clothes still hung loosely on his body. He still had a gaunt look, but he felt healthy.

He sat and poured a glass of water. "Hey, everyone."

The return greetings were cordial, but Jerry felt a definite tension in the room. Jail taught Jerry to sense things like that. That was how he'd survived. The Lord protected him by showing him when to remove himself from approaching evil or harm. It had taught him to spot cons or when people tried to take advantage of him.

Life had changed for Jerry. Days and nights were fleeting. He vowed to live them wisely before God. He saw the church and his duties differently now. He'd been complacent and at ease. His service to the Lord had been mundane and routine. He'd grown comfortable in his space. He wanted… needed a change. His eyes darted from one elder to the next. He studied them, trying not to be resentful. No one had called or visited, except Dave.

Dave rushed in and took his seat. "Sorry, I'm late. Jerry, glad you could come. How are you feeling?"

"Eager to get back to service."

Dave shifted his body. "That's what we wanted to discuss with you." Dave shot a glance to each man around the table. "As you know, Larry filled in as head elder while you were away." He cleared his throat. "We decided to make his position permanent. Now, this has nothing to do with you or your situation. We just feel...."

"It's all right, Dave," Jerry interrupted. "You know I support whatever and whichever way the Lord leads you." Jerry smiled and rose from his chair.

"Uh, Jerry, we're not finished. Please, have a seat." He waited for Jerry to sit. "We're not throwing you to the side." Dave threw a nervous glance around the room. "Jerry, how do you see yourself serving here?"

Jerry took a long breath and glanced at everyone. "The Lord taught me a lot while I was in jail. At first, I was bummed out. You know, the usual 'Why me?' attitude. That lasted all of a week. There were guys in there who had committed serious crimes. They knew they were going away for a long time, a lot of them for life. At first, I judged them, criticized them for the stupid choices they'd made. There were some whom the system had railroaded. The hopelessness in their eyes made me grieve for them.

"The funny thing is, I had gotten away with a crime I committed fifty years ago. I was a hypocrite for judging those men. If justice had prevailed back then, I'd be in prison for life. God changed my perspective. I saw those men as lost sheep instead of savages. I started a Bible study. God had shown what an incredible opportunity I had. We spent every day, sometimes twice a day studying His word. It was awesome. It took me days to do a book that normally would have taken months to go through. We completed almost the entire New Testament in a month.

"Some of those men got out of jail and turned their lives around. Some of them found jobs, married, and started families or reconnected with families. They all found churches to serve in. That's what excited me the most. Not one of them has returned to jail. The others, who are doing long stretches of time, serve in various ministries within the jail, helping the chaplains, visiting churches and ministries. Some have started their own Bible studies. That doesn't mean they don't have their challenges, but those men learned how to serve the Lord where they are.

"I said all that to say that working with those men taught me to make every day count. I want to work more in the field, with people, teaching God's word, helping people find their place in God's will. So, I think your decision is timely."

Jerry couldn't tell if the board members were stunned or relieved. They shot glances at each other, and Dave let a grin slip out. "This is timely, Jerry. We haven't had a chance to talk about this, but... wow, look at how the Lord works. What we wanted to talk to you about is taking over the church plant ministry."

Jerry's eyes widened. "Church-planting?"

"Yeah, while you were away, Eddie retired and moved to Florida. You were on my heart for the position."

A smile burst through Jerry's cheeks. "I think God has been preparing me for this."

* * *

Ruby poured a cup of coffee with pursed lips. Flopping onto the couch, almost spilling her cup, she sighed and sipped. I leaned back and folded my arms. "What's got you in a frenzy?" I suspected it had something to do with Alicia. "Well, what's bothering you? You've been fretting all morning."

"I'm thinking about Alicia."

"What about her?"

"You know, she's dating a white boy."

"She's not dating anyone I'm aware of. What's your problem with that, anyway?"

"She can't find someone black to date?" Ruby shot me a double-take. "You, of all people, should agree with that."

I shifted in my chair. "That might have been true a while ago, but God has shown me not to judge people based on their skin color. Besides, she lives in an all-white area and goes to an all-white church. What do you expect? But, I don't think they're dating. They're just friends."

She rolled her eyes. "Well, he dropped Deshon off at my house. I didn't like that."

"He's a godly man. If they were to date, I think he'd be perfect for Alicia."

"Um-hm. Wait until you see your great-grandkids. At least, they'll have good hair."

"I'm not going to dignify that."

Ruby turned up her nose. "Changing the subject… when are you coming back to West Florence?"

"I can't go back there."

"Why, 'cause it's an all-black church?"

Drawing my brows in, I shot her a look. "It has nothing to do with color. I asked the Lord to place me in a church where the people love Him, teach His word and don't see color. I asked Him to put me in a place where I could be useful."

Ruby chuckled. "Fat chance on finding a place like that. You must be planning on going to heaven soon, because that doesn't exist down here."

"I refuse to believe that. I have hope in God and His grace

to change hearts." Ruby smacked her lips and geared up for a rebuttal, but the phone rang. Shaking my head, I brought the phone to my ear. "Hello. Hi, Tammy, how have you been? What…? Oh, my…. oh, my…. Let me know when you have the arrangements. Okay, bye."

Ruby watched me hang up the phone. "What's wrong, Mama?"

"That was my friend from my old church. Their new pastor suddenly died."

"That's terrible. Did you know him?"

"No. I left the first day he came. That's something. They're without a pastor now."

* * *

Nancy's invitation to lunch was unexpected but very much welcome. I hadn't seen the Adams' in a while. I missed their fellowship. I'd get the chance to spend time with them. I told Nancy they didn't have to come up and get me; I'd drive down. I wanted to spend time with Alicia and Deshon. Nancy told me if it got too late, I could stay at their house. Dorothy called and told me she'd love to come, but she was working and felt she had to stay home with Timothy. She felt the Lord was getting through to him. I hoped so—only the Lord could get through to him.

The drive down wasn't as bad as I thought it would be but was still long. I hated to drive long distances these days. Ruby usually drove me where I needed to go. By the time I'd arrived, I was sure I was spending the night. Nancy rushed out as soon as I drove into the driveway. "Katie, I'm glad to see you," she said, squeezing me a good while.

"Where's Jerry?"

"He had some business to take care of. He'll be back in a while. It's just us two."

"Where's Alicia?"

"At work. She was mad I pulled rank and made her work while I fellowship with you. Deshon is at school. She'll pick him up on her way home. Let's go inside."

"Y'all have decorated since the last time I was here. This is nice. I like it."

"It was time."

The snacks were tasty. I feasted on pepperoni wraps Nancy had thrown together. She filled me in on what had been happening in their lives. She started telling about what was going at Grace Chapel when Jerry drove up. A wide smile stretched across my face when he walked into the house. I stood, he gave me a hug, and we sat on the couch.

"I'm glad to see you, Jerry," I said.

"Thanks, Katie. What's been going on with you?"

"I received a sad phone call yesterday. The pastor of my former church passed away."

"I'm sorry to hear that. Was he the pastor who moved away?"

"No, the one who took over after he left."

Jerry drew back with a curious stare. "So, they're without a pastor?"

"Yes."

Nancy took over the conversation as Jerry drifted away in his thoughts. I didn't know what he was thinking, but I suspected it had something to do with South Bay Baptist. Maybe he thought about sending flowers or something. Whatever it was, he pondered hard, and knowing Jerry, he wouldn't stop until he reached a resolution.

* * *

Another Sunday, and I was home alone. I missed church. I missed fellowshipping with my Christian family. It was time to serve again. It was time to use the gifts God had given me to mentor young girls, teach a Sunday school class, or get back involved in jail ministry. I might even join a praise team somewhere. It's not like I'd have many days left. Whatever time I did have, I wanted to spend serving God.

Where would I go? What church would I attend? A bright reflection bounced off my face. Rising from my chair, I walked over to the window and peeked out. Jerry's truck brought a smile to my face. I hadn't seen him in a month. Sometimes I hated his new position. It kept him very busy, but he loved it. I had the door open before he knocked.

"Hello, Katie," he said, giving me a big hug.

I returned the hug. "Hello, my brother. Where's Nancy?"

"She's at church."

When he didn't offer any more information, I motioned to the couch. I sat in my chair, happy to see him but surprised by his visit. He usually called before showing up, and it was Sunday, when he usually was at one of the churches he'd planted. He sat with a mannish grin.

"What brings you by? In the neighborhood?"

"I have a surprise for you, but I need you to come somewhere with me first."

"Now?"

"If you don't mind. I really want you to see this." He must have read the hesitation on my face because he poured the charm on even more. "I promise you, you won't be disappointed."

"All right."

Jerry loaded me into his truck. I felt as though I were on top of the world, his truck was so high. He beamed about the church-planting mission he was involved in. I'd never heard of a church so busy with starting other churches. I found it intriguing, mostly because Jerry was engrossed in his work. He had found his niche.

"Katie, I am excited to be planting churches. Like the Lord said, 'The harvest is great, but the laborers are few. Pray to the Lord of Harvest to send laborers into his field.' I've planted one church in Calabasas, and we have one scheduled to open in Sun Valley next year. But I'm really excited about this church. This is an entirely different direction than we've gone."

I wondered what he meant. Why was this church more special than the other churches he'd planted? I hadn't paid attention to where we were going until he pulled into the parking lot of South Bay Baptist Church. As much I wanted to be angry at Jerry, my heart actually yearned to go inside to look around the church. What changes had they made? Most of all, I wanted to see my old church family. Most of them were gone, but those who'd stayed, I wanted to see them. I looked at Jerry, waiting for an explanation.

"Before you get angry, let me explain."

I nodded.

"I've told you I've talked to Dave and the board about changing our ways. In fact, I've made it clear that we had to stop planting churches in white suburbs only. They agreed but were cautious 'bout appearing to be condescending."

"Why would they think that?"

"Well, they just didn't want to be reacting... like hiring a black person just to say they hired a black employee. I assured them we'd let the Lord lead us. When you told me the pastor here passed away, my spirit exploded. I knew that was the open door. I prayed about it, then came here, met with the elders, and told them what was on my heart."

"Which was what?"

"To bring this church into our church family. This is the first, of many, churches that will cross over cultural lines. We've started on the path so that, I'm proud to say, we'll be fulfilling the Lord's command to go into all the world and proclaim the gospel. I'd like you to be a part of this fellowship, Katie."

"Me?"

"You've been too long away from church. You will make a perfect fit for what the Lord is doing here. I know you feel it in your spirit."

I looked over toward the church; I'd never thought this would be the place I'd come home to. A man walked out of the church toward us with a smile on his face. I assumed he was one of the elders from Grace Chapel. He looked to be in his thirties, neatly groomed, wearing Dockers and a button-down shirt.

"Here's the new pastor," Jerry said, anticipating my reaction. "He's the Lord's choice. I'm confident of that. I wanted to bring a black pastor aboard, but then I thought, skin color shouldn't matter in choosing who should shepherd God's flock. What does the Lord want? After much prayer, I knew he was the one. He has a heart for the Lord and for people."

I relaxed my face with a sigh, looking at my new pastor. "The Lord's will be done."

About the Author

The writing bug bit Lynn late in life when Beverly, his wife, kept urging him to pursue writing. He finally listened to her wisdom and developed his passion for writing Christian fiction. Lynn has a strong passion to write stories with a strong message of Christ to strengthen and encourage believers in their walk of faith.

When not writing, Lynn enjoys cycling and works as a Stationary Engineer for the state of Illinois. He has a passion for teaching through the Bible verse by verse. Lynn and Beverly live outside of Chicago and have five adult children and thirteen grandchildren.

Made in the USA
Monee, IL
13 August 2020